CW00665398

THE MODEL SPY

BASED ON THE TRUE STORY OF TOTO KOOPMAN'S WORLD WAR II VENTURES

MARYKA BIAGGIO

MILFORD
HOUSE

an imprint of Sunbury Press, Inc.
Mechanicsburg, PA USA

MILFORD HOUSE

an imprint of Sunbury Press, Inc.
Mechanicsburg, PA USA

For information about special discounts for bulk purchases, please contact Sunbury Press Orders Dept. at (855) 338-8359 or orders@sunburypress.com.

To request one of our authors for speaking engagements or book signings, please contact Sunbury Press Publicity Dept. at publicity@sunburypress.com.

FIRST MILFORD HOUSE PRESS EDITION: March 2022

Set in Adobe Garamond Pro | Interior design by Crystal Devine | Cover by Christina Fenwick | Cover photo: George Hoyningen-Huene, *Vogue*, © Condé Nast used with permission | Edited by Sarah Peachey.

Publisher's Cataloging-in-Publication Data
Names: Biaggio, Maryka, author.
Title: The model spy : based on the true story of Toto Koopman's World War II ventures / Maryka Biaggio.
Description: First trade paperback edition. | Mechanicsburg, PA : Milford House Press, 2022.
Summary: Celebrated model Toto Koopman had beauty, brains, and fame. When the winds of war swept Europe, she gave up the life of a bon vivant and threw herself into the world of espionage. As she spied for the Allies and the Italian Resistance, both Mussolini's and Hitler's forces hunted her.
Identifiers: ISBN : 978-1-62006-780-2 (softcover).
Subjects: FICTION / Historical / World War II | FICTION / Thrillers / Espionage | FICTION / Biographical.

Product of the United States of America
0 1 1 2 3 5 8 13 21 34 55

Continue the Enlightenment!

To the brave and dedicated, then and now, who fight
and continue to fight for democracy.

The opposite of love is not hate, it's indifference. . . . And the opposite of life is not death, it's indifference.

—ELIE WIESEL

Many people have asked: Where did I find the courage to throw myself in danger's path? But now that my life lies shattered in ways I could never have envisioned, the question I ask myself is how much of my life was shaped by others, both those brave and depraved? The fact is, the war changed how I saw myself—and all of humanity.

———

I was an impetuous little girl, full of the spirit of adventure and not a little bravura and spunk. The Java of my childhood was filled with floral-scented breezes, the chatter of macaques in a canopy of trees, and the lushness of big-leafed jungle plants. I roamed freely and felt as safe in the nearby fields, jungle's edge, and military enclave as in the embrace of my family.

I awoke to my singularity early—and suddenly—at age six. I hadn't yet developed that sense of self-awareness borne of reflection. I merely soaked up experiences with the people in my world—my brother and our parents, the servants, family friends, official visitors, and the odd stranger who happened by our low-built home.

I wasn't altogether oblivious to my uniqueness; I was simply too busy bounding from one exploit to another to take the measure of it. Nor did I absorb the praise my parents cast my way—my mind merely sped over compliments. What use did a busy child have for approbation? For all I knew, a Dutch father in a smart military uniform and an Indonesian mother wrapped in a sarong were as common as the emerald splendor of a tea plantation or the bounce of oversized raindrops on dusty paths. I thought servants bustling from house to yard to barn, gathering fruit for the breakfast table, and flinging open the shutters on warm mornings inhabited all the nearby homes.

By age six, I spoke Dutch and the Malay common to the East Indies and took it in stride when my father explained that I, like my older brother, would be schooled in English, French, and German as well. To me, it was unremarkable that my skin matched neither my mother's fawn brown nor my father's pale sandstone but rather a blend of the two. The pats on the head that visitors bestowed when I chirped hellos and recited my daily exploits assured me I was lovable, even admired, and that not a soul I might ever encounter would think me unworthy of affection and regard.

Yes, there was much I didn't understand then—much I would not only learn, but fathom the weighty import of: that by a stroke of fate I'd inherited the sleepy-lidded eyes of my mother, the slender uprightness of my father, and the glistening blue-black hair of my grandmother; that I was blessed with the certitude of forebears who had lived long and well enough to pass on their legends and wisdom; that the eyes of men and women would follow me, often with wonder, sometimes with envy, when I walked down Paris's runways; and that all my gifts wouldn't be enough to shield me from the horrors and brutality of war.

JAVA

OCTOBER 1914

I was shaken from my childhood dreaminess on my sixth birthday. My mother proudly wrapped me in a sarong decorated with purple and red flowers, and my father invited me to accompany him to the commissary.

"Come, Toto," he said. "You can help me carry the supplies."

I ran ahead, pattering on the packed dirt path, keeping to the shade of the flame-of-the-forest trees, and whizzing past the white picket fence. The commissary in Salatiga's Dutch military compound was one of my favorite places. I loved walking its aisles and admiring the goods: wheels of Edam and Gouda cheese; a wooden barrel of pickles; tins of sardines, anchovies, and miniature sausages; lavender-scented soap wrapped in tissue; and tins of tooth powder with flowery red lettering.

I tugged the screen door open and headed for the candy display—chocolate and licorice all the way from the Netherlands. The lightweight door fluttered shut behind me, its latch closing with a satisfying click.

"You, what are you doing here?"

The gruff voice surprised me. I looked behind the counter. I'd never seen this man before. His uniform was just like the one Sergeant De Roos wore, white trousers with blue-striped seams and big round buttons on his linen shirt, but he wasn't the red-cheeked De Roos. His mustache swooped downward, and his bushy eyebrows grew together like a stretched-out caterpillar. He looked as mean as a snarling dog.

"I'm shopping," I said.

"You can't shop here. Get out this minute."

The man darted from behind the counter and headed toward me. He grabbed my arm, sunk his fingers into it, and yanked me toward the door.

"Ouch," I hollered.

My father swung the door open. "What's the meaning of this?"

The man shook me by my arm. "This little heathen was grabbing things off the shelves."

"I was not, Daddy." I struggled against the man's grip.

"Unhand her this minute," said my father.

The man released me, and I ran to Father. I flung my arms around his waist and pressed my cheek against the cool metal buttons of his uniform.

Father cupped his hand on top of my head. "This is my daughter, Sergeant, and I expect you to treat her with respect."

I was what many called a green Dutchman—half Dutch and half Indonesian. Never before had anyone suggested I was less deserving of respect than other children of the Royal Netherlands Army. But now, the whispers among the officers' Dutch wives as they regarded me took on a sinister import.

My father turned me around to face the man. "I think you owe my daughter an apology."

"Of course, Colonel. I'm sorry, miss."

To hide the defiance seething inside me, I forced a shy smile. Father wouldn't have approved of me talking back.

That evening at the dinner table, my father told my mother what had happened. It pleased me to know he was angry this man had belittled me.

My mother huffed, "When will the world be free of such foolish and ignorant men?"

—•—

My father procured horses for the Dutch Cavalry, so we didn't live among the other officers in Salatiga's military enclave but in a nearby home with a large plot of land, a garden of many vegetables, and banana, cherimoya, and fig trees. Our servants tended the house and garden, and I was especially close to my nanny, Djim, who was like another grandmother to me. She taught me about Javanese legends, the names of many different jungle plants, and all the kinds of snakes, especially the ones to avoid. I loved her colorful *kabajas* and the heavy, dangling earrings she wore. She dressed each day as if she might be summoned before royalty. My mother, too, always dressed immaculately, in white linen Javanese garb, her blouse held together with a gold chain of jeweled pins. When my father wasn't in his smart-looking military uniform, he wore a high-buttoned white cotton shirt and starched white trousers.

Our village lay in the hills below the mighty Mount Merbabu. Salatiga is higher in altitude than the low-lying perimeter of Java, so we didn't suffer the kind of sweltering heat that visited the island's lower elevations. It even got chilly enough some nights to need a blanket to sleep.

The jungle surrounding Salatiga was home to a great variety of animals: the Javan Languor with a tail longer than its chestnut-brown body; baby-faced macaques; the biggest lizard in the world, the giant Komodo Dragon; a one-foot-high mouse-deer; and many, many beautiful birds. There was a big gecko, the Tokay, that croaked like a frog, and if you heard it croak seven times, you could make a wish on it. Some animals were dangerous, like panthers, boa constrictors, rhinoceros, and tigers, though they rarely approached people. Our parents warned Henri and me to watch out for the king cobra, the most venomous snake in the world, and if we ever saw one, we were supposed to stand very still before slowly backing away.

I loved the tiny beige tjik-tjak lizards that climbed all over the walls and ceilings of our home, making clicking noises. They did no harm and even helped by eating the dreaded mosquitoes that sometimes found their way through the screens. Insects of many shapes and sizes crawled hither and yon, and all our furniture was from the hardwoods of Java because termites would quickly chew through softer wood. One family from the Netherlands had insisted on bringing their piano to Java, only to have its legs turned to sawdust by invading termites.

One of the greatest wonders of Java is the Borobudur temple, an ancient Buddhist temple in the middle of the jungle. I grew up a mere winding path from this monument, which rivals all the world's natural wonders. Its stone surface is carved with exquisite scenes from the life of Buddha. It is so rich in detail and construction that it surely took more engineering and artistic know-how than Egypt's pyramids.

There were many stories told by natives about the flying fox, the biggest bat in the world, with a wingspan as wide as a man is tall. When they flock to fruit trees to feed, they are very noisy, screeching and chattering like a thousand babies. The Javanese people believe the flying fox possesses special powers of sight. If one crossed your path, it meant you had a big change coming in your life and that you should open your heart to a new vision.

A flying fox crossed my path once, when I was still a youngster. And, yes, it foretold a new chapter in my life.

JAVA

I experienced two great sadnesses during my mostly carefree childhood. The first was saying goodbye to my pet baby elephant, and the second was leaving my parents to attend boarding school in the Netherlands. In the summer of 1921, Father drove my mother and me from Salatiga to the train station in Ambarawa. From there, Mother and I were to take the train to the port of Batavia—a seven-hour trip covering almost five hundred kilometers.

At the train station, Father sat me down on a bench and took my hand. "You are going on a grand adventure, to a place that is very different from what you're accustomed to. At least you will have Henri to help you."

"I can't wait to see Henri." I gave my father a sure nod, trying to show courage.

He smiled wryly. I think he saw through me. "Be wary of those who cast a disapproving eye on you. They may call you many things—foreigner, Belanda Indos, half-breed. Do not argue with them. They are the misguided ones. They may tell you you don't belong, but you must be brave and find your place in the world. Do you understand?"

I looked into his green eyes. They were much like mine—streaked with a burnt brown that gave them a penetrating quality. "Yes, Daddy. Only I hate to think I won't see you and Mother for a long time."

"You'll never be far from our hearts, and you'll have letters from us. We'll miss you dreadfully, dear one, but you have many things to learn. I know you'll be an excellent student."

When the call to board came and Father embraced me one last time, I couldn't stop myself from crying. I honestly didn't know when I would see him again.

My brother had written about the busy avenues and sturdy buildings of the Netherlands, but it pained me to be leaving my beautiful homeland. I doubt many children could claim a childhood as rich with adventure, exotic plants, and wild animals as that which I experienced.

Now my mother and I sat side by side on our swift-moving train, gazing out on the lovely landscape of Java: beautiful terraced rice paddies; bursts of red, orange, and purple flowers; fields planted with tobacco, indigo, and sugar cane; and train depots where the occasional Dutch soldier boarded, Javanese in turbans and sarongs mingled, and station workers steered carts with oversized wheels. I looked longingly at the spine of mountain peaks our train passed by, not knowing when or if I would ever return to my island paradise or see my parents again.

I was bound for a school in Bloemendaal, a city on the outskirts of Amsterdam. When I boarded the steamship *Kawi* and embarked from Batavia's port for the Indian Ocean, rounded the Horn of Africa, passed the palm trees of the Suez Canal, traversed the azure Mediterranean, endured the English Channel's choppy waters, and sailed into Amsterdam's harbor, I was only twelve years old.

AMSTERDAM

JUNE 1923

I was in my friend Nora's bedroom trying on new dresses when her younger sister, Anneke, asked, "Why do you want to learn Italian?"

"Because it is a beautiful language," I said. "More musical than Dutch, German, or English. Even French. And I imagine Venice is as lovely as Paris, except more unusual because of its waterways. I've seen the paintings by Canaletto, and one day I will live there. After I see Paris."

I was sixteen and could hardly wait to be free. I had excelled in foreign languages at school, and once I mastered Italian, I'd be fluent in the five important languages of the Western world. I yearned to travel Europe and sample its capitals and historic cities. Yes, Java and its wild jungles, lush landscape, and Buddhist and Hindu temples had fascinated me as a child, but now I wanted to see the other side of the world—the Western cultures that also reached back centuries, and the paintings and architecture that told their stories.

During my Bloemendaal education, I lived at the boarding school but spent many weekends at the De Vries home in Amsterdam. They had lived in Java for many years, which is where my family met them. The two daughters in the household, Anneke and Nora, were older than me by two and four years. Their father was a military attaché, and they often traveled to Paris with their parents and reported back on its wonders. They also showed off the clothes they bought and hairstyles they adopted, which I was quick to copy.

A few days earlier, I'd worn a slender dress and flesh-colored stockings to school, and my teacher had taken me aside. "Toto, your choice of attire is drawing attention. And the girls are talking about your hairstyle."

I wore my hair in the short wavy style popular at that time, not in the usual tight braids of Dutch girls. I smiled at Miss Janssen. "None of them has said anything to me, miss."

"I don't imagine they will," she said. "But do you truly wish to set yourself apart so?"

"Not at all," I replied. "It's a simple matter of dressing as I wish." What did I care about her opinion? Or those of my classmates? The styles pleased *me*.

Nora stepped back to see how the dress I tried on fit. "And what will you do in Paris and Venice?"

"I'll explore the avenues, the shops, and the museums."

"You can't go traipsing all over Europe by yourself," Anneke said. "Girls don't do that. It's dangerous."

"Don't be silly." Nora was more daring than her younger sister—and tall and slender like me, so I easily fit into the clothes she acquired in France. "Toto belongs in Paris. She could be a model if she wanted."

"But you need to be careful," Anneke said. "Some people can't be trusted."

"Let me tell you a story." I glanced from Nora to Anneke. "When I was only three, a man came knocking at our door. The man's dark-as-night eyes bounced about like a hungry wolf's. He wore a dirty shirt, with the cuffs turned up, and his face was deeply tanned and as leathery as cowhide. In a raspy voice, he asked to speak to my father.

"Ordinarily, I liked welcoming visitors to our home, but this man frightened me. I flung my arms around my mother's neck and screamed at him. Mother was flustered, so she told him he must come back later and slammed the door on him. Father wasn't home at the time, but later he explained this man was only bringing trouble and should never be permitted in the house. After that, my mother and Djim told me some people could see into the souls of others and that I was one of those people. So, you see, I know how to take care of myself."

It was the spring of 1923, and I was soon to graduate from Bloemendaal School. Next, I would attend finishing school in London, as my parents had arranged, but it was Paris I'd set my sights on. Nora and Anneke had filled me with stories of the city's beauty and, given the gowns, accessories, and hairstyles they brought home with them, spoiled me for any other place—other than Venice.

But by the time I finally found my way to Venice, all of Europe was at war. Italy was one of its hotbeds, and I wasn't there to explore. I was hiding out.

LONDON AND PARIS

1923–1934

After I graduated Bloemendaal School, I moved to London for finishing school. I'd insisted on a school that emphasized not only social graces but also academics. I happily threw myself into studies in art, history, literature, and geography and mastered Italian under the tutelage of a Florentine.

Then in 1928, at nineteen, I moved to Paris. Mr. De Vries, the father of my dear friends Nora and Anneke, provided an introduction to an executive in Le Bon Marché's catalog department. I couldn't have asked for a better stepping stone, even though my job was merely clerical. I assisted with the production and mailing of the catalog, which showcased French styles and sold fabric and patterns to fashion houses and Europe's finest seamstresses. I learned about the famous designers of Paris and purchased chic "seconds," clothing from designs tested by the seamstresses who worked for the catalog. My salary was sufficient to afford a tiny apartment in the 17th Arrondissement on Boulevard Berthier. It wasn't suitable for entertaining, but, no matter, I spent little time there. I was building a new life in Paris.

I had only worked at the catalog for five months when the assistant to *Vogue* magazine Editor Michel de Brunoff contacted me. Would I like to model for *Vogue*? That was the beginning of a thrilling time in my life. While I donned elegant gowns, makeup people fawned over me and photographers posed me. Pictures of Toto Koopman in the latest fashions circulated around the world. I proudly sent a few issues to my parents.

They wrote back: "You've blossomed into a beautiful young lady, and we understand the fashions are up-to-date and sought out by Paris's most fashionable women. But we had hoped for a more reputable life for you. You are intelligent and well educated. Surely it is neither prudent nor wise to display yourself so audaciously, even immodestly, for the world to see. Please give some consideration to your prospects. You have great promise. We wish only the best for you."

I understood their concerns. Modeling was not considered an honorable profession, but I enjoyed dressing in the latest fashions. I liked mixing with Paris's haut monde, and I reveled in their smart conversation.

At a party at Le Meurice Hotel marking the release of the 1930 spring and summer collection, I met Coco Chanel.

"Coco and Toto," she said, brandishing her cigarette like a magic wand, "with such names, we really must work together."

"A pleasure to meet you," I said. "And I must add your new line is simply out of this world."

"You'd look absolutely stunning in my little black dress. Those legs of yours are made for showing off."

True to her word, Coco hired me to model her designs. I was the first biracial model in the industry—not that I allowed that to define me. I suppose if I'd not first modeled for *Vogue*, the color of my skin might have been a disadvantage. But fortune smiled on me, and both *Vogue* and Coco Chanel embraced what they considered my "exotic features." I simply acted like I belonged, flaunted my strange beauty, and dared any detractors to shun me. But no one did. No, Paris's smart set celebrated me.

Coco's designs fit me like a glove. My svelte figure showed off the gamine dash and elegance she strove for in her fashions. But I did not like Coco. She was haughty and demanding and smoked like a locomotive. Whenever she fitted me, she brushed her hands over me like I was a possession, not a person. One day, after only six months in her employ, I'd simply had enough of her grasping and glomming and stormed out.

I was not without employment for long. Main Bocher hired me to work at his salon on Avenue Georges V. He involved me in all aspects of showcasing his designs: I walked the runways at shows; I was photographed in the latest for fashion magazines; and I gadded about Paris in his elegant gowns. I also modeled for customers who called at the salon, including Daisy Fellowes, who I found rather cheeky. We got on famously.

The constantly on-the-go style of living pleased me. I only slept and spent evenings at my apartment, when I bathed and dressed for whatever entertainment the night held. I mixed and mingled at all the hot spots and freely took lovers, some with titles. I researched my own family's history and discovered I was descended from a Belgian family of nobility.

So I started telling people I was a baroness. Everyone threw their pedigree around those days as a kind of currency for admission to high-society circles. Famous photographers, including George Hoyningen-Heune, Edward Steichen, and Cecil Beaton, shot me, and pictures of me graced *Vogue*'s cover and the best fashion magazines of the day. Before long, Mainbocher designs and I were the rage of Paris.

Monsieur Bocher was a real gentleman. He had a broad forehead, wavy brown hair, and a serious countenance that was handsome, welcoming, and also nondescript. I'd first met him at *Vogue*, where he was a fashion editor, and someone there told me he'd engaged in intelligence work during the Great War.

One day, when it was just the two of us in the fitting room, I said, "Tell me about your war experiences."

"That was long ago and a world away. I have a new life now."

"And I'm grateful for that. But where did you learn French, and how did you ever get involved in intelligence work?"

"I've always adored everything French. I began studying the language when I was quite young, in school in Chicago. As for intelligence work, it, shall we say, found me. In 1917, I was serving with the American Ambulance Corps in France, arranging the transport of wounded Americans back to the U.S., and I learned certain troubling things." He paused to kneel and tug at the skirt of the two-piece suit he was fitting me in.

"You can't stop there. You're just teasing me."

"Yes, well." He casually tossed his head in that unassuming way of his. "It seems German operatives were selling narcotics to American soldiers, gouging them rather deeply. I became concerned about the number of wounded soldiers showing up with opium stashes—and serious addictions. So, I reported it to the colonel in charge of my unit. Next thing I knew, the Intelligence Corps put me to work gathering information on the operatives."

"How dangerous was it?"

"Who can say? I put myself out as a music student looking for opium and handed over names and descriptions, working my way up the ladder of suppliers and disrupting the network. That was in 1917. I suppose if the war had dragged on much longer, they would've caught up with me."

"You're a man of great compass. And courage."

"War." He shook his head as if lamenting some miserable news. "If there's such a place as hell, I glimpsed it then."

As both of us were soon to learn, the seeds of another war were in the making. In the 1930s, more and more defectors fled Germany. Many of these émigrés were Jewish professionals and artists. I—and all of Paris's café society—welcomed them with open arms. And when I learned that Hitler had declared a boycott of Jewish shops and was persecuting his political adversaries, I, like them, detested him for it.

LONDON
1934

soon tired of modeling work. It had served me well for a time, and I'd earned enough money to afford a sort of vagabond independence. When a friend in the film industry encouraged me to try acting, I returned to London, auditioned for a role, and won a part in Alexander Korda's *The Private Life of Don Juan*. I was to be one of the many mistresses of Don Juan, who was played by Douglas Fairbanks. But I found acting as tedious as posing for photographers—waiting, waiting, waiting, shooting, and more waiting. I walked off the set one day, and Korda terminated my contract.

But I loved mingling with the acting set. Tallulah Bankhead, who'd starred in many London stage productions over the years, happened to be vacationing in London. I met her at an opening night party, and we became lovers. She was marvelous—audacious, witty, and wild. When we showed up at the premiere of *The Private Life of Don Juan*, her with lipstick to match her flame-red hair, me in a Schiaparelli gown, both of us in expensive furs, we made a bigger splash than the film. Yes, we set London tongues to wagging, driving around in her Bentley, flitting from one party to another, flaunting our glamour. We appalled the punctilious (hah, who cares about their hollow morals) and fascinated the imaginative (just as I would have it).

But, alas, an affair as intense as ours was destined to flame out before long. Besides, she had film contracts to honor in Hollywood. We went our separate ways after only four months, but I dare say we packed those months with more dash and mischief than many a lifelong marriage ever sees.

It was through Tallulah that I met the man who, perhaps more than any other person, changed the course of my life. We were attending the Royal Caledonian Ball at the Grosvenor Hotel, a formal affair and the highlight of London's social season.

There we were, standing on the edge of the dance floor, taking in London's most celebrated as they showed off their tuxedoes and floor-length gowns—and doing a bit of strutting ourselves—when a rather squat older man approached.

"Miss Bankhead, I'm delighted you've joined us. Though I've missed you on the stage."

"All the more time to enjoy London's offerings." She held her hand out to him and, as he accepted it, said, "Toto, may I introduce Max Aitken. Max, this is Miss Toto Koopman."

"Charmed, Miss Koopman," he said.

I offered my hand. "Delightful to meet you, sir."

"Oh, Toto, 'sir' will never do. Max is a lord. Lord Beaverbrook. He also happens to own all of London's big newspapers."

I had heard of Beaverbrook. Everybody who was anybody had. He ran the *Daily Express*, *Sunday Express*, and *Evening Standard*.

"Oh, bother," he said, "for the purposes of this evening, I'd rather be known as an entertaining host." He turned to me and asked, "Do you live here in London?"

"At the moment, yes."

"Our Toto," said Tallulah, looping her arm in mine, "is a world traveler from Java by way of Amsterdam and Paris."

"I didn't mean to imply you're unknown to me, Miss Koopman," he said. "I was merely inquiring about your current residence."

That was the beginning of my liaison with the fifty-five-year-old Lord Beaverbrook. I was twenty-five at the time. He was a widower and a billionaire press baron. Such a fascinating man—not in the least handsome, with a broad nose and toad-like face, but as magnetic as Chevalier.

Lord Beaverbrook pursued me, and I hesitated not at all to accept his attentions. Shortly after Tallulah ran off to Hollywood, I found myself spending many an evening with the brilliant and worldly Lord Beaverbrook. I imagine to the outside world we seemed rather like chalk and cheese—him being a fireplug of a man with warts marking his complexion.

But our association served us both. Dinner parties in his London suite, handsomely appointed in beaux-art style, were an education in and of themselves—in the politics of both Great Britain and the Continent, the arts scene, and the denizens of society's upper echelons. Beaverbrook's social connections stretched far and wide. Everybody who climbed or wished to climb the social ladder, including political influencers, artist hopefuls, and businessmen on the rise, sought his imprimatur or tried to rub elbows with him.

Oh, the people I met—the renowned Baroness Moura Budberg, British Intelligence officer Stewart Menzies, authors Rudyard Kipling and H.G. Wells, and the famous conductor Herbert von Karajan, to name a few. I wanted for nothing—I traveled all over Europe, attending operas in Bayreuth, Rome, Milan, and Vienna, befriending Lord Beaverbrook's many associates, and broadening my own circle of friends and acquaintances across Britain and the Continent. It was all terribly fascinating and intoxicating: learning about Europe's political players; associating with ambassadors and members of parliament; and soaking up news of political maneuvering.

But I was no kneeling student to Max's wealth and influence. My fluency in several languages served his ends as well. Each day he had at least a dozen newspapers delivered to his breakfast table. On mornings that found me at his London mansion, Stornoway House, he dispensed with his usual interpreter and relied on me to translate stories in the *Berliner Morgenpost* and *Il Messaggero*. He was a true student of world politics and never spared me commentary on the events of the day. A man of such influence could say what he wished to whomever he wanted, but he had the sagacity to parse his comments in public and use his power to benefit his news empire and political agenda.

But Beaverbrook did not hold back with me—I'd won his respect by not bowing down before him and by proving I could be as discreet as he was. The two of us agreed that Europe was on a dangerous path at that political moment. And as I traveled Europe, with and without him, I made it a point to take the measure of the storm brewing on the Continent, especially the currents circulating among the power mongers of Italy and Germany.

ROME

SEPTEMBER 1935

"Toto," Max called as he entered the suite. "We go to Rome tomorrow. Be packed by ten."

Our trip would be no sightseeing tour. At Max's prompting, Benito Mussolini had invited us to visit his residence, Villa Torlonia, in the heart of Rome. We traveled by Lord Beaverbrook's private plane, which was flown by his personal pilot, a Swissman of German extraction.

Max explained we'd meet with Mussolini that evening, spend one night at his villa, and return to London in the morning. "I have newspapers to run. And little appetite for Mussolini and his ilk."

It was because of "his ilk," Hitler in particular, that Max had sought a meeting with Mussolini. By September 1935, Hitler's actions had raised concerns among Europe's leaders. He'd consolidated his political power and brutally suppressed any rivals, taken control of the Saar region, and, in violation of the Treaty of Versailles, announced the rearmament of Germany. It looked to all the world as if he were preparing for military action.

An aide to Mussolini met us in a sleek black Mercedes and whisked us from Rome's airport to Mussolini's estate. Now it was Max who leaned on me. He knew not a word of Italian: Lord Beaverbrook didn't bother himself with such mundane matters.

"Ask the driver to take us by the Colosseum," he said. "I like to imagine the spectacle of the gladiators and lions."

I interpreted the request. It seemed the driver didn't understand English, but Max was not one to take foolish chances. He reached for my hand and whispered in my ear—as if he were merely conveying some sweet nothing— "It'll put me in the right frame of mind to joust with our host."

When we entered the grounds of Il Duce's sprawling enclave, the driver pointed out its various buildings—the family's palatial residence, an Orangerie, and a theatre. The road circling the grounds showed off the estate's extensive gardens, an impressive tower, and many sculptures.

Our driver parked in front of a building with a portico and turrets, hopped out, and opened the car door for us. "The Casina delle Civette quarters have been readied for you."

The driver carried our baggage inside and showed us around. Large windows afforded excellent views of the grounds, and stained-glass windows and scenes in majolica decorated the interior.

"Please," he said, "make yourselves comfortable. A servant will come for you at five."

An hour later, we were escorted to the main residence. Along the way, we crossed paths with a handsome, middle-aged man in sharp military dress trotting to his car. He paused to greet us. "You'll be Lord Beaverbrook and Toto Koopman. An honor to meet you," he said with a slight bow. "I'm Il Duce's son-in-law, Galeazzo Ciano."

Quickly I translated, then offered my hand. "A pleasure to meet you."

Max heartily shook his hand and said, "I hope you'll be joining us this evening."

Again, I translated.

"I will, most certainly." Ciano brushed a hand to his forehead in a casual salute. "Until then."

As Ciano slid into his car, Max gave me a confidential, leering glance. I knew just what he was thinking: That, my dear, is fresh prey. We'd spoken of Ciano's recent promotion to Minister of Foreign Affairs—and his obviously cozy relationship with Mussolini. Max had no compunction about me using my wiles to extract information.

The servant walked us up the imposing stairway of Mussolini's residence, a stairway rising to an entry lined with columns reminiscent of the Pantheon.

Mussolini met us in the expansive entryway. He was a balding, thick-jawed man, dressed in a smartly tailored blue suit with a red-and-blue-striped necktie. Mussolini had a way of throwing his legs out as he walked that lent him an air of absolute self-confidence, even though he was of mere middling stature: My five-feet-eight-inches roughly matched his height. His eyes put me in mind of a lizard's—close-set, beady, and darting, as if he was lying in wait. I didn't trust him.

He and his wife, Rachele, toured us around the main floor. Every room in the residence displayed the best of Italian art and craftsmanship—glossy marble floors, lovely frescoes, painted ceilings, crystal chandeliers, and sculptures nestled in little alcoves. The dining room alone could have seated twenty.

The four of us, plus Il Duce's personal translator, exited the villa's backside and seated ourselves. The rear terrace overlooked a reflecting pool lined with slender potted cypress. Aperitivi were served, a bright-red Campari concoction prepared with flair by Il Duce himself. We discussed the fine fall weather, the beauty of the estate, and the upcoming opera season. It was all very ordinary, like neighbors meeting on a back porch, albeit a grand one. I knew Max was anxious to get to the business at hand. Still, Mussolini never would have guessed this, for Max offered genuine praise for the lovely villa, thanked him for our comfortable quarters, and laughed easily when Il Duce mock-teased his wife about taking a lesson from my *bellissima* dress and shoes.

Ciano joined us for dinner, as did his wife. Afterward, the wives left us so we could adjourn to the business part of the visit. When Max indicated he wished me to serve as his personal translator, Mussolini seemed displeased.

"But my translator will suffice," he said.

"I respect your wishes to have him present," said Max. "But let me assure you, Toto is very efficient and discreet."

Il Duce relented, and the five of us retired to a sitting room furnished with carved-wood and red-upholstered chairs.

"The British government," Max said, "is well aware you are the leader Hitler trusts the most. And confides in."

Max and I knew that the relationship between Mussolini and Hitler was complicated. Hitler admired Mussolini's 1922 March on Rome and had tried to emulate it during his rise to power. Although they publicly praised each other, Mussolini thought Hitler crude and unsophisticated. Il Duce considered Italy far more advanced than Germany in its art, cultural heritage, and political system. The two men had first met in Venice in June 1934, and Mussolini had made no secret, at least with his inner circle, of having found Hitler's tirades childish and annoying. Still, the more brazen Hitler became, the more Il Duce took notice of his maneuverings and declarations. Hitler's success in building up his military did not escape Il Duce, and he didn't want Italy left behind should Hitler march on sought-after territory.

Mussolini slid a hand over what hair he had, even though it was neatly slicked back. "Perhaps, but I cannot claim to be privy to all Hitler's plans."

Max narrowed his eyes and nodded slightly. "I'm sure you agree his actions raise concerns. Great Britain is worried about his order for twelve submarines. What exactly does he need a fleet of submarines for?"

Il Duce hunched a shoulder as if to make light of the question. "Perhaps he simply wants to ensure shipping in the Mediterranean. As you know, we do a brisk trade with Germany. It is advantageous to both our countries."

"Still," Max said, "he claims his military is only for defensive purposes, that he is a peaceful ruler. But his build-up makes little sense when no country is planning any offensive against the German people or the country's borders."

All these speculations were nothing new. This line of conversation continued for a time, with Il Duce occasionally making side comments to his son-in-law, sometimes jesting about Hitler's admiration for him and other times ensuring Ciano understood he intended to maintain the upper hand with Hitler.

Then Max came to the point. "Can Britain count on you to help manage Hitler's ambitions for territory?"

Il Duce shifted in his seat, and Ciano fixed his eyes on his father-in-law.

"Of course, we are true friends of Britain," Mussolini said. "But your government has negotiated directly with Hitler. For instance, there's your naval pact. Why do you need me to play interloper?"

"We certainly rely on such official actions, and direct negotiation is not out of the question. We only appeal to you because of your special relationship and influence with Hitler."

"Our Grand Council formulates official positions." Il Duce cocked his head in Ciano's direction.

Ciano thumped a hand to his knee. "Most assuredly. This is the official arm of the government. And the Council has discussed its position toward Hitler."

Max turned to Ciano. "May I ask what the official position is?"

"At present," he said, "we are watching closely, not just his words but also his actions."

Max set his jaw and nodded, encouraging Ciano to elaborate. I liked Ciano; he obviously took care to mark Il Duce's words, but his expression conveyed an open sincerity, his eyes a watchful intelligence. His high brow met a squared-off hairline, and a straight, regal nose emphasized the pensive measure of his countenance.

"It is true, what you say," said Ciano. "Hitler says one thing, but his actions don't always fall in line with his words. You can count on Italy to work closely with Britain in matters concerning the security of Germany's neighbors."

"I'm pleased to hear that," said Max. "May I convey this message to Prime Minister Chamberlain? He will be keen to hear of your willingness to stay in step with Britain."

Ciano leaned back in his chair and, knitting his fingers together, looked to Il Duce.

"We would expect you to convey our sentiments to the Prime Minister." Il Duce picked up the crystal decanter of grappa. "May I offer you more?"

At the close of the meeting, Ciano escorted us back to our lodgings and offered to tour us around the grounds.

"It's such a lovely evening," he said. "There's enough moonlight to see the gardens. Would you like me to show them to you?"

Max patted the hand I had cupped under his arm. "My dear, please, why don't you? I believe I'll turn in."

As we strolled along, Ciano pointed out the enclave's theatre building. "The theatre is used for retreats, when we wish to be at our leisure and discuss policy."

"Does the entire Council meet here then?"

"No, it is more informal groups." He clutched my elbow and guided me toward a path through the garden. Under the pale moonlight, the white flowers along the pathway—roses and daisy-like blooms—glowed. He asked, "Are you Lord Beaverbrook's official translator?"

"Perhaps his primary translator. He has one or two others he can call on."

"I can tell you are close. Do you perform any other services? Are you an aide of sorts?"

I chuckled at his open curiosity about my relationship with Max. "I suppose it would be most accurate to call us close friends. And you, your relationship with Il Duce must be complicated, with you serving in an official capacity and also being his son-in-law."

"Yes, fortunately, we get on very well. We meet almost every day."

"You are perhaps his right-hand man, then?"

Now it was his turn to laugh. "I suppose I am one of many who would like to claim that position."

When he walked me back to our quarters, he asked, "Since you will come to see the opera next month, would you join me for a private dinner? We could continue our discussion of Italy's relationship with Britain."

When we said our goodbyes, he gave me the card of his private secretary. "You can contact him in advance to arrange our meeting."

A month later, I met Galeazzo Ciano at an apartment in central Rome. Max himself had encouraged my affair with Mussolini's son-in-law. But the irony of it all, as future events were to show, was completely lost on him.

CHERKLEY COURT

everal months after our meeting with Mussolini, Max and I motored to his Cherkley Court estate, twenty miles from London in the Surrey hills. It was to be a quiet retreat, with just the two of us and Stewart Menzies, the Assistant Director of British Intelligence. At the time, Menzies was schooling me in intelligence gathering. Max had asked him to tutor me after my first assignation with Galeazzo Ciano, and I welcomed the opportunity to learn from a master.

"She can be a valuable asset," Max had told Stewart. "God knows she's proficient enough in languages. She should learn how to protect herself."

Of course, I agreed. After all, I was consorting with Il Duce's son-in-law, who operated a mere arm's length from Mussolini and high-level German officials. Now that I had tasted political intrigue, I thought it advisable to learn how to procure secrets and fend off danger.

Max's country estate was the perfect place for my lessons in spying. Stewart Menzies could easily claim a holiday in the country. Keeping guests to a minimum ensured no one else would learn I was being schooled in espionage, and the four-hundred-acre grounds offered privacy from the outside world. Anybody who didn't know Stewart would never have suspected him of being a master spy. He had a dowdy look about him—with his pale blue eyes, sandy hair, bowler hat, and blasé black suit.

There was just one complication that weekend. Max's son, Max Aitken, Jr., showed up unannounced, claiming he'd decided on a whim to escape to the country for a few days. Most people referred to him as Little Max, but I called him MJ, short for Max John. Since MJ didn't know Stewart Menzies was tutoring me, we needed to take precautions to keep him from learning about my lessons. Max, Stewart, and I had all agreed on the strictest terms of secrecy about my training.

The fact is, I was both annoyed at MJ for showing up and pleased to see him, though I kept my feelings to myself. I'd first met Lord Beaverbrook's son in 1935 at Max's Stornoway House in London. Dashing hardly began to describe him—he was handsome and smooth-complected, quite the opposite of his father, with one arched eyebrow, as if he were perpetually on the hunt for mischief. Women flocked to him at parties, for he was clever and quick to laugh. He did resemble his father in one way—he, too, could be a cad. Not surprisingly, his father chided him about his tendencies to flit from one love affair to another and to flaunt his rakish side at parties, which, in my opinion, made him all the more entertaining.

Max was quite blind to his own faults but readily spotted them in others. He thought MJ too flighty and given to life's pleasures, though he himself had done his share of pleasure-seeking. He'd also spoiled MJ, who benefited from the family wealth in many ways. MJ was an aviator with his own private plane. His father had set him up in a penthouse on Portman Square and granted him a hefty allowance, which MJ freely flashed about. I was immediately attracted to MJ, but at the time, Max and I were preoccupied with political matters, including not only our communications with Mussolini and Ciano but also with British politicians about Italy's invasion of Abyssinia and the threat of aggression by Hitler.

In 1935, MJ had been commissioned as a captain in the Royal Auxiliary Air Force. This, at least, his father approved of. So, dinner that evening was taken up with talk of British, Italian, and German military prowess.

Over the filet mignon entrée, conversation turned to the invitation Hitler had extended to Max. Hitler had learned of Lord Beaverbrook's meeting with Mussolini and invited Max to Berlin. Apparently, he was keen to show off his military installations and imagined that Beaverbrook would present the ideal opportunity to broadcast his military might to the world.

"It's a good thing I've got a steely disposition," Max said. "Hitler is supposedly a most disagreeable conversationalist. Even Mussolini finds him insufferable."

Menzies tipped his wine glass to Max. "Think of it as your patriotic duty. Take your best photographer. If the man wants to strut for the world, you might as well get pictures of his installations."

MJ said, "Bring me along. I'd like a look at his fleet."

"Don't be ridiculous," Max said. "You're a military man. Let's not be obvious about it."

"Hmph," MJ said. "Speaking of being obvious, you're a newspaperman."

"It's best you stay behind," Max said to his son. "Toto can come to translate."

"Oh, I don't know, Max," I said. "You saw the fuss Mussolini made about me interpreting for you." The truth is, I didn't want to meet Hitler. I loathed everything he stood for, and I was disinclined to pretend otherwise.

Max said, "I'll simply insist, as I did with Il Duce."

"Won't your pilot do? He'll be flying you over anyway. And he's a native German speaker."

"We'll discuss this later," Max said. He hated to argue in public. Later he'd try to order me to accompany him. The fact is, in addition to my distaste for Hitler and Germany's atmosphere of belligerent nationalism, I had another reason to beg off. Weeks earlier, MJ had invited me to attend *Lohengrin* at the Royal Opera House, the tenor Lauritz Melchior being a particular favorite of mine.

That evening, when I was alone with Max, he broached the topic again. "I'd like you to go to Berlin with me."

"I'd really rather not. You can do without me."

"Of course I can, but I prefer to have you as translator. Your presence takes the edge off. It'll look more like a casual tour than an intelligence-gathering mission."

"There's no need to camouflage your intent. Hitler's only too eager to show off his military."

"I'm asking you to come. I don't want to argue about this."

That's how it was with us those days—him trying to strong-arm me and me having to assert my independence.

"Neither do I. And I'm not coming."

"You can be most disagreeable. And ungrateful. I thought you enjoyed meeting dictators. And their spawn."

"That's a rather crude way of putting it." I barely suppressed a huff. "I'm not your assistant. And I'm not going."

I spent Saturday afternoon walking the grounds with Stewart—in misty rain—being further schooled in how to manage live and dead letter drops, spot and shake a tail, identify rendezvous spots, escape a chokehold, and handle a gun. (But there'd be no shooting today since MJ might ask about the noise.) Stewart always insisted I wear trousers for our "walks around the estate" so we could practice some of the physical moves. He'd even taught me how to kill with my bare hands or a knife. When I said I could foresee no situation in which I'd be forced to crush a man's trachea or slice his throat, he explained I must be prepared nevertheless and that the first time was always the hardest.

We also discussed how I might create a convincing cover, though we agreed I was probably too well known to engage in such artifice, except under unusual circumstances. Still, Stewart impressed upon me the importance of understanding the little quirks and customs that would help me blend into my surroundings. I learned to use fabric instead of paper for messages hidden on one's person—since fabric didn't make noise as paper did. The whole process was exciting and chilling at the same time. But Stewart praised my progress in the art of espionage: "You're an excellent student, with just one liability—your fame as a model. But that may not matter in commoners' circles, and you're smart enough to turn it into an asset."

While Stewart and I walked the grounds, Max kept MJ out of the way, probably criticizing him for his latest act of brazenness. What Max didn't know then was that MJ and I were seeing each other and, in fact, had fallen in love. After I'd first met him, I couldn't get him off my mind—he was delightfully engaging and light-spirited. As it turned out, he felt the same about me. We'd kept our affair very hush-hush, but soon I'd need to extricate myself from Max's iron clutches, and it'd only be a matter of time before all of London learned of my affair with MJ. The plan was for me to break it off with Max in the next week and, afterward, for MJ to tell him of our involvement.

None of this would be easy. Max was one of the most insufferably jealous creatures I'd ever met. Early on, he'd been reasonably respectful of my time and autonomy, but lately he'd become exceedingly demanding, expecting complete loyalty and fidelity. The mighty Lord Beaverbrook might have understood the minds and machinations of Europe's rulers, but he didn't understand me. All my life I'd been the different one, neither Dutch nor Javanese, neither wealthy nor destitute. I'd not had the luxury of gradually learning the rules of high society by proximity or parental tutelage. I'd survived, even thrived, by making a quick study of the beau monde. In a way, I held the advantage, for I'd learned not only how to comport myself among them but also how to exploit their foibles.

I did have some qualms about leaving Max; he'd taught me so much about world politics and introduced me to many high-level politicians. Still, I couldn't have borne his possessiveness much longer, even if I hadn't fallen for MJ.

MJ and I knew difficulties lay ahead, but we didn't anticipate the intensity of Max's reaction. Or that he'd try every trick he could think of to keep us apart.

LONDON

MARCH–JUNE 1936

"Max, we need to talk." We retired to his parlor, and I swung the French doors closed behind us. This room was plush and cozy— with its wingback chairs, smoke stand, and oil paintings of the gentle English countryside. Yes, I'd benefited from Lord Beaver-brook's wealth and influence, but none of that mattered anymore. "I'm leaving you. I want my freedom. I hope you'll understand."

His puffy cheeks splotched with redness. "I should've seen this coming. You've been nothing but contrary lately. And insolent."

"I don't want a scene. I'm grateful for your generosity, but I won't be ordered about."

"You didn't mind when I gave you money for gowns and travel."

"Please, let's dispense with the melodrama. Ours has been an equal exchange. And I'm nobody's possession."

"You'll regret this. You can't just discard me on a whim."

But my decision was no whim. I gathered the few belongings I kept in his apartment, and that was the end of it.

A week later, MJ broke the news to his father that he and I were involved. I met MJ for dinner afterward, just the two of us at the Grill in the Carlton Hotel—one of the first times we were seen together in public.

MJ pulled my chair out for me. "If only you could've heard him. I've never seen my father so incensed."

"He doesn't take kindly to being shown up, does he?"

"He raved like a crazy man, spewing a flock of epithets. He referred to you as 'that Negress.'"

I exploded with laughter. I couldn't help myself. "That's the best he can come up with? After he carried on with this so-called Negress?"

"He says to tell you you're persona non grata with him. And not to expect any more favors."

"You mean he's written me out of the will?"

"Hah," MJ laughed. We both knew the idea of me being in Max's will was preposterous. "He says I'll soon tire of you, and you'll be crawling back to him, like everybody else."

I took his hand. "Your father's in store for a great deal of disappointment."

MJ and I were crazy about each other. At the end of the month, I gave up my cramped apartment and moved into his penthouse. But Max's jealousy knew no bounds. He barred mention of me in his newspapers' society pages, had his informers tail us around London, and ranted to anybody who'd listen about my "loose morals" and "unscrupulous conduct." Since Lord Beaverbrook had introduced me far and wide around London, my affairs with the father and son made for tantalizing gossip.

That I took lovers as I pleased and whenever I wished should not have come as a surprise to anyone, including Lord Beaverbrook. Since I was famous for my glamour and impunity, not just in London but in Paris and beyond, he should have known I'd not let anyone treat me as property, not even him.

But it seemed nothing would convince Beaverbrook to give up his smear campaign.

When MJ and I showed up for the Royal Caledonian Ball in May, the door-man intercepted us. "Sir, I'm sorry, but I have strict orders not to admit you."

"This is bloody ridiculous," MJ said. "Let me speak to my father."

"I'm sorry, he's occupied at the moment."

I didn't wish to give Max the satisfaction of seeing MJ upset over us being blackballed. I took MJ's arm. "Look, we're all dressed up. Vivian and John are probably having a quiet evening at Vivian's. Let's pop in on them."

Reluctantly, MJ backed down, though not before leaving a message for Max. "You can tell my father he's gone too far this time. And when word gets around, he'll be the one who looks petty and foolish."

What a fuss Max and his entourage made about MJ and me. For heaven's sake, was this modern-day London or some hidebound medieval village? I refused to succumb to the shallow judgments of men like Lord Beaverbrook, who put no restrictions on their choices of lovers. As best as I could tell, Max, a man of supreme self-assurance, had never done battle with his conscience. Why should I?

BERLIN

n August, I flew to Berlin to attend the Summer Olympic Games. MJ accompanied his father to the games; needless to say, I was not invited to join their entourage.

MJ was none too pleased about me attending. "I don't see why you'd even set foot in Germany. My God, Hitler's a maniac."

"It's the event of the year. Why ever would I miss it? After all, you're going."

I'd kept my interest in gathering intelligence from MJ. Stewart Menzies had long ago instructed me to maintain secrecy—not just to protect myself but also those around me. Not that I had any spying assignments these days. Beaverbrook had probably tried to poison Menzies against me. Still, I reasoned, if I uncovered any valuable information, I could pass it on to Menzies. He was the consummate professional and would likely put country above Max's slur campaign.

"I don't like it, Toto," MJ said. "With all the propaganda about Aryan purity. I don't think it's safe for you."

"Oh, dear, you're worrying more than necessary. It's not like I'll be wandering the streets by myself."

I arranged to rendezvous with friends from both Paris and London at the Hotel Adlon. The taxi ride from the airport to central Berlin was quite a spectacle. The city was awash with Nazi banners and gleaming with modernity. Window boxes bloomed with red geraniums. Hitler clearly wanted to impress the athletes, officials, and fans flocking to the games.

On my first evening in the city, my friend Herbert von Karajan called for me at my hotel. We strolled to a restaurant with a view of Brandenburg Gate and chose an outdoor table. Herbert looked quite dapper, dressed in a tan suit with a white shirt and stylish red tie, his shock of black hair combed straight back, and his dark-brown eyes dancing with joie de vivre.

He pulled out the chair for me. "Do you find the city much changed since your last visit?"

Eight months earlier, I'd attended his debut performance of Beethoven's *Fidelio* at the Berlin State Opera. His introduction was a triumph—Germany was in love with their charismatic new conductor. A mutual friend had informed me of Herbert's membership in the Nazi Party. When I mentioned this to him, he'd said, "Do you think I'd have been appointed concertmaster if I hadn't joined the party? I'm just doing what I need to do to advance my career. I can assure you I'm not on back-slapping terms with Adolf."

I sat and arranged my hands on my lap. "The city is remarkably transformed, though I've been told the change is recent."

"Still, the people are happy. You can see it everywhere. They're taking pride in their country again."

"So, you are pleased with Hitler's policies?" I'd been reading the Berlin papers earlier in the day and had noticed the unflattering coverage of the American athlete Jesse Owens.

"For the most part," he said.

I thought it best not to press him on Hitler's views about race. A waiter appeared at our table and saved me from this line of conversation.

The waiter asked, "Would the gentleman and lady like a drink?"

Herbert turned to me. "What would you like?"

"Shall we have Champagne?"

Herbert turned to the waiter and asked, "What Champagne are you serving?"

A man at a nearby table of four said in a loud voice, "Surely you're not going to serve that woman."

The other men at the table laughed.

The waiter turned his back on them and stammered, "I'm . . . I'm sorry. We have Perrier-Jouët 1933. Would that be acceptable?"

"Waiter," the man called. "I asked you a question."

Herbert's jaw tightened. He spoke softly to the waiter. "Why don't you send the manager over before you bring the Champagne."

I reached for his hand. "Herbert," I said, "let's just ignore them."

"No, I'll not allow this." He turned to the waiter. "I insist on speaking with the manager."

I shifted in my chair, inching closer to Herbert. I leaned toward him and said, "This, I'm afraid, is the sort of conduct Hitler's policies encourage."

"I fear you're right."

Herbert had words with the manager, who turned to the table of trouble-makers. "Please, gentlemen, I ask you to respect the privacy of the other diners."

I heard chairs screeching against the concrete sidewalk. The loud-mouthed man in the party spoke. "We don't wish to dine among such filth."

At that, the party stormed off.

Herbert sighed. "I'm sorry for the embarrassment. It was uncalled for."

"Perhaps they thought me a Negro—like Jesse Owens."

"I don't know what they thought, but I regret not being able to protect you from such treatment."

I changed the topic, inquiring about the upcoming opera season and his travel plans. I shared news about mutual acquaintances. When I circled back to the matter of government policies and asked if he was happy with his move to Berlin, he said, "I'm happy with my post at the State Opera. I enjoy the city's musical offerings. The rest I ignore."

The city filled up over the next few days, and I accompanied a party of five to the opening ceremony. It was full of pomp and fanfare—trumpeters playing from the ramparts, a lean, muscular flame-carrier running into the stadium to light the torch, and Hitler opening the event to booming applause and Heil Hitler salutes. The stadium was completely packed every single day. When Jesse Owens won his first event, confusion rippled through the stands, with some cheering wildly and others sitting in stunned silence. But the crowd slowly warmed to him, and when he took his third gold medal, the whole stadium erupted into cheers. But I doubt Hitler applauded Owens' triumph.

One evening I dined out with a group of friends, some French, some Germans, many of whom had left Germany. They minced no words about Hitler's policies, reporting on book burnings and assassinations of political rivals.

"What books are they burning?" I asked.

"All books by Jews," my German friend explained, "and anything with the least whiff of criticism. The great philosophers and many novelists."

"Can you get me a list? I'm especially interested in any Italian authors."

"Yes, I can write something up for you."

I told them about my experience at the restaurant my first evening in the city and added, "Not once in Paris or London did anyone make a scene over my skin color."

One of the German men at our table said, "They took down all the 'Jews Forbidden' signs before the games. But, mark my words, they'll go back up again when the world is no longer watching."

Anise, a Parisian friend of mine, said, "I'm just glad I live in a country that doesn't bow down before a murderous dictator."

Berlin may have put on a good face for the Olympics, but I'd seen the ugliness lurking beneath the surface. I left Germany before the games concluded, full of outrage over what I'd seen and heard. I feared not only for Germany's Jews but for others like me—people who didn't fit the perfect Aryan mold.

LONDON

1936–1939

eaverbrook's harassment of MJ and me went on for months that stretched into years. It was inconvenient and sometimes annoying, but MJ and I tried to laugh it off. We were in love. What did we care about his father's desperate recriminations? In late 1936, we were granted a few months of reprieve while everyone was preoccupied with Edward's abdication and marriage to Wallis Simpson.

Then, one summer day in 1937, as I entered the lobby and headed for the stairs to our penthouse, I noticed a husky man peel away from the post he'd been leaning against. He fell in step behind me and closed the distance to four feet. His out-of-style suit strained at his bulging belly, and he looked for all the world like a thug.

MJ was out at the time, and this man made me uncomfortable. I didn't want to let myself into the penthouse and risk him forcing his way in after me. In all likelihood, he only meant to frighten me, but I hated to take any chances. I needed to shake him. As I reached the second floor, I saw a couple approaching the stairs. I didn't know them but had exchanged greetings with them in the past.

I piped up with, "Hello, darlings, let me walk down with you. We haven't chatted in forever."

They must have spotted the man behind me and gleaned my meaning because, as I turned and fell in with them, they warmly inquired about me. The stalker, thwarted in whatever he might have planned, pretended nonchalance and, a few minutes later, made his way back down the stairs and out the door.

When I told MJ, he said, "The old fool doesn't know when he's beat. Let's get out of here and make his spies work for their money."

MJ and I flew off to Spain for a long holiday, and we managed to foil Max's informants for a time. But when we returned to London, the harassment started up all over again. Max had ordered mutual friends and acquaintances not to invite us to their parties, not even to galas and benefits. He slurred me in his social circles and generally played the righteous moralist.

After all this smearing, many of his acquaintances shunned us. I admit I missed conversations with ambassadors and politicians about the political changes sweeping Europe. But I cared little for the shallow people in Max's inner circle, and MJ and I made our way just fine among our friends and the younger set—mostly artists and free spirits who loved us all the more for the iconoclasts we were.

We carried on as we pleased amid the censure Beaverbrook rained down on us. In fact, all the adversity perhaps had the opposite effect Max strived for: MJ and I came to feel protective of each other and grew even closer. There was even a certain sport to our affair, what with his father downright scandalized over MJ stealing *his* lover.

What did I care about gossip when there was no limit to the wealthy and attractive men—and women—who accompanied me to the opera, plays, and soirées? And MJ agreed. Ours was an arrangement that afforded each of us complete liberty. MJ had the occasional fling, as did I. But we always came back to each other.

Then, in June 1939, MJ surprised me with a marriage proposal. Of all things, marriage.

"Really," I said. "I'm happy with things just as they are. Why ruin what we have?"

He'd actually knelt in front of me. "To pledge ourselves to each other, live in wedded bliss, and stop the wagging tongues."

"And what if I prefer unwedded bliss?"

"Look, we love each other—I want you in my life always."

"You'll have to give me time to think about it."

"Meantime," he said, rising, "I'm going to discuss it with my father. Perhaps him knowing we're serious enough to consider marriage will end this ridiculous campaign of his."

"I suppose it couldn't get much worse."

———

But in that, I was proved wrong. A few days later, Max summoned me to a "highly confidential meeting." He told me that if I married his son, he'd cut him off—and disown him for good.

"How could you be so cruel?" I asked. "MJ is completely unaccustomed to any other sort of life."

"If you decide to marry, both of you'll have to learn to live like paupers. As long as I'm alive, he'll never secure work in any high-level position."

I'd thought hard about MJ's proposal, and I couldn't imagine marrying him—or anyone else. Still, I'd never admit this to Max. At the moment, I only wanted to do battle on MJ's behalf. "You know MJ may be headstrong enough to defy you anyway."

"That's where you come in, my dear."

"I can hardly believe you're being so small-minded about all this."

"I have my reasons," he said. "And a proposal for you."

We were meeting at Baroness Moura Budberg's apartment. Both Max and I had remained on good terms with her, and she'd promised us privacy. Max had made it clear I was not to tell MJ of the meeting beforehand. Now he added more conditions.

"If you agree to neither inform my son of our meeting nor marry him, I will give you a generous allowance for life." He reached into his inside suit pocket, extracted a folded paper, and placed it on the coffee table between us. "One-hundred-twenty-five pounds a month."

My God, he wanted to buy me off. With that sum, I could live comfortably anywhere in the world. I picked up the paper and read it.

. . . a cheque for 125 pounds to be drafted from the bank account of Maxwell William Aitken on the first of each month in perpetuity and sent to Miss Toto Koopman at the address of her choosing. She is to keep my agent at the Bank of England informed as to the address it is to be sent to, but that address may not be the same as the residence of one Maxwell John Aitken.

I am not particularly proud to admit that I signed the agreement on the spot.

LONDON

"Yes, I suppose I am selfish." I hated doing this to MJ, hated the coolness in my voice. But everything had changed. I couldn't wed him, and he wouldn't stop asking. It seemed he wouldn't be happy unless I agreed to marriage, and I knew that'd be disastrous for him. His father would cut him off—completely and forever. Without his father's money, I feared MJ would flounder and flail.

Two months after I'd signed the agreement with Max, I was still living with MJ, but I felt suspended in a kind of miasma. I'd not given Max an address to send his monthly checks. That seemed like such a big step, albeit one I'd need to take sooner or later.

All summer, I'd been a riot of feelings, ever since learning that my mother, far away in Java, had passed. It was as if her death opened doors in my mind that I'd shuttered over the last several years—my years of diversion and adventure with MJ. But now, all the ghosts rattling behind those doors assailed me.

I'd tried living with one man, and I did love MJ, but I'd made a mistake. This life didn't suit me. I felt stifled, shut out of the world of political maneuvering and secret trading, especially now that portents of war pervaded the Continent. In March, Hitler had seized Czechoslovakia, and Great Britain and all of Europe feared his intention to march on Poland.

MJ leaned forward in his chair, knitting his fingers together. "This makes no sense, Toto. I know you love me."

It would have been so easy to open my arms to him, to put this off another month, even another week. But no, I couldn't let him see I still loved him: He'd only sweep me into his arms and crush my resolve.

"I can't stay. I'm not the same person anymore."

He winced and swung his head aside as if I'd slapped him.

I wanted to beg his forgiveness, to explain it crushed me to hurt him so. But I couldn't. It was more than not wanting to marry, more than Max's condition I not reveal our agreement. My life with MJ had begun to feel aimless: the late-night dinner parties and oh-so-clever conversation; my friend Vivian and I taking ourselves off on "proper shopping sprees"; MJ forever proposing a rich new diversion—a holiday in Venice or chemin de fer at the Monte Carlo tables. For weeks, I'd tried busying myself at the usual pastimes: carousing with friends at the 400 Club; enjoying the occasional high tea; and losing myself in shows, plays, and movies. But I couldn't shake the nagging sense that my life had become inconsequential—that nothing I was doing made a pebble's worth of difference.

He stood, paced a few steps, and stopped. "You're upset over losing your mother. You just need more time."

"It's not that." At least not in a way I could explain. By the time I'd received word of my mother's death, the funeral in Java was over. I'd never see her again. I could only revisit the memory of our parting—that day when I left Java for school in the Netherlands, when my mother's lovely brown face glowed with good cheer, pride, and sorrow. I could still feel her arms wrapped around me as she whispered in my ear, "Look at you, my bright little beacon, going out into the world."

And now, somehow, I sensed my mother's presence. It was as if, when her body died, her spirit blazed up, more luminous than ever, and took hold in me, noiselessly urging me on to some fresh destiny.

I met MJ's pleading eyes. MJ—with his rakish raised eyebrow and Romeo charm—looked different to me now. My disquiet had cast a sheen of triviality over him. "Everything has changed."

"*We* haven't." MJ took my hand. "Tell me I don't make you happy."

I let him curl his fingers around mine. "I can't marry you. I'd never make a proper wife."

This expensive penthouse, set up as our home and gathering place for friends, suddenly reeked of coarse sentiment. The mauve Queen Anne love seat, a gift to me from his father—before MJ and I became lovers. The compact mahogany dining set we'd purchased: "We'll never invite more than four for dinner," I'd explained. "Even that's a test of my culinary talents." The sleek chrome floor lamp he'd surprised me with on my thirtieth birthday. Yes, I'd miss it all, but I couldn't live like this anymore.

What did MJ have to offer once the whirl of madcap love and utter surrender to its delights died down? The thrills of turning heads—my slender physique clad in Paris chic and handsome MJ, the dashing RAF man and son of one of England's most wealthy men—had soured into empty superficiality. Of course, gadding about Europe and partying in its capitals alongside my charming MJ entertained. But the amusement and gratification paled when compared to meetings with heads of state and their entourages. I needed purpose in my life. And I'd settled for mere diversion.

"To hell with marriage," he said. "We'll just go on as before."

"*I* can't." I looked up at him. "I'm sorry. It's over."

He beat the air with a fist. "Mark my words, as long as you wander, you'll never be happy."

My stomach seized up. I sprang from my seat and rushed to the entryway table. Grabbing my purse, I called to him over my shoulder, "I'll fetch my clothes later."

I let myself out and bounded down the steps. I could stop at Vivian's apartment for a while, but that was no definite kind of plan. Whatever would I do now?

LONDON AND FLORENCE
AUGUST–SEPTEMBER 1939

That afternoon, I took myself off to Kew Gardens, hardly noticing when I covered the same ground, meandering along its walkways until my feet throbbed. When the chill wind unleashed a needling drizzle, I scurried to the Palm House and sheltered in its humid warmth.

Poor MJ. I worried about him, but he'd have our social set to comfort him. Let them vilify me if they wished. It might nudge him out of his grief.

And I had enough to worry about. For years I'd given myself over to pleasure and its distractions—until laughter and luxury bound me like an unthinking habit. I couldn't end this senseless careening from one gay event to another as long as I stayed in London.

I plopped down on a bench and tugged off my shoes. My parents hadn't approved of the life I'd led in Paris. Or in London. Why had I settled for a modeling career? And now the frivolous life of a gadabout? I'd disappointed them. Because I could. Because I'd been gifted with the slim figure of an Egyptian goddess, because Paris's modeling houses found my tawny skin exotic, because the rich and celebrated welcomed me to their soirées.

I'd lost my way.

The words my mother spoke when we parted came back to me: "Don't be afraid, my little love, take courage. Make your ancestors proud." At this very moment, my mother and ancestors were looking down on me, and one day I would meet them in the land of the many.

I'd wanted to make my parents proud, wanted them to believe I was courageous. But I'd never counted myself as such. Perhaps adventurous—like back in '34 and '35, while I worked alongside Lord Beaverbrook at power-broking. Such heady encounters I'd been privy to, sitting beside him while we conveyed the sentiments of Mussolini and Ciano to Stewart Menzies. It was all so satisfying. I believe if my parents had known of these endeavors, they would have been proud.

I missed those thrilling times as Lord Beaverbrook's political co-conspirator. My life had meant something then. I'd glimpsed the inner world of deal-making, the secrets behind government machinations, and the motives and greed that fueled dictators and their hangers-on. During my brief romance with Herbert von Karajan, I'd observed Hitler's skill in commandeering artists for propaganda purposes. At the Berlin Olympics, I'd gathered stories about Nazi persecution of Jews and subversives.

And now, with all of Europe worrying about Germany's fearsome military, with Hitler tidily annexing Austria, and with prospects for war on the Continent heating up, what was I doing—except standing by in the face of it all? If only my intelligence-gathering hadn't been the result of happenstance: my association and travels with Lord Beaverbrook. Because the days of collaborating with him were over.

What could I possibly accomplish on my own? Nothing while I cavorted about London. That much was clear.

———

Two days later, with the outlines of a plan in mind, I invited my friend Randolph Churchill to a quiet dinner at the Lion's Head Pub, a dimly lit, dark-wooded eatery in Kensington that guaranteed anonymity.

No sooner had Randolph and I slid into a corner booth than he asked, "Just what happened between you and Little Max? The poor fellow's stunned. And heartsick."

He probably intended his reproach to sting: Randolph and I had once been lovers, though for only a few months. He claimed he was mad for me, but I never felt a lover's spark for him. Yes, we had a terrific time gallivanting around London. Playboy that he was, the young and dashing welcomed us to their parties. In the end, we parted amicably and, thankfully, brought off a friendly truce.

"I simply couldn't go on with that kind of life," I told him. "And—not that you'll believe this—it's tearing me up, too."

"Come now. There's more to it than that." Randolph shot me a knowing smirk. "Or it wouldn't have lasted what—three, almost four years? That's a record for you, isn't it?"

"MJ started going on and on about marriage, but I'm not the marrying kind."

"I heard the old scandal monger threatened to cut off MJ."

"I wouldn't doubt it for a minute," I said, wondering how word of that had gotten out. Perhaps Max himself had threatened MJ. It'd be like him to drive another wedge between us, just to ensure his grand plan to keep us apart. "Do you honestly think MJ could manage without his father's money?"

Randolph rapped his knuckles on the table. "What about *you* and Beaverbrook's money?"

Beaverbrook had sworn me to secrecy about our financial agreement. But I couldn't hold back everything, not when I wanted Randolph's help. "Suffice it to say we have a confidential arrangement."

Randolph's eyes glinted playfully beneath his scrunched brow. "Come, Toto, you can trust me with your secret."

"I refuse to limp along beside MJ when I can't give him what he wants, not without subjecting myself to suffocation by marriage." I glowered at him. He could be such a bloody bounder. "And, actually, I do have a secret to hash over with you."

That seemed to get his attention—and curiosity—for when the waiter arrived to take our order, Randolph rushed him along. "Yes, man, Guinness and shepherd's pie is what I said."

He leaned in. "A secret? You sphinx, do tell."

While I was retrieving my belongings from the penthouse, I'd happened on a week-old letter: Friends from Hungary had invited me to join them on an art-hunting expedition in Florence. That had made up my mind. "I'm going to Italy. To gather intelligence."

Randolph wagged his head as if to shake off disbelief. "To spy?"

The sconce dimly lighting our ruddy-stained booth accentuated Randolph's prominent jaw and patrician forehead. It gave him a look of sturdiness, but I understood his weakness: He hated operating in his prominent father's shadow but nonetheless strove to please him.

"I believe that's what I said. And you're going to help." If anyone could assist me, it was Randolph, with his father, Winston, closely allied with the House of Commons and the Committee on Defense.

"Look, you're just the sort that could manage it, what with rattling off French, Italian, and whatever else when it suits you. But Christ, Toto, it's dangerous. If you're restless, why not go back to modeling?"

I rolled my eyes. "Do you have any idea how dreadful it is to be dressed up and paraded in front of a camera? For hours on end? I'm not some walking, talking sculpture."

"Restless is one thing, foolish another."

With an impatient cluck, I shook my head. "Do you imagine I take this lightly?"

"Have you any idea what you'd be letting yourself in for? Intelligence work takes patience and plotting." He pulled the corner of his mouth into a smirk. "You couldn't even fulfill that movie contract."

Oh, Randolph, I thought, is it any wonder I left you after three months? "Acting is merely modeling with movement—being trotted out on a set like some showpiece. I've got a brain, you know, and convictions."

"I suppose you think that's all you need."

"There was a time I actively gathered intelligence on the Continent. The flotsam method it's called: collecting open-source information from locals, noticing troop movements, and such. For Beaverbrook. And the British government." Vienna, Berlin, Rome, and Milan—I'd hopscotched all over Europe, establishing contacts, tossing off casual questions, and keeping my eyes and ears open. I'd fed my findings to Beaverbrook and his government contacts. Few people besides Lord Beaverbrook knew this. Just Stewart Menzies, Chief of Secret Intelligence Service, and, now, Randolph.

"Why put yourself in such a position?" Randolph asked. "With Fascism and Nazism on the rise."

"I'll be deuced. You've just answered the question."

"Look, you could easily go on living the high life, if not with MJ, with any number of men who'd line up to court you."

I interwove my fingers and tapped my thumbs together. "The fact that you and men like you think that makes me an excellent prospect for intelligence work."

"There's a whole section of the government devoted to intelligence. Leave it to them. You're a damned amateur."

I saw no need to bring up my training with Stewart Menzies at British Intelligence. I knew it was always best to reveal nothing more than the most essential information, even to those one trusted. Another tactic was always to convey confidence.

I glared at him. "If you're trying to dissuade me, it's not working."

"Christ, if the Nazis throw people in jail for not saluting, imagine what they do to spies. Can you picture yourself in an interrogation room with some sadistic bastard?"

But I wasn't going to Germany, and I needed Randolph's assistance. I might have prevailed on Menzies to support my mission, but in the years since I'd trained with him, Beaverbrook had likely polluted him with unflattering stories about me. I needed Randolph and his father's connections with the British government. Winston Churchill could grease the wheels for me with Stewart Menzies.

I braced my spine against the booth's back. "Randolph, I don't need you to evaluate my suitability. Just to ask your father how I can best serve in Italy. And, of course, to consider this matter strictly confidential."

— —

In under a week, I'd tidied up my London affairs and arranged to have mail and checks routed, avoiding MJ the whole time. When I discussed my plans with friends, I simply pretended I was off on another opera-hopping junket. Naturally, the more nervous and politically astute asked: "Whatever reason can you have to leave England at such a time?" I made light of their inquiries, playing down the prospects of another war: "Nobody has a taste for it, not after the debacle of the Great War."

With Winston Churchill's approval and orders in hand, I set off for Florence. Within days of my arrival, disturbing headlines rocked Europe: On September 1, GERMANY INVADES AND BOMBS POLAND; and on September 4, BRITAIN AND FRANCE DECLARE WAR ON GERMANY.

FLORENCE

OCTOBER–DECEMBER 1939

forced myself to wait three weeks before sitting down, with pen poised, at the narrow secretary in my Florence hotel room. I should write to one or two London friends. They would expect it.

MJ, my dearest,

Florence is all I remembered it to be—full of old-world allure, its churches resplendent with Renaissance art, and the River Arno flowing as quietly as a summer breeze. It all brings to mind our wonderful month here two years ago.

I have joined Reka and Tamás at a comfortable hotel not far from the train station, in a delightfully Florentine neighborhood. We three spend our days scouring the city for paintings and sculptures. They're on the hunt for notable works by the lesser contemporaries of Giotto, da Vinci, and Michelangelo. What a heavenly pastime it is! Surely you recall the galleries here and how I could never get enough of them.

I yanked my pen off the page. I couldn't tell him the city's charms only heightened my frustration. That I was desperate to gather intelligence for Britain. That Germany would have been the more logical destination except for it being so much more dangerous. That he was right: Only lily-white Aryans could blend in there, and the sleepy veil of my eyelids and tint of my skin would attract scrutiny. So, Italy it must be. I mustn't write about these matters. Not with him in the RAF. What if he were shot down and interrogated? It would be one more thing for him to worry about—or be tortured into telling.

My darling, I wrote, *everywhere I go, I'm reminded of you, of how much I miss you, of how I long to speak to you.*

I slapped down my pen. I mustn't go on like this. It would only tempt MJ to come running. I rubbed a hand over my forehead and studied the lines I'd written. Then I tore up the letter.

A week later, I tried again.

> *Dear MJ,*
>
> *I hope you're well and enjoying fall in London. We've had a long stretch of cold, clear weather here. Quite lovely for dashing about.*
>
> *The art hunting has gone swimmingly. Reka and Tamás acquired a sculpture of Saint Stephen and two lovely paintings, both of Old Testament scenes. We spent several days admiring them before they shipped them home.*
>
> *The three of us have made a quest of sampling Florence's finest ristorantes. What a departure they are from London's middling fare. The delectable sauces, the fresh vegetables, the succulent pasta, even the inexpensive wine. They're all simply incomparable.*
>
> *During one of our gallery outings, we happened upon a lovely young woman from Düsseldorf who's studying Italian language and art. Elisabeth and I hit it off famously. Just last night, over dinner in her apartment, we spent the entire evening debating the merits of La Scala and the Wiener Staatsoper, pitting Verdi against Puccini, and arguing about if or how one could separate Wagner's scurrilous conduct from his beautiful music. It was awfully good sport.*

I paused and read over the words. Oh my, I thought, I might as well be writing a distant cousin. And I really ought not to name people I meet: It would not surprise me if my letters were intercepted and inspected. I destroyed that letter, too.

Reka and Tamás departed in mid-November, leaving me lonely but not aimless. I read every newspaper I could get my hands on, something I'd had little time for during my weeks of art hunting with my friends.

The newspapers provided much to ponder, what with Hitler having persuaded Mussolini to sign the Pact of Steel, rendering Italy a hornet's nest of political and military maneuvering. It seemed most Italians feared war and hoped Hitler wouldn't drag their country into the mire. Still, wartime propaganda pervaded the newspapers. Before the rationing of meat and coffee, newspaper articles extolled the virtues of vegetarianism and the harmful effects of coffee. One morning in November, all the shop windows in Florence displayed posters declaring, "Il Duce is always right. Il Duce knows everything, sees everything, remembers everything."

The more I learned, the more useless I felt. I'd made no progress insinuating myself into a circle of anti-Fascists. But it was not something to be rushed—I must establish credibility and prove I could be trusted.

I knew Italy seethed with a variety of anti-Fascist movements, and Churchill himself had described the politics of Italy's factions "as convoluted as tunnels beneath the Vatican." Randolph said that when he'd exclaimed, "There are tunnels under the Vatican," Winston had replied, "How in the world would I know?"

I finally decided it'd be best to sever the last tenuous link to my London life. In December, I wrote a letter to MJ. Hardening myself against tenderness, I referred to our time together in the past tense, thanked him for the wonderful adventures we'd shared, and lied a little, telling him my new life in Florence greatly pleased me. This letter I posted.

But of course, the letter was a sham. I had no wish to return to London, but I still missed our life together: his delight in my stylish attire; our game of collecting colorful expressions wherever we visited; and his boyish, carefree laugh. The only thing that came close to pleasing me at present was my friendship with Elisabeth. Our time together distracted me from pining over MJ, though, in my private hours, I sometimes bemoaned the comfortable and exciting life I'd left behind.

All I knew for sure was that I wanted to find a way to fight Fascism, but I had only the vaguest idea of how I might do that.

FLORENCE

I n January, I took up the study of Italian art at the University of Florence. It was one small step. After all, I needed to claim some occupation to cover up any intelligence work. And this one came quite naturally to me.

So now I studied alongside Elisabeth. Today, the two of us strolled the corridor of the Art Building, past sturdy office doors carved with graceful scrollwork. I breathed in the dry and musty scents of old books and fracturing plaster. The smells transported me—they reminded me of learning and erudition.

We'd scheduled a meeting with one of Elisabeth's professors, Alfonso Frascati, a grandfatherly art historian full of stories about the old masters. I never missed a chance to attend his after-hours talkfests about Giotto, Brunelleschi, and Masaccio. He seemed to take an interest in me, too, for we often gravitated toward each other and had even traded barbs about Mussolini's "loutish speechifying" and "juvenile hero worship."

As Elisabeth and I made our way down the hall, I peeked at the notice boards posted on the walls, eavesdropping on notes, photographs, and articles professors had pinned up. Elisabeth was a wonderful friend—unassuming, warm, and intelligent, though not in a shallow sort of way. She possessed a sensibility and sense of decorum I admired and prized.

We stopped at Professor Frascati's office door, and my eyes widened. "Look what the professor has put up."

Elisabeth studied the drawing, which appeared to be from a magazine. "It's . . . striking. And original."

The picture's black lines swirled around roughed-out faces of men, with the blocky heads diminishing in size until they and the lines converged in the middle. How ironic. I'd just been thinking: Here I can forget the Fascist propagandizing and the Blackshirts roaming Italy's streets. In fact, being on campus reminded me of those years of innocence in Holland and England, when I devoted myself to reading the great poets and philosophers, learning languages, and laughing with classmates at our severe teachers. Then I'd spotted this.

I poked my chin toward it. "Can you still say art is above it all?"

"I didn't mean it *must* be above politics," said Elisabeth. "Only that it's sometimes best to pretend it is."

"That's something else altogether." Of course, I'd wondered about Elisabeth's political leanings. She clearly evinced no love for the Nazis. But I doubted she engaged in any direct activity against them. And if she did, she covered her tracks well.

Elisabeth leaned close to the drawing. "The vanishing point is like a swirling black sun—or an obscure swastika."

I pulled back to study the effect and smiled. "Look how the men's expressions are all the same—gruff and haughty."

The professor's display of this sly drawing thrilled me. After four months in Florence, I'd only gathered intelligence on propaganda flyers and the occasional arrest of an insurgent. Of course, I mustn't rush my introduction to partisan groups—I'd only risk undermining the cause—but now an idea came to me. I'd speak to the professor. Today, if possible. The way his eyes sparkled when we spoke of political matters convinced me of his shrewdness—and courage. Besides, he was Jewish. All that, and now this drawing, marked him as a likely anti-Fascist.

Elisabeth knocked on Professor Frascati's door.

He called from inside, "Who is it?"

"Elisabeth Freitag. And Toto."

Footsteps thumped behind the door. It swung open, and a stern-faced Blackshirt poked his head out. "The professor is busy. Go see someone else."

Through the door's narrow opening, I glimpsed the professor's desk and the bookcase behind it. One of the shelves had been emptied. On top of his desk sat two boxes heaped with books.

My mouth parched to cotton dryness. I reached around Elisabeth and said, "But we have an appointment."

The Blackshirt thumped his thick boot against the door, stopping it short. "Who are you?"

Elisabeth edged me aside. "We're his students."

"He's busy now," he said.

I wanted to face down this ignoramus, brush him aside, and greet the white-haired professor with the respect he deserved. But I knew I dare not.

"I see," said Elisabeth, backing off and easing me away as she did so.

The door closed, and I clapped a hand to my chest. I whispered, "The Fascists—they're removing him."

Elisabeth gripped my arm and guided me down the hall. "We mustn't draw attention to ourselves."

"Come," I said, "we were going to visit the Basilica Santa Maria Novella anyway."

Elisabeth and I slipped out onto the neighborhood's odd-angled streets. But I could think only of what was happening to Professor Frascati—and of my father's lesson on dignity when I was six and the commissary clerk called me a heathen. Afterward, Father had told me, "You mustn't allow the ignorance of petty minds to beat you down, my little charge."

Everything in me raged against what I'd witnessed. I probably shouldn't have said a single word to the Blackshirt. Then there was Elisabeth. I trusted her as a friend, but I imagined her circumstances were complicated. After all, she required the permission of the Nazi government to study in Italy.

On our walk, I held back. I'd not force the topic of the professor on Elisabeth.

But it was Elisabeth who brought it up. "Such a shame," she said. "I didn't believe Italy would do this to their Jews, too."

"I thought he might be exempt because of fighting in the Great War."

"Who can trust the Fascists?"

"*Sì*, they're like Nazi factotums."

Elisabeth slowed her step and turned to me. "It's upset you terribly, hasn't it?"

The image of the wire-thin professor intimidated in his own office by a pile-of-rubbish Blackshirt sickened me, but I paused before responding. "The surprise of it shocked me."

"I admire him, too, but one mustn't show such emotions." Elisabeth had a low and soothing voice, like a cat's purr. "Do you agree?"

"Unfortunately, I do." I'd come so close to finding a like-minded comrade in the professor. That and the injustice being done to him disturbed me.

Elisabeth nodded. "In Germany, when people tried to intervene, they too became targets."

I had followed the advance of anti-Semitism in Germany: first, the laws denying Jews citizenship and prohibiting marriage between Jews and Aryans;

and then Kristallnacht. "I wouldn't be surprised if Mussolini mimics Hitler's policies against the Jews."

"I truly hope he won't," she said.

The hints of sympathy Elisabeth dropped emboldened me. "What good is all the art in Italy if this country harms its own people?"

"Yes, it's unjust. But one can't simply react."

We came upon a stretch of bumpy cobblestones, and my block-heeled shoes shifted unevenly with each step. I took Elisabeth's arm to steady us. My plan to speak with the professor had been upended, but I trusted Elisabeth. It was time to open up to her. "If there was some way to help Italy's Jews, would you?"

I felt Elisabeth's arm tense as she turned to me. "Of course. But I'm only a lowly student. Not even Italian."

"Perhaps I can think of a way." First, I'd track down Professor Frascati and speak to him. If necessary, I'd recruit Elisabeth's help—and, to keep her out of danger, never reveal too much to her. "You're German, and that gives you certain advantages here."

Elisabeth cupped her hand over mine. "You're quite serious, aren't you?"

"Terribly," I said.

Elisabeth patted my hand. "Then I know someone you should meet. I will arrange a dinner for us."

———

I left Elisabeth and hurried back to the campus. I had an idea I wanted to discuss with the director of the library. I found him at the circulation desk studying a stack of index cards.

"Signor Peruzzi, would you kindly advise me on a research project I am undertaking?"

He looked at me over the rims of his half-moon glasses. "*Si*, I will be glad to help."

"Can we speak in your office?"

"Of course."

I followed the tall, balding director to his office, where he invited me to sit.

I perched on the edge of my seat. "I am interested in books about art history written by Jewish authors."

"Why Jewish authors?"

"Because I am concerned about the scholarship by these experts. That their books may be removed from the library."

He steepled his fingers. "I assume, *signorina*, you are enrolled at the University."

I used my formal name, the name I was registered under. "Yes, I am Catherina Koopman, studying art history."

"And may I ask why you think these books may be removed?"

"Do you know Professor Frascati?"

"Yes, of course."

"I was at his office a few hours ago. A Blackshirt was supervising the packing up of his office."

The director nodded gravely. "I see. And are you Jewish?"

"No, but I care about literature and the people who write it, as well as those like yourself who preserve it. You no doubt know about the book burnings in Germany and the censuring of books deemed critical of the regime. And that the Nazis are taking control of publishing presses all over Europe, including here in Italy."

"Of course, I know. What are you proposing, *signorina*?"

"I would like to help you hide books that may be destroyed. We could identify households that can store them."

"That would take them out of circulation."

"Isn't that better than them being lost for good?"

He twirled the wedding band around his finger and studied me. "How do I know I can trust you? That you would not report me for hiding books?"

"I would help transport them for safekeeping. I would be putting myself at risk doing this. That is how you know you can trust me."

He leaned back in his chair. "You must give me some time to consider this research project of yours."

"Certainly. May I visit you again next week?"

"*Si*, I will expect you then."

———

Three days after Professor Frascati's removal from the University, Elisabeth introduced me to Dominic over dinner at her utilitarian apartment. She referred to him and me by first names only. When I leaned in to greet him, I caught a mixture of scents—hair oil, burning wood, and an earthiness like mushrooms. He struck me as a serious and reflective sort, with thick, workman-like hands, stocky legs, and a broad forehead. Like a watchful animal, he spaced his feet wide and held himself steady and still. I caught him eyeing my clothing, perhaps disapprovingly: My stylish indigo dress hugged the lines of my slender hips and contrasted sharply with the baggy fit of his wool sweater and shiny-with-wear pants. This man obviously cared more about practicality than style.

Over dinner, we danced around the topic of allegiances. While Elisabeth played political matchmaker—"You should know that Toto and I share a deep admiration of Italy and its working people"—Dominic quizzed me about politics and my life in London.

He held his wine glass in mid-air and gave it a little bounce. "Tell me, what do you think of how Chamberlain is managing the German threat?"

"He wants to placate the upper class and the royals. They don't want another war. But I disagree with his concession policy. Appeasing a bully like Hitler only encourages him to push for more."

"But don't many in Parliament think Fascism is a good way to fight Communism?"

I knew some segments of the Italian resistance favored Communism, but I didn't. "I disagree with both political systems—they rely on the repression of freedom. I say Fascism should be opposed simply because it is cruel. And Hitler and Mussolini must be unseated because they are depraved dictators."

His expression remained impassive throughout the evening, so I couldn't guess if I'd passed his test. After dinner, courtesy demanded he walk me to my hotel. I braced myself for more scrutiny.

It was a chill January night, and Dominic walked briskly beside me, his hands thrust deep in his coat pockets. He'd been inquiring about my upbringing in Java. "This older brother of yours, what does he do?"

"He's a banker. Working in Amsterdam now. Why do you ask?"

"Families, they are important," he said, shrugging. "After your mother died, why did your father leave the military?"

"He wanted a change." I began to grasp the motive behind his questions. "He's in business now, in Java, with the Royal Dutch Airlines. He stays out of politics. Is your family here in Florence?"

"Only my sister." He scratched his neck and rushed his words as if to dismiss the matter. "Our parents are gone, and our brother, too."

"I'm sorry to hear that."

Out of the darkness, two Blackshirts emerged, walking toward us. The sight of these Fascist enforcers always put me on edge, but after the dinner discussion about resistance work, I felt especially wary. I steadied my gait. "The Blackshirts, they creep about everywhere, don't they?"

Dominic pulled a hand out of his pocket and casually took mine. "It's better this way."

I stepped closer to him and matched my step to his. "One must be as brazen as they are."

"*Si.*" He lowered his voice, pretending at a lover's intimacy. "I have a story for you. About a friend's encounter with a Blackshirt."

I glanced at his sturdy profile and nodded.

"This friend, he's a crazy writer. He stays up all night writing and sleeps all day. He told me he was walking his dog a few weeks ago, around midnight, when a Blackshirt stopped him and asked what he was doing out so late."

The Blackshirts, their heads bent in conversation, strolled past us, and Dominic continued, "My friend calls his dog Bruno because he's strong and big-chested and looks mean. But really, he's gentle and affectionate."

Dominic withdrew his hand and reached for a cigarette.

I took his arm, aware the Blackshirts need only turn around to check on us.

He lit his smoke and took a drag. "We turn onto Il Prato to get to your hotel?"

"*Si*, it's not far now." We rounded the corner and strolled on quietly, putting distance and buildings between ourselves and the Blackshirts. I let go of his arm. Three- and four-story apartment buildings lined the streets, and lights glowed in a few curtained windows. But we were alone on the sidewalk. "What happened to your friend?"

"While he was explaining he couldn't sleep, Bruno cocked his leg and pissed on the Blackshirt."

I couldn't help but cackle, and that set him off, too.

Later, when I lay alone in bed, it occurred to me that his story might have been a test to see how I would react. If so, I believed I'd passed. Santo Cielo, *had I finally found a way to join a partisan group?*

I hoped so. And maybe, just maybe, Dominic could help me with the requests Winston Churchill had made—to infiltrate one or more Italian Resistance groups and report on their level of support and effectiveness countering Mussolini's propaganda campaigns. Also, if possible, to gather information about Italy's military—its equipment, troop movements, and preparedness. I was excited. Maybe I had finally found an anti-Fascist group to join.

——

I visited the library director again the next week, as I had told him I would.

"Signorina Koopman," he said, tapping his fingertips together. "I understand your last residence was London?"

He must have looked up my student file. "Yes, I lived there for several years before coming to Italy."

"What brought you to Italy?"

"First, I must ask why I should trust you, Signor Peruzzi."

"Because I am an anti-Fascist. Anybody who cares about learning and values freedom would be. I'm a librarian, *signorina*. Do you need to know more?"

"No, I wouldn't have approached you if I hadn't suspected your allegiance to anti-Fascism. As for why I came here: I hoped to make some difference, to stand up to the dictators who are pushing war and demagoguery."

"Why books?"

"They are a way to preserve knowledge and defend freedom. When I saw Professor Frascati being removed from his post, I started worrying about books by Jewish authors, as well as other banned books. The thought of them being heaped onto a fire disgusts me."

"Have you spoken with anybody else about this idea of yours?"

"No, I have not."

"You understand this is a dangerous thing you are proposing?"

"Yes, if anyone comes to raid the library, you could say you have already disposed of prohibited books. Out of loyalty to the regime. If they even ask about this, which we can't know."

"That would mean keeping track of all the hidden books so they can be retrieved when it is safe. Pulling the cards from the catalog repository. And doing so quietly and carefully."

"Of course. I could be your assistant."

He inhaled deeply, as if steeling his resolve. "Very well. We might as well get to work. But first, come with me."

He walked me to a kitchen in the back of the library and made us coffee, which was not readily available then. But he had somehow managed to keep a supply on hand.

I took a sip of the rich, dark coffee, savoring its creaminess. "Thank you," I said, holding up the cup. "This tastes as wonderful as a glass of Champagne on New Year's Eve."

That was the beginning of our campaign to save library books. And Professor Peruzzi told me he would also set up a network of librarians to warn each other of any raids. I was very pleased with our project, but I told no one else about our work.

FLORENCE

JANUARY–MARCH 1940

One week passed with no word from Dominic. Then two. I asked Elisabeth if she'd heard anything. But no, she had no idea if or when Dominic might contact her or me: "I'm not a member of the movement, only a friend on the outside."

Perhaps it would take more than a casual dinner meeting to warrant an invitation to join Giustizia e Libertà. The only thing to do was wait.

Then, one February afternoon, a messenger arrived with a note from Dominic. Could I accompany the messenger to a meeting place? When, I asked? Right now. The abrupt notice was no doubt designed to foil any attempts at treachery. I'd obviously not passed all of Dominic's tests. But at least he was offering another chance.

I went with the messenger to Palazzo Strozzi. Dominic met us there and escorted me across the Arno to a building in the San Niccolò neighborhood. We climbed the stairs to a third-floor apartment, where a man met us. Dominic introduced Nemo, a wiry, thick-haired fellow who wielded a toothpick like a miniature cigar.

"Sit, please," Nemo said, motioning to a chair at the kitchen table. He sat opposite me. "We have some questions."

They offered no drink, not even water. The cramped kitchen was lit only by a dim-bulbed ceiling lamp. I couldn't see anything beyond a dark hall. It appeared this apartment, with its out-of-the-way location and gloomy atmosphere, was a perfect place for interrogations.

Dominic sat diagonal from me and lit a cigarette.

Nemo plucked the toothpick from his mouth and waved it like a baton. "You must understand we're taking a chance on you. So, we expect you to hide nothing from us."

"*Si*, you need only ask."

Nemo angled his tall frame over the table and shot questions at me: How did I learn Italian? What other languages did I speak? How long did I work for Coco Chanel? How much was I paid for my photographs in *Vogue*? Why did I quit modeling? For what reasons did I move to London?

His pointed questions showed good familiarity with my history. Some of these details Dominic had learned over dinner at Elisabeth's apartment. But others, he and Nemo must have ferreted out on their own, like what modeling houses I'd worked for in Paris, what magazines my photographs appeared in, and my liaisons with Russian aristocrat Alexis Mdivani and Nazi-party member Herbert von Karajan. They'd clearly put effort into scrutinizing my occupations and relationships. I was impressed.

I squelched my resentment at Nemo's gruffness—I suppose they wanted to observe my reaction to interrogation—and answered with honesty and sang-froid. "*Si*, I was on intimate terms with von Karajan for some months and traveled around Germany with him. I saw first-hand how Hitler used artists for propaganda purposes. It was enlightening. And infuriating."

Nemo leaned toward me and, cocking his head this way and that, held my gaze. "You were in Berlin for the Olympics?"

"*Si*." I imagine they'd discovered this from the society pages in London or Berlin newspapers. Or from an informant.

"Accompanied by whom?"

"I traveled alone but met some friends there."

"What friends?"

"People in the fashion world. And also those who traveled the opera circuit. Many of these people I had first met in Paris. And they introduced me to their friends in Berlin."

I flattened my hands on the table and looked at both of them in turns. "They all told the same story—just before the Olympics, the Nazis cleansed the city of all its 'Für Juden Verboten' signs and decorated the avenues with blazing swastikas. They even ordered residents to display window boxes with geraniums. But before the outside world showed up, they were beating and humiliating Jews in the streets."

"Did you meet with any government officials then?"

"Not on that occasion. But I had on a previous visit, in November of '35."

Nemo shot a glance at Dominic and shifted in his chair. "Tell us about that."

"I was traveling with Lord Beaverbrook. He's . . ."

Nemo waved me off. "We know who he is. Who did you and Beaverbrook meet in Berlin?"

I spoke slowly, meting out my words. "Werner von Blomberg, the Minister of Defense. I was Beaverbrook's interpreter for the meeting."

"And what was discussed?"

"Mostly military matters. I believe Hitler extended the invitation so Blomberg could tout Germany's flourishing military. Blomberg had worked hard to build up the army. That's probably why Hitler promoted him to Minister of Defense. He bragged about purging the Reichswehr of Jews the previous year, ahead of Hitler's order to do so. He apparently assumed we'd admire his actions against Jews, as if all of Europe agreed with the Nazis on this."

I paused to let that sink in. Nemo and Dominic studied me and held themselves still as stones.

I brushed my palms together. "But mostly, he rattled off numbers and showed us charts to demonstrate the rapid growth of all branches of the military. I suppose Hitler hoped Beaverbrook would carry word of his military prowess back to the British government. Of course, that's exactly what Beaverbrook did."

Nemo twirled the toothpick between his fingers. "Do you still have access to any German officials?"

"No, I no longer associate with Beaverbrook. I haven't since several months after that meeting."

Nemo asked, "Do you have any contacts in the British government?"

"Yes, I do." Now it was my turn to take control—and exercise caution. "I think it best not to reveal who those people are. But I have a means of sending messages back and forth—to high levels of the government."

Nemo placed the toothpick in the corner of his mouth and eyed Dominic.

Dominic drummed his fingers on the table and asked, "Why do you want to work for the resistance?"

"Because everything in me rages against what Hitler and Mussolini stand for. They and their henchmen are hateful snakes, ready to consume anybody who stands in their way. As if they are fit to judge. As if they're not the evil ones. They presume a power they're not fit to wield."

Dominic poked his chin out. "And nothing else?"

Damnation, I thought, *is that not enough?*

Dominic raised his eyebrows into a just-answer-the-question cast.

I plunked my forearms on the table and leaned over them. "I believe these regimes are a grave threat to the people of Europe. Hitler and Mussolini jeopardize not only peace but the fabric of human decency. They intimidate with their power and brutality. They aim to cow people into either looking away from or participating in their inhumane practices. They want to turn people against each other for their evil purposes."

I paused to gather myself. The kitchen smelled of cigarettes, garlic, and a blend of sweat and lived-in clothing—the scent of ordinary Italians going about their daily lives, only now under the watch of Fascism. "And also because my soul demands it."

Dominic squinted at me. "The work is dangerous. You must prove yourself worthy. The lives of many are at risk."

"I understand. And I promise I can help. Just give me a chance to show you."

"What if you were caught and tortured? Could you swear never to give up my name?" He circled his gaze around the room. "Or this place? Or my comrade here?"

"You are courageous to do this work." I imagined myself being kicked and beaten. I wanted to believe I could withstand brutality. Only I hoped it wouldn't come to that. "I would never dishonor your courage with cowardice."

"It's not easy to withstand torture," said Dominic. "Nobody can predict how they'll react. But we expect at least a day of resistance. To give others a chance to avoid capture."

I nodded. "I would strive to do better than that."

"If you swear allegiance to Giustizia e Libertà, you must do so absolutely, with all your body and soul. Can you do this?"

"*Si*, that is what I wish to do." I did want to fight the Nazis and Fascists. Could I be smart and sly enough to avoid capture and torture? Yes, I assured myself, this I could do.

———

On the walk back to my hotel Dominic strode briskly, all man about his business. "I will take you on as an assistant. But I'll make introductions to others only as necessary—to protect you and them."

His pace forced me into long, ungainly steps. "Those are exactly the reasons I don't reveal my British contact. But let me assure you: I *will* be of service."

"Then you will read our circulars first? To learn what we believe, what we do?" There was none of the convivial tone he'd struck that evening after dinner at Elisabeth's.

"Yes, but I already know you're trying to depose Mussolini." I didn't need lessons on anti-Fascism, only on its many facets. It'd take time to acquire the information Churchill had requested. Why not start now? "And that you subscribe to liberal democracy, though other partisan groups have different philosophies."

He snuffled and trained his gaze straight ahead. "We also work with our American branch. They provide some funds. So, we need someone who speaks good English. And German, too. That's how you can help."

He'd sloughed off my comment about the movements' political positions. Did he intend to use me only as a translator and transcriber? I evened my voice to quell the annoyance ruffling me. "Certainly. But the more I know, the more helpful I can be."

"I'll tell you what you need to know." He flapped his hand. "Don't worry about it."

So much for inquiring about Italy's various resistance groups, their leaders, and their following. *I mustn't force this,* I told myself, *I can learn as I go.*

Over the ensuing weeks, I accepted the string of menial assignments Dominic set for me. When he wished to pace and think out loud, I typed his ideas so he could shape them into articles. I mostly translated German materials for him, newspaper articles and circulars out of Berlin, and wrote messages in German, apparently to be relayed to an informer safely tucked away somewhere. I imagined in Switzerland.

Each week, Dominic and I spent a few afternoons and one or two evenings together, but he treated me like a secretary and avoided personal topics. I understood he was overburdened—given his post as a journalist at *Principî* newspaper and his role as local leader of Giustizia e Libertà.

Still, my position as hireling grated. Did he not trust me? Or was he only giving me menial tasks because I was a woman? Whatever the reason, I couldn't bide my time much longer, not with Galeazzo Ciano's visit to Florence—and my chance to act decisively—mere weeks away. I must somehow temper his intransigence and elevate my standing.

Little by little, I tried to pierce his hard-boiled exterior. When I reviewed one of his articles, I playfully chided, "What do you mean '*sbarazzarsi di*'? That's too formal." When he responded, "I'm the journalist here," I rattled the page and said, "If you want to show you really mean 'to hell with the autocrats,' say '*abbasso*' instead."

Then the Royal Navy seized the German merchant ship *Altmark* and freed the British prisoners hidden in its hold. Dominic remarked, "Finally, your British friends are doing something about the Germans."

I winked and said, "Yes, I tipped them off."

With a look of astonishment, he asked, "What do you mean—tipped them off?"

"I'm joking, Dominic. You know what a joke is, don't you?" But none of my presumed familiarity, flattery, or teasing smiles budged him from his role as stern supervisor.

———

The more time I spent with Dominic, the more he fascinated me—with his seriousness, his dedication, his inscrutable depths. He was unlike anyone I'd ever known. He eschewed the superficiality of style, spoke only after thinking, and wrote with searing, penetrating intelligence. Something about him challenged the very things I questioned in myself: my dedication to my beliefs and the superficiality of my past endeavors. Did I have the kind of courage and conviction I sensed he possessed?

One evening when he visited my hotel room to request my assistance, I found myself looking at him with fresh eyes—as a person mystified by the singleness of another, as if he were a riddle unto himself.

He handed me a note. "I need this translated by morning. For our messenger."

"I'll do it right now. You might as well wait. And relax, which you don't do enough of." I plopped down at my secretary and gestured to the upholstered chaise and small stand in the corner of my room. "Help yourself to some grappa."

I bent over at my desk and studied the note, acutely conscious of his presence, as if he were emanating an electrical charge. I carefully interpreted and wrote out the message—setting up a rendezvous in Milan—aware all the time of him sipping and taking in the room. Feeling his eyes on me stirred a new sensation in me, a kind of shy uncertainty. When I finished, I folded the message and placed it in an envelope. I rose and walked to the chaise, easing down beside him.

I motioned to the grappa bottle on the side table. "Pour a little for me, please."

He poured and handed me a glass. "You're a fascinating woman. But, of course, you know that."

I smiled and looked into his eyes—their deep mahogany, their unique hazel striations. "And you a man of much mystery."

He leaned close and cupped his hand over my cheek. "I wonder: What kind of magic might you work, you beautiful spy?"

FLORENCE

MARCH 1940

I lay awake beside Dominic, alert and jittery, imagining how the coming day might unfold. Our night of seduction had ignited an affair, a sort of tentative dance between us, as if Dominic had finally admitted to a stifled attraction but refused to completely surrender to it. As for me, it was love, a new kind of love that made me want to know what his every sigh meant, why he wrinkled his brow, how his mind worked—everything about him.

I knew I should have guarded against allowing passion's entanglements to complicate my work. Menzies had advised me not to mix romance with espionage. But I couldn't help falling for Dominic. I told myself we were partners in this venture, that no lover's quarrel could possibly diminish our devotion to Giustizia e Libertà. That our intimacy meant we shared our dreams and hopes. That love would keep us from betraying each other and those we cared about.

Still, I hoped our newfound affinity would convince Dominic to trust me with some missions—beyond message writing and translating. But it hadn't yet done so. Although he spoke more openly with me about the cause and its campaigns, he continued to insist I stay behind the scenes.

I plumped up my pillow and rolled onto my back. The corner streetlamp cast a beam over my upright wardrobe and the dresser top, landing on the glossy pearls dangling from my jewelry stand. Except for the cold wind swirling down the alley, all was quiet. But in a few hours, with the break of day, the piazza would fill up. Blackshirts would take over the cafés, goading each other with their bluster and bombast. Women in shawls would scurry about their chores, the odd one grinning at a favorite Blackshirt but most studying the cobblestones. Shopkeepers would put out their baked goods, produce, and wares, smiling the same *buongiorno* to all. And workers, pretending to ignore the Blackshirts roving their streets, would hail friends with slaps on the back.

Dominic turned onto his side, bracing himself on an elbow. "You're not sleeping."

"No, I love the stillness," I said. "Finally, the city rests."

"Are you worried about something?"

Chill air nipped at my neck. I tugged the blanket snugly around me. Not now, I couldn't tell him now about my plan for the coming day. He might try to stop me. But I'd have to confess afterward, so I might as well pave the way. "I want to do more. You're not giving me the chance to show what I can accomplish."

He stroked my cheek with the back of his hand. "Everyone has their place. We must all work together."

"I can do more than write messages. You insult me by holding me back."

"Just wait. For when you can do something important."

I suspected this was his way of putting me off. "Do you doubt my ability?"

A sensation I recognized from childhood—a kind of plucky pride—washed over me. I remembered feeling it while I leaned against the smooth trunk of an old banyan tree, surveying the valley and imagining myself at the center of the universe. Were all children so confident? Or was it merely that I'd led a carefree childhood—with my father telling me to be proud of my exotic heritage and my mother encouraging me to venture out into the countryside. How I treasured those sultry days in Java, running on dirt-packed roads past rice fields and tea plantations, splashing in the lake, and romping with my pet dogs and baby elephant. It had all made me sure and unafraid. Weren't those precisely the qualities of a good spy?

Dominic's breath puffed against my forehead. "Why would you want to court danger?"

Would he ever quit asking about my reasons for joining the resistance? I'd explained I couldn't bear the Nazis persecuting Jews and the Fascists punishing people for daring to criticize them. That hadn't satisfied him. He kept picking away at me, digging and probing. But this was no time to show my exasperation, not when I was poised to prove my worth. So, I came up with yet another motive. "I wonder how they can be so depraved."

"Do you hate them?"

I caught myself unconsciously running my thumb and forefinger against each other and stopped, scolding myself for showing disquiet. "I keep hoping there's some humanity in them, that they're not completely evil."

"But you must hate them. To protect yourself."

"Let me tell you a story. When I was a little girl, my mother and I visited a friend on a coffee plantation. This woman was very wealthy and collected

Japanese artifacts. She displayed one, a ceremonial Japanese javelin, on a red lacquer stand in the entryway. It was the first thing I noticed when we arrived, and I yearned to touch it, for it was dangerous but also shimmering and graceful. Believing it had special powers, the Javanese house servants bowed each time they passed it. The lady of the house saw my fascination and thought it best to put the javelin in storage during our visit.

"That night, I awakened to a baby's cries. When I reported the crying in the morning, our hostess told me there was no baby in the house and that I had merely dreamed it. The next night I again heard the baby crying. It was no dream but the piercing wail of a real baby. When word of this circulated among the servants, they explained it was the javelin crying for its freedom and begged their mistress to restore it to its place of honor. She acquiesced, and the crying stopped. My mother told me the javelin was speaking to me and that it would always watch over me because I had answered its plea."

Dominic scrunched up a corner of his mouth. "And you believe it will protect you now?"

"I believe there are forces we cannot see."

He ran his palm across my ribs, over the hollow of my stomach, and curled it around my hip bone. "I don't want you taking risks."

"*You* take risks." I brushed a lock of his hair over an ear. "Why shouldn't I?"

"Because you are not some obscure person."

"The Fascists don't care that I was a Paris model."

"Don't pretend with me. You know important people in London. You were often seen with that Lord Beaverbrook."

It was true. Beaverbrook was well known, as was my association with him. His ownership of the *Daily Express*, *Sunday Express*, and *Evening Standard* rendered him as influential as any politician. "But all the photos of me are from my modeling work."

"That's a problem, too. You could be identified."

"Women have certain advantages, you know." We'd covered this before: how I'd been schooled in politics by Beaverbrook and ambassadors; how I'd been trained in espionage and gathered intelligence while I traveled the Continent.

But I had no intention of telling him about my affair with Randolph Churchill. After all, the care with which I guarded secrets had earned me the trust of many. I had, however, informed him of my occasional liaisons with Mussolini's son-in-law, Galeazzo Ciano, which we'd conducted with the utmost discretion. That he needed to know. It would also make it easier to explain what I was about to do.

"Still," said Dominic. "You're suspect because you're not Italian."

"My Italian is as good as any countryman's."

"If only that were enough to keep you—and those around you—safe."

I sighed. His skepticism annoyed me, but I'd soon put it to rest.

"You're so delicate," he said. "It makes me want to protect you."

In the end, he was like most men, putting great stock in muscle and bravado. He didn't understand how a woman could use a smile or alluring words to dazzle.

"It's the middle of the night," I said. "We should sleep."

Dominic stroked my cheek. "You mustn't question me about this."

My kiss landed on his temple. "We'll talk more later."

———

I woke to Dominic slipping away from my side.

He whispered in my ear, "No need for you to get up so early."

From the thick-posted bed, I watched him button up a gray wool shirt and pull on baggy brown pants. I'd grown accustomed to his rough-hewn look—the unkempt, wavy black hair, solid five-ten frame, even the contortion of the two fingers injured building a rock wall. I liked how he held me, enveloping my tall slenderness in his compact strength. It made me feel wanted.

I turned on my side to admire Dominic's transformation. He'd traded his journalist's jacket for farmer's attire. "The people in Turin will say to each other: Look at this peasant come to the big city."

The lines around his deep-set brown eyes crinkled. He flung his coat over his shoulder. "*Grazie* for the fine compliment."

"I'll see you Friday evening?"

"*Sì*," he said. "I'll think of a private place for dinner."

"May you have much success." I couldn't help but think: And may I, too.

He leaned over and kissed my forehead. "I'll leave by the alley."

"I know. You always do."

DISPATCH FROM FLORENCE

13 March 1940

Subject spends many days each week with a female German student (GS) at the University of Florence. She often accompanies GS and other art students on outings to churches, museums, and architectural sights. The students do not appear to engage in partisan activities, but they consort with some Italians who could be partisans. Subject also meets regularly with a male Italian journalist (IJ). They may be having an affair. My evening activities preclude scrutiny of the nature or frequency of their meetings. Please advise as to priority of assignments.

WD

FLORENCE

MARCH 1940

I stood at my hotel window, looking out on the patchwork of bone-colored buildings. A late morning rain pelted the tile roofs, turning their burnt-coral hues to dun browns. Below, passersby hunkered into their coat collars and stepped briskly along the sidewalks. It wasn't the most pleasant weather for an outing.

I ate a late lunch at the hotel's café, spent a long hour on my chaise longue catching up on newspapers, and took a steaming bath. After plucking my eyebrows into high arches and waving my hair, I chose an elegant but unobtrusive outfit—a black sweater with billowy sleeves and a slim black skirt. I tied the sash of my wool coat around my waist and set out for Elisabeth's apartment on Via Zara.

Elisabeth ushered me into her second-floor flat. "*Entra, entra*. This rain is miserable."

I shuttered my umbrella, and we greeted each other with kisses on the cheeks. Elisabeth wore a modest black dress, its drop-waist style dated but somehow fitting on her squat, fleshy frame.

Opening my coat to reveal my outfit, I said, "Aren't we chic in our uniforms?"

Elisabeth winked. "A proper pair of Blackshirts."

On our walk to the Palazzo Vecchio, I offered my arm, and the two of us fell into a matched step under our shared umbrella. Blackshirts swarmed in full force amid the few Florentines braving the inclement weather.

"So, you will play the dashing and daring one this evening," I said.

"I shouldn't have agreed to this. You know that's not my style."

Yes, Elisabeth was the shyer and more diminutive of us. My friends in Paris and London would've considered us mismatched, but I refused to count appearances as the sole coin of esteem. "Hah," I said, "as if playing the wall-flower is my forte."

Elisabeth clucked. "Well, if you expect me to speak up, you'll have to keep quiet for a change."

"Just pretend it's like any other night we're out with friends."

"Honestly, Toto, let's not play childish games."

I tossed my head back and laughed. I loved my friend's candor. Some women held me at a distance, as if I were a rival, but not Elisabeth, whose liveliness made up for her plain looks—the button nose, abbreviated chin, hair braided and wrapped atop her head. And I trusted her. She couldn't risk engaging in partisan activity—she relied on the German government's permission to study here. But she did not shrink from sharing her views, which resonated with mine. We knew we could count on each other's discretion.

"I'm just trying to find the right sensibility for us," I said. "So, I can be demure, and you can play the proper go-between."

"That's me," said Elisabeth, "always the messenger, never the sweetheart."

<hr>

As we entered the hall, our heels clicked on its muted-red floor and melded with the host of voices ricocheting off its lofty walls and gilded ceiling. Oversized frescoes of Florentine battle scenes lined the side walls, and gleaming marble busts were perched on solid stands beneath them. Nothing but the city's most palatial salon, the Hall of Five Hundred, would do for Galeazzo Ciano, hero of Italy's Abyssinian conquest. In 1936, after his service in that campaign, Mussolini had awarded him a Medal of Valor and pressed him into service as his Foreign Minister—or, as Dominic put it, "*numero uno* errand boy."

Elisabeth and I arrived nearly two hours before the rally and secured seats halfway back in the audience section. Ropes blocked off the elevated stage at the head of the hall, and signs indicated it was reserved for city officials, the military, and school and university personnel. Mussolini loyalists crowded into the audience rows, buzzing with excitement. No doubt, they relished the chance to brag about their brush with the Foreign Minister. Still, I reasoned that Elisabeth and I weren't the only ones pretending at devotion to Mussolini and his underlings.

The Fascist government spared no measures drumming up the public's devotion or, at the least, docility: A week earlier, newspapers reported the arrest of three Turin agitators for acts of treason. I knew their "crime" consisted of producing a circular taunting Mussolini for signing the Pact of Steel. The text, which Dominic and I had read together, declared "Keep Italy at Peace" and claimed Hitler had used the Pact to turn Mussolini into his leashed dog. Dominic had laughed when I said, "He may be a leashed dog, but he froths at the mouth when he speaks, just like his master."

After introductions from three local grandstanders, Galeazzo Ciano strode to the head table, his step sure and measured. The crowd rose to its feet, clapping and stomping. Ciano wore a wide leather belt around his trim waist, and colorful bars crowded the breast of his uniform. A leather strap running diagonally across his torso showed off the prideful lift of his chest. Once at the podium, he nodded with grave formality to those on his sides. He seemed more stern or severe than when I'd last seen him, his manner tinged with melancholy—or perhaps it was the weight of responsibility.

He held up his palms, acknowledging the clamorous welcome. How mysterious, I mused, are the forces of loyalty and power. Ciano had never struck me as a blind follower. But now I wondered: Had his marriage to Mussolini's daughter irrevocably swept him into Fascism's orbit? Or perhaps he'd sought out this union because of the power it promised. When he lay naked beside his wife, did he dare confess any misgivings about her father's grand plans? I doubted he took delight in enforcing the government's cruel orders. Then again, Dominic claimed Ciano had plotted the assassination of Giustizia e Libertà founder Carlo Rosselli. So maybe he had a brutal side after all—or had no choice but to obey orders from Il Duce.

And what about me? In 1935, after Ciano had arranged for us to meet privately, we'd easily fallen in with each other. I'd been his secret, albeit occasional lover, for four years now. But how well did I know the man? He was a Fascist, and I hated Fascism. Still, he trusted me, he'd confided in me, and his revelations had proven accurate. His gallant bearing and carefully chosen words had tempted me into mining his depths. And Beaverbrook had encouraged me, practically salivating at the prospect of me procuring state secrets from Ciano.

But it was not Fascism that Ciano spoke of this evening—at least not directly. No, he praised the grandeur of Italy and its past: "We are a country united in purpose. . . . Soon Italy will rise to its old glory. . . . We shall once again be an august nation of trade. . . . With Franco, we have secured the western Mediterranean as our waterway, and we will keep it free to serve our country's industries. . . . In the words of Il Duce, 'There is a single faith: the love of country; there is a single will: to make the Italian people great.'" Ah, such doltish aphorisms Mussolini spouted; he was like an elephant giving birth to a mouse.

Only after Ciano had exalted Italy to the majesty of yesteryear's Roman Empire did he relinquish the stage to his aide. This man delivered what I surmised was the intended message: "We will build an army, navy, and air force to rival that of any country. Our young men will gladly join this supreme effort, and their mothers and fathers will glow with pride. Their countrymen will laud their sacrifices and take up their places in the fields and factories."

After the speeches, Elisabeth and I nudged our way through the departing crowd to the front of the hall, where we approached a cluster of some thirty Blackshirts in uniforms emblazoned with yellow-striped insignias. Elisabeth headed toward a man glancing our way and asked to speak to the commanding officer.

He escorted us to a bulky man with a chunky face and large ears.

"*Signor*," Elisabeth said, offering her hand. "I am Elisabeth Freitag."

"*Signorina*." He bowed his head and accepted her hand. "Consul Reitano at your service."

Reitano turned to me. I dropped my head and looked down.

Elisabeth said, "Allow me to introduce my friend Catherina Johanna."

To obscure my identity, I'd decided to use my official first and middle names—not the whole truth, but also not a complete lie. I dipped my head in greeting and feigned shyness.

Reitano turned back to Elisabeth. "You are German?"

"*Si*," said Elisabeth, "but I'm learning Italian. It is not too *atroce*, I hope."

"No, I understand you well, *signorina*. What can I do for you?"

Elisabeth removed a wrapped package from her purse. I had selected an expensive pair of leather gloves, supple and expertly stitched, and attached an envelope with a note tucked inside: *My dear Galeazzo, I offer these gloves as a token of our enduring friendship. If it is your pleasure, I would very much like to see you. All my admiration and respect, Toto*

Elisabeth held out the package. "We'd like to present a gift to Minister Ciano. Would that be possible?"

The plan was contrived but necessary, for Galeazzo preferred to avoid tipping anyone off to his romantic liaisons—especially local Blackshirts who loved nothing more than trucking in rumors.

The officer signaled to another man, who rushed up to him. Reitano ordered him, "Take this and see if Minister Ciano would like to meet the ladies who brought it."

The officer trotted off, and Reitano clasped his hands over his protruding belly. He seemed nervous, as if unsure of how to behave in the company of women. Perhaps he'd been too long steeped in the business of brutality. Finally, he spoke. "Our guest does us a great honor visiting Florence."

Elisabeth asked, "Will Minister Ciano stay here long?"

"No," replied Reitano. "Tomorrow, he speaks in Livorno."

It occurred to me that I could put all of us at ease by letting out a tiny detail about Galeazzo. I smiled at Reitano. "That is his hometown. They'll give him a warm welcome."

Reitano bent his head to catch my eye. "And you, what is your nationality?"

It was too difficult to explain my Dutch/Javanese ancestry and too danger-ous to reveal I'd most recently resided in London. The last name I'd used was Dutch, and since my tawny skin might dispose him to think me part Algerian, I thought it expedient to claim France as my home—and prudent to avoid intricate deceptions. "I'm Dutch, but from Paris," I offered, letting the silence fill up.

Reitano glanced to the front of the hall, scanning the Blackshirts milling about the chamber. He turned back to us. "What brings the two of you to Florence?"

Elisabeth said, "We're studying art and art history."

"It's a good place for that, isn't it?"

"The University has many esteemed professors," said Elisabeth.

Reitano tightened his cheeks into a smirk. "You mustn't believe everything they say, *signorina*."

I wondered: Was Elisabeth baiting him? The intelligentsia and Blackshirts regularly taunted each other. Elisabeth knew that.

And then I smiled to myself as Elisabeth deftly bailed herself out: "But you forget I'm German, Consul Reitano."

Reitano chuckled. "*Si*, so you said."

Reitano eyed me, so I put on a conspiratorial smile, reminding myself of Dominic's warning: You must consider them evil. Still, Reitano struck me as more of an oversized buffoon than a scheming adversary. What evil, I won-dered, was he capable of?

Rocking back and forth on his heels, Reitano again surveyed the stage area. "Ah, here he is."

The officer marched up to us and addressed Elisabeth. "Minister Ciano wishes me to give you this note."

I waited until Elisabeth and I strolled onto the street before I stopped to read Ciano's message: *The Royal Suite, second floor at the Grand Baglioni. 10 PM. My guards will let you pass at these words: I am meeting a Pisces.*

Elisabeth glanced at the note. "I don't even want to know what it says. I just hope you know what you're doing."

"Better you not know. Now, what about that dinner?"

———

"Ah, Toto, how long has it been?" Galeazzo took my hands and swept me into an embrace.

The glow of quick and easy intimacy warmed me. "Since Rome, almost a year and a half ago."

"And what brings you to Florence?"

"I've been here since September, studying Italian art. And enjoying the company of a dear friend."

He tilted his head and flashed a knowing smile. "Which of your many friends is that?"

"A young German lady from Düsseldorf. Who loves opera as much as I do." I squeezed his hands. "It's awfully good to see you."

He led me to a plush couch decorated with red and gold pillows. "You're looking marvelous. You must tell me about all your adventures."

The velvet, floor-length drapes, Galeazzo in a burgundy smoking jacket, the softly lit cream wallpaper, and our delicate, bell-shaped grappa glasses all spurred a rush of memories: of those years I'd traipsed around the Continent, staying in hotels with double-slipper copper tubs, listening to jazz in smoke-filled clubs, and sharing fine wine with diplomats, artists, and wealthy businessmen. My life was so different now. And it wasn't just the war. Something in me had shifted, too. I felt insignificant in the face of all the forces rocking the Continent, and I wanted more than ever to make some difference.

I told Galeazzo of my travels, reporting last on my visits to Germany. "Wagner's *Ring Cycle* in Bayreuth was a revelation, the best imaginable venue to hear Wagner. But, sadly, some of my favorite Berlin clubs have closed. Like the Romanische Café."

"Berlin," he nodded. "I'm on my way there now."

"When did you last visit?"

"In September."

"And how did you find it?"

Galeazzo swung one leg over the other. "Remade, I should say. Flush with Nazi swagger."

"*Si*, Hitler has changed everything." I brushed my palms together and thought a moment. "He's serious, isn't he, about expansion?"

"Completely. Poland won't be his last conquest."

"The world is getting so complicated," I said with a touch of huff. "With France and England declaring war, and Italy caught in the breach."

Galeazzo drummed his fingers on the couch arm. "Il Duce knows we're not ready for war."

"But doesn't Hitler wish to draw Italy into the military action? Isn't that what the Pact of Steel is all about?"

"I'm carrying a list of demands to Hitler. In hopes Germany will supply us with more coal and oil."

Still, I wondered, why had the evening's rally focused so pointedly on building up the military? "Isn't it more a matter of when—not if—Italy will go to war?"

"In all likelihood. A few of us on the Grand Council have apprised Il Duce of the slow rate of equipment production. He doesn't like to hear this, but we've told him that we must first think of Italy's people. And not send our men to battle without the best tanks and planes."

"Why does he not like to hear these things?"

He off-handedly flared a hand. "He wants to share Hitler's triumphs. And get his help securing the Mediterranean for our shipping."

Ciano hadn't revealed anything terribly sensitive, but I knew I must project some naïveté to draw him out more. I asked, "Can't Italy ship freely now?"

"That's the irony. Britain only impedes us because we trade with the enemy."

I couldn't help but worry: How angry would Dominic be when I revealed this liaison? And how far must I go with Galeazzo to keep his confidence? I relaxed against the couch back and spoke. "Surely, Britain would rather not fight Italy—or see Italy join the fight."

"*Sì*, I have it from them first-hand." Ciano regarded me with a one-eyed squint. "Tell me, what do your friends here in Florence say about the prospect of war?"

His connections with British officials didn't surprise me. He had nurtured these ties years ago. But him asking *me* about his countrymen's opinions—that did surprise. "My friends are students of art. They worry about both their future and Italy's. They would not welcome war."

"You'll not tell them about our meeting?"

"And upset the delicate balance of our debates? Heavens, no," I said. "And I've not forgotten the pledge I made long ago."

"So, you are still loyal to me, with the whole world changed?"

"And always will be." How easily I lied—though for a cause—but belaboring the point would only have invited suspicion. "I can tell you're troubled by all this."

"Hitler has us by the throat. We told him we couldn't be ready for war until '43, and he claimed to understand. I believe now he only said that to lure us into signing the Pact of Steel. Since he took Poland, the situation is complicated."

I eyed him over the rim of my glass. "What do *you* want?"

"I'd like to keep us out of war. But I can't say this publicly. And certainly not to Il Duce. I'm in an awkward position."

We were on familiar terrain again, him commiserating with me, freely revealing himself. He still trusted me, and I still cared about his struggles. It gave me confidence. "Do you have any allies on the Grand Council?"

He rubbed a hand over his chin and sighed. "Not enough."

If nothing else, I could confirm Pietro Badoglio's position. He was already high on my list of prospects to pass along to Churchill—even if Dominic derided him as a toady. "Surely Badoglio stands with you?"

"*Si*, but he's an opportunist, always watching which way the wind blows."

I knew this about Badoglio. And how he always managed to keep clear of blame. "You can still use him for your cause. Because you, too, always know the way of the winds."

"Ah, Toto," he said, with a show of his palm, "this is why I love our little talks."

"I understand you. I truly do."

"I only want to do what's best for the people of Italy."

Galeazzo had honor and mettle, and I admired him for it. "This meeting in Berlin will be difficult for you. Carrying Mussolini's message when you don't want war."

"*Si*, I'm forced to give these speeches glorifying war, and all the time, my love for Italy fights with my obligation to Il Duce. And I don't trust Ribbentrop or Hitler. They've deceived us in the past. I would rather trust Britain."

"Can you say what costs Italy would bear if it remained a nonbelligerent or broke with Germany?"

He paused and stared into the void, his expression melancholy and distracted. "If only I could know the future. If only I could reason with Il Duce—without fear of being gagged."

FLORENCE

APRIL 1940

I milled about the piazza, watching for Dominic. He'd insisted we take separate and meandering routes to his apartment—so we could avoid attracting attention. Tugging my scarf forward to better hide my face, I casually scanned the street. There he was, turning a corner and heading toward his building. I sped up to meet him on the doorstep.

"Roasted chestnuts for us," I said, handing a crinkled brown bag to him. On my way, the honeyed scent of roasting nuts had lured me to a street vendor, and I thought a present might help my news go down easier.

"*Grazie.*" He swung the door open, motioning me into the building.

We trotted up a flight of stairs and into his apartment. I hung my coat on the rack beside the door. "This sister of yours, will I ever meet her?"

"It's to protect both of you that I don't introduce you. But she teases me: 'You rascal, I know you have a lover.'"

"Why not tell her you're meeting someone from the newspaper?" I glanced around Dominic's apartment—at the grainy kitchen walls stained with cooking oil, the sturdy pots and skillets dangling from a metal rack and, opposite the chipped-up enamel stove, the thickset wooden table and chairs.

"It's better she thinks it's a lovers' rendezvous. She'll worry less that way."

Simmering smells of thyme, bay leaf, and root vegetables filled the room. Dominic's sister had prepared a simple meal for us, a rabbit stew with turnips and carrots, and Dominic brought out a bottle of Chianti Rufina. I had only visited his apartment south of Santa Trinita bridge twice before. I was not accustomed to such quarters: the primitive cooking stove, minimal electrical wiring and lighting, and narrow windows. But its rustic rooms pleased me—the way a quaint but dated art gallery might.

"*Salute*," Dominic raised his glass across the pocked table and tipped it to his lips. "Mmm, a good wine."

I let the viscous liquid seep over my tongue, its taste bright as cherries. I shelled a chestnut for him.

He plunked his glass on the table. "What is this big news you have for me?"

"After the rally on Wednesday, I met privately with Galeazzo Ciano."

He coughed the chestnut out of his mouth. "No. Tell me this isn't true."

"It is. He invited me to his suite. At the Grand Baglioni."

Dominic slammed his fist on the table. "And you didn't tell me before? Do you have any idea the trouble this could cause?"

"Ciano will reveal nothing. He'll keep our meeting secret—because of our history."

"Your history, you call it? You mean your love affair."

"Yes, and if I'd told you before, you would have forbidden it. We'd have missed the opportunity it presented."

"What opportunity? For him to bed you?"

I braced my hands on the table edge and pushed back, screeching the chair legs against the wood floor. "No, to hear about Mussolini's plans. And I will leave this minute if you keep treating me like a tramp."

He ran his hand over his forehead as if trying to wipe away his dismay. "Look, I'm the leader in Florence of Giustizia e Libertà. Do you know what that means?"

"I have my own connections. And that means something, too."

"Are you saying you won't cooperate with me?"

"No, but I don't take orders only from you. I have work to do, too."

"How can I trust you when you defy and deceive?"

"Because we want the same thing."

"But now I don't know where your loyalties lie."

"Loyalty is not like a pie, with only so many pieces. I am loyal to both you and the British government. They want the same thing you want."

"I'm the one who knows the situation here. Better than the British."

"And I can help. With my connections."

"You can't just go off on your own. You endanger my comrades and me."

"You would have stood in my way. And I was careful."

"That's no excuse."

I sat down, plopped my forearms on the table, and leaned toward him. "You mustn't treat me like some underling."

"In the future, you must inform me beforehand."

"I will—if you respect me and treat me as an equal, instead of someone to be ordered about like a child."

"*Basta*." He bit his lip and glanced to the side. Was this such a hard pill for him to swallow? "Tell me what you learned from him."

"I will. Over dinner."

With a sigh, Dominic rose and brought the kettle to the table. He ladled stew into our bowls, noisily clunking the spoon against the pot. "How did he treat you? Does he trust you?"

I waited until he sat down. "Yes, I believe he trusts me. But he didn't reveal anything new or helpful. He said Hitler's invasion of Poland is forcing Mussolini's hand, that Mussolini will hold off on a declaration of war because the military isn't ready yet."

"Did he explain how they'll prepare the military?"

"He gave no details."

"What else?"

"Mussolini fears Britain and France will interfere with Italy's shipping channels." I reached for my wine glass. "I didn't press for details. Next time I might do so. It's been a while since we met. I didn't want to arouse suspicion."

I couldn't bring myself to betray Galeazzo's confidences about his differences with Mussolini. Besides, those quandaries were personal. "Of the political situation, he spoke only in generalities. And even then," I added, "about things we already know."

Dominic cleared his throat. "For these things we already know, did you go to his bed?"

"No." I stared unblinking into his eyes, holding my wine glass in mid-air. "It was late. I told him I had to go. He said he needed to rise early."

"Humph," he muttered. "What about the meeting at the hall? What was said there?"

I recounted Ciano's speech and his aide's rallying words. "They reserved the meeting square not only for the military and city officials but also for teachers and professors."

Dominic snorted. "Next, they'll raid the classrooms and haul the schoolboys off."

"If Il Duce believes he can rally Italy behind him for the sake of history, he's a fool."

Holding his spoon over his bowl, Dominic smirked with disgust. "Mussolini and his bootlickers think Italy can be a great military power. That's worse than foolish."

"One of these days, he'll fall." The room felt stuffy. I loosened my blouse collar. "I hope you had success in Turin."

Dominic flapped an open hand as if shooing a fly. "It might be better not to tell you about that."

"But we should share what we learn."

With a dismissive bounce of his head, he said, "Some things are too dangerous for you to know."

"How dare you. We're partners in all this."

"There's no need for you to get upset."

"Why won't you tell me?"

"If you're questioned, the Blackshirts won't care that you're a woman. And Ciano won't risk himself to save you."

"Do you think I expect his help?" I glared at him. "I want the Fascists out, too."

Dominic shoved his bowl aside. "And I want that thug Ciano held accountable for murdering Rosselli."

"Are you accusing me of divided loyalties?"

"How do I know you won't trade secrets with him?"

It was like a slap in the face. "That's outrageous."

Dominic leaned over his elbows, closing the distance between us. The lines at the corner of his eyes compressed. "Then tell me everything you and Ciano spoke of, not just what you wish to tell."

I eased back in my chair. "All right. I've not given you all the details—but only because they may not matter." I told him everything I recalled, holding back nothing about Ciano's differences with Il Duce.

When I finished, he thumped his fist on the table. "And why did you not tell this at first?"

"I didn't consider his doubts about Il Duce and his position of import."

"But they might be. Rifts in the regime could be exploited."

"Yes, you're right."

"And do you understand why I might question your loyalty?"

"*Si.*" I felt chastened. Protecting Galeazzo's confidences may have kept me safer, but it did not serve our cause.

"Next, will you decide to go back to your rich friends in London?"

I dropped my jaw and blinked hard to clear the shock. "No. I've made my choice."

"Every action must be carefully weighed. Lives are at stake." Dominic paused as if collecting himself and refilled our wine glasses. "I will tell you nothing about Turin. The matter is settled."

"You're doing me an injustice." I hardened my gaze. "Why?"

He said nothing.

"I can get information to the British government. Together we can make a difference."

Dominic stared at me, his mouth pressed shut.

I thumped my clenched fist on the table. "I have Jewish friends. Hitler is persecuting them. And now Mussolini proclaims his own Manifesto of Race, like a dog after his master's pat. I care as much as you about the people and principles at stake."

"Do you have the slightest idea what the Blackshirts could do to you? Or me?"

"Of course I do."

"How can you? You've never been tested."

Shoving my chair back, I stood and yanked up a blouse sleeve. "Look at my skin. Men want me at their side, and as long as they have me, they tolerate this. But when I demand the same freedoms they have, they call me a filthy half-breed. Or a debauched whore. Will the Fascists round *me* up next because they hate the color of my skin?"

Dominic avoided my gaze.

"Listen to me." I waited for him to look up. "I made a pledge. To you and Giustizia e Libertà. I stand by it."

Dominic bit his lower lip.

I walked to his side, gripped his jaw in my palm, and lifted his face. "I promise you: I will never betray you or our cause."

"There are unknown dangers."

"Am I nothing because I'm not a man? And you, have you been tested?"

Dominic's chin twitched. Quickly, he tightened his jaw.

But I'd seen the crack in his courage. I dropped my arms and stepped back. "You're afraid, too."

He hung his head. Was he ashamed I'd seen his fear?

I softened my voice. "You've never told me: Why do *you* do this?"

He studied his fisted hands.

"Tell me, Dominic."

He looked up, his eyes gleaming. "Because my brother died for no reason in Abyssinia. And my sister's husband, too. Because Mussolini and Ciano's rats assassinated Rosselli—just for his ideas."

I stroked his shoulder.

"I want freedom," he said. "And revenge."

"Then let me fight beside you."

"First, I must trust you—to death if it comes to that."

I knelt before him and wrapped my hands around his. "I know what I do is dangerous, but I will not turn back."

He leaned over and rested his forehead on my temple. Tenderness welled up in me, coursing between us until I could no longer discern where I ended and he began. Nor did I care. Now, we would work as one.

NICE

MAY 1940

Wrapped in the nonchalance of a model on the runway, I strolled from my hotel to the nearby rail station and boarded the train bound for points north. Up the coast it sped, through Genoa, arriving six hours later in Ventimiglia, the last stop before Italy's border with France.

Usually, I enjoyed train trips, allowing myself the pleasures of reading, scenery-gazing, and dozing, but not this time. Anxiety over my first intelligence hand-off dogged me, and I spent much of my time rehearsing scenarios of apprehension and escape. If intercepted, my notes about military equipment, though carefully hidden, would expose not only me but also Dominic. As if simple worry was not bad enough, I understood that too much fretting carried its own risks. Did a fox deliberate before it pounced? No, I told myself, of course not. I must be like the fox. Like my code name, Cher Fox.

An announcement blared through the loudspeaker: "Continuing passengers, please remain in your seats. Do not exit." I clasped my hands together on my lap and listened to the murmur of fellow passengers and, outside the train window, the clatter of baggage carts. Several rows ahead, a train official moved down the aisle, requesting passports. I concentrated on the questions he asked, considered my answers, and retrieved my passport.

"Passport, please, *signorina*."

I handed him my Dutch passport, my expression rich with humility, and spoke softly. "It's a fine day for travel, isn't it, *signor*?"

"*Si*." He flipped open the passport, studied it, and eyed me. "What is your destination?"

"Nice." Anticipating his next question, I offered my answer with a glance to the side, as if prevailing on his discretion. "I'm meeting a friend for a holiday."

"Will you be returning to Italy?"

"Oh, yes. I'm studying in Florence."

"Very well." With a flick of his hand, he returned my passport and shuffled on.

As simple as that. And to think of the time I'd spent mulling over how much makeup to put on and whether to crimp my hair—when all I needed to do was dissemble a bit, cover up in a coat, and, like an old Italian woman, wrap my head in a shawl. Then again, I was pleased I'd decided on a stylish Rochas dress jacket and slim skirt in cobalt. Beneath my long coat, I felt like my old self again—the glamorous Toto Koopman off to meet an old friend.

———

"Toto," Randolph called from the platform, rushing up to me. "You're looking perfectly marvelous."

I dipped my knees to set down my suitcase and embraced him. "Starting already with the flattery, are you?"

"Hah," he laughed, adjusting his hat to a rakish angle. "And you, my dear, are flirting with a married man."

"Such marvels you men can be. Look at you—the charming rogue, tamed and with a wife at home."

Randolph motioned to the side with a bounce of his eyes toward a couple of beefy men. "Let's be off. These bloody minders make me nervous. They're forever warning me about lurking enemies."

He picked up my suitcase, and I followed him beneath the Gare de Nice's arched roof and through its high-ceilinged station. Ah, I was in France, the beautiful sunny south of France, with wildflowers blooming in the hilly countryside and tangy ocean scents wafting on warm breezes. Already I breathed easier. What a difference a border made—the melody of the language, the mansard-roof architecture, the elegance of the women's attire. The Wehrmacht might be storming France's northern border, but one wouldn't know it by the relaxed atmosphere here.

"Come along," Randolph said, heading toward an automobile pulling up to the curb. "We have rooms at Hotel Westminster."

———

Randolph had arranged for us to dine in his suite. "It's the only way," he said, "we can speak freely without putting up with those bloody minders. Or German spies."

Before dinner, I strolled the Promenade des Anglais, rattled through an evening newspaper (with the ominous headline "Netherlands Queen Wilhelmina
Evacuated To London"), and changed into a dinner gown. Refreshed, I took
the stairs to Randolph's suite. I'd announced when he dropped me at my room:
"Darling, I know you never travel without your Ballantine's, but I'm dying for
some tiny-bubbled Champagne."

It was chilling when I arrived. As he plucked it out of a chrome bucket, the
ice tinkled invitingly. "Shall I uncork it?"

"Please," I said, standing at his corner window. "What a lovely view—the
promenade in the slanted sun. I can even imagine it painted in shimmering
oils."

"This is the only hotel I'm comfortable staying at just now. What few guests
there are are mostly Brits."

I swung around. "It doesn't look good for France, does it?"

Pop, the cork exploded. "Not at all. I can only stay one night. Parliament's
all tied up in knots."

I walked to Randolph, who stood by the liquor cabinet. Atop it sat a
near-full bottle of Ballantine's whiskey and the chrome bucket dripping with
condensation. I took the glass of Champagne he offered. "The border crossing
was surprisingly easy."

"It won't be for long." Randolph tipped his glass to mine. "Here's to saving
our asses."

We took up opposite ends of the curvy couch and caught up on news about
our lives: Yes, he was enjoying his service in Parliament, which pleased Pamela
since it kept him in London most of the time. So far, he found marriage "to his
satisfaction."

I had to chuckle. "That's not a terribly resounding endorsement."

He winked. "Marriage has its comforts, not that you'd ever admit it."

"Have you, by chance, been commiserating with MJ?"

We laughed, like old chums sharing a secret.

"How is MJ?" I'd written to him twice, early on, but he'd only responded
to my first letter. It was probably for the best.

"Pamela and I introduced him to an American friend of hers. He likes her
well enough for gadding about."

"I hope she makes him happy." Of course, I occasionally thought of MJ and
our times together, but preoccupied as I was with other matters, memories of
our affair and London escapades paled in significance. And now I had Dominic.

"Did you know," Randolph said, "that my father asked Lord Beaverbrook to serve as Minister of Aircraft Production?"

"I hadn't heard." An amused grin overtook me. "He certainly has the wherewithal. Especially if it involves strong-arming his adversaries—and aides—behind closed doors."

"Ah, well, about the Cabinet, I'm afraid I have some bad news for you."

I plunked my glass down on the table. "What do you mean?"

"The Cabinet has forbidden women from serving on the front lines, in any capacity. Including espionage work. It's too dangerous. And they're not protected by international laws on war."

That took my breath away. "I can't believe this. While I'm risking my neck in Mussolini's Italy, these old men sit around a table issuing ridiculous pronouncements. While I walk streets patrolled by *squadristi,* they're safe in London."

"Yes, I'm sorry. I wanted to tell you in person."

"Well, you should at least show them what I've got."

"Yes, yes. I might as well."

"They owe me that much."

Randolph refreshed our Champagne and sat down, leaning over his knees toward me. "All right. What can you tell me?"

I decided to give him the less important information first—and save the best for last. "I attended a rally in March, where Count Ciano spoke. Mussolini's aides are traveling around to whip up the appetite for war. Conscription is at high steam, as are exemption requests. But that's probably no surprise."

"Not really."

"I'm working on the list of key contacts for your father. Chief of Staff Pietro Badoglio is high on it."

Randolph swung one leg over the other. "What else do you have?"

"The government is signing military equipment contracts with all the big producers, and *clientelismo* is in full force in the businesses."

That got his attention. "Even with Mussolini looking over their shoulder?"

"He needs them," I said. "Fiat and Ansaldo have convinced Il Duce that they're the only ones who can design and build heavy military equipment, so they get the contracts. And they know how to fatten their profits—they just claim their workers are ready to strike. Which the workers would probably be glad to do since so many are anti-Fascists."

"Do you know what they have in production?"

"Fiat is making more CR.42 biplanes."

Randolph nodded solemnly. "Any idea how many they're producing?"

"My contact tells me three hundred."

"Do you know what bases they're deploying to?"

"No, but this should interest you: Fiat is building a new tank, the M13/40, to replace the older model. I don't have numbers on that, but I do have the design." I reached into my purse, pulled out a quarter-folded paper, and spread it on the coffee table.

He looked at the drawing, then jerked his head up. "My God, you carried this across the border?"

"In a hidden purse compartment."

He shook his head, like a parent torn between disapproval and admiration. "A regular boffin you are—and as intrepid as ever."

He leaned over the table and studied the penciled design. I'd redrawn the print Dominic showed me, including specifications of armor thickness, primary and secondary armaments, engine style, and operational speed and range. I'd rather enjoyed mastering all the mechanical minutiae.

He asked, "Are they building these in Turin?"

"Fiat is building the V8 engines in Turin; Ansaldo is assembling the tank in Genoa."

"And the CR.42s?"

"They're built in Turin."

Randolph leaned back and draped an arm over the couch back. "Excellent, simply excellent. Your contacts have good information."

"I believe I can keep it coming. If the Cabinet will deign to accept intelligence from me."

"We can bloody well use this intelligence. To hell with the damn rules."

"There's more where that came from."

"We'll need to think of a different way for you to get reports out. The whole Continent is likely to ignite in short order."

"So, you'll make my case to your father?"

"Yes, I will."

"I appreciate that, Randolph."

"We need someone in Italy. And you've provided more than any other agents on the ground there."

"Yes, you can count on me to keep it coming."

"My father's not one to stand on ceremony. He'll be pleased with this information."

"Tell me, how's your father bearing up?" News of Winston Churchill's rise to Prime Minister had made headlines in Italy. And, I imagined, the whole Continent.

"He said the most incredible thing to me a few days ago." Randolph got up to retrieve the whiskey bottle. "Care for any?"

"No, thank you."

Randolph leaned against the liquor cabinet, crossed a leg over his shin, and rested a toe on the carpet. He cut a dapper figure, and I imagine he knew it.

"I went up to his bedroom one morning to hurry him along. He was shaving at his basin, hacking away with his old valet razor. He put me off: 'Sit down, dear boy, and read the paper while I finish shaving.' After a few minutes, he piped up and said, 'I think I see my way through' and went right on shaving."

Randolph poured himself a whiskey and brought the Champagne over to freshen my glass. "I had to ask him: 'Do you mean we can avoid defeat or that we can beat the bastards?' He said, 'Of course I mean we can beat them.'"

"Amazing," I said, "Can he really manage it?"

Randolph held up a finger on the hand grasping the Champagne, urging patience. He plunked the bottle in the bucket and strolled back to the couch, like an actor playing the scene for effect. "I told him I was all for it, but I didn't see how he could do it, not with the German juggernaut on the rise. By this time, he'd dried and sponged his face. He turned around to me and said with great intensity: 'I shall drag the United States in.'"

"Really?" I asked. "But how?"

"I asked that, too. All I got was, 'Wait, and you'll see. It's my ace in the hole.'"

"And if the U.S. won't come in?"

Randolph plopped down on the couch and twisted toward me, bracing a hand on his knee. "The Nazis could march all over us."

"Does your father agree it's as dire as that?"

He nodded with sad resignation. "Look how easily they took the Low Countries. And the Luftwaffe probably has three to four times as many aircraft as the RAF."

"My God, that's frightening."

"Italy's no great industrial or military power, but they have a strategic location and can add to Germany's might. So, anything you can give us may help."

I placed my glass on the side table and swiveled around to face him. "Then we'd better discuss how I'm to get reports out."

FLORENCE

AUGUST 1940

N o sooner had I closed the door than Elisabeth handed me a letter. "For you. It came this morning."

The neat, thick-penned script gave away the writer's identity—Galeazzo Ciano. It'd been five months since our rendezvous after the rally, and I'd begun to think it unlikely I'd hear from him. "I'm a little surprised he's written. Considering the circumstances."

In June, Italy had declared war on Britain and France. Shortly afterward, France had fallen, and, only days ago, the Royal Air Force had unleashed attacks on Turin and Milan, targeting some of the factories I'd told Randolph about.

"I hope it doesn't signal trouble." Elisabeth worried her hands. "Come, sit down and read your letter."

Elisabeth had given me permission to use her apartment address for communications with Ciano. We reasoned that the Fascists would neither suspect nor detain a German citizen—or scrutinize her mail. As we seated ourselves on the couch, it caved in the middle, sliding us elbow to elbow. I slit the envelope, tugged out the note, and flapped it open.

5 August 1940
My dear Toto,
I have some business in Florence on August 21 and would love to dine with you that evening. I'll send a message later about where we can meet.
I hope you're enjoying your art studies,
With affection,
G, your faithful friend

Looking up from the note, I said, "He wants to meet for dinner."

Elisabeth twisted around to face me. "Will you risk it?"

"Of course." I couldn't say no—to either him or the opportunity such a meeting presented.

"But it could be dangerous."

"It's just as dangerous to decline," I said. Still, Elisabeth was right. This was a new game I played: consorting not merely for nibbles of intelligence but also as a member of the resistance. "I can manage it. This wouldn't be the first time I've been under the microscope."

"I suppose." Elisabeth rose. "I haven't even offered you a drink. Your usual?"

"Please. And I must thank you again for letting me use your address."

"It's too risky for you to get such mail at your hotel."

"I know, but I don't want you to risk any more than necessary. I'll make a different arrangement for any future communications."

"Yes, but do you think it prudent to continue seeing him and doing your partisan work?"

"I must risk it this time at least. He has summoned me."

Surely, I could handle an evening with Galeazzo. After all, I could count on him to take measures to keep the meeting secret.

Elisabeth handed me a Campari. "Is it possible Ciano suspects you of partisan activity?"

"He can have no evidence. I've kept myself in the shadows."

Besides, I'd managed before in the face of accusation. During my first year with MJ, while the scandal reached a scorching pitch, I scoffed at Beaverbrook's vicious attempts to ruin my reputation. Not bad practice, really, for my present circumstances—befriending a rugged Italian journalist, a lowly art student, *and* a high-ranking Fascist. Anyone who knew my past would have brushed it all off: That Toto keeps such—shall we say—eclectic company. What a rebel she is.

Not that it mattered what people thought or said, except insofar as I needed cover—because now I was consorting with a lover who'd become the enemy, Mussolini's Foreign Minister and son-in-law. And, at the same time, ferrying intelligence about the manufacture of military equipment to Randolph and the British government. And hiding banned books.

I sighed. "I suppose I'll have to tell Dominic. He'll likely be more vexing than Ciano."

Elisabeth patted my hand. "Love sometimes complicates our lives, doesn't it?"

"I knew it would. But we couldn't help ourselves." I smiled sadly. "Now I, like Tosca, have a Cavaradossi to protect."

———

"Ah, Toto, glamorous as always," said Galeazzo, rising from his seat to pull out my chair. "And what a ravishing green your eyes are in that dress."

As he kissed my cheeks, I took in the room. "Dear me, if we had an orchestra, we could waltz."

Our lone table sat in the middle of a room large enough to accommodate twenty diners. Galeazzo had obviously asked the hotel to arrange a private room for us, and he'd also stationed his guards at the doors. But no, I'd told myself, this was no trap—merely protection against any anti-Fascists plotting his assassination.

He leaned jauntily to the side in his wing-back chair. "I rarely have a usual dinner out anymore."

"Such are the costs of prominence."

He grinned. "It also has its rewards."

We chatted over glasses of Vermentino. It'd been sweltering in Rome for weeks, he told me, and Florence was a welcome change. Yes, his children were fine. Indeed, the family often visited Villa Torlonia, and Il Duce always stole some time to dote on his grandchildren. Watching them together gave Galeazzo great satisfaction.

A waiter arrived to acquaint us with the chef's offerings.

How strange it all was. Galeazzo had once been as innocent as his children. Now, as a devotee of Fascism, he must believe some greater good justified its brutality, including the assassination of Carlo Rosselli. And could I condone killing for the resistance? I'd been trained to use a Browning HP but chose not to carry one. I hoped I'd never be forced to differentiate between the culpable and the innocent. Galeazzo's children were innocent. Was his wife, too? What about ordinary military officers caught up in the fight? This war confused the usual lines of morality. Mussolini was the only one I was certain about—he was a small man whose greed for power demanded the deaths and persecution of many. And Hitler, too, of course, a megalomaniac if the world ever knew one.

The waiter left us, and I asked, "I imagine you're terribly busy, with the country at war. Have you resigned yourself to it?"

"We have our objectives. It's simply a matter of keeping them in front of Hitler and Ribbentrop."

"Do they listen?"

"Now that we've honored the Pact of Steel, we have a right to present our goals, which I'll do at the Vienna Conference."

He said it so matter-of-factly, as if it were as routine as setting up a chessboard. Was it a change of heart? Or was he testing me? "And your goals and Il Duce's are one and the same?"

"I am Il Duce's servant. And Italy's Foreign Minister."

His taciturn manner—toward the war and Mussolini—warned me off more questions. I lifted my wine glass. "Then, I must wish you success in Vienna."

It was astonishing, really. Italy officially at war alongside Germany, and Ciano shuttling between Il Duce and Hitler and his minions. Still, Italy's place in the military and political landscape was complicated, with Hitler turning the tables on Mussolini: During Hitler's rise to power, he'd spoken openly of his admiration for Il Duce. But since then, the Führer had wrested complete control of Germany and conquered Czechoslovakia, Poland, Norway, France, and the Low Countries. Now Il Duce struggled to keep pace with the Nazi war machine—and garner his countrymen's support for the war.

"And you," he said, twisting sideways to cross a leg, "I'm surprised you've stayed so long in Florence. What keeps you here?"

"I love this city—the art and architecture, its glimmers of the Renaissance." To say nothing of plotting resistance maneuvers and selling my most valuable jewelry and furs to support Giustizia e Libertà. I shot him a mischievous grin. "And you must agree, neither Paris nor London are terribly inviting just now."

"Göring's only sending his bombers and fighters after strategic targets. Not London."

"Luftwaffe bombs are falling all over Britain. London could be next."

"I can't say. Still, it's not like someone as wild as you to stay long in one place."

"Wild, you say?" Tilting my head, I arched an eyebrow. "I'll take that as a compliment."

He flapped his hands apart and held them open. "Truly, I'm curious. Who do you spend your time with here?"

"I've fallen in with the art crowd. I first came to join some Hungarian art collector friends. Through them, I met art dealers and students of art. A few musicians and painters, as well." I was not, I reasoned, giving anything away by revealing what he already understood of me. And I didn't believe I was under surveillance. "Artists and opera-goers suit me, as you know."

"And have you traveled much since being here?"

I told myself: This isn't an interrogation, just casual conversation. Give away a little, but not too much. "Not at all since the declaration of war. It rather dampens the urge to trot about."

"So, you'll stay indefinitely?"

"As long as it pleases me."

Galeazzo wagged his head like some doubting Thomas. "Don't you miss your London friends?"

"I left a broken heart in my wake. It's easier not to dip back into those waters."

The conversation continued along lines that mystified me. Galeazzo displayed none of the tortured sentiments he'd expressed in March. He balked at speaking about the war in detail yet showed bald curiosity about my activities and views.

Did he suspect me of spying? I kept my manner relaxed and convivial, but my skin prickled with fear. Do not forget, Dominic had warned, this man is a murderous thug. You are only a plaything to him. Of course, I'd conceded, Ciano would not tolerate a whiff of betrayal. I'd promised Dominic I'd tread carefully.

After dinner, Galeazzo invited me to his suite and made his intentions clear: "I have regretted our brief meeting so many months ago. Let us enjoy each other tonight."

There would be no escape. I must humor him—even if I gathered not a crumb of intelligence. Six months ago, this encounter wouldn't have carried the risk it now did—with me firmly planted in the ranks of the resistance. And if I'd stayed in London, I'd not be courting such risk. Why had I changed my life so drastically, shifted like a pendulum from indulgence and freedom to danger and calculation? True, I detested Fascism and Nazism, but could I make any difference by placing myself in the middle of the mêlée? I could only hope I'd not been overly reckless, that I'd not merely succumbed to my craving for novelty—and that my actions would be of some value.

He led me to the bedroom of his suite, sat on the bed, and commanded me to stand before him. Lifting my foot, he removed one, then the other, of my snug-fitting heels. Deliberately, he undressed me, peeling off my sleek pastel-green dress, silk stockings, and bra and panties. He ran his hands over my shoulders, my breasts, my hips and thighs. Keeping his gaze trained on me, he kicked off his shoes, threw his jacket and shirt aside, and unbuckled and yanked off his belt.

Standing, he encircled me in his arms, jerked me to him, and forced my torso to mold to his. "You will be mine tonight?"

Throw away thought and deliberation, I commanded myself, be the sensuous animal, and nothing more. I brushed my lips over his ear. "All for your pleasure."

And after giving myself to him, I wanted something to show for it. Something to tell Dominic—even though he'd likely rage at me for pressing my luck.

I nestled my head against his shoulder and smoothed a palm over his sturdy chest. A bracing menthol aftershave mingled with his musky sweat. "You once asked me if you could speak confidentially with me. May I ask the same of you?"

"I'll give you the same assurance you gave me." His arm looped under my neck and over my shoulder. He lifted and dropped his hand against my arm as if to signal assent.

Or was it a move calculated for that effect? For all I knew, he'd been playing cat and mouse with me all evening. If he did suspect me of partisan activity, what better way to disabuse him than to make a minor confession? And extract some information in the process. "Some of my friends here and in London are Jewish."

His shoulder hunched slightly. "That doesn't surprise me."

I knew Ciano had grown up in Livorno and had many Jewish friends there. In 1936, after anti-Semitic articles landed in several Fascist newspapers, he'd made a public statement claiming that the government's attitudes toward the Jews remained unchanged. Did he still hold that position? I said, "Some have lost their jobs."

"The place of our Jews is different than the German Jews. Here they live among us. As our neighbors."

"But that didn't stop Il Duce from releasing his Manifesto of Race." I would never forget Alfonso Frascati's removal from the University because of Italy's laws about Jews. And he was only one of many. I'd met several Jews in London who had fled Germany. My dear friend Conrad Veidt left with his Jewish wife just before Goebbels purged the film industry of Jews. The brilliant director of *Don Juan,* Alexander Korda, with whom I'd worked briefly in London, told me that he too had been forced to flee. Escaped Jewish Poles spoke openly of Nazi campaigns against them, and many suspected similar crusades in every other country under Hitler's control.

"And," I continued, "he enforced the new rules about their employment."

"*Sì,* but the Jews are of little consequence to him now. He has more pressing concerns."

"Does Il Duce intend more campaigns against them?"

He jerked his head back to take me in. "This is official policy you're asking about."

"I would do nothing to harm you or the people of Italy. And some of these people are Jews."

"I advise you not to make yourself an enemy of the state."

"You yourself put Italy and its people first. You've said so to me. What's wrong with me doing the same?"

"It's not wrong to consider the Jews. But you mustn't defy the government. Or me."

I smoothed my palm over his chest and sought the spot where I could feel the thump of his heart. "I know you don't hate the Jews. We're the same that way. So, I cannot defy you."

"I don't wish to argue with you about this."

"Just tell me: Will Il Duce order more acts against them?"

He gripped my chin between his finger and thumb. "We'll speak no more of this."

I detected no antipathy in his tone, only the mild exasperation of a put-upon friend. I hoisted myself up on an elbow, leaned over his chest, and whispered in his ear. "Tell me."

He slung me onto my back and rolled on top of me. "I cannot say," he murmured and smothered my mouth with a forceful kiss.

But in his own way, he'd answered my question. And I doubted, after this evening, that I'd ever again hear from him.

FLORENCE

A year earlier, when I'd witnessed Alfonso Frascati's removal from the University, I'd resolved to track him down, to both console him and seek his counsel. But I'd had no luck doing so, and I'd found a way to join the resistance without his help. Then one evening, while Elisabeth and I were out dining at a neighborhood trattoria, in walked the rail-thin, white-haired professor. I ran to him, and we embraced like old friends.

"Professor, I'm so glad to see you. Won't you join us?"

He pulled up a chair. "Ah, Toto and Elisabeth, I have missed our lively discussions."

What had he been doing these many months, Elisabeth asked? Besides staying out of sight, he explained, some private tutoring. Two bottles of wine later, talk turned to the plight of Italy's Jews.

Lowering my voice to be sure no one else could hear us, I told Elisabeth and the professor what I'd surmised from my last conversation with Galeazzo Ciano—without revealing the source of this intelligence. "I believe Mussolini is planning more campaigns against Italy's Jews."

"I'm not surprised," the professor said, smoothing his hands over the floral tablecloth. "Not after he issued the Manifesto of Race. Mussolini is nothing if not Hitler's lackey."

After dinner, the professor and I dropped Elisabeth off at her apartment.

We turned onto the street, and I took his arm. "About the Manifesto," I said. "What can be done to counter Mussolini's campaigns against Italy's Jews?"

Along the boulevard, street lamps and window lights cast shadows through tree branches rattling in the wind.

He stared straight ahead. "Why would you want to get involved?"

"Not you, too," I said. "Why does every Italian man I know doubt my sincerity?"

"Perhaps to keep ourselves safe. Everyone is suspect these days. Everyone a possible informer."

"Look, I was outraged when you were removed from your position at the University as if you were an enemy of the state. What you may not know is I have many Jewish friends, and I'm determined to do whatever I can to undermine measures against them."

"I'm pleased to hear this, but I'm sure you understand I must be careful about my associations."

"Then let me make some inquiries. Will you meet me for dinner next Wednesday—at the same trattoria?"

I told Dominic of my encounter with Alfonso Frascati and asked if there was something we could do. That was when I learned that the professor was also a member of Giustizia e Libertà. I convinced Dominic to join us for dinner the next week.

When the professor saw Dominic, he embraced him warmly. And then me. "If Dominic trusts you," he said, "so do I."

The three of us huddled over a corner table. Candles on the tables and dim wall sconces lit the small trattoria. Its dark atmosphere lent an aura of intimacy to the diners, and the cook and waiters were all family. I felt safe here.

Our *primi* plates were served, and the professor tasted his gnocchi. He smacked his lips and put his fork down. "I have learned that the Directorate for Demography and Race is ordering cities to update their lists of Jews."

I shook my head. "I'm not surprised. First, they'll get their lists cleaned up; then they'll use them against the Jews."

"I've been thinking of a plan." The professor circled his gaze between the two of us. "First to warn Jews in other cities and then to break into Florence's Municipal Registry Office and remove the list."

I thumped my hands on the table. "I want to help."

Dominic, being the local leader in Florence, needed to approve any such plan. He stopped twirling spaghetti around his fork. "Do we know if the Jews are in imminent danger?"

Professor Frascati hunched a shoulder. "I've heard nothing beyond the order to update lists."

I turned to face Dominic. "This is a good time to act. No one would expect such a raid since no news is circulating about any actions against Jews."

The professor agreed. "I think the time to strike is now, before Mussolini's next pandering move to ingratiate himself with Hitler."

Dominic brushed his forehead. "Fine, but you must plan carefully so no one will be caught. And Toto can only help with planning, not acting."

"I will agree to that," I nodded. "It's only worth doing if done well."

"*Si*," said the professor. "I'll find the right people for the job."

Alfonso chose three others to join us. We decided we'd need at least two weeks to develop a reliable log of activity in the vicinity of the municipal building. We analyzed means of entry and the traffic in and out on both weekdays and weekends. Alfonso tapped a connection to a former city official for information about where in the office we could find the list of Jewish citizens. I prevailed on a sympathetic widow whose apartment afforded a good view of the preferred entry point, the Registry's rear window, and we kept watch over it. One of us paced the surrounding area at night and discovered there were no guards stationed nearby, only occasional walking patrols, though never between two and five in the morning. Apparently, even strutting Blackshirts retired to their warm beds on cold winter nights.

Our squad planned to strike during a typical lull in Blackshirt activity, on Friday, January 31, at 2:45 a.m.

DISPATCH FROM FLORENCE

19 January 1941

Subject and IJ continue to meet often, typically for dinner. He some-times accompanies her to her hotel and does not leave until morning. Over the last week, she has spent several evenings a week at an apartment on Via della Condotta. She meets four men there, always late at night. The group's activities are suspicious and may be partisan.

WD

FLORENCE

JANUARY 1941

The day before the raid, I prepared to travel to Genoa to make a dead drop. Randolph Churchill had arranged for the pickup at a previously scouted location, and there was little for me to do in Florence now. Alfonso would ably oversee the Registry Office raid. Since the plan was to abscond with the list of Florence's Jews and leave as few traces as possible, we hoped to delay discovery of the theft over the weekend. Still, if officials learned right away that the list was missing and anyone suspected me of involvement, I'd have an alibi. And Cher Fox had important intelligence to convey.

I donned unassuming travel wear and accoutrement, a subdued charcoal wool suit, light makeup, no jewelry, sensible walking shoes, and a beat-up suitcase. Inside my hidden purse compartment, I carried a list of Italian submarines and battleships in port at Taranto harbor. I'd worked with Dominic and his Taranto contacts to gather technical information about their condition and state of repair since the British bombardment. Ticket in hand (for important trips I always purchased my ticket in advance), I let myself out by the hotel's alley door to avoid scrutiny. What chilly weather, I thought, glad I'd chosen my fur-collared, mid-calf wool coat. I headed toward the street behind the hotel and rounded the corner.

Two Blackshirts leaning against the building turned toward me. One was Reitano, the hefty officer I'd met months earlier at the Ciano rally. I pretended, in single-minded hurry, not to recognize him. The other one, scruffy and unshaven, tossed his cigarette to the sidewalk and ground it out with a toe. They pushed away from the wall and blocked my passage. I smiled absently and stepped into the street.

"Signorina Koopman," Reitano said, stepping aside to intercept me. "May I ask where you're going?"

"Ah, Consul Reitano," I said with a gentle nod, "nice to see you again. I'm bound for the train station."

"And you are traveling where?"

I had my ticket. I couldn't lie about my destination, not that it was incriminating in itself. "Genoa."

"We must ask you to come with us."

"But I don't wish to miss my train."

"I'm sorry, we must escort you to jail for questioning." He moved to within three feet of me, opened his palm, and pointed in the direction opposite the station. The coarse-looking man came up to my side, smirking like a schoolyard bully.

My heart thumped wildly. What could I do? Certainly not run or dispute their order. But the intelligence I carried—I must get rid of it. "May I drop my suitcase in my room first?"

"No, I'll carry it." Reitano stepped forward and took it from me.

Flanked by the Blackshirts, I could do naught but consent to the route they guided me along. Think, I commanded myself, find out what you can. Trying to quell my screeching anxiety, I steadied my step and breathed evenly. Turning to Reitano, I said, "Consul, I have no idea what this is about. Why am I being detained?"

"I'm not able to say, *signorina*." From his haughty height, he looked down on me. "I do wonder why you gave a different name when we met."

"What do you mean?"

"You said you were Catherina."

"My passport shows that Catherina is my first name. Toto is my father's nickname for me. Surely that's no crime."

"That's not for me to decide."

"Consul, I'm quite baffled by all this. Can you tell me anything to explain this mistake?"

"No, *signorina*." He stared ahead, his expression impassive.

He either wouldn't tell or didn't know. He was obviously following orders, and Blackshirts were nothing if not deferential to high command—braggarts and bullies on their own, but dutiful and ingratiating in the face of authority.

I must try another strategy. We were approaching a neighborhood café that I sometimes frequented. Maybe I could invite them in, then distract and evade them somehow. Or pay the bill not just with lira but also with the report. I could signal the waiter, with whom I had a friendly rapport, that I was in some trouble. Better to let him destroy the intelligence than allow the Fascists to discover it.

I angled my face to Reitano. "Where are you from, Consul?"

"Sicily."

I turned to the coarse fellow. "And you, officer?"

With a gravelly voice, he said, "Sicily, also, but a different village."

"How are you finding Florence?"

Reitano snorted. "Too cold. Right now, the sun is probably shining in Sicily."

"No sun is not healthy," said the other. "I'm turning white like a ghost."

"Can't you request to be stationed nearer your homes?"

"Hah," said Reitano. "You don't understand the Milizia Volontaria. It's not as voluntary as the name says."

I touched his arm. "But I'm sure you find the service gratifying?"

He hunched a shoulder. "It's not bad. I can send money to my family."

We came to the café. "*Signori*, I would love a coffee. Would you allow me to buy for us?"

Reitano frowned. "*Grazie*, no."

"I insist."

"No, we have orders."

"Surely there can be no harm in a coffee?"

"It is not permitted."

There'd be no escaping. I was wasting my breath on these two. They'd caught me, and I had no idea how or for what. Surely it wasn't the trivial matter of my name. Had someone leaked information about the Registry Office raid? Not likely—few people knew, and those who did were trustworthy. Had someone in Giustizia e Libertà been arrested and interrogated? I'd heard nothing of the sort. Might it be the courier in Genoa? No, the British Secret Intelligence thoroughly vetted and trained their agents. Might there be a double agent in my midst? Or had I roused Ciano's suspicion? *Oh, Mother, please watch over me now. So I can make you proud. Send me courage.*

We entered the Florence jail, a drab brick building with a reputation as a holding facility for anti-Fascists. Consul Reitano escorted me to a windowless room barren of anything but a clunky desk and two solid chairs.

"You can sit there." Reitano pointed to the wooden chair in front of the desk and plopped my suitcase down inside the room. Then he stood blocking the doorway, as if he expected me to bolt. But there was no window, no route of escape whatsoever.

A forceful voice cut through the leaden silence. "You may be excused, Consul."

Reitano gave way. In walked a man of perhaps forty in a smart black uniform with silver buttons: not a Blackshirt, rather much worse—a military officer of the Carabinieri branch. A sour lump burned at my gullet.

He swung the door shut and held himself upright in front of me. "*Signorina*, I am Captain Donati. May I see your passport?"

"I'm pleased to meet you, Captain." I extracted my passport from my purse and handed it to him, pulling back my hand to avoid exposing its quiver.

He marched to the other side of the desk and sat. Opening the passport and flattening it on the desk, he flipped through the pages, then turned back to the identification page. "Catherina Johanna Koopman. You're perhaps better known as Toto Koopman?"

Summoning attentive serenity, I leaned slightly toward him. "That's the version of my name I usually go by."

"You planned to travel somewhere today?"

"*Si*, to attend a lecture at the University of Genoa." One should always carefully think through one's cover story. It helped the words roll out easily.

"What lecture?"

"By an expert in Etruscan art."

"Who is this expert?"

"Franco Barra. Have you heard of him?"

He sloughed off my question with a scrunch of his cheek. "How long did you plan to stay?"

"I thought I might have a nice dinner in Genoa and return in the morning."

"And who were you to dine with?"

"Myself." I smiled affably. "I'm one of those women who's perfectly capable of dining alone."

My response did not amuse him. "Did you plan to meet anyone in Genoa?"

"No, Captain. I have explained the extent of my plans."

"You, a world traveler, know no one in Genoa?"

I allowed the hint of a chuckle to escape. "I'm flattered you know something of my reputation. But I actually don't have acquaintances in every city on the Continent."

"*Signorina*, do you expect me to believe you were on a lecture outing and nothing else?"

"Yes, Captain Donati, and I don't understand why I'm here. Can you tell me, please?"

"I will ask the questions." He inhaled sharply. "Why were you going to Genoa?"

"It's as I've explained." I bounced my clasped hands. "Now, I must get to the station. I've already missed one train."

"Do you not understand? You're under detention."

"Really, Captain, this makes no sense."

He plopped his forearms on the desk and leaned toward me. "Do you deny ever engaging in subversive activity?"

"If that's what you believe, you are misinformed."

"We expect you to cooperate with us."

"It's not a question of cooperation. I'm a private citizen, and I wish to travel to Genoa. Now, may I go?"

"No. A guard will search you, and then you'll be transported to San Vittore Prison in Milan."

This was the worst possible scenario. If they found the intelligence hidden in my purse, my clandestine activities would be revealed—and I'd be charged with spying. Had Alfonso or Dominic also fallen under suspicion? If interrogated, I mustn't breathe their names. Ever.

An old shame gurgled up in me, harkening back to an incident when I was only nine. My brother, Henri, had ridden off on his horse late at night to meet some friends. I'd overheard him and his school chums planning their mischief—a swimming party with girls. And when our parents asked me if I knew anything, I'd betrayed him and revealed the lake where they'd gathered. Which meant Henri was not only scolded but also embarrassed in front of his friends. Because of me.

But I was just a youngster then. And it would have been wrong to lie to my parents. The matter before me now was much clearer. And the stakes higher.

The captain marched out of the room, pulling the door shut behind him.

I sighed. *Please, my crying javelin, lend me your protection.*

DISPATCH FROM FLORENCE

30 January 1941

My informant reports subject was arrested today and transported to San Vittore Prison in Milan.

WD

MILAN

FEBRUARY 1941

The two officers transporting me to San Vittore Prison ordered me to take the seat by the window. They plunked down opposite each other in the train compartment, forming a barricade between me and the door. One, a restless, lanky-armed youth, pretended I was invisible, all the time blathering like a youngster showing off for a girl: Such a grand time he'd have roaming Milan's city center; when he got home, his brutish brother would only brag about whatever he'd done that day; he'd buy his mother a nice present; that'd shut up his lout of a brother.

Their inane conversation only heightened my squirming agitation. I must get rid of the intelligence I carried. The guard who'd stripped and searched me at the Florence jail emptied my purse and combed through its contents but failed to detect the hidden compartment. If they discovered the papers at the prison, they'd try to extract the names of accomplices and prosecute me as a spy. And no doubt torture me.

I must find a way to destroy the paper; I must work around these two. There had to be a way. I hid my face behind a newspaper, pretending to absorb the words, reminding myself to turn the pages occasionally. Meantime, the officers babbled on. Whenever I shifted my position or turned a newspaper page, the older, jowly one eyed me. No doubt they'd been ordered to guard me closely. Surely, they knew they'd be held accountable if anything went awry with my transport.

During a lull in their banter, I asked if I might have a glass of water. With a show of irritation, the young pup fetched it for me. During his absence, the other officer lit a cigarette and stared at the exhaled streams of smoke, as fascinated as if he were examining some intricate machine.

A while after guzzling the water, I asked if I might visit the lavatory. They studied each other, as if unsure how to manage this request.

Forcing evenness into my voice, I said, "Officers, I really must relieve myself."

The pup escorted me down the narrow train aisle. Nemo was on this train—the man who'd first interrogated me with Dominic. I hadn't seen him since that evening. He'd looked up as I passed him, and we briefly caught each other's eyes. He no doubt noticed the officer trailing me.

The young officer checked the lavatory, apparently to determine if I might escape through the window. I could probably have flattened myself and wriggled through the window. But the speed of the train rendered such a maneuver perilous. Besides, a successful escape would have branded me a subversive and, possibly, endangered Dominic.

During the luxury of these few private minutes, I dug out the paper evidence. Should I cast it out the window? No, someone might see the paper flakes flying. I could ingest it. Then I thought: What if I passed it to Nemo? He could get it to Dominic, who'd then know of my arrest. Maybe Dominic could somehow convey the intelligence to British authorities. It was risky, but I decided to try to leave the list with Nemo.

Upon exiting the lavatory, I attempted to get the guard to lead the way back to our seats. But he insisted on following me, and now his eyes would be on me the whole time. I slowed my step as we neared the seat I'd spied Nemo in. I stumbled, bent over, and crammed the palmed paper between the arm of Nemo's chair and his thigh.

Righting myself, I said, "Excuse me, *signor*."

He nodded. "Of course, *signorina*."

We passed by Nemo. I was so relieved—to get rid of the paper and leave it in safe hands.

Back in the compartment, I watched the frozen scenery whiz by—dingy brown fields, here and there a patch of snow, and trees skeletal against the murky sky. I'd passed off the list, but fresh worries flooded me: *What would the courier in Genoa conclude when the drop from Cher Fox failed to materialize? Poor Dominic, he'd worry terribly when Nemo told him of my arrest. He might scuttle the Jewish registry operation out of fear of apprehension. Heavens, I was hungry. Was it possible mine was not the only arrest in Florence? Please, not Dominic, anybody but Dominic. They would torture him. Or worse.*

It was seven in the evening when we arrived at Milano Centrale, where a driver awaited us. How different Milan looked from the backseat of a car.

The shops were shuttered and their windows dark, so I could only imagine the clothing, hats, and jewelry I'd once shopped for in the city. My escorts sat one on each side of me, obscuring the side views. Through the front window, I watched headlights and street lamps looming and dissolving like markers lining a tunnel.

The officers handed me over at San Vittore Prison. A slouching warden issued a scratchy prison suit, appropriated my clothes and personal effects, and marched me to a cell, a cement cubicle with a table, basin, wooden-barrel toilet, and cot. Stench clung to the toilet, which quite possibly hadn't been cleaned since its installation. I detected no source of heat. *At least, I thought, the prison's thick walls will block out the harsh winter wind.* Then I felt a draft and looked up—at the broken pane on a barred window high on the wall. I could only hold my nose, use the toilet, huddle on the cot, and do my best to keep the thin wool blanket tucked under my feet and shoulders.

———

The next morning a guard opened the sliding metal gate to my concrete cell and marched me down the corridor. I was in the women's block; its sullen occupants looked up at me as I passed, their expressions questioning and solemn. The hallway opened onto an open area from which other corridors fanned out. Dear God, I hoped they wouldn't torture me. The guard marched me to a wing with solid doors, perhaps to offices or interrogation rooms. The guard swung the door to Room 141 open and motioned me in.

A man sitting behind a desk said, "Please be seated, Signorina Koopman. I am Colonel Brambilla."

My inquisitor, for I imagined I would soon be subjected to the next level of interrogation, was an older man in neat military attire with a sonorous voice. His bushy mustache stood out like an afterthought on his narrow face.

His wooden desk was thick and substantial, and on the wall behind him hung a portrait of Il Duce. He folded his hands and smiled pleasantly. "I hope your trip was comfortable?"

"As comfortable as an unexpected journey can be."

"I apologize for the sudden intrusion in your life. You are, perhaps, busy with your current occupation."

If this was his strategy, I could easily play the congenial conversant. "I must confess, Colonel, I'm quite baffled as to the reason for the intrusion."

He held up a hand as if to stave off my question. "What, may I ask, is your current occupation in Florence?"

"I'm taking my leisure and also studying. Art and art history."

"You have no official business there?"

"No." I relaxed in my chair. "Can you tell me, Colonel, why I've been detained?"

"It's simple, really. We wish to discuss a certain matter with you."

"I can't imagine what that might be."

"I understand you know Lord Beaverbrook?"

Why were they asking me about Beaverbrook? This made no sense. I thought it best not to admit we'd been lovers or that we'd traveled together, although these matters were common knowledge in some circles. "Yes, we are acquainted."

"If I'm not mistaken, you were on intimate terms with him for some time. Have you maintained contact with him?"

So, the colonel possessed an accurate grasp of my relationship with Max. But why would they care about that? Then it dawned on me—Max was now a part of Churchill's government. "No, I've not seen him since '35."

"Can you tell me exactly when you last spoke with him?"

I paused to consider. Actually, I did remember—it was in May, just after King George V and Queen Mary's silver jubilee, after Beaverbrook learned MJ and I were lovers. But I'd not betray the significance of my relationship with Max by recounting such an exact detail. "It was sometime in the spring of that year."

The colonel went on to impress me with details of my break with Beaverbrook and liaison with his son, speaking in the sure manner of a professor expounding a theory. Then he asked, "Have you had any contact with Beaverbrook or his son since coming to Italy?"

"None with Lord Beaverbrook." They might have intercepted one of my letters to MJ, and I had no reason to hide anything about him. "I corresponded briefly with his son, MJ Aitken, in the months after my move to Florence, but that was over a year ago."

"What was the nature of your communication with this MJ?"

"Oh, it was personal, really. About where I was living, the friends I'd met, the art galleries we'd toured. That sort of thing."

"Have you communicated with either man by phone or messenger since taking residence in Florence?"

"No."

"You are aware Beaverbrook is Britain's Minister of Aircraft Production?"

This was what they wanted to interrogate me about? Perhaps they didn't have any evidence of espionage after all. "Yes, I learned of that shortly after his appointment."

"And have you exchanged any information about Italian political or military matters with him or any other representative of the British government?"

"No, Colonel, and all I know about these matters is what I read in the newspapers."

"Do you deny operating as a spy for Britain?"

I nodded gravely. "*Sì*, I deny it."

"We will uncover no shred of evidence that reveals you are a spy?"

"No, Colonel."

"Even though you would make an excellent spy?"

I tossed my head. "This is perhaps something we disagree about. I'm quite content with my life as it is."

"You mean your life of leisure?"

"And of study."

"Would you say you're sympathetic with Italy and its people?"

"Yes, I have many Italian friends. And Florence is an exquisite city."

The colonel paused to stroke his mustache, then looked up at me. "It cannot be inexpensive to live in a hotel, dine out, and attend the opera whenever you wish."

"No, but I manage."

"It does, however, require not a little money?"

"Of course." Beaverbrook's bank sent the checks to my hotel. I could only hope they wouldn't intercept the next one, due to arrive in a week or so.

"And you are not at present serving the British government in any way?"

"No, I am not."

He smoothed his fingertips together and pointedly locked his gaze on me. "Assuming you're being truthful, I believe we have something to talk about."

MILAN

FEBRUARY 1941

A guard visited my cell late that morning. "Here is your suitcase. You can change out of your prison clothes for your meeting with the colonel."

What was this "something" the colonel wished to discuss? Certainly not my release. They wouldn't have transported me all this way only to set me free—unless someone was interceding on my behalf, which would explain me being allowed to don my clothes. Or perhaps they only wished me to believe this. Then they could name my compatriots and trick me into incriminating them.

Be careful, I told myself, you must play the watchful sentry. And steel yourself. For some sinister plan is no doubt in the offing.

A matron led me to a dank room with a rust-stained bathtub. I bathed in the guard's disinterested presence and then dressed in the outfit I'd packed for Genoa, a sleek midnight-blue dress. As the matron walked me back to my cell block, the clink of utensils against tin plates sounded down the hall. But no lunch tray awaited me. Bloody hell, I was hungry.

An hour later, Colonel Brambilla escorted me to another wing of the complex. Judging by the smells wafting down the corridor, we were approaching the prison's kitchen. I lifted my nose and inhaled. My tastebuds tingled at the steamy scents of simmering onions and sage.

The colonel showed me into a private room which held some dozen tables, most with four upholstered chairs around them, a few with only two. A roomy table awaited us, set with cloth napkins, sturdy but comely glasses, a bottle of Dolcetto, even ornate silverware. Black and white photographs of Milan city scenes lined the milk-colored walls. This, I imagined, was the functionaries' dining room.

The colonel pulled out my chair for me. "You mustn't think of me as the enemy, *signorina*."

"That would, perhaps, be easier were we not meeting in a prison." I summoned the image of my protective javelin. I pretended to rest it on my lap, clutching the handle with my right hand and brushing its sharp edge with my left.

"I can't blame you." He swung his gaze around the room. "This isn't exactly La Scala."

"Ah, La Scala." I let my mind wander over its interior—the intimate oval expanse, its golden decor. "Last time I was there, I saw *Turandot*, with Rosina Storchio. An absolutely searing performance."

The colonel poured wine for us, and I watched its red ribbon glisten as it streamed from the bottle's lip to the glass's waiting mouth.

He asked, "Tell me, why did you move to Florence?"

So, it was to be like Turandot's riddles. I must outsmart the colonel to save myself—by playing the breezy raconteur. "I have always loved Italy. Still, it was an impulsive decision. Prompted by an invitation from friends."

"*Cin cin.*" He tipped his wine glass toward me. "And you will stay, even with the war?"

"Yes, that's my plan." My heart leaped at the prospect of returning to Florence—and Dominic. But clearly, the matter was more complicated, or I wouldn't be here in San Vittore. I took up my glass and sipped. The wine's luscious, crushed-berry flavors lingered on my tongue. But I must mind my hollow stomach.

Brambilla rocked his clasped hands, like a pastor enjoining a stray congregant. "Are your loyalties perhaps strained? You've lived in Paris and London. Surely, you still have friends there."

"Of course. As well as in Italy and Germany."

"Tell me, then, exactly who are you loyal to: Britain and France or Italy and Germany?"

I imagined holding the javelin over my head and declaring: I am in charge here. I angled my head in a considered mien. "To peace, Colonel."

He reclined in his chair and raised a finger, signaling to someone.

An aproned man swung through a windowed door and approached. He set plates of tomato-glazed gnocchi before us. The smell of the sauce penetrated my nostrils; with a painful ache, saliva exploded in my mouth. I'd had only a weak imitation of tea for breakfast, no lunch, and no dinner the night before. Calmly I gripped my fork, scooped up a gnocchi nugget, and delivered it to my mouth.

The colonel eyed me, lifting his fork and holding it in mid-air. "But you must choose, Signorina Koopman, whose peace you wish to live under."

I chewed and swallowed before responding. "I only wish for a speedy end to the warmongering."

"And who would you have win?"

"The ones who would deliver permanent peace."

"Come now. Such coyness doesn't suit you—you who've mixed with the likes of Minister Beaverbrook."

Slowly and deliberately, I took up another forkful. The gnocchi—firm and chewy—must have been made of potato. Swallowing, I let the macerated bits slide down my throat. "In all honesty, I prefer not to mix politics with friendship, not with Beaverbrook or anybody else."

"You no longer have the luxury of avoiding choice. You see, Italy and Germany will bring peace to all of Europe." He scooped up a forkful of gnocchi and gobbled it down.

"I see no signs of peace, only war."

"But war is upon us, and it would be best if Churchill realized Britain cannot win."

My aching stomach embraced each swallow. Eat and drink slowly, I commanded myself, and keep your head. "No one wins when blood is spilled."

"It's Churchill who has the blood of his people on his hands."

I said nothing and focused on my meal. The food, like glowing coal, radiated relief from my stomach, through my torso, to my arms and legs.

"The Rome-Berlin Axis has a plan," he said, applying his napkin to the sauce flecking his mustache. "Il Duce has just returned from Berghof. I can tell you Hitler's forces will assist the Italian army in Greece. Our opponents cannot withstand such combined might."

Was it possible Germany would conquer all of Europe? I recalled Randolph's concern that the Nazis could walk all over Britain, especially if America declined to join the war effort. And Churchill hadn't managed to persuade Roosevelt to do so. "Then, I hope the victories will be swift so the new rulers can show magnanimity to all."

"I'm pleased to hear this from you." He flared an upturned hand. "Because you can help."

"You flatter me, Colonel. I'm of no importance to you, Beaverbrook, or anyone of consequence."

Again, the colonel signaled the kitchen. Our next course arrived—a steaming slab of pork loin decorated with rosemary sprigs. This was the best meal I'd eaten in months. With meat in scarce supply and pasta, rice, and flour rationed, it might be my last real feast for a long time.

With an agreeable nod, I took up fork and knife and cut a less than dainty portion of pork. I chewed, relishing its juicy meatiness. At the moment, I could imagine no temptation greater than this. Would he whisk it away if I refused to cooperate?

The colonel cleared his throat. "You're a well-traveled and sophisticated young lady, *signorina*. It's a pleasure dining with you."

"And I'm grateful for your kindness, Colonel."

"You must know you're perfectly suited to assist us."

"I'm sorry." I cut off another piece of pork. "But I don't see how."

"It's all arranged. First, you'll return to Florence and help us uncover enemies there. Then you'll go to England—to learn about aircraft production and as many other military matters as possible. We have agents there to work with you. And, of course, we'll pay you very well."

I imagined letting my javelin drop point-first, pierce the tabletop, and vibrate fiercely. *You, Colonel, are a fascist weasel, and I will take up all my weapons to fight you. You will not turn me.*

No, I'd never spy for them, never betray Dominic or any of the others. But now, with me resisting cooperation, they'd probably not release me either. *Santo Cielo*, I implored, what's to become of me?

The colonel poured more wine for us. "I'm pleased you're giving our proposal careful consideration."

I wanted to cast dignity aside and shovel in every last bit of food. Instead, I forced myself to calmly chew my meat and wash it down with swallows of wine.

"We'll treat you very well." He opened his palm and motioned to my plate and wine glass. "Like this."

I eased my fork and knife down on the table. "I must think about this, Colonel. About whether I wish to involve myself in this way."

"I see." He pitched his head back and nodded gravely. Taking up his fork, he invited me to do the same. "Then, let us enjoy this fine meal."

I followed his lead, but as my appetite sated, my shame grew: Was I so weak that I chose a few mouthfuls of meat over decisiveness?

No, it wasn't that: I'd never help the Fascists. Since forsaking a life of leisure, finding Dominic, and serving the resistance, I felt more complete than ever before, as if for the first time in my life, my beliefs and actions fully harmonized. The test was easy. Plateful upon plateful of delectables were not sufficient to sway me.

And the choice was clear. What kind of government sanctioned brutality against its people? What kind of men rounded up Jews like cattle? What kind of leader demanded absolute authority and killed detractors? They all sickened me—Hitler, Mussolini, and their enforcers, including Colonel Brambilla.

I just didn't want to refuse him yet. What harm could there be in enjoying a meal? I'd indulge in this temptation with the full knowledge that I'd not succumb to it. Scooping up another mouthful of meat, I thought, *it's awfully charitable of you, Colonel, to give succor to the enemy.*

Over a cup of strong coffee and cannoli dessert, the colonel renewed his campaign. "I truly don't understand why, if you love Italy and its people, you would refuse to work with us."

I cleared my palate with a sip of coffee, reveling in the sensation of fullness. "Let me tell you a story from Java. There was a leopard, a young Sunda leopard, who knew the time had come for him to leave his mother's care. 'I will go now,' he said, 'to seek my own territory.' He wandered through the jungle of his rollicking days and, at jungle's edge, came to a river with forest trees arching over its rippling waters. Here he lay down to rest and keep watch for prey. But the long journey had tired him, and he dozed off. The chattering of monkeys awakened him. In the trees above, a family of long-nosed monkeys screeched and gestured—at him. 'Why are you screaming at me?' he asked.

"One of the monkeys, a large male with a fire-orange head and whip-like tail, bounded to an overhead branch. 'You are new here. Why have you come to hunt us?'

"'I am seeking fresh territory, and this one suits me. It has both jungle and grass expanse, all the better for me to hunt.'

"'I know a perfect place for a beautiful and strong leopard like yourself,' the monkey said. 'A place where you can be king among the leopards. It is full of stupid chattering monkeys and tender young crocodiles.'

"The leopard stood and stretched, reveling in the rippling of the muscles beneath his spotted fur. 'Where is this place?'

"'Across the plain and over the saddle between the mountains, to the rich jungle on Mount Merapi's north slope. There you will find a paradise waiting for you. Just the place for a king of leopards such as yourself.'

"The leopard set off, marching across the expanse of grass and climbing the slope of Mount Merapi. His stomach ached with hunger, but on he pushed, certain he would find plentiful game in this new jungle paradise. He stopped to rest on a rocky rise. As he slumped onto his haunches, he noticed a Komodo

Dragon on a high rocky ledge across from him. 'What are you doing in my domain?' asked the giant lizard. 'This is no place for a leopard.'

"'I am seeking the paradise on the other side of Mount Merapi.'

"'Yes, that is the place for an unrivaled hunter such as yourself,' said the lizard. 'There you will find lizards so busy sunning themselves they will not see you sneaking up on them.'

"The young leopard pushed on, loping down the slope of Mount Merapi. Before him lay a lush jungle. Yes, he said to himself, this is my jungle paradise. Then he heard a roar and hiss. Looking to his side, he saw a large Sunda leopard, the biggest he'd ever seen, charge him. This mighty leopard lunged and swiped at his flank, gashing him. Blood trickled from the slits left by his claw marks.

"'This is my territory,' said the mighty leopard. 'Begone, or I will kill you.'

"Hungry and defeated, the young leopard retreated, traveling back over Mount Merapi to the edge of his old domain.

"So, you see, Colonel, conquest is not always as easy as it seems, and sometimes it is better to accept one's circumstances than to seek false kingdoms. This is how I choose to live, peacefully and without challenging greater forces."

Of course, all this was a lie—but what choice did I have with the Fascists trying to enlist me?

MILAN
FEBRUARY–MARCH 1941

n the ensuing days, Colonel Brambilla continued to court my cooperation. Only now our discussions took place far from the prison kitchen—in a barren interrogation room, with me again dressed in a coarse prison suit. Over and over, I told him: "No, I can't work for you. I refuse to lend assistance to any war machine." When the colonel tired of questioning and cajoling, he simply relegated me to my stinking cell and instructed me to "Use the time to consider our most generous offer."

That first week in San Vittore, taken up with days of monotonous interrogation and nights of solitude, tried me in many ways: with the cut of separation from Dominic, the miseries of hunger and cold, and the torment of not knowing my future. My captors housed me at the end of the wing, depriving me of contact with the other prisoners. From my marches to and from the interrogation room, I gathered that there were only fourteen women in this section, though it could have housed over thirty. Since the women's cells were spread apart, they communicated by hollering down the hall. Their talk consisted of comments about the awful food, gossip about a Milan neighborhood a few of them shared, and smutty insinuations about the guards. If any were resistance workers, they concealed it well. I wanted to feel some kinship with them, I wanted to know if they were partisans, I wanted some reassurance I was not alone. But none of the women reached out to me, and when I asked what news they had of the war, my pleas were met with silence. Maybe they feared I would turn on them.

On the sixth day of interrogation, Colonel Brambilla told me, "*Signorina*, I must say goodbye to you. I regret we have not come to an agreement."

My God, what did he mean? Would I be relegated to indefinite imprisonment? Or worse?

For days after that, I remained alone in my cell, the cold biting me, the stench clinging to my nostrils, the small rations of bread and watery soup hollowing out my stomach. No one summoned me for questioning. If only I could feel Dominic's arms around me—even for a moment—so I could hear him say he loved me. Or take up pen and paper and write to my mother about my sacrifice and circumstances. With that thought, the realization of my mother's death struck me anew, pushing up my gullet like a hard fist. I crumpled over with a whimper. *Someone, please talk to me. Save me from this disorienting unreality.*

I marked the days of aloneness on my cell wall. After twenty-three days, I was desperate for some human contact—even Colonel Brambilla's interrogation. Loneliness ate at my soul. That night I tossed and turned—agitation and misery feeding my frenzied yearning.

By morning I had again found my footing. *This is what they want—to make me desperate. I mustn't allow it.* That afternoon a guard deposited me in the usual interrogation room, but no one awaited me this time. After an hour, a German officer appeared—in a *feldgrau* uniform with the distinctive angled pockets of the SS.

God save me; the Fascists had turned me over to the Nazis.

"*Ich bin* Lieutenant Wolff," he announced, marching up close to the narrow table and standing wide-stanced before me. His barrel torso and puffy red face suggested he spared himself no small amounts of beer and sausage.

I nodded. "*Guten Tag.*"

He sat and pitched his briefcase onto the tabletop, revealing nails and cuticles gnawed ragged and red. "You are highly regarded in many circles, *Fräulein*. You know important people, many who fight against Germany."

"Yes, I have many friends, but they're common people, peaceful people."

"Do you include Lord Beaverbrook in that category?" His nostrils flared when he spoke, as if he were on the verge of bursting into a rage.

"I've had nothing to do with him for ages."

He pitched his head back to an arrogant cock. "Yes, but when you did, you were quite familiar."

"As I said, Lieutenant, that was years ago." I hoped he would not bring up others, like Randolph Churchill or Ambassador Koo, associations that would have given away my proximity to high-level British and French officials.

He unsnapped the latches of the briefcase, extracted a paper, and slapped it before me. "Then, what is this?"

I recognized it—a check from Beaverbrook's bank. I'd worried they might intercept the mail delivered to my Florence hotel. If they'd been tracking the mail, they knew these were regular payments. But why did they believe it was from Beaverbrook? The checks never bore his name. With a toss of my head, I said, "That? It's merely an allowance."

"And what are you being paid for?"

I could do worse than insinuate the truth. "It's a private and personal matter."

"Who is it from?"

He was so close I could see the whisker follicles on his fleshy face, the hairs of his sparse eyebrows, the pulpy insides of his nostrils. "I must confess, that is the private part."

He smirked. "We know it's from Beaverbrook."

Perhaps they knew, perhaps not. It didn't matter. "I've given my word not to reveal who it is, Lieutenant."

"Such a simple thing as money from a former lover, you cannot reveal in private?"

"No." The bare room, with its cement walls and metal table and chairs, chilled me. I wanted to hug myself for warmth but refused to reveal my discomfort.

"Then I can only conclude it's not as simple as you say. That it's payment for spying."

Shaking my head, I released an airy huff, hoping to convey simple exasperation.

He thumped a fist on the table. "You will answer when I speak to you."

The rattle of the table shocked me. I snapped my head up. "With whom and why I made this agreement is immaterial to the political situation or the war."

"That's not for you to judge."

I turned my head aside, avoiding his gaze.

"Very well, *Fräulein*, I won't waste my time on you." Like a pompous orator, he brushed a hand across his mouth and stood, straightening to a full stand. "You will serve Italy and Germany. You speak the languages. You know our cities. It's elementary, something you can easily do."

He loomed before me, bulky and steely-eyed. *He is nothing but a brute trying to intimidate*, I told myself. "I have explained to Colonel Brambilla I cannot do this."

"You're not being asked to cooperate. You're being told to do so."

I composed myself, turning my face up toward him. "I won't, Lieutenant."

He yanked his arm back and swung it at me. His palm landed hard on my cheek. My head reeled.

"You dare to defy both Mussolini and Hitler, you black bitch."

The sting shocked. My eyes watered.

He slapped again, harder, sending me flying off the chair.

I crashed on the floor, shoulder-first. Pain streaked down my arm. Pulling myself up onto all fours, I crawled back onto the seat, hunching in on myself.

"Too high and mighty, are you?" He gripped my jaw in his hand, jerking my head up. "You will do this. You've whored before."

I cast my gaze downward to avoid his glare.

With a violent thrust, he released his grip on my face. "Do you know who sent me here?"

The room's cold air, the pain in my shoulder, and a rush of apprehension convulsed me. I braced my arms over my torso to still the shiver.

He leaned over and brought his face close to mine. The Iron Cross on his breast pocket swung like a pendulum. His cheeks turned red with fury. "Reichsführer Heinrich Himmler. That is who invites you to serve. Does that name mean anything to you?"

So, it was Himmler who commanded him to force my cooperation. And Himmler who he feared. An urge to shatter the facade of enmity, to speak to him as one human to another washed over me: *You are only cruel to me because you dread what retribution Himmler might visit on you. There's another way. Listen to me. We are both trapped in this ugly war. You don't need to do this.*

I could tell him no amount of humiliation or torture would win me over, that we might as well bare our souls to each other. That if he revealed his fear, he could find solace in me, that I would sympathize with him. And I could help him think of what to tell Himmler. Surely not every man who served Hitler was evil.

I stilled my expression and looked up at him. His eyelids narrowed to unblinking slits. No, he was beyond my reach. Himmler was his god and master. I glared back at him. He had revealed his weakness—fear. So, I must show him he did not frighten me. Even if it heightened his horror of the punishment Himmler might unleash on him. Even if it pushed him to greater cruelty. I mustn't succumb to the same base cowardice that drove him. For then, he would know he'd mastered me, just as Himmler had mastered him.

He yelled, "Do you not understand? Are you stupid?"

I clamped my lips shut and studied a pattern in the peeling paint on the wall: the cracked center of a paint bubble. It resembled a star, a star in Italy's night skies, skies that shone over all of Europe's citizens. *I'm not the only one who defies you. You and your kind are nothing but cruel, cowardly cretins. Honor means nothing to you.*

"Germany is on the march," he said, stomping a boot on the floor. "You will serve the mightiest of nations."

I will lock you out of my mind. You cannot enter here. I won't give in. I withdrew into myself, refusing to speak. He admonished and scolded, slapped and hollered, grabbed my chin and whispered his commands. For how long, I did not know.

I built a wall around myself: *I am my own fortress. Where are you, Dominic? Ah, I see you now, your jaw clenched, your lips pressed together, those deep, earnest eyes gazing into mine. I feel you guiding me: Have courage. Speak not a word. Think of all the others who suffer at the hands of these curs. Yes, Dominic, I stand shoulder to shoulder with you. We outnumber them. You, Dominic, are real to me, not this Nazi toady. I am solid as stone. No Nazi will break me. Ever. For my mother and all my ancestors now watch over me. From them, I take strength.*

Finally, he stood back, rubbing his hands together, as if to signal he'd reached some verdict. "You've obviously chosen sides. I'm warning you: If you've spied for the enemy, we'll find you out."

A guard marched me down the long prison corridors and back to my cell. I slumped sideways on my cot and pressed my stinging cheek and aching shoulder against the chill wall, letting its coolness lap at the burning pain. The clicking heels of the afternoon guards sounded down the corridor, the ones who made a sport of badgering me. I sat upright and stared at the side wall.

The guards stood at my cell door, looking in on me.

"*Signorina*," the one with the crooked nose said, lewdly thrusting his pelvis, "Did you have a good time with our German friend? Or do you like the Italian men better?"

Not to be outdone, stubby legs chuckled. "I can bring you some fresh hot water for washing, *signorina*. Would you like that?"

I knew they'd never show me such kindness. I played deaf and dumb. If I responded, they'd only find fresh ways to torment.

"We will help you wash," he sneered. "All your secret places."

I budged not at all.

"She's a standoffish one," the crooked-nosed guard said to his mate. He turned back to me. "Tell me, do spies shit like everyone else?"

Both of them laughed, as did a few of the women, and they shuffled off, chuckling as they receded down the corridor.

God, I felt helpless. And abandoned. *You were right, Dominic. I've never been tested like this, never known this sort of abuse. Not me, with parents who loved me dearly and indulged me with pets of all kinds. Not the one who floated through schoolgirl years among well-bred Dutch and English girls. Not the person who was handed a modeling career and dressed by Paris's most renowned designers.*

How drastically my life had changed, from comfort to torment. Could I hold out in the face of this treatment? With only weak tea and thin soup for nourishment, weariness and hunger were sapping my strength. The bread—hard and dry, likely passed over by the guards and kitchen workers for days—needed soaking with broth or saliva before I could swallow it.

I dreaded the prospect of another day with Wolff. Perhaps I could agree to cooperate, gain release, and tell Randolph and the Intelligence Service I couldn't serve anymore because I'd been compromised. Then I could live in London again, amongst my old friends. Or would that put them, too, in danger? No, that couldn't work. Once my noncooperation was exposed, the Nazi spies and informers prowling all of Europe would hunt me down. And silence me for good.

Even if I could evade the Nazis—perhaps by fleeing to America—brief imprisonment followed by unconditional release would mark me as a traitor. And I'd be forced to abandon my efforts to assist Britain and the Italian Resistance. Never again would I see Dominic. It'd break my heart. It'd confirm his worst fears about me. And mine about myself—that I lacked the courage for the choice I'd made.

———

In February, cold like the lowest level of hell descended on northern Italy. The prison's units reached out from a central body, like the extremities of a giant spider. The cold assaulted me from both sides of my leggy corridor. During the long stretches of solitude, when no guards could see me, I danced the Charleston to stoke my body heat. And that made me ache for a thumping-good band and the dance floor at the Savoy Hotel.

I had no visitors. I wrote a letter—after careful deliberation—to my brother, Henri, in Amsterdam. It would look suspicious if I wrote no one, for my jailers would conclude I wished to avoid incriminating comrades. And this was true. I dared not write Dominic or Alfonso, not even Elisabeth. But a relative, that would be expected. And perhaps Dominic would even contact my brother for news about me. For his and my brother's sake, I wrote a letter full of reassurance: *I believe the authorities will soon realize my detention is a mistake. I'm a threat to no one and wish to have nothing to do with this terrible war. I only want to be free to rejoin you and my friends. Meantime, I'm fed reasonably well and am in good spirits. So, you mustn't worry.*

If Henri received my letter, he didn't respond. Or if he did, my captors blocked any delivery. Next, I wrote a letter to my banker in London, asking him to hold my monthly checks. I'll be damned if I was going to allow the enemy to abscond with my money.

On the first Monday of March, Wolff once again summoned me to the interrogation room. He had long ago given up on recruiting me to serve as an agent. Instead, he'd attempted to extract information about my purported spying activities, though I'd steadfastly refused to admit any such work. I braced myself for another round of interrogation and abuse.

But this day, instead of adopting his usual threatening stance, he seated himself across the table from me and slung one leg over the other. "I'm finished with you, *Fräulein*. You're completely useless."

I said the first thing that came to my mind, perhaps unwisely. "Will Herr Himmler be annoyed with you?"

"You shouldn't flatter yourself that he thinks you of any importance."

"I'm pleased to hear that, Lieutenant, and sorry if I've caused you inconvenience."

"I'm sure you're not in the least sorry. But soon, you'll regret your refusal."

At that moment, I knew I'd not be released. In their efforts to recruit me, Brambilla and Wolff had revealed a great deal about Italian and German war plans—and guessed that my sympathies lay squarely with Britain. Three months of refusing to cooperate had only heightened Wolff's disdain and cruelty.

"What will happen to me now?"

A sadistic smile spread over his plump face. Hell and damnation, I'd played into his hands. He rose from his seat, strolled to the door, and opened it. Turning to me, he said, "I will personally see to it that you never go free. You're being sent to Camp Bolsena. May you rot there."

DISPATCH FROM MILAN

8 March 1941

Authorities believe subject has been operating as a British spy. They have transferred her to Camp Bolsena detention facility.

WD

CAMP BOLSENA

MARCH 1941

M y stomach churned as the lorry reeled through a narrow-streeted section of Bologna. Finally, the vehicle halted, and I swallowed down the bile sloshing up my gullet. Five new prisoners were ordered onto the benches in the lorry back. One was a woman—a slight, older woman who stayed close to a round-shouldered man.

I signaled the couple to wedge in beside me. Shifting toward the cab's hold to make room for them, I muttered, "*Ciao, signora, signor*. My name is Toto."

"I'm Maria." Coils of the woman's gray-brown hair dangled around her angular face. "And this is my husband, Beppe."

The transport's two guards took up their stations at the open end of the lorry. One brandished his submachine gun and announced, "Remember, no quick moves. Or I will use my gun."

I didn't doubt it. I had no choice but to give myself over to the resigned torpor that gripped me. The lorry threaded through narrow streets, lurched onto a paved road, and headed south on a smooth highway stretch of Italy's spine. Now that we traveled a straight length of road, my nausea abated. I was close enough to Maria to see the sinewy flesh of her throat and the turquoise veins lining the bony hand grasping her husband's. Maria and her husband must have been in their sixties. There was something about them, perhaps their frailty or the way they clung to each other, that sent a surge of sympathy through me—and a desperate ache for camaraderie. I was no longer alone. Others, like me, were bound for this uncharted purgatory.

I asked Maria, "Where are you from?"

"Bologna," she said. "And you?"

"Florence. When were you arrested?"

"Last week, in Bologna."

Could they be companions to me? I wanted to ask why they'd been detained. I wished I could share my sickening fears with them. But I'd been warned: If captured, be leery of other prisoners, especially those seeking information about clandestine activities or even what you've been interrogated about. They might betray you by trading information for preferential treatment or release.

I said nothing more, nor did Maria or Beppe. I gazed absently out the back of the lorry, at the ribbon of road behind us, the rough brush and haphazard hills, the receding horizon. *This backward view is like my wretched confinement,* I thought, *robbing me of my future and leaving me to agonize over how I got here.*

Two hours later, we passed through a village. The sign on its backside displayed its name: Viterbo. An old man hoeing a garden plot stood and peered into the back of the lorry, pivoting and fixing his gaze on us. He shook his fist and hollered, "Traitors."

Dannazione eterna, I cursed; even an ordinary peasant reproaches us. Could he be a betrayer himself, informing on his fellows to ingratiate himself to the Fascists? Or perhaps he was an outcast—like the runt of the litter forced to lick and scrape to survive. Has the world gone so wrong that even the lowliest turn on each other? Damn the Fascists and their wicked ways.

The lorry topped the crest of a hill, and below I spied two runways and four neat rows of military aircraft. I nudged Maria and caught Beppe's eye. "Look."

Beppe leaned forward. "That's Viterbo Air Force Base. We're north of Rome, about one hundred kilometers."

Minutes later, the lorry drove through a sturdy metal-grate fence and halted. Come my turn, I hopped off the truck. Three guards herded the lot of us toward a boxy brick building and lined us up. I stood close to Maria and Beppe, hoping to bolster and be bolstered by them, and furtively appraised the yards and buildings. At the sound of a deep rumble, I looked up. Arrays of zooming fighters and roaring-engined bombers—the white cross of Italy's air force emblazoned on their tails—striped the cloudless sky, no doubt off on an easterly mission, perhaps to Greece. Prison camps, I reasoned, surely they're one of the few places not targeted for bombing. Look at me—trying to find some small recompense for being locked up.

Gray-uniformed guards steered us toward a row of brick structures, some with identifying placards—a compact "Headquarters," a two-story "Guards House," and a "Canteen"—and two sprawling unmarked buildings. These structures lined one side of the compound and stared down ramshackle wooden barracks arranged in four rows and extending eight-barracks deep. Fences nearly as tall as the intermittent observation towers secured the perimeter. The towers' wide windows looked down on the camp's dirt-packed grounds, fenced walls, and brush-spotted exterior. Wind whipped around the buildings, stirring up dust from the bare earth.

So, this was the detention camp Wolff hoped I'd rot in—unless I could escape. But by what route? The camp's fence ran along an exposed strip of bare earth, making it impossible to hide any digging. Attempts to clamber over the loops of barbed wire atop the fence walls would present another risk: entanglement. Anybody trying to dig under or climb over the fence would surely make an easy target for the lookouts.

Guards marched us one at a time into the headquarters building. When I reached the head of the queue, a guard ushered me into a cramped room. I stood before a bulky official in a tight-fitting brown uniform. Looking up from his desk seat, he asked, "Toto Koopman?"

"*Si*, officer."

He dropped his clipboard to the desk. "Take off your clothes."

What could I do but comply? I removed my wool coat, my only remaining personal possession, and placed it on the desk. I stepped out of my shoes, pulled my scratchy prison top over my head, and stripped off my pajama-style pants.

He motioned toward my underpants. "Those, too."

I took off my last bit of clothing and crossed my arms over my breasts. Is this necessary, I wondered, or is it an exercise in humiliation?

He stood and came up behind me. "Bend over. Hold your ankles."

With a shiver, I folded over and reached down, gripping my ankles. Of all things, what came to mind was a circus act I'd seen in Amsterdam when I was a schoolgirl. I'd cringed watching a bear forced to dance on his hind legs and then sit on a tiny stool and clap his immense paws.

The guard wrapped his large hand around my hip bone, sinking his thick fingers into my flesh. "Don't think I enjoy this."

His gloved hands spread my buttocks and checked the folds of my private parts. I shivered at the roughness of his touch.

"You can stand again," he said, whipping off his gloves. He grabbed a dull-blue gown off a shelf. "Here."

I yanked on my underpants and slipped the gown over my head.

He flicked his arm toward the door. "We're done here."

Would I be allowed to keep my wool coat? I whisked it off the desk and turned to leave.

"Uh, that coat," he said.

"Yes, officer?" I swung toward him.

"Give it here."

I held it out, scrunching the waist with one hand. "It's very small, hardly of use to anyone else."

He took it from me, turned the pockets inside out, and checked the lining. "Fine. Keep it."

"*Grazie, signor.*"

He humphed sourly, as if to assure me he meant no kindness.

I rejoined Maria in the hall, and a guard marched the two of us across the yard to a barrack three down in the second row.

"Take those bunks there." The guard pointed at two stacked bunks near the front of the narrow structure. "Leave your personal items and return directly to headquarters."

The guard marched out. I stood beside Maria taking it all in. A narrow window beside the door we'd entered let in a slant of light, and the smell of dank wood permeated the room. Two rows of bunks lined the windowless side walls—thirty-two beds in all—most of them neatly covered with flimsy wool blankets. Five unmade beds revealed makeshift stuffed mattresses, and the two designated for us each held a folded blanket. A few of the beds showed signs of occupancy: a folded sweater; a scarf hung over a bunk post; a pair of boots tucked under a cot. What were these other women like, I wondered, and what kind of company did they keep? This, at least, was better than a cold cell at San Vittore. Here I'd have barrack mates, all of them, like me, probably political prisoners.

Maria walked up to the stacked beds designated for the two of us and jiggled a corner post. The bunks swayed slightly. She stood examining them, her spindly arms and legs sticking out like twigs from her baggy prison gown. The sight of her reminded me of an anniversary photo my father had sent me a few years ago: My mother's gaunt and drawn appearance in it had surprised and saddened me.

I went to Maria's side. "I'll take the top bunk."

"*Grazie.*" Maria smiled impishly. "I'm afraid of high places."

I chuckled. "You and I, we're going to get on just fine."

I slung my wool coat over the bunk post and flared the sides of my dingy-blue camp gown. "It fits like a gunny sack. Whoever designed this ought to be sent to prison."

Maria looked down the aisle. "I see no toilet. And only that washbowl for cleaning."

A metal bowl sat on a bulky wooden table at the end of the row of bunks.

"What's through that door?" I headed to the rear of the barrack.

Maria followed me. Just outside the back door, we discovered a shack that shared a wall with the barrack. I swung the door open. Ugh, a dug-out latrine, a filthy, smelly space with a square hole in the floorboards to squat over. I clamped a hand over my nose to block the waft of excrement. Slats under the roof eaves let in some light and ventilation, but not enough to clear out the putrid stink welling up from the hole.

"I'll test it for us, Maria." I shut the door, squatted on my haunches, and groped the walls. There was no handle or railing to grip.

I took in short breaths and huffed them out, clenching my nostrils against the stench. In the hole below, flies buzzed annoyingly.

My God, I thought, how long will this war go on? Brambilla and Wolff had claimed that German and Italian forces were overwhelming Greece and that Germany would soon invade Britain. But my Fascist and Nazi interrogators would naturally want me to believe they were on the winning side. Still, if their reports were accurate, Germany and Italy had surged and might soon win the war. And if that happened, the best I could hope for would be a lengthy detention. The worst I chose not to contemplate.

CAMP BOLSENA
APRIL–JULY 1941

t was three weeks after my arrival, in the deep of night, when bursts of gunfire rattled the quiet. I bolted upright on my cot. The beat of running feet—of perhaps three or four people—thudded in the yard. I hopped down from my bunk and ran to the window.

Maria threw off her blanket. "What's happening?"

From the rear of the barrack, Rosa, our self-appointed matron, barked, "Everyone, stay in your beds. It's trouble."

I shuffled back to my cot, cocking an ear toward the door. I heard a distant holler, "Over here." Then silence.

Eventually, I slept again. I dreamed of dashing madly around London, a hellish version of London crammed with crooked streets and steep hills, frantically searching for something, though I didn't know what. I stumbled upon my father and asked what he was doing in London. He told me he and my mother lived there now. But, I said, Mother is dead. No, he replied, you're wrong. She recovered from her illness and wonders why you haven't visited her.

When the morning horn blared, I woke up feeling guilty and groggy, raw from the haunt of loss. *Mother, I miss you. I wish I'd visited you one more time. I could cry now from wanting to see you.*

I stumbled through the morning routine. On the way to the workhouse with the others, I spotted a lump in the open yard. *Please, no,* I thought, *they can't have shot someone.* As I came closer, I saw it was as I feared—the corpse of a man, his limbs sprawled at awkward angles, his clothing caked with dirt and blood.

When everyone assembled for roll call after the early work shift, the man was still there, a look of terror frozen on his gray face. I could tell by the trail of scraped boot heels that he'd been dragged to the spot. Nausea heaved up in me. I'd never seen a dead body, and the sight of this straggled-out man, his pained grimace exposed to all, sickened me. I swallowed down the bile burning my gullet.

The commandant circled the corpse, angling his head this way and that. Taking up a position beside the body, he faced the assembled prisoners. "This Greek here, he tried to crawl under the fence. See, you cannot get out. Unless it's your own life you wish to escape."

The commandant seemed to revel in lording this man's killing over us, no doubt to frighten us into subservience. Even the attending guards held themselves stiffly in his presence.

He singled out a stooped prisoner in the front row. "Your job today is to dig a grave."

My fellow prisoners and I tucked our heads, intent on showing deference or avoiding scrutiny. Disgust as putrid as the rot of decay coursed through me. *You bully, are you so obsessed with disobedience and defiance that you refuse to show any compassion? I will make a study of you and this camp. To keep myself safe. To help everybody else here. And to plot my escape.*

—

Over the ensuing weeks and months, I watched and learned what I could— about the routine, the commandant, anything that might be of use. The guards seemed intent on enforcing the camp's strict order and maintaining its fixed seven-day-a-week work schedule. Rumor had it some were failed pilots relegated to camp duty. Still, in hopes of finding a sympathetic man among them, I nodded and held the gaze of passing guards, but they responded with stony silence.

I'd even heard reports that the camp's superiors disciplined guards for not enforcing camp rules. One of my barrack mates, Silvia, worked in the infirmary and saw a guard hauled off to headquarters for giving extra food allotments to an elderly man. It puzzled me that this guard's kindness was punished. So many Italians resented Mussolini's tyrannical rule, his rush to war, and the conscriptions tearing husbands and sons from families. I would've expected some guards, who were also victims of Mussolini's ruthless war, to sympathize with the prisoners. Could it be that the commandant's rules forced the guards into complicity with his cruelty?

Or perhaps the guards were harsh because Greek prisoners, who likely numbered over seven hundred, predominated in the camp. Maybe the guards looked on these men as the killers of their brothers and comrades and wanted revenge. Of all the prisoners, the Greeks fared the worst. I spoke no Greek, but it was easy enough to observe their treatment. The guards assigned them the most difficult task, forcing them to dig large stones from the rocky terrain, haul them to the compound, and build a mounded-rock fence, a lame exterior fence that served no purpose.

Not that the rest of us—the twenty-nine women housed in my barrack and the few hundred Italian men—fared much better than the Greeks. The Italian men, who were likely either deserters or presumed partisans, toiled at quarry work and road-building and were sometimes transported to nearby factories. We women weren't subjected to the back-breaking labor foisted on the men but rather to long, tedious days of cooking, working in the infirmary, serving in the canteen and officers' and guards' quarters, and washing the military's laundry. I was assigned to the laundry, where I worked alongside six of my barrack mates.

If only I could trust my fellow prisoners or tease a touch of compassion out of a guard or two, I might gather some news of the war. But, no, from what I could tell, the guards consorted with prisoners only to encourage them to report any violations.

And that meant some prisoners might be spying for the guards. I even suspected that the haggard-faced Rosa, who lorded an assumed authority over our barrack, cooperated with the guards. All the women gave her wide berth and, not surprisingly, divulged little about themselves to her or each other. I imagined all my barrack mates had probably engaged in subversive activity: For what other reason would an Italian woman find herself in a detention camp? But instead of this fostering trust and camaraderie, a climate of suspicion hung over us.

I railed against the ugliness of imprisonment—its callousness, the mind-numbing sameness of the days, the pervasive mistrust. *Santo Cielo*, I wanted out. But after nearly four months in the camp, I'd conjured only one possible escape plan. And it would have required a level of cooperation that seemed completely out of reach.

———

One warm June night, perhaps around eleven or midnight, a slight shifting of my bunk beams roused me from sleep. I held still and, out of the corner of my eye, I saw Maria creeping out. I guessed she planned to meet her husband, whose barrack was one over and six down from ours. Although these two barracks were situated in the inner rows and shielded a bit from the observation huts, she and Beppe were courting considerable risk.

I didn't hear Maria return, but when the 4:30 a.m. wake-up horn sounded, Maria was back in her cot. Out of bed I scrambled, issuing my usual *"Buon-giorno."* The first time I'd done this, only a few had muttered a reply. But gradually, it'd become a habit until, like today, all responded in kind, which I considered a minor victory for civility.

The day began as usual: the queues to the washbasin and latrine; the march to morning assignments in the laundry building or canteen; the guards' sporadic checks; and roll call before breakfast. Nothing unusual. Only in retrospect did one minor incident stand out, and then only after the events of the day unfolded.

During roll call, one of the guards approached Maria, gripped her by the arm, and steered her to headquarters. I looked for her at breakfast, afterward in the laundry room, and at the evening meal. Only when we returned to the barrack that night did we find her—hunched over on the floor, her hands chained behind her back and secured to a bunk post.

We all clustered around her.

"Curse these damnable *cafones*," I muttered under my breath. I lowered myself to a knee beside Maria. "What happened?"

Crusts of tears streaked her face. "Three days confinement. And no food."

Rosa, standing over the huddle of six crouching around Maria, asked, "Why?"

Maria dropped her head and said nothing. It was then I remembered: After our groups split in the morning, mine to the laundry room, Rosa and the others to the canteen, Rosa had held back. Had she been waiting for an opportunity to speak, unseen, to a guard? Yes, it all made sense now.

I twisted around and stared up at Rosa.

She returned my glare, her mouth held tight and one eye asquint, like a marksman sighting a target.

Riveting my gaze on Rosa, I shot her through with silent accusation. A charged hush fell over the barrack. I turned back to Maria. "Let's wriggle these chains up so you can lie on your bunk."

"*Si*, do what you can for her," said Rosa, walking off.

Silvia and I worked some slack into the chains and repositioned Maria on her bed. But the chains bound her closely to the beam, and she could only curl up crosswise on her cot. Through the night, I heard her shifting in search of some small comfort.

In the morning, I pushed to the head of the washing line, scooped a handful of clean water, and brought it to Maria.

She gulped it down. "Can you tell Beppe? And make sure he hasn't been caught?"

"*Sì*, I'll tell him you are being strong and brave."

Over the three days of Maria's confinement, several of us cared for her. I pocketed rags from the laundry to clean her messes. A few other women snatched bits of bread and slipped them to her. While she ate, her guardians and I stood near, shielding her, aware we risked punishment for bringing food to someone under orders of deprivation.

All this time, I knew the source of Maria's trouble, and I suspected most of the others did, too. Finally, Maria's chains were removed, but I swore to neither forget nor forgive Rosa for betraying her. I churned with anger and disgust at Rosa and could think only of how I might undercut her and loosen her grip on the barrack. So, I hatched a plan.

I waited two weeks—enough time to pretend I'd forgotten Maria's punishment. On the evening walk back to the barrack, I came up beside Rosa and asked, "Would you like me to give your undergarments a proper sudsing? I could sneak them in amongst the laundry."

Rosa hated uncleanness and charged the young woman in the bunk above hers with washing her panties. But there was no soap in the barrack, so a rinsing was all they got. Rosa thought a moment, perhaps taken aback by the offer. "No."

"It's no trouble. I'd like to do this for you."

Rosa nodded. "But if you're caught, I know nothing."

Soon I developed a schedule for laundering everyone's undergarments, avoiding detection by slipping them inside the sleeves and pant legs of uniforms. How could Rosa protest when she, too, benefited?

Next, I took to pilfering potatoes from the guards' store so the kitchen workers could thicken the prisoners' soup. None of the few that knew—except Maria—dared thank me for these acts for fear of angering Rosa. In fact, they probably sensed that Rosa considered me a rival and decided it was wise to shun me. Or maybe they ignored me so they could feign innocence if I were apprehended. Whatever the reason, most of my barrack mates kept their distance and treated me with indifference. I may have seduced Rosa into a quiet collaboration, but the aloofness of the others—who I only wanted to protect and defend—still stung. In the midst of these many who should have upheld at least silent allegiance to one another, I felt painfully alone.

I kept telling myself the risk of helping others was worth it—that I helped not just for the others but for the sake of my soul. And sanity. Still, I cursed the guards, especially the higher-ups. They'd won. They'd succeeded in pitting prisoner against prisoner.

In the face of the guards' and Rosa's malice, I could only trudge through the monotonous routine and meditate on how to maintain my composure and sanity: *I must keep up my spirits, I mustn't let the cruelty of this place reduce me to selfishness. Or blind me with hatred. I beg you, Mother and my dear ancestors, show me how to be as constant as the stars. Teach me how to defy this barbarity.*

CAMP BOLSENA

AUGUST–NOVEMBER 1941

We prisoners never knew when or why we might be ordered on a march around the camp's perimeter, only that the guards used the occasion to scour the barracks. Why they bothered to check for contraband made no sense since we were thoroughly searched upon arrival and permitted no visitors. Perhaps they feared someone had fashioned floorboards into weapons or hoarded valuables received in mailings or the occasional Red Cross package. Or maybe the commandant simply enjoyed watching the prisoners and guards jump at his command.

The latest decree came late one August afternoon. "Out, out," called two guards bursting into the laundry building. "To the yard."

We stumbled out into the hot yard and joined the procession. I squinted under the bright sun and trudged through the grit stirred up by our many feet. A few paces ahead, I noticed a gangly, narrow-faced man loping sluggishly among the Italian men. I didn't recall ever seeing him before. Purple bruises mottled his face and arms, earned, I imagined, during an interrogation. Judging from their livid hue, it was a fairly recent one.

I wove my way to his side. "You're new to the camp, *si*?"

He nodded and regarded me quizzically. "Where are you from? Your accent is unfamiliar."

His soft-spoken manner and hunching nonchalance put me at ease—as if a mutual friend had just introduced us. I replied, "I'm not Italian. But I've been living in Florence."

His sentence came out like a sigh. "Florence, it is a city of great beauty."

"If they let me out, I will go straight back there."

"I'm from a nearby village, Pistoia."

I said nothing. We neared the corner observation tower. A guard leaned out the window, surveying the lot of us.

He asked, "Have you friends in Florence?"

I needed to warn him. And protect both of us. I kicked a clod of dirt and studied the ground. "It's not good for us to talk too much. The guards might think we're plotting."

He plunged his hands into his pockets, and we walked in silence for a time.

Speaking under his breath, he said, "I know a fellow journalist in Florence. Dominic Bianchi."

My heart thudded. Why had he named Dominic—and so baldly, as if throwing out the name of a resistance leader carried no risk? Was it possible he'd succumbed to torture and was now spying on me, perhaps to expose Dominic?

But I had sought him out, not vice versa. "My name is Toto."

"I'm Luca Rospigliosi."

He'd not hesitated to give his full name, a prized coin among resistance workers—and their enemies. Yes, I decided, I could take a chance on him. "Do you think we'll see the moon tonight?"

He shot me a crafty grin. "If so, I hope no raven passes its face."

I wanted to scream with delight. I wanted to kiss his cheeks. He'd answered with the secret signal of Florence's Giustizia e Libertà.

———

Luca and I took care to avoid the appearance of fraternizing. Still, we snatched what time we could—on the forced marches or during the relative disarray of prisoners forming and breaking for roll call. When we came under the guards' scrutiny—in the canteen or on marches—we feigned disinterest in each other. On occasions that afforded opportunities to talk, we walked one behind the other, muttering with our heads bowed. When we wished to speak at length, we mingled among the Greeks and used a hodgepodge of Italian, French, and English.

During my nine-month captivity, I'd only gleaned broad strokes of news from other prisoners—that the Luftwaffe was mercilessly bombing London and that Japan had signed a pact with Germany and Italy. After being deprived of daily and detailed reports, I'd stored up a torrent of questions. But I chose carefully because my time with Luca was limited. First, I asked about Dominic.

"I haven't seen him in nearly a year," Luca said. "But I've heard nothing of an arrest or troubles for him."

"I'd like to get a message to him, but I don't want to write directly."

"We'll think of something. Words always find their way."

On a September day when rain obscured the guards' view and beat down on the hunkered-over prisoners, Luca and I walked side by side. Had he, I asked, heard of a raid on Florence's Municipal Registry the previous January? No, he said, but that didn't imply failure: If it'd been successful, both the Fascists and perpetrators would have hushed it up. I told him about my detention in San Vittore, and he revealed the reason for his arrest: He was suspected of producing propaganda that mocked Mussolini's military missteps.

"It's true," he said. "The British captured over one-hundred-thousand Italian troops in Africa. Hitler laughs at Mussolini behind his back, and still, Mussolini plays his lap dog."

"Has America joined the fight?"

"No, but they passed a law promising military aid, even if Britain can't pay for it."

Over the following weeks, I gleaned much from Luca about recent events: Yugoslavia's defeat and partition among Germany, Italy, and others; the sorry state of Britain's coffers; Italian Communist and Socialist groups' appeals for resisters to unite and depose Mussolini; and Germany's surprise invasion of Russia.

Luca said, "Some of Churchill's countrymen denounced him for warning Russia."

"I don't like the communists either, but somebody's got to stop Hitler."

"Churchill is nothing if not a pragmatist," said Luca. "He told his critics, 'If Hitler invaded Hell, I would make at least favorable reference to the Devil.'"

I chuckled at that but said nothing of my friendship with Churchill's son, Randolph. I did wonder if Randolph, or anybody for that matter, knew of my whereabouts. If they did, were they considering ways to get me out of this place? Then shame overcame me, shame over considering myself special or more deserving of release than any of the others.

One day in early October, after camp guards singled out numerous prisoners and marched them in for questioning, the camp buzzed with speculation: Had some event prompted Mussolini and his henchmen to seek new evidence of spying or betrayal? Perhaps this was my chance to seek out the intelligence Winston Churchill had requested, even though I lacked the means to get word out.

When the evening roll call broke up, I headed straight for Luca. "Is it possible there was a coup?"

"I doubt it. Mussolini's grip is tight."

"Do any of the resistance groups have the resources to overthrow Mussolini?"

"Not now."

"But if they united?"

"Possibly."

Instead of breaking off as we passed the women's barrack, I stayed beside him. It was dark. Maybe I could escape notice. "And if they did, who would be the leader afterward?"

He said, "That is like trying to find the biggest fish in a lake."

"Would the other groups accept Spinelli's federalism?"

"No, that's too great a leap."

"Would the resistance groups tolerate an insider? Like Badoglio?"

Before he could respond, a guard waved me off. "You, get to your barrack."

The next morning, a guard pulled me from roll call and walked me to headquarters. In the same cramped room where I'd been processed into the camp, two officers of the Servizio Informazione Militari grilled me: What do you know about aircraft production in England? Nothing. Who hired you to spy for Britain? Nobody. What were you doing in Florence? Meeting friends and studying. Surely you and your friends discussed the war. Yes, but our talk was of local matters. What local matters? The sacrifices the people made, the poor food supplies, the bombing of Genoa. (I took pride in having played a role in the bombing of Genoa's factories; I'd passed on intelligence about tanks being assembled there.) My inquisitors persisted: Among students and university people, you were no doubt privy to talk against Mussolini. No, I said, the people of Italy accept Mussolini; he has done much good for them. Is that all they say? And that they want the war to end so they can have the old times back. And who are these friends? I will not name these ordinary people; they are of no interest to you. Yes, you will. No, I refuse to drag innocent people into this. What do you know of this man Luca Rospigliosi? That he is imprisoned here in the Italian men's barracks. We know you speak to him; what do you discuss? The beauty of Florence. They kept me in the interrogation room all day without food or water, but I never deviated from my denials or refusals. My questioners obviously had no solid evidence of any partisan activity to use against me. After a full day of questioning, they passed me over.

Luca fared far worse. Him they beat, mercilessly, but not so badly that they couldn't drag him back the next day and start all over again. Before arriving at Bolsena, he'd withstood one round of torture, and I hoped they'd not break him now and force him to reveal Dominic's partisan work. But mostly, I feared for his life. One day they might go too far. It was time, I decided, to spend what little influence I had in the barrack and implement the escape plan I'd hoped to use myself.

After morning roll call on what would be Luca's fourth day of beatings, I sought him out as he limped, crumpled over, out of his row. I whispered, "I know a way to get you out. Do you want to risk it?"

"*Si*, I will. I must."

"Sneak to the women's barrack tonight when it's dark." I must be brief. Guards could be watching us. "In the morning, I'll get you out on the laundry truck."

That evening in the barrack, I called the women together and announced my plan. "This is something we must do for Luca. I've told him it's all arranged. His life is at risk."

Rosa beat the air with the back of her hand. "No, we won't do this. It's dangerous. And foolish."

To hell with honesty and honor, I told myself. There was only one way to get around Rosa. Stepping up on my bunk beam, I shook my fist at her. "If you undo this plan, I'll report you for stealing potatoes."

"Hah," Rosa smirked. "You're the one who steals them, not me."

It was true. I had stolen potatoes for the prisoners' soup. I'd tried to hide this from Rosa, but she'd found me out—and quietly lorded it over me. I had worried for weeks that she might report me. I could only hope she enjoyed stoking her potbelly enough to keep quiet.

I decided to risk it all—Luca's escape and my place in the barrack. "But all the others here will say you're the thief."

I looked first to Maria, pleading with my eyes. My heart thumped at my eardrums. I looped my arm around the bunk post to steady myself.

Maria nodded. I turned my gaze on Silvia, lifting my brow in silent appeal. Silvia nodded. So did the woman at her side. Like an uncoiling spring, nods swelled the circle. With each assent, I dipped my head in thanks. Come the end of the voting, every single woman had joined me. I wanted to howl with delight. I wanted to thrust my fists to the sky. Instead, I kept my expression grave.

Rosa reddened. Any moment she might explode with anger and manufacture some fresh threat against her mutineers. Think, I commanded myself. You must save Luca.

Muffling the swell of conquest rising in me, I fixed myself with serenity. "Rosa, if your life were in danger, I would do the same for you. Everyone here matters."

Rosa snorted dismissively. "Do it, then. But you'll regret this."

I bowed my head to Rosa. "*Grazie.*"

A hush fell over the barrack as Rosa stomped off. I heaved a sigh and glanced around the assembled circle—at the faces shining with satisfaction, relief, and admiration. I met their waiting eyes, patting my hand over my heart. Such sweet victory, such sweet revenge. I'd brought the barrack over to my side.

———

Maria gave me the bottom bunk that night. I tossed about, wakeful and alert, waiting for Luca. Finally, the door creaked, and I bounded out of my bed. Taking Luca by the hand, I led him to my cot. "It's agreed. Everyone here will help you."

He sat down on the bunk and looked up at me. "It's a good plan?"

"*Sì*, it is." In the dark, I could only imagine the yellow and purple bruises on his face. "Get in bed now. We'll keep each other warm tonight."

He shucked off his shoes, pulled the blanket over himself, and held it up. Huddling in beside him, I circled an arm around him and tugged him to me.

He relaxed his head in the hollow of my shoulder. "Tell me your plan."

"The laundry lorry comes in the morning. We'll hide you on it."

"If I get out, I'll thank you every day of my life."

"Just live. Go back to your work. And if you can, get my messages out."

"*Sì*, I will."

"And you will get out. I promise."

He said, "I told my bunkmate I was crawling off to die like a dog."

"Too bad the guards won't find a body."

"Let them suspect cannibalism."

I chuckled faintly and patted his shoulder. "You funny man. Sleep now."

He huddled close, molding himself against me and fitting his hand into the cove below my sternum. His warmth seeped into me. I cupped my fingers over his. Such sweet communing—like that of mother and child or lovers after union. The lean lines of his chest and belly curled against my side, softness to softness. His breathing lapsed into a sleeper's steady draw, pause, and release.

I usually welcomed sleep after the monotony of the workdays and prayed for it to eclipse night's haunting hopelessness. Now I didn't care if I slept at all, so delicious was the sensation of our bodies warm against each other.

I woke with a start at the sound of the 4:30 reveille. We hurried through the morning routine—the quick-moving latrine line and face splashing. Then all of us surrounded a crouching Luca and tramped through pre-dawn's dark toward the laundry building. When the canteen contingent broke off, my group kept Luca in the center of our pack. Once inside the laundry room, I hid him under a stack of dirty sheets and towels. I joined the others, filling the washing tubs and rolling the baskets of clean laundry onto the loading dock.

Maria stepped outside to see if any guards were watching. When she gave the all-clear sign, I summoned Luca. "Come, hide behind this basket. When we load it on, flatten yourself against it to get onto the lorry. Jump out at the crest of the hill."

"You're taking a great risk," he said. "I thank you with all my heart."

"Once over the hill, they won't be able to see you in their mirrors."

He took my face in his hands and kissed my forehead. "You're an angel, Toto."

"Hah," I said. "There's a lot you don't know about me."

The laundry lorry arrived, and I helped Rosa and the others unload the dirty laundry. Slowly, we wheeled the first basket of fresh clothes onto the truck. I hopped off the dock and headed for the drivers. I only needed to distract them for a few minutes. "*Per favore*, *signori*, can you spare a cigarette? Just one?"

The men regarded each other dubiously, and the young, swaggering one said, "Why not?"

He shook out two cigarettes, offering me one. He struck a match and held it up to light mine.

But I'd only cough if I tried to smoke it. "Oh, no, I wish to save it for later."

He laughed and lit his cigarette. "Ah, *signorina*, you want to share it with your lover?"

I would give it to Rosa, I thought, *to thank her*. Shyly, I looked down. "Please don't report me."

The older man smirked, "Just don't burn any holes in Il Duce's uniforms."

"Il Duce's uniforms? But isn't this laundry for the airbase?"

"*Mamma mia*, no." He plopped his foot on the lorry's runner. "You think the military gets such clean uniforms and sheets? These are for Rome."

I'd seen the uniforms. They were nothing fancy. And they certainly weren't Il Duce's. But what did that matter? I reached out and touched the fur collar of the younger one's wool jacket. "What a fine jacket. Are you a pilot?"

"Soon I'll go into training."

The older man playfully punched his arm. "That's why you haul laundry back and forth. To learn how to fly over the hills."

"When the war's over, I'll know how to fly. What'll *you* do?"

"Stay alive, you blockhead."

A guard emerged from the headquarters building and headed toward the laundry dock.

"You, there," the guard called. He'd spotted me talking to the drivers.

I stuffed the cigarette up my sleeve. My gaze darted between the drivers. "Please, don't give me away."

The younger driver smiled and hollered to the guard. "She's just reporting on the loading. No problem here."

"Come on, Gemo," the older fellow said, nudging his hat up. "Can't keep Rome waiting."

I backed away from the drivers, and they hopped into the cab. Off they drove, down the road in front of headquarters and toward the gate. The lorry exited the compound, bounced onto the bumpy country road, and climbed the hill signifying Luca's freedom. I smiled with pride and pleasure.

CAMP BOLSENA

NOVEMBER 1941–MARCH 1942

The day after Luca's escape, Rosa took up her post at the head of the washing line and announced: "If anyone ever threatens me again, I'll report all of you for helping that man escape." She shook a finger at me. "Especially you, for risking everyone's necks."

I couldn't help myself. I flew at Rosa. "Who do you think you are?"

Rosa spat. "The one that watches out for everybody here."

I grabbed a handful of her garb and twisted it into a knot. "You only watch out for yourself."

"Let me go, you reckless whore."

Maria and Silvia rushed forward.

"Don't." Maria grasped my arm. "Don't fight."

Outrage boiled up in me—at Rosa's treachery and the wretchedness of this bloody hellhole. "I know you talk to the guards. You don't fool me."

Silvia pushed in between us. "Toto, let go."

Reluctantly, I released Rosa's gown.

"Get her away from me," Rosa hissed.

Maria and Silvia yanked me to the end of the line. I allowed it, but inside I seethed: I hated everything Rosa stood for—cowardice, greed, and malice. I wanted to fight it out with her.

Maria spoke quietly. "Don't make it worse than it already is."

"I can't help it. She's an insolent bully."

Silvia shielded us from view and spoke lowly. "We know that. But she could report you."

"This place is driving me mad."

Maria cupped my cheeks in her hands. "You mustn't let it."

"She's using Luca's escape against me. Forcing us to collaborate in her gutless conspiracy with the guards. Rendering me useless."

"Stop," said Maria, gripping my shoulders. "Don't let her rule you like this. You must keep your head."

Silvia smoothed a hand over my arm. "Maria's right. Think of yourself. And the rest of us."

With a sigh, I let my shoulders drop.

We got on with the morning routine, and I plunged into laundry duty, cursing under my breath with each flail and wring of a uniform or sheet or shirt.

Maria came up beside me. "Listen to me. It could've been worse. Don't you see that?"

"How?"

"Rosa could've ruined Luca's escape."

"I even gave her a cigarette from the driver."

"You are the generous one, not her," said Maria.

"Ungenerous? She's worse than that. She's dangerous."

"She only wants her rule over the barrack back."

"So she can turn you in again?"

"We don't know she did that," Maria said. "And even if she did, I forgive her. Can't you?"

"No."

"Then look what you did. You saved Luca's life."

Yes, Luca could carry on with his work. Our work. He might even get my messages to Dominic and Elisabeth. "That's because you and everybody else helped. Now Rosa lords it over all of us."

"Stop this, Toto. It does no good."

Maria reminded me now of my mother, who never let up when she had a lesson to teach. And I didn't want to upset Maria. "Fine, let Rosa think she's in charge."

Maria smiled at me. "*Si*, what does it matter who's first in line?"

I nodded.

"We'll watch out for each other, you and me," she said. "Just like we've been doing."

"*Si*, Maria, we'll do that."

That seemed to satisfy her. But damn it, I hated rotting away in this camp. It made my blood boil. It'd been three years since I'd set out to make a difference in this awful war. And what had I accomplished? A handful of intelligence reports passed on, my furs and jewelry sold for Giustizia e Libertà, some books saved, and a plot hatched on Florence's Registry that, for all I knew, had failed.

If I'd never left London, I'd be there now, taking shelter beside my friends. Surely, I could have found a way to aid the war effort from there. Instead, I languished in a camp run by cold-blooded Fascists.

Had I been a fool to think I'd make a good spy? I was Toto Koopman; I'd consorted with Britain's now Minister of Aircraft Production; I'd been photographed by Europe's most famous. Was it any surprise the Fascists and Nazis cut off my career as a spy and partisan after one short year? They'd reduced me to this—to a miserable prisoner who could do them no harm.

I hated every single one of them. And I hated Rosa, too.

———

In the weeks and months after I wrangled with Rosa over Luca, nobody in the barrack dared mention his name. Nor did word of his escape circulate among the other prisoners—probably because no one wanted to risk being accused of abetting an escape. The camp commanders, perhaps loath to admit they'd been duped, had probably decided to tamp down rumors by making little of it. They also began searching all vehicles entering and exiting the camp, foiling any hope I could make a similar break. Not that Rosa would have allowed such a plot to take root.

On Christmas eve, after a blessedly short workday, the barrack gathered around a candle to sing carols.

Maria tugged at my sleeve. "Come, join us."

"No," I said. "I'd rather not."

I climbed up onto my cot and stretched out. I'd have nothing to do with this religious celebration—not while Rosa led the carols. The mawkish songs—about adoring shepherds, angelic voices, and Jesus, light of the world—aggravated me all the more. How dare Rosa sing about love and light?

I cursed Rosa for quashing my will to fight. But what good had my lofty convictions done me? Or anybody else? Could convictions save me or any of us from the twelve-hour workdays or the cruelty and deprivations of this place?

This camp was killing my spirit. And if I weren't careful, it'd kill my body, too. The best I could do was keep myself safe. I must at least do that much.

When the caroling ended, Maria came over, stood on the bunk's lower rung, and propped her elbows on my bed. She leaned close and whispered, "Everyone is wondering what's wrong with you. It's our savior's birthday."

"I'm not Catholic, Maria. Not even Christian."

"It doesn't matter. Don't you believe in some goodness?"

"I see little of it in this place."

Maria latched onto my arm. "You mustn't give up."

"What does it matter?" I pulled out of Maria's clutch, and a twinge of shame shivered through me, a familiar and nauseating shame. I'd felt this way before—as a child when I'd begged my parents not to send my baby elephant away, even though I knew it was best for my beloved pet to rejoin her kind.

I shrugged it off. This was different: Selflessness mattered little here. I had no control over anyone's safety or fortunes.

"Toto, please, we all need you."

I stared at the ceiling to avoid Maria's eyes. "It's not my concern anymore."

"You're the only one who can stand up to Rosa."

"And if I do, she'll punish all of us."

Sleep evaded me for hours that night. Then I dreamed. I was a child again, hiking beside my mother through a towering stand of grass. Mother held my hand and chanted sing-song melodies, songs I'd heard my grandmother sing a long time ago. A howling wind roared up, carrying my mother's voice away. Low clouds swept in and cast a shadowy pall over the trees and brush. Mother and I pushed on into a tangled jungle of twisted branches. Then my mother was gone. Mama, Mama, I called, pushing through the thorny branches, scratching my arms bloody. Rain pelted down, falling in sheets and drowning out my voice. The ground turned into a vast swamp, sucking my bare feet deeper and deeper into the muck. The more I flailed, the more the mud enveloped me, gripping me like powerful claws.

"Toto, Toto." A hand shook me.

I woke with a start.

Maria stroked my arm. "You were dreaming."

Sweat beaded my brow and the valley between my breasts. A chill shot through me. "It was a nightmare."

"Are you all right?"

"Yes, yes."

My heart thudded against my ribs. I rearranged my blanket and stilled myself. Aftershocks of dream-desperation rattled me. I was afraid, afraid of what would happen if I didn't get out of this place.

At the blare of the morning horn, I woke feeling clammy and adrift, haunted by desperation and loneliness. Had everyone I'd ever known or loved deserted me? No, I had a few friends here. I slipped out of my bunk and knelt by Maria. "Forgive me, Maria. I gave in to pity. I just don't know how to help myself anymore. Let alone the rest of us."

"Just be strong, like I know you to be."

Maria was right: I mustn't surrender to hopelessness. It had crept up on me and sucked me into a morass of self-pity. Only I felt so helpless and useless, like a lame workhorse shuttered away. What good was I to anyone? The heartlessness and depravity of this camp suffocated, little by little, my dwindling supply of hope.

———

All the prisoners in Camp Bolsena suffered that cold winter. The wind whipped through the barrack's wood-slat walls. At night, Maria and I paired up in one narrow cot to share the heat of our weakened bodies. Come morning, I welcomed the constant motion of work to warm my fingers and toes. But the labor left my belly aching for fuel, and the cycle of cold, cruel days numbed my mind. So, I traipsed through winter's short-of-light days, sullen and confused, and railed at the feckless passage of time. As for Rosa, over those freezing months, we settled into a sort of stalemate, neither of us challenging the other or doing anything that helped or harmed our barrack mates.

One piece of heartening news reached us in December. We learned that America had declared war on Germany. But conjectures about whether they would make a difference ranged wildly between hopefulness and pessimism.

In February, prisoners across the camp noticed that the influx of new captives had stalled, but we had no way of knowing why. When we bent over the meal table or retreated to our cots, we whispered speculations. Perhaps new camps had been constructed to accommodate the ever-increasing numbers of prisoners. Or maybe the war had shifted to air and sea campaigns that took few captives. Or—dare we hope?—British and American forces were on the march, and they were now the ones taking prisoners. Oh, for some news. I would've traded a day of meals for the front page of *The Daily Express*.

One evening in early March, the guard coming around with deliveries called my name. What could it mean? In my fifteen months of captivity, I'd received nothing from the outside world. I walked to the front of the barrack. The guard held out a letter. I looked at the handwriting. "My God," I whispered. "It's from Elisabeth."

My fingertips tingled as I took the envelope. The air in my ears buzzed. I wanted to fling my arms to the sky and scream with excitement. But no, I told myself, don't. Don't reveal yourself. You know nothing of the letter's message or what it might portend. Don't stir up curiosity. I murmured a simple *grazie* and, avoiding the eyes of my barrack mates, retreated to the privacy of my bunk.

How did Elisabeth know where I was? Perhaps Luca had gotten a message to her. Or maybe she'd made inquiries of the authorities. *Santo Cielo,* someone knew my whereabouts. No longer was I hidden from those I loved. And if Elisabeth knew, Dominic did, too. Now I could reach out to Elisabeth. Would it be possible, with Elisabeth or Dominic's assistance, to devise some escape?

The letter was unsealed, no doubt having been opened and examined. Elisabeth knew well enough to keep her report brief and neutral, but I lapped up every word as if it were the richest cream.

My dear Toto,

I am so sorry I have not been able to visit you. Please know that I often think of you and hope we will soon be able to resume our lively discussions of Giotto, Masaccio, and da Vinci. In June, I am moving to Perugia to continue my studies and begin work on the thesis. I will write about the famous painter Perugino, who decorated Perugia's Sala ole Cambio with his frescoes. You can mail letters to me in Florence or at my Perugia address, which I include below.

Our friend Domenica misses you and sends her love. Do not lose faith, Toto. We will not give up hope for your release.

Your loving friend,

Elisabeth

How clever of Elisabeth, I thought, to change Dominic's name to a woman's. I read the letter twice more and slipped it under my mattress. As far as I knew, Elisabeth engaged in no partisan activities. And now I was glad of it—if she were investigated, the Blackshirts would find no evidence against her. That meant she could be my friend now, without fear of consequences.

I lay in bed hoping this letter might be the first step to freedom, all the while cautioning myself: Don't torment yourself with the unknown—or the improbable. But I couldn't shut down the gushing torrent of hope. My so-called resignation cracked, and I saw it for what it was: a barrier I'd erected to hold back expectancy. I wanted out. So desperately I understood that slain Greek prisoner's attempt. And I pledged: I *will* get out. I'll devote myself to this. I'll find my way back to Dominic and my comrades. So I can fight on.

CAMP BOLSENA AND BEYOND
MARCH 1942

Two weeks after I received Elizabeth's letter, a guard pulled me from canteen duty. "You, come with me."

My legs turned wobbly; tremors of panic fluttered through me. I thought of Luca's terrible beatings. Steady, steady, I told myself, focusing on each small step. At the door, I turned and shot Maria a questioning glance.

She folded her hands in a prayerful pose and mouthed, "Be brave."

The guard marched me to headquarters, into an office with a desk so uncluttered it appeared unused. The Fascists apparently preferred not to document their iniquities. Over the next half hour, the room filled with twelve other prisoners, men with cropped hair and the same droopy prison garb, most in their thirties or forties, a few at the other reaches of years. I was the lone woman.

Furtively, I glanced at the men. I recognized in their glances my own vigilance, in their hand-wringing, my own churning fear. We stood in the cramped office, shifting from one foot to the other, warily appraising each other.

I sidled up to one of the men and whispered, "Do you know why we've been summoned?"

He cleared his throat and glanced over his shoulder. "No, I do not know these other men."

The man beside him leaned in and hunched his shoulders in a questioning way. Perhaps none of us knew the reason we'd been gathered.

I nodded in resignation and looked out through the room's small box of a window, at Lazio's mounded trees, rolling green slopes, and here and there a terra cotta home tucked among them. Ordinary people lived there: peasants who worked their orchards and gardens; families who supped together; men and women who were free, even if tyrannized by the watch of ruthless Fascists—unless they themselves were traitors to their countrymen.

Would I ever again laugh or dine with someone I could trust? Studying the wispy clouds racing over the hills, I cursed the capricious winds that blew to unknowable places. Blast this fate. Even if I escaped this place tomorrow, would I know who to rely on or where to go? Perhaps Elisabeth would take me in. Or would my presence endanger her?

An officer in a gray-green uniform marched in. The gold braid on his cap and bold black markings on his jacket revealed a higher rank than that of an ordinary camp officer.

Regarding us with a tucked head and hardened brow, he took up a sheet of paper and called, "Are you present, Toto Koopman?"

"*Sì.*"

With business-like efficiency, the officer read down the list, accounting for each prisoner. He folded the paper and tucked it in his chest pocket. "You're being transferred. Obey the guards' orders and there'll be no trouble." With a peremptory nod, he turned and marched out.

One of the guards directed me out of the headquarters building. "You're to clean out your bunk area."

As he and I crossed the expanse to the barracks, I said nothing: Anyone could observe us there, and I imagined my escort would not like to be seen conversing with me. With each steady step, I mustered my concentration. It was a transfer, then, for these men and me. Why had we been singled out? I must find out what this move augured. Perhaps I could break free along the way.

I pushed open the door to my empty barrack. How I'd yearned for a mere hour by myself here—to write a letter or pry up the floorboards and see if I could dig my way to freedom. But this transfer forced me to rethink everything. Bloody hell, I hoped it was a transfer. And not some pretense for perfidy.

After a glance at the guard's name badge, I hurried to my cot and began stripping it. "Can you say, Officer Rossi, where we're bound?"

He twisted his head around, taking in the women's barrack, even sniffing the air. Yes, I imagined the women smelled different from the men. Not clean—our bodies sweated just like the men's, our clothes absorbed the same filth, and the closest we got to a bath was lice powder treatments. But we emitted our own smells, too, like the metallic tang of menstruation. Or perhaps it was the rot of our wretchedness he scented. Or my tart fear.

Absently he answered, "Massa Martana detention camp."

I plopped my pillow atop the folded blanket. "But why must I leave? I've caused no problems."

With a dismissive toss of his head, he said, "We don't keep your kind here."

I tucked Elisabeth's letter into my gown pocket and draped my coat over my shoulder. "What do you mean, my kind?"

"So, you play innocent?"

I walked to the door and stood with my back to it. "I can't say, officer, without hearing your accusation."

He smirked. "Partisan scum."

My belly overran with the acid of dread. So, they persisted in this belief, though they'd never confronted me with any evidence—because they'd not uncovered any.

Basta, I thought, *call me a spy. Punish me as a partisan. Only don't kill me. I want to live. Reckless fate, tell me this isn't some ruse for a firing squad. Please, please, let me live.*

———

The guard allowed me no chance to say goodbye to Maria or the others, not even time to write a note. My barrack mates wouldn't know what fate awaited me. But neither did I. Clues, I must try to pick up clues. As my fellow prisoners and I stood waiting for our transport, I mingled among them and whispered: "We're bound for Massa Martana. Any idea why?"

No, each answered.

Even if we were all suspected spies, why move us to a different camp? Unless they were turning us over to the Germans. *Please, anybody but the Nazis, hang every one of them by their devil's tails.*

Guards lined the thirteen of us up behind a lorry similar to the one I'd arrived on. An unexpected chivalry put me first in line, and I chose a spot against the cab, where I could avoid the gusty spring wind and the lorry's exhaust and be near the gap between the canvas canopy and the truck's cab. Once all the others had stepped on, two guards took up positions at the rear.

The lorry rambled down the dirt road and out of the compound. I checked the gap in the canvas covering the rear compartment. It was narrow, but I might be able to squeeze through. If the guards dozed off, I'd dare it. But the chances of that seemed unlikely. Perhaps if all the prisoners worked together to overtake the guards, we could escape. But that didn't account for the driver, who was likely armed, or prisoners who might refuse to fight. Still, I wanted to try, which meant taking a chance on the man next to me.

He was light-complected, with bristles of silver hair poking up on his smooth, shiny head. Something about him struck me as not typically Italian—perhaps the way he pitched his head back, as if deep in meditation, or crossed his legs at the ankles. His bearing was formal, even refined.

I leaned toward him. "A guard said they're transferring us because we're partisans."

"They'll think what they want, God help us." He spoke with no discernible foreign accent but rather like a northern Italian.

I asked, "Where are you from?"

"Milan. And you?" He turned to face me. His green-streaked irises and black pupils dazzled with intensity and ken.

"Most recently, Florence," I said.

He asked, "Did you learn anything else?"

The guard diagonal to us shouted, "You two, no talking."

We shut up. I would try to speak to him again later.

I closed my eyes and let myself roll with the lorry's pitch and lurch, conscious of taking comfort in jostling against my companion. We were comrades now, and I wanted to believe this thread of connection I felt was mutual.

As for escape, it seemed completely unrealistic given the guards' vigilance. I had no choice but to give myself over to dumb hope. As the lorry advanced over the smooth, curving road, I summoned the faces of my loved ones, all as remote as gallery portraits. I missed Dominic, his fervor and tenacity and the way he held me close at night. If only I could visit my father to reminisce about Mother. Or chinwag with my brother about childhood memories. Curse it all anyway—this not knowing, this unpredictability, these whims of our capricious captors. What a blasted unlucky time to be alive, with this wretched war raging. And no sign of anything like justice or civility to keep us safe from the likes of Hitler and Mussolini.

I gazed out the back of the lorry at expansive rolling fields punctuated by rows of cypress trees. The fields slowly gave way to modest-sized plots, some bare, some sprouting sturdy jade-green stalks. I supposed it was a good sign that we'd passed through the sparsely populated countryside, where a firing squad could have quickly dispatched us.

In the distance, a village with a spiking church tower and cream-colored buildings spilled down the hill. I leaned forward and lengthened my arms over my shins. Slowly I pulled out of my stretch and glanced at the guards. One of them slouched in his seat, his eyelids drooping, and the other stared off into the countryside.

I asked my companion, "Do you know where we are?"

He muttered, "I believe that's Todi on the hill."

He was, like me, a supposed partisan. Perhaps he had some fresh intelligence. "Do you know," I asked, "if America is helping Britain?"

"*Sì*, they're sending troops over now. Their generals are planning strategy with England."

The first words that came to me were those Maria uttered when freed from her chains. "Holy Mother of God, thank you."

He murmured, "Bless you, my child."

I jerked my head around toward him. "You're a priest?"

"*Sì*."

MASSA MARTANA
DETENTION CAMP

MARCH–MAY 1942

The lorry slowed and steered through the metal gate of a compound. I should've been relieved it was, as I'd hoped, merely a transfer. But I couldn't help silently fuming at the foe who now pulled the strings of my life. What I wouldn't give to know who this dastardly conniver was, so I could imagine someone yanking him from his haughty perch. It'd be a great service to the world if he—and everyone else up his chain of command—spent the rest of their days in prison. What kind of men imprisoned people for no reason? What kind of justice granted no challenge or legal recourse?

Waiting guards marched me and my fellow prisoners to a two-story building, an outworn brick structure, perhaps once an academy, that the Fascists had requisitioned for their purposes. As we climbed a set of stairs, I slowed my step to take in the view from a window on the landing. Roads zigzagged among the camp's brick barracks in a checkerboard grid. The grounds were as barren as those of Bolsena, and the brick walls also high and foreboding. But something seemed different here: the layout and signs of humming industry—a crew of prisoners repairing a damaged wall section, another group bouncing along in the back of a lorry—suggested a more workman-like than punishing atmosphere.

Guards assembled us in a room with a blackboard, and an officer of perhaps fifty sauntered in and took up a position before us. I couldn't help staring at him. One side of his face squashed together as if he'd long ago suffered a bludgeon blow. All his features skewed off-kilter: his cheeks formed different-sized triangles; his mouth slanted sharply; one side of his brow caved over a crumpled eye socket; and his other eye opened wide as a lira coin.

He searched the faces of each of us as if daring us to shrink from his disfigurement. Tucking a thumb in his belt, he said, "At Massa Martana, we have strict rules, and I expect everyone to obey them to the letter. You have important work to do, and I won't tolerate any treason or plots to escape."

He put on a bulldog scowl. "Especially from proven partisans."

———

Over the next few weeks, I scrutinized the camp's operation and discerned that its guards did indeed operate on a different ethic than those at Camp Bolsena. Although they enforced long workdays and strict order, their treatment of prisoners wasn't as capricious. True, whenever guards opened the gate or transported prisoners from one area to another, they kept especially close watch. But they generally interfered with workers only when someone slacked off, as if their highest priority was ensuring the prisoners accomplished their various jobs: sorting metal scraps; planting and tending a large garden; mending military uniforms; repairing roads and buildings; preparing food; and tending the sick.

The women in my barrack received me with dispassionate but polite interest, as if I were just one among their many—like travelers waiting at a train station. One of them, Luisa, a gaunt, sallow-cheeked woman, offered me a few pieces of advice, like how to slip away with thread for personal mending and from whom to buy, in the complicated exchange system of the camp, soap for the biweekly showers. My barrack mates seemed to regard each other with a sense of shared, albeit unspoken, hardship. From what I could gather, no one like Rosa lorded power over us. Still, I knew better than to let down my guard.

So, here I was, in a new camp, forced to start all over on devising an escape. And I missed Maria and Silvia. I wouldn't have thought I'd grow close to my sister prisoners—but I had—and the abruptness of our separation galled me. The Fascists had robbed me and countless others of life's ordinary pleasures: the leisurely breaking of bread; easy, uncomplicated conversation; and so-long-until-later partings. I hated everything they stood for.

This war made me both leery of and desperate for comrades, like the man I'd met on the transfer, Father Pavesi, who invited me to call him Father Matteo or even Matteo. Of all the people to pine for, I'd chosen a priest, a man sworn to celibacy. But botheration, the man could've passed for an aging Valentino. Don't be foolish, I told myself, there's no room here for such frivolities as flirtation or romance. Still, I yearned for his companionship, which was all I could afford anyway. The last thing I needed was one more person to add to the collection of loved ones now lost to me, like Dominic, Elisabeth, and my father and brother.

I'd spoken briefly with Father Matteo only on two occasions since our arrival—on the third Sundays of the month—after the monthly Mass for prisoners, during the time allotted in the schedule for devotion or exercise.

After today's Mass, under clear May skies, I caught up with him. "May I walk with you, Matteo?"

"I'd like that," he said.

We struck out on a path that hugged the wall. He clasped his hands behind his back, hunched forward, and swiveled his gaze toward me. "You didn't attend Mass. Do you not practice any religion?"

"What's religion? Besides empty ceremony and dubious belief?"

"At the least, you can share with the others."

"Ceremony is vacuous. Why waste time on the motions?" Or, I thought, talk of them. I had little patience for debating religion, but he was a priest.

"Ceremony is how we share and honor belief."

"When I was young, my father took us to services on Easter and Christmas. Just for the show of it, he said. He never schooled us in the faith, but he's as charitable and honest as any man I've ever known."

"Did he teach you to believe in God?"

"He taught us to be fair-minded and loving. Can you learn those things kneeling in a pew or chanting Latin?" Such Sundays I'd enjoyed as a child in Java. While our father supervised the cleaning of the horses' stalls and checked the tack, my brother and I chummed around, refilling the water trough and grooming the horses. Once we finished the chores, the three of us saddled our horses and rode a loop that took us past terraced fields and the edge of a lush forest. It was then that Henri and I coaxed stories out of our father about his military service. I especially liked his amusing account of how he'd chastised a missionary caught forcing baptism on a village of reluctant Javanese. No stuffy church ceremony could compare to that.

"And," I added, "he respected my mother's beliefs in spirits and ancestors— her brand of Javanese Buddhism."

"You haven't answered my question," Father Matteo said. "Or explained your beliefs."

I paused when we reached the wall's corner, at a spot sheltered from the brisk wind. Leaning against the bricks, I felt the warmth of their stored heat. I studied the dry-packed earth of the camp, smelled the dust lifted by the wind, and took in the rows upon rows of dreary wood barracks—all the same except for the numbers on their fronts. Here I stood, in a walled camp, my closest companion a handsome man more intent on converting me to Catholicism than revealing anything of himself. And now he challenged me, as if to suggest that giving myself over to some unseen savior might dissolve the boundary between us or solve some unspoken problem.

"My mother's beliefs probably influenced me more than my father's."

He crossed his arms and settled onto his heels. The sun at his back accented the genteel oval shape of his head. "Belief in spirits and idols?"

I looked into his expectant eyes, and defiance reared in me. Who was he to judge me? This Christianity of his offered naught but false hope. "As if your beliefs are any different."

Father Matteo flinched, speechless for a moment. He paused, brushing a hand over his mouth before speaking. "You must pardon me if I've given offense."

"Come, let's walk," I said, taking his arm. I hadn't meant to sound so harsh. "In a way, I did partake of ceremony with my mother. We made pilgrimages to the ancient temples. And I took comfort in the rituals honoring our ancestors and the wisdom of lives lived."

"Tell me more."

"My mother saw the sacred in all things: flying and four-legged creatures, trees and grass, rivers and mountains. She taught me one must venerate one's spirit by observing and controlling actions and thoughts. And by setting aside arrogance, pleasure, and material things."

"That's not far from the Christian command to honor one's body as a temple of the holy spirit."

"I learned something important from her: Only through restraint can one master and exercise control over the inner and outer selves." But I refused to confess that I'd lost sight of how to follow my mother's instruction, that contempt for my captors gripped me as tightly as a fighter's fist, that each day I struggled to find a way to rise above my bitterness.

Matteo picked up his pace as if we had someplace to hurry to. "You don't mention God. How can you have a religion without God?"

I reached out to slow his step. "My parents lived their beliefs. They were dignified and honorable. Isn't that more important than the worship of an unknowable god?"

Matteo squinted an eye at me. "It is belief in the Holy Father's goodness that gives the faithful hope."

"And where is the Holy Father now?" I wagged my head from side to side, taking in the expanse of the camp. "When so many need him?"

"We cannot know the ways of our Lord."

I kicked at the path, stirring up dust. "Nor, it seems, the souls of our enemies."

"It's your soul I'm concerned about."

"I'm not asking you to save my soul. Only to be my friend."

We walked on in silence. Our talk had unsettled rather than heartened me. Growing up, I'd not reflected on my parents' instruction but rather taken it in stride. Now I understood they'd tried to teach me to conduct myself with dignity and courage, especially in the face of ignorance. And I was failing. I wanted to be honest with Matteo, as honest as I might be with a trusted friend, yet I feared showing weakness.

Finally, he spoke. "Then I shall be your friend. And I will pray for you, whether you wish it or not."

What I wanted more than prayers was friendship. And the fortitude my parents had tried to instill in me. Yes, I could see my likenesses to them in my character. I carried both of them in me—not just my mother's tawny skin and oval eyes or my father's tall, slender build—but also their sensibilities and spirits. Only their lessons eluded me now—like some shimmering haze I couldn't grab hold of. Yes, they'd quarreled at times. My father insisted on speaking up in the face of injustice, and my mother believed in the power of quiet example. And now I argued with myself over these very matters and found myself frozen in some sort of spiritual wasteland—incapable of taking any action, unable to determine how I might combat the depravity around me.

But I sensed Father Matteo wouldn't understand all that, even though he was likely a fellow partisan. Besides, we dared not share our partisan activities. And I wanted his friendship. "If only prayers could give me the courage to fight on and the wisdom to know how."

"That's a great deal to ask. I suggest you, too, pray for these things."

I wanted to be the person my parents raised me to be. I wanted to embody their equanimity and dignity. What a sight the four of us must have made in public: my mother in a colorful, loose-fitting batik dress, my father in his smart cavalry uniform, and my brother and I tagging along in whatever august garb we'd chosen for the occasion. Our parents proudly showed us off, stood up to those who derided us as half-breeds or green Dutchmen, and taught us how to respond gracefully to uncouthness or insult.

I caught and held his gaze. "One thing I can say: My parents gave me the instincts to see the ungodliness of Fascism."

"I would hope people of all faiths agree on that."

The siren sounded, calling us to our workstations.

"But they don't, do they? The Fascists are Catholics, too."

"We can talk of this later." With a brusque shake of his head, he hustled off.

I looked up to the sky, where my mother's spirit dwelled, and imagined my father at my side. *Mother and Father, I don't know how to make sense of Hitler and Mussolini's policies of prejudice and punishment. I try to believe those who carry out orders to torture and kill aren't evil themselves but rather misguided or warped by fear. But what can I do to fight them? Please give me the strength to face this savagery. Because I'm lost now; I can't see beyond my outrage.*

On my way to the metal-sorting room, I spotted a feather and picked it up. A small, brown- and white-striped feather. I held it to the sky and rolled it between my fingers. "It is you, Mother, telling me to free myself from hatred. I will try, I promise. Only I feel so full of despair. And useless."

DISPATCH FROM MILAN

11 April 1942

Subject transferred to Massa Martana Detention Camp. Considered an enemy of Italy. No options for release. This camp permits visitors. Please advise as to next course of action.

WD

MASSA MARTANA DETENTION CAMP

JUNE–DECEMBER 1942

S oon Elisabeth would be nearby in Perugia. For days I fretted—while I worked at culling metal scraps and when I lay awake at night—about what to write to her. Finally, I settled on a simple note, something that couldn't possibly be considered seditious, and gained permission to post it.

12 June 1942
My dear Elisabeth,

It was a great joy to receive your letter, and I hope you'll pardon the delay in my response. I've been transferred to the Detention Camp in Massa Martana near Todi. The commandant and guards here are reasonable and fair. We're allowed visitors, so I hope you'll come and see me. Of course, the authorities may realize at any moment that my imprisonment is baseless, and then I'll be the one visiting you. Meantime, you know me well enough to understand I'm carrying on as usual, making myself of use here and, in so doing, demonstrating my sincere respect for the Italian government.

I trust your art studies are progressing well. How can they not when Italy is home to so many of the world's greatest artists?

I send wishes that you are well and thriving,
Affectionately,
Toto

In late June, I was moved from the metal-sorting room to the camp's sizable vegetable garden. Each day, from first light to mid-day meal, and afterward until dusk, I knelt among my fellow prisoners, cultivating and weeding. Over that first week, the sun and fresh air lulled me into something akin to happiness, a sort of meditative abandon. I didn't even mind the dirt that lodged beneath my nails or the ache in my back.

Then came the rain, soaking my hair and clothes, turning the grounds into a mud bath, and reminding me I was a captive. And toiling amid all this bounty tempted to distraction: the rows of tomatoes, cauliflower, and peppers; the tender leaves of spinach and beet greens; mounds of flourishing potatoes, carrots, garlic, and turnips; and bushy vines of beans and zucchini. As the spinach was pulled and loaded into crates, I yearned to stuff handfuls into my mouth. When we harvested the garlic in early July, I salivated at the thought of its pungent bite. But little of the garden's yield showed up in the camp's kitchen. The soup was a bland concoction, portions were stingy, and my gnawing hunger constant. Apparently, the garden didn't provision the camp but rather the army or government workers.

One afternoon, I noticed a prisoner slip a carrot into his pocket. As I watched for a chance to pilfer some spoils for myself, a guard marched down the row, yanked this man out of his crouch, and dragged him off. It was too risky, I decided, stealing in the light of day with guards watching from every corner.

As the months wore on, I nurtured alliances with two women in my barrack, Luisa and Marianna—not friendships of disclosure or plotting but of an understanding to neither ask nor expect too much from each other. It was self-reliance the prisoners here prized, at least those who had the health and means to practice it.

Still, like the others, I revealed little about myself and steered clear of allusions to partisan activities. Only with Father Matteo did I feel somewhat safe, although with him, too, I refrained from discussing my past political work. The two of us mostly confined our talk to the current state of the war, religious debates, and the workings of the camp. While each of us had hinted to the other of our desire to escape, we proposed no plan, as if we understood that plotting carried risks, risks that sharing only magnified. But I imagined we'd make a good team. He was strong and reticent, the type that could be trusted to act judiciously. So, although I was still new to this camp and the possible avenues of escape, I promised myself I'd keep trying to find a way out.

Late one August evening, as the women in my barrack bedded down, someone started a game of concocting nicknames for the camp's disfigured commandant. Seizing on the levity, I tossed off, "I'll wager no one's ever escaped under Commandant Cockeye's watch."

Luisa, who'd been at the camp for nearly two years, said, "They've tried. Guards discovered a tunnel under one of the men's barracks last fall."

I said, "At Camp Bolsena, they shot a man trying to get over the fence one night."

Marianna's eyes darted from me to Luisa. She asked, "What about the tunnel? Did they find out who dug it?"

Luisa said, "They hauled everyone in that barrack to the yard for public questioning. None of the prisoners would name the instigators. They shot the lot of them—twenty-eight men in all."

A hush fell over the barrack. I said, "So much for tunneling. It'd be safer to commission the Hindenburg."

A few snickers greeted my jest, though I decided I'd best abstain from any more public references to escape. But I wouldn't give up trying to break out. Each passing month placed me at higher risk: What if the Fascists somehow tricked a resistance worker into naming me? And with each day in captivity, I wasted away a little more—from lack of nourishment and constant labor.

To mark the time—and beat back the numbing monotony of the unvarying work routine—I acquired a sheet of paper and drew a makeshift calendar of rows and columns. Each month, I erased and redrew the week's dates, hoping every day might bring me closer to freedom. Surely this nightmare couldn't go on much longer. The fact that the war was dragging on so long after Hitler's initial lightning strikes suggested that his conquests were slowing, perhaps even reversing. But about the war, I only garnered snippets of information from fellow prisoners, and how could any of us verify what we'd heard?

———

On September 27, a guard ushered me into the hallway of the administration building.

A seated official greeted me. "Number 10027? Toto Koopman?"

"*Si.*"

"You have a visitor. The rules are no touching and no passing of items. If you exchange any goods or solicit prohibited information, we will terminate the visit. Do you understand?"

All I understood was that I had my first-ever visitor. For that, I would have agreed to any rules. "*Si,*" I blurted.

He pointed down the hall. "Last room on the left."

I hurried to the visiting room. Inside, four guards stood watch. The tuneless ping of conversation bounced off brick walls. A long wooden table took up the middle of the room; prisoners sat on one side and visitors on the other. And there was Elisabeth come to visit.

"Elisabeth," I called out, rushing to the seat across from her.

Elisabeth had changed little. Her face retained most of its plumpness, her eyes shone brightly, and her cheeks flushed a healthy pink. I slapped one hand to my heart and splayed the other on the table. "I can't tell you how happy I am to see you. You look marvelous."

Elisabeth's features flittered with surprise, quite likely, I imagined, at my changed appearance. Yes, my face was thinner, and my limbs leaner, but I was also more muscular. Surely, I wasn't so terribly altered: Elisabeth was simply accustomed to seeing me made up and stylishly attired.

Elisabeth clapped both her hands around mine. "My dear, how are you?"

The guard behind me hollered, "No touching."

Elisabeth withdrew her hands.

I flapped my palms outward in a look-at-me invitation. "Wonderful. No disease, no broken bones. I've kept my svelte figure."

Elisabeth chuckled. "I've missed you terribly. You and your knack for irony."

I could've cried from the swell of happiness. "Seeing you, talking to you like this—you can't imagine how many times I've wished for this moment."

"My God, it's been a year and a half."

"It feels like a lifetime."

"Is there anything, in particular, I can bring you?"

"I was told we couldn't exchange items."

"But I'm allowed to leave things for inspection or mail them."

"I'd love some real food. I've been craving cheese, like a hunk of salty pecorino to sink my teeth into." At the very thought, my saliva glands twinged.

"I'll do my best. So much food is rationed now. Or unbelievably expensive."

"Yes, I forget. The hardships of war, they hurt everyone." I rested my forearms on the table. "How is Domenica?"

"I saw her shortly before I left Florence. She's well. And busy as ever."

"You must send her my love."

"Yes, I'll write to her tomorrow."

The guard behind me shifted down the row and took up a position ten feet away.

I lowered my voice and asked in German, "How goes the war?"

"All maddening ups and downs," Elisabeth spoke softly in German. "The Italians destroyed Britain's last two battleships in the Mediterranean. The Germans bombed Malta to rubble. But the Russians have held Moscow. They're pushing the Germans back."

"On balance, who's winning?"

Elisabeth gave a sure nod. "The Allies will prevail."

A guard on Elisabeth's side of the table rushed up to her. "You two, only Italian is allowed. I must terminate your visit."

I begged, "No, please."

Another guard came up behind me and grabbed my arm. "Get up."

It was unfair. We'd had so little time. I steadied myself against the guard's bearish grip and looked to Elisabeth. "Will you visit me again?"

"*Sì*, when I can find transportation."

The guard yanked me up and over the bench.

I called over my shoulder, "And write?"

Elisabeth reached out her hand as if we might touch. "I will."

With the guard steering me, I stumbled out of the room. So much was unsaid. I'd had no chance to ask Elisabeth about the possibility of a release. As for the guards—the imperious asses—let the devil take them all.

———

Over the rest of that fall and on to winter, my life revolved around Elisabeth's visits. I imagined her going about her daily life, mere miles away. She was free. She could spend her days as she pleased. She could study and write her thesis. I craved her company—the gleam of compassion in her eyes and the hope she nurtured.

Elisabeth was my one reliable source of information about the war. True, she and I had to wait for moments when guards could not overhear us, but we'd learned our lesson, and Elisabeth managed to telegraph bits of news in concentrated bursts. Plus, we developed a rough code: Germany we called Wilhelmina; England, Constance; and America, Betty.

In early October, I gave Elisabeth my brother's address and asked her to write to him. Perhaps, by routing mail through Germany and avoiding censors, Elisabeth could get news to and from Henri. Several weeks later, Elisabeth traveled to Florence to meet secretly with Dominic, to convey my report on Luca Rospiglioso's escape and ask Dominic about the chances of a release.

Afterward, Elisabeth reported that no one had heard from Luca Rospiglioso; Dominic hoped the Fascists hadn't recaptured him. And, yes, the

Registry Office raid had come off as planned. Elisabeth explained that I mustn't rely on the slim possibility of release or help with an escape but should instead learn what I could in the camp and watch for chances to escape. I decided to keep an eye out for a reliable and sympathetic (or reliable and corrupt) guard who I might bribe.

Some of the news from Elisabeth was heartening. The Italian Communist Party had distributed a manifesto urging workers to slow production of military materials. People across the country were growing impatient with the rationing and war losses, and many workers planned slowdowns and strikes. If only, I quipped, that also applied to detention camp guards.

Elizabeth brought encouraging news in late November: The Americans had launched their first major offensive, in French Morocco and Algeria, with a force quite likely to overwhelm. If only I could raise a glass of Champagne with Randolph: Your father has brought America on board. Three cheers for Winston Churchill.

Five days before Christmas, Elisabeth made a surprise visit. I was in the infirmary, where I'd been working since October, when a guard came to fetch me. Fresh snow had fallen the night before, thickly blanketing the tin barrack roofs and casting a dull hush over the grounds. Over a foot deep, it promised to linger for months. Only around the chimneys of the headquarter building and guards' housing did the snow show signs of melting.

As I hurried along a pocked path, rims of snow collapsed onto my legs and ankles. Once inside headquarters, I stomped and brushed the snow off my pant legs and creviced leather shoes. Elisabeth sat waiting in the visitors' room, looking cozy and stylish in a black wool coat with a fox-fur collar.

"I mailed a package for you last week," Elisabeth said. "Did you get it?"

"No, I received no package." I hugged myself to ward off the chill, soaking up the relative warmth of the room. If I stayed long enough, my shoes and flimsy pants might even dry out.

"Oh, dear. It was a calendar, socks, and panforte. If I'd known I'd be coming again before Christmas, I'd have brought it instead."

I pictured the panforte, dense and sweet, full of nuts and fruit and spices. How wonderful it would have been to sink my teeth into its richness and share some with Luisa and Marianna. "Well, I'm sure you'll soon receive a thank-you note from the guards."

"I'll count on it," said Elisabeth, tucking her cheek into a mock smile. "Do you get cold here?"

"Only when I'm not working."

"And at night?"

"We've been issued a second blanket."

Elisabeth compressed her lips. Her throat rose and fell with a swallow. "I received a letter from your brother."

"My Henri! How is he?"

Elisabeth's words stumbled out. "He's . . . he's fine."

"There's something wrong, isn't there?"

"I'm sorry to tell you. Your father died this past July. In a Japanese detention camp. He was too ill to leave Batavia before the Japanese overran it."

———

Gone—my dear, kind father. This cruel war had robbed me of the chance to comfort him in his last months. And if I hadn't been locked up in this cursed camp, I might have even helped him flee ahead of the invasion. But innocents be damned, Hitler, Mussolini, and Hirohito must conquer their empires. Why had so many failed to thwart the rise of these depraved dictators?

I couldn't even share my grief with my brother. So, I plodded, bitter and distracted, through my hours in the infirmary, only forgetting my grief when I gave myself over to comforting the sick.

Late one night, a few days after Christmas, I bent over a prisoner who'd cut his leg in the metal-sorting room, trying to calm his fevered thrashing. His wound had festered, poisoning his body, and now his heart beat fiercely against his bony ribs. I smoothed my hand over his brow and muttered, "I'm here with you." But the miserable desperation of life's last grasp trapped him, and he writhed and railed against death. When he dropped into unconsciousness, I summoned a guard. "He won't live through the night."

The guard agreed. "I'll call a priest."

The guards never troubled priests from nearby towns for last rites, instead summoning one of the camp's priests. This time, it was Father Matteo.

While Father ministered to the man, I held his slack hand. Matteo finished the last rites, returned the crucifix, candle, and oil to their storage box, and started up out of his seat.

"No," I said. "I can put it away. Please sit with us awhile."

He sat down again, facing me across the patient's bed.

I asked, "Do you think he heard your prayers?"

"It doesn't matter. God heard."

I studied the man's pallid face, his expression finally calm. "Is his death a mercy or a tragedy? What would Christ say?"

"We cannot know God's ways or reasons."

Something inside me went limp, as if my heart were sagging. "How can we even know there are ways or reasons?"

"I've tried to explain it to you, Toto. We can only have faith."

The image that haunted me of late—my father, alone in some miserable camp, reaching out to me—rose before me, and a torrent of sadness flooded me. "My father died last July."

"I'm sorry, Toto."

"It was after the Japanese took over. They put him in a detention camp, even though he was weak with cancer. He probably died a miserable death."

"I know you loved him very much."

"And I couldn't be with him." A vice-like force gripped my chest. "And this war keeps on killing. For what?"

"I can't explain it. Who can?"

I hunched over the man and looked into his fleshy lids. "*Sì*, I know that only too well."

"We cannot know God's design for any of us."

I looked around, taking in the infirmary, every one of its beds occupied. As winter had dragged on, more and more prisoners had contracted pneumonia. There weren't enough beds in the infirmary for all of them. If brought here earlier, the relative warmth of the infirmary might have saved some. Instead, their coughs worsened in their freezing barracks, and only when they collapsed from weakness were they brought here. "Can God have a design when this happens?"

"Your fury at God is misdirected."

"My fury at Mussolini hasn't done any good, either."

"Don't," Father Matteo said. "Don't torment yourself so."

"How can you believe in God when the Fascists ruin all these lives?"

"I believe in the goodness of God. We're all tested. Even Jesus was tested."

"Aren't the Catholic guards and all the other Catholic Fascists violating God's will?"

"In so doing, they blacken their souls."

"Don't they have confessors? Don't you and the other priests stand up to them?"

"The confessional is not the place for that." Father Matteo reached out and gripped my hand. "This bitterness of yours. It helps no one. What would your father have you do?"

His question, so unpredictable and sudden, startled me—like a flash of bright light. I closed my eyes and summoned a picture of my father. I imagined him taking my hand and holding my gaze, imploring me with gleaming eyes: "Put your anger to work, Toto. Honor your mother's brave spirit. Stop and think. You are smart enough to find a way forward."

I opened my eyes and squeezed Father Matteo's hand. "Thank you for making me think of what to do now."

"So, I am your friend after all, not just a priest whose religion you resist?"

"Yes, you're my friend. And a fellow partisan." Of course, it was more complicated than that. But I had neither the luxury of time nor hospitable circumstances to expand on that. Because he was a priest, his religion and vows constituted a wall between us. Then it dawned on me: I could make use of Father Matteo's priestly status—to carry on my work. "Tell me, can you find out who Pietro Badoglio's confessor is?"

"I think so. There's a monsignor from Rome in the camp."

"Good. That may prove valuable." And if I obtained this information, I'd find a way to get it out.

"Valuable? How?"

"You know it's best not to discuss these matters."

He brought my hand to his lips and kissed it. "This is the Toto your father and mother would be proud of."

I looked into his eyes, aglow with compassion I neither expected nor knew how to acknowledge.

MASSA MARTANA
DETENTION CAMP
JANUARY 1943

Under the unchanging January sky of clouds, I marched to the infirmary, cold and hunched over. This month marked two years since the Fascists had captured me. Ten months since they'd transferred me to Camp Massa Martana.

Over seven hundred days of my life had been squandered. In that time, thousands of others' lives destroyed: brothers, fathers, and husbands forced into grisly slaughter; frightened boys pitted against blundering soldiers; and innocent bystanders annihilated by promiscuous bombs. All to feed the wanton appetites of Hitler, Mussolini, and Hirohito for glory and empire. Three men, it took just these men—and the countless minions who executed their cruel orders—to turn the world upside down.

Only by believing the Allies would vanquish their enemies could I go on. Because here I was, trapped, unable to help myself, let alone others. No, I mustn't torture myself about matters I couldn't control. I must be grateful to be alive, grateful I might live to escape.

With each beat of my shoes against the uneven frozen ground, pain coursed through my soles and inflamed my chilblains. I burst through the door of the infirmary and paused to soak up its sudden warmth. Taking in the rows of beds occupied by the hopeful and despairing, I thought: *Father died in a place like this, in a camp designed to cage and confine. And here you all are now, far from your loved ones. I am the one who must be strong for each of you, my mortal family.*

A man who lay nearby turned his lolling head toward me. With trembling fingers, he lifted an arm and reached out. Something about his expression struck me—his face was pallid yet serene, his eyes so gray they were nearly translucent, and his pupils were fixed and steady. That look, eyelids drooping but gaze direct as a beam, shot through me, as urgent as a baby's cry.

I hadn't thought of music—that comforting old friend—in ages, but now strains of Wagner's "Liebestod" shuddered through me, ethereal and transcendent as wisps of fog. I knelt by the man and wrapped my fingers around his hand. He relaxed into my grip. I cupped my other hand over the man's cool cheek.

Death, I will not shrink from you. In you, I will find the purpose to live. For this is what it means to love. And love will conquer hate. It must. Finally, I saw how to rise above my bitterness and hatred. I even grasped the wisdom of Father Matteo's words: It is faith in goodness that gives us hope.

MASSA MARTANA DETENTION CAMP

FEBRUARY–JUNE 1943

n early February, word raced around the camp: Germany had surrendered to Russia. Was it only a rumor? No, everyone claimed it was true. Luisa's daughter even confirmed the news during a visit. And judging by the guards' hectic conferences and preoccupied manner, it portended fateful change. Maybe, just maybe, the tide had turned. Maybe Germany and Italy were in retreat.

I asked Elisabeth at the first opportunity during an early March visit. "What does it mean, Russia defeating Germany?"

"It's hard to say. Hitler vows to fight on. And Mussolini is cleansing his cabinet of those he doesn't trust."

That was as much as Elisabeth could convey, but it was enough. I dared not hope for a speedy end to the war. No, I cautioned myself: You must take matters into your own hands. You must watch for a chance to escape.

March brought not only signs of spring—garden duty for me, the sprouting of weeds around the grounds, and the scent of effluvium long trapped in cold latrines—but also a sort of buzzing impatience among both prisoners and guards. The women in my barrack openly prayed for the end of this miserable war. Some dared to speculate the whole camp would be disbanded; others rushed to tamp down what they considered wild speculation. The guards huddled in small groups while they kept watch, ignoring what must have been a standing order to avoid distractions. The commandant limited visiting days to two a month, perhaps fearing he'd lose control over the increasing numbers of visitors.

I wrote Elisabeth, informing her of the changed visiting policy, and took to stopping by the mailroom frequently to drop off letters to her and check for any letters from her. A few different guards staffed the office, and one was actually polite, even affable. Whenever I found Nino Voci there by himself, I ventured a few kind words.

"Nino, is your home far from here?"

Nino, a lanky youth who appeared to be no more than twenty, wore a wooden leg, which was especially evident when he tried to stand, for he listed to one side while his artificial foot sought solid ground. "*Sì*, Camini, in Calabria."

"Why are you posted so far from your village?"

"There's no camp there, and I don't qualify for the regular army."

"That's good. Your mama doesn't have to worry too much," I said, coaxing a shy smile from him.

I also risked more and more with my friends, Luisa and Marianna, as they did with me. They discussed their homes and families. Luisa, a widow even before the war, would go back to her daughters and grandchildren in Perugia. Marianna evaded questions about her husband (I imagined he, too, was an imprisoned partisan) but said she would return to Faenza to care for her younger brother and sisters. I told them Florence was my destination. Only I doubted it'd be wise to return there; my presence might endanger Dominic, Alfonso, and my other comrades. Still, the prospect of freedom sustained me. It mattered little where I ended up. That I could decide later.

Gradually and tentatively, prisoners across the camp speculated about how the war might end. One Sunday in April, while I walked the yard with Luisa and Marianna, talk turned to the popular subjects of post-war Italy, what sort of peace it might have, and how life would be different after Fascism.

"The end could come soon," I said, though I knew better than to hope for too much. "Eventually, Mussolini's generals will tire of following his suicidal orders."

Luisa walked between the two of us, hunched forward in the crouch of the elderly. She'd weakened noticeably in the last several months, so now Marianna and I each took her by an arm to help her along.

Luisa said, "If the Action Party captures Mussolini, they'll let the people try him."

Marianna caught Luisa's eye. "They should join with the Communist Party and the other resistance groups to depose Mussolini and rebuild Italy."

Ah, I thought, *now the allegiances of my fellow prisoners surface.*

"Hah," said Luisa, tossing her head to clear stray strands of gray hair from her face. "You think the Allies will let Italy decide its fate?"

I said, "Churchill and Roosevelt should seek unconditional surrenders. To show the world this can never happen again."

"It's Germany they should punish," said Marianna. "Hitler's the one who wanted to take over all of Europe."

I said, "We'll see the true mettle of the victors when this is all over."

"They can start by breaking down the walls of this miserable place," said Marianna.

"Amen to that," chimed Luisa.

———

I had a brief letter from Elisabeth in May, but it said nothing of when she might next visit. I surmised Elisabeth, too, was caught up in the foment sweeping Italy—the workers' strikes and general unrest.

Finally, in June, after an absence of nearly three months, Elisabeth again visited. "I'm sorry it's been so long. I came last month; there were so many in line, they turned me away."

"The visitors are coming in hordes. They smell change."

Elisabeth bounced her gaze off the guard strolling behind me. "And I've been preoccupied with my studies."

Oh, my, I thought. *Will we only be able to discuss humdrum matters?* "When will you complete your program of study?"

"I wish I knew. There are so many distractions." Elisabeth, usually the picture of patience, drummed her fingers on the table.

I sensed Elizabeth wished to convey some message. I leaned back in my chair, adopting a detached bearing and hoping to signal the guards that our conversation meant nothing. "So, the thesis must wait?"

"I've had to go to Florence to meet Professor Frascati."

Why, I wondered, mention the professor? The Fascists had long ago banished him from the university. He could serve no purpose in her formal studies. I asked, "And how is the professor?"

"He's very sad these days. He's no longer writing about art history, and you know that gave him much satisfaction."

I still couldn't grasp what Elisabeth might be communicating. Perhaps she was referring to the occasional partisan circulars Alfonso wrote for *Principî.* "Do you mean those art essays Domenica sometimes asked him to write?"

"Yes, sadly, there's no place for his essays anymore."

"No place?" Could it be—*Principî* shut down? "Has the journal closed?"

"Yes, that university office they used for the journal ran out of money."

My God, that is what she meant. But Dominic wouldn't close the press unless forced to do so. I bent forward and probed my friend's expression. "But it meant so much to Domenica."

"I just don't know any other way to tell you this." Elisabeth angled her head into a sympathetic slant. "Domenica is dead. It happened at the office. A terrible accident. While she was moving some supplies."

"No," I gasped. "It can't be."

"It is terrible to lose someone so young and healthy."

I slumped over the table and clutched my stomach, trying to contain the crushing anguish washing over me. "I can hardly believe this."

Elisabeth nodded and sat quietly.

Tears pushed against my eyelids. I stifled a moan surging up my gullet. Don't cry, I told myself. I concentrated on inhaling and exhaling, slowly and deliberately.

The guard behind me held stubbornly to his post.

Elisabeth placed her hands on the table and wove her fingers together. Bowing her head, she whispered, "I'm so sorry."

I cupped my palms tightly on my lap, hiding them under the table, summoning composure. I mustn't show weakness; some of the guards took pleasure in sniffing it out—as if it justified their baseless grip on authority. I shook off my distress. "When you next visit Florence, you must convey my condolences to her family and those who knew her."

"I will. They're all in shock. No one even wants to go near the office to put things in order."

I knew that probably meant the Blackshirts had destroyed the printing press. They'd shut down *Principî*. And probably murdered Dominic.

Fast on the heels of that thought came another: Might Dominic have been tortured into naming comrades? I asked Elisabeth, "Did she suffer much?"

"No. She died quickly."

After my visit with Elisabeth, I marched back to the garden plot, knelt between the rows, and plunged my hands among the tender tomato plants, tugging out the weeds trying to choke them. I allowed some tears to dribble out, then told myself to stop. The day was warm, and I'd not take water again until dusk.

Thoughts of Dominic raced through my mind—about what he might have felt his last minutes, whether he'd had any warning. Perhaps he'd fought to the death rather than allow them to capture him. It would have been like him, to be brave when the final test came. He wouldn't have wanted to give his comrades away. My dear, brave Dominic.

Still, the Fascists might hunt down others in Florence. If anyone named me, I'd never be released, not unless the Allies prevailed—*and* reached the camp ahead of the Fascists.

The Fascists. Such bloodthirsty miscreants, murdering Dominic because he worked to free his country from their perverse grip. Who gave this order? Mussolini himself probably didn't bother with the thousands of partisans trying to undermine him, but, instead, charged his underlings with ferreting them out. Why did they obey him? To curry favor, to ensure their place among his lackeys, or to avoid the same fate as his enemies?

If I'd come face to face with Dominic's murderers, I'd have fired on them— to save Dominic and myself. At least I'd been trained to do that, almost without thinking. And if I'd killed someone, could I be sure it was not an innocent, someone like Nino who'd been forced into service? Bloody hell, I hated the horrid vagaries of this war—how it turned black and white into ever-darkening shades of gray.

No, I'd not torture myself with such riddles. What I knew for sure was that Dominic, a brave and righteous man, was dead.

Dominic, my darling, I will do all I can to avenge you. I don't have the means now. But I promise you: I'll never give up trying.

DISPATCH

3 July 1943

The commandant of subject's camp has clamped down on visitors. No viable release or escape strategies yet identified.

WD

MASSA MARTANA DETENTION CAMP

JULY–AUGUST 1943

By late July, sun baked the yard's grounds to rusty brown, and news of Italy's manifold military defeats spread. Sweating guards paced nervously as they watched over us. Barrack inspections increased, and the commandant suspended visits. Rumors circulated that outsiders conducting business with the camp (produce buyers, coffin makers, and, undoubtedly, black marketers) had started haggling for better prices.

The charged atmosphere naturally agitated us. We completed work assignments hastily. We speculated wildly about the unsettled state of the camp: Because of all the strikes in the cities, the military was afraid prisoners, too, would rise up; the commandant didn't trust the guards to keep order in the visiting room; Mussolini was losing his grip; if there was a coup, the guards might turn on the commandant.

Now is the time, I thought, *to be watchful, with the camp in relative disarray.* I ached for freedom—and revenge—with a longing as fierce as hunger. Damn the bloodthirsty fascists who'd ordered Dominic's assassination. For what empty end did they kill? With each outrageous murder of their own citizens, they proved their dissolute lust for power. Surely, many of the Italian people saw this—that Mussolini and his thugs were their enemies, not the champions they'd claimed to be.

In late July, at a time Nino Voci was likely to be alone, I visited the mailroom. "Why all the excitement, Nino?"

"You haven't heard? Yesterday Mussolini was overthrown."

Hell and hallelujah, finally. And now, the assignment Winston Churchill had given me meant something. "Who has taken over?"

"Today, Pietro Badoglio. Tomorrow, who knows?"

"Will the prisoners be released?"

"There's no word on that."

Amazing. At last, Mussolini was ousted. And Badoglio in. It was as I'd hoped: someone the British might work with, someone who'd be keen to side with the victor and spare his neck. I'd learned a great deal about Badoglio from Galeazzo, and now, if only I could establish some communication, I could get this information out.

When I returned to the barrack, I discovered news of Mussolini's downfall had already spread through the camp: "Have you heard? Il Duce is out. The King had him arrested."

That marked the beginning of weeks of news and conjecture: The Allies had invaded southern Italy and seized Sicily. Soon they would liberate the camp. The end of the war was in sight.

My fellow prisoners and I waited, abuzz with anticipation. Still, nothing happened, not until mid-August, when guards posted notices on the canteen building: "Prisoners will be released at noon on Thursday, with exceptions as listed." Everyone crowded around the announcements, scanning the prisoner numbers, whooping or muttering prayers of gratitude when they found they weren't on the exemptions list.

I elbowed my way through the throng to the list of well over a hundred numbers. That'd be about one in twenty prisoners. Most of us would be released! Once close enough, I scanned the columns.

And there it was—my number. Curse my bloody bad luck. Why? Why must I stay? I clamped my jaw and turned to walk away. *I must think of a way out, perhaps on release day; the camp will be in chaos then.*

As I edged back through the clot, I caught myself. I'd forgotten to check for Luisa's number. She'd been moved to the infirmary and was too weak to venture out. I stood on tiptoes and squinted at the list. No, Luisa's number wasn't on it. At least *she* would go free.

The guards had apparently given up on getting us to our assignments. Prisoners scurried, like a colony of busy ants, around the camp. How could this throng be contained for three more days? Why not let them leave now?

I rushed to Father Matteo's barrack. He wasn't there. Perhaps he'd gone to his work assignment at the canteen. It'd be like him—to get on with the cooking and food preparation. Everyone still needed to eat. First, I stopped at the infirmary to give Luisa the news.

"In three days, you will walk out of here." I cupped my palm over Luisa's cheek. Her cool skin drew the heat from my hand.

"You, too." Luisa's mouth clucked with dryness.

"No, I'm an exception. I stay."

"Why?"

"I wish I knew." Would the Fascists keep the camp open with its population so reduced? It made no sense to run a big camp like this for only a hundred-some prisoners.

Luisa looked at me through slitted eyes. "Water."

I fetched a cup of water from the bucket, braced Luisa up, and held the cup to her lips. "We must get you strong again. For your family. Shall we get word to them about your release?"

"*Sì.*"

"After you eat, we'll write a letter."

I found Father Matteo in the canteen kitchen, washing utensils, metal bowls, and pots.

I sidled up to him as he cleaned one of the stubby-bladed knives allowed only in the kitchen. "Can I help?"

"No, it's not allowed." Matteo hunched over the grimy washbasin and spoke under his breath. "Do you believe it? Finally, prisoners released."

"I'm on the list of exemptions." I whispered, for guards always kept a close eye on the kitchen workers—especially today, perhaps wary of rebellion.

Father clanged a pot against the basin and rushed out his words. "Me, too. And Badoglio declares the war will go on."

A darting-eyed guard approached and questioned me. "What are you doing here? This isn't your work duty, is it?"

"No, I'm from the infirmary. I'm ordered to bring a pot of stew to the sick." The guards called what we ate stew, but it was only soup.

"Then get on with it." He bounced his head toward the door.

I ladled some soup—it looked like a broth with turnips or potatoes and onions—into a kettle, covered it, and lugged it out the door. Weighted down with the load, I walked, wobbly and wide-legged, to the infirmary. I fed Luisa as much as I could get her to swallow and begged paper and pen off the infirmary guard. It took nearly a half-hour to get a letter written; Luisa was too weak to speak in anything but short bursts.

Finally, I addressed the envelope to Luisa's daughter Gina and delivered it to the mailroom. "Nino, will this go out today? It's to Perugia."

"*Si*, that's a one-day delivery."

———

On the day of release, hundreds of prisoners thronged the gate, edging forward with their puny bundles of belongings, animated and charged with chattery energy. I squeezed through the columns of gray-uniformed prisoners and made my way to the infirmary.

"Luisa, it's time. I'll walk you to the gate."

"I'm too weak." Luisa raised herself on an elbow and yanked at the bottom of her shirt. "Take my number. Get yourself out."

Santo Cielo! A chance to get out. All I had to do was exchange shirts with Luisa. I could blend in with the crowd and flash Luisa's number at the guard. No more days of fear and deprivation, no more wasting away. I'd be free.

Careful, I told myself, *you must think this through.* "But your daughter will be waiting for you. She'll expect you."

Luisa spoke with wispy faintness. "Call for Gina Lanzi. She's short, with red hair."

Oh, the shame I felt—over being so tempted. If Luisa didn't get out now, she'd probably die here. But if she went home to her family, they might nurse her back to health. Or maybe her illness had already doomed her to mere weeks of life. But me, I had work to do; I should get out. I might not get another chance like this.

Only it meant weighing the value of my life against Luisa's, and something about that repulsed me. "No, I'll walk you to the gate."

Luisa flopped down. "I'm too weak."

"I'll get some help."

I set out at a lope. Had fate intervened for me? If so, I ought not to dismiss this opportunity. For months I'd racked my brain, trying to think of a way out. And now, Luisa had handed it to me—a short and simple walk to freedom. Surely, she wouldn't have made the offer if she didn't mean it. It could work. All I had to do was keep calm, allow the guards to check Luisa's number, and recite her name.

Unless they caught me sneaking out in Luisa's place, then neither of us would be released. *Mio Dio,* I must think, I must sort this out.

I found Father Matteo in his barrack. Out of breath, I sucked hard at the stuffy air. I couldn't decide what to do. Then again, I was here, wasn't I? Had my legs made the decision for me? "Come, I need your help. With Luisa."

I dragged along beside Matteo as we rushed to the infirmary. My legs and lungs ached from the exertion, and still, I hadn't decided, at least not definitely. I could ask Matteo what he thought about Luisa's offer. But, no, even forming the question felt crass and hypocritical, as if I were plotting a Judas kiss.

I sat Luisa up in her bed, hugged her slight body close, and slowly lifted her. Matteo looped Luisa's arm around his neck and wrapped his arm around her waist. I took her other side, and together we trudged along the dirt-packed path, weaving among the barracks. Whenever my energy flagged, we stopped to rest, then propped Luisa up between us again and shuffled on.

We lowered her to the ground at the edge of the assembled clot, where she sat and crumpled forward over her knees. Matteo started into the crowd, turning to say, "Stay here. I'll find someone to help."

I sat down beside Luisa and pulled her close. "You'll get well now, my dear Luisa. Your daughter will take care of you."

Matteo returned with two men. "They're from Perugia, too. They'll get her out the gate."

"My daughter?" Luisa asked.

One of the men stooped by her side. "We'll help you find her."

I hugged Luisa and kissed her cheeks. "You're a brave woman. I'll miss you."

Luisa whispered to me, "Thank you for your goodness."

A twinge of shame brought tears to my eyes. I'd come so close to erasing all the kindnesses I'd ever shown Luisa.

The two men made a basket of their arms, lifted Luisa, and disappeared into the mingling crowd.

Father Matteo and I dropped back and took up a position where we could watch the prisoners funnel out. Small groupings shuttled through the checkpoint, like sand trickling through an hourglass, and dispersed into the excited crowd outside the gate. I could hear the shouts and cheers of the reunited, gleeful as children on holiday.

I leaned against the wall. A crushing wave of despair engulfed me. I could have been among those leaving. Instead, I'd surrendered myself to uncertainty. Was it that Nazi Lieutenant Wolff's order that kept me imprisoned? For all I knew, a fate worse than imprisonment awaited me—hanging over my head like the damnable sword of Damocles.

Matteo, with eyes fixed on the departing crowd, spoke as if to no one, "I tried to buy someone else's number to get out."

My breath escaped. He was confessing to me. Confessing the very transgression I'd considered. "And you were refused?"

He dropped his head; his shoulders caved. "Yes, and now I must live with my shame. And pray for forgiveness."

I'd never seen him so helpless, as withered as a boy who'd failed the first test of manhood. "I was tempted, too. Luisa offered to let me use her number."

Matteo turned to me, his expression a map of humiliation. "But here you are. May God grant me as much compassion."

I smoothed a hand over his shoulder. "It's this place and the depraved Fascists who rob us of our humanity."

He crumpled into my arms. "I'm afraid. Afraid of what this place is turning me into. Please share your courage with me."

All the tears I'd restrained—over the loss of my father and Dominic, over my struggle not to take Luisa's place—broke. I clutched him close and spoke through my thickened throat, "And I need your belief in some kind of goodness now. Or I won't be able to go on."

"May God give me the faith to share that with you."

"I'm afraid, too."

Matteo rested his cheek on the top of my head. "Let me do penance by showing you I can be strong for both of us, my friend."

I pulled back enough to lift my face to his and meet his eyes. "We'll take care of each other now. We must. For we don't know what the Fascists have in store for us."

MASSA MARTANA DETENTION CAMP

AUGUST–SEPTEMBER 1943

The rest of the day, the guards and remaining prisoners rattled around the camp like dazed inhabitants of a dying village. The commandant hastily reshuffled prisoner duties, and I was told to report to the garden in the morning to help bring in the last of the harvest and clear out the wilting greenery. Preparing the garden for another planting season struck me as ridiculous, with the future of the camp so uncertain. Perhaps, in the wake of Mussolini's fall, the commandant wished to bolster his precarious command by carrying on like a good soldier.

How lonely the camp felt that evening. My barrack was reduced to two, myself and the petite, dark-freckled Marianna. Had Marianna's proclivities for Partito Comunista doomed her? Bloody hell, I didn't know why I was being held, let alone any of the others.

Marianna sat down on the cot across from me. "Will you take a different bed?"

"I'm ill accustomed to so much choice." I looked around at the empty beds, the bare walls, the floor worn smooth from shuffling feet. Quiet hung in the air like a thick cloak. In the stillness, the stench from the barrack's dug-out toilet clung all the more to my nostrils. "The bed in the corner might be quiet. Or the one under the window could be cooler at night."

Marianna swiveled her gaze around the barrack. "Who knows how long we'll be here."

I put on a wry grin. "Maybe we should put up some nice wallpaper and a few paintings. Bring in fresh flowers every day."

Marianna smiled weakly. My attempt to cheer her had failed. Her shoulders rose and fell with a thick sigh. "I heard the Germans are coming to take over the camp."

"Heaven help us," I said. "We can only hope that's not true."

—•—

The day after the big release, following the morning roll call, I caught up with Father Matteo on his way to the canteen. "There's a rumor the Germans will take over the camp."

"I heard the same from a barrack mate."

"Marianna had it from a guard. I should see if Nino knows anything more."

"We've got to get out of here." He shook his head. "Can you find out when the Germans will move in?"

"I'll try. Do you have a plan?"

"Not yet. But we must come up with one."

My thoughts turned to Marianna, whom I knew to be a dedicated partisan. If I helped anyone out, it should be her. But Matteo and I had pledged to take care of each other. Only I didn't know if I could count on him. Would a priest have the courage—or conviction—to fight if it came to that?

I marched off to garden duty and knelt in the rows, plucking out carrots and beets, tossing them in a wooden crate, and dragging the cumbersome load behind me. Signs of fall's onset surrounded the camp—the smell of dying leaves, the crackle of desiccation, and the slow-to-warm morning air. All that and a heart-sinking dread weighed on me. I'd heard the reports: of the cruelty and destruction the German war machine visited on the vanquished.

At the mid-day meal, I gulped down a larger than usual helping of farro gruel—the kitchen hadn't yet adjusted to the greatly reduced number of prisoners—and scurried to the mailroom. On my way there I spied the mail lorry leaving. The mail was still moving.

Nino was not alone. Another guard sat on his desk, smoking and making jolly talk. They turned and eyed me.

"Good afternoon," I said. Damn, I couldn't pump Nino for information. I needed an excuse for turning up. "I'm expecting a letter today."

Nino stood and strolled to the back room, where the mail was sorted. I eyed the floor and shifted my weight from one foot to the other. I preferred to make myself unknown to guards, except any that might be sympathetic, like Nino.

I could feel the guard's eyes on me. I clasped my moist hands in front of me to quell their quivering.

He asked, "Where are you from?"

"Florence."

The bulgy-eyed man swung his leg loosely from the knee; his boot clicked against the desk. "No, I mean, where were you born?"

I hated this question, loath as I was to give out information that might arouse curiosity. But Nino was still checking the mail. Maybe I could get him off this topic. "Indonesia. You sound like you're from the North."

He ignored my unspoken question. "Your Italian is good. Where did you learn it?"

"As a schoolgirl." I lifted my gaze long enough to catch his eye. "When do you get to leave the camp?"

"Maybe next week."

Nino, with his lopsided gait, came to the doorway. "No, nothing for you today."

"Grazie," I said, turning sharply and hurrying off.

God rot them, I thought, the guards have so little to do now they just entertain each other. But at least I'd gathered some sense of when the Germans might arrive.

And then an idea struck me. Perhaps I could escape on the mail lorry. It'd be risky; it'd require good timing, luck, and Nino's cooperation, albeit unintended. But I couldn't succeed without a man to play the role of guard. I'd need Matteo's assistance. And with the Nazis on the way, I had no choice but to risk it. And little time to waste.

———

Two days later, Father Matteo and I visited the mailroom, just before the midday delivery. I had told Matteo we'd need a knife, and he'd managed to swipe one from the kitchen. It was a blunt-nosed thing, but better than nothing, and we'd decided he should be the one to wield it.

I'd asked him, "Can you use it if necessary?"

"I think so."

I could only hope his nerves wouldn't fail him. "You'll have to wrestle Nino under control. I'm not strong enough now."

Blessing of blessings, we found Nino in the mailroom by himself.

Nino, friendly as ever, greeted us with a smile. "Hello, Toto, Father."

"Nino," I asked, "can we help get the mail ready?"

He gave me a puzzled look; prisoners weren't allowed to sort mail. "It's already done."

"Can we see?" Matteo asked, heading for the forbidden back room.

"No." Nino quickly stood to block Matteo's way. He faltered on his wooden leg and gripped the desk edge to keep his balance.

Matteo twirled around to Nino's backside. He snared Nino's neck in the crook of his arm and held the knife to his throat. I lunged and grabbed the gun from his holster.

"Don't move," Matteo commanded. "I've got a knife."

I pulled back a few steps, aiming the gun at Nino. "Just do as we say. We don't want to hurt you."

Nino stiffened. "What do you want?"

"We only want out of this place, and you're going to help us."

"I won't."

"You will," I said. "Take off your uniform."

"And if I don't?"

Matteo brought the knife to Nino's throat. "I'll slit your throat."

"You won't get away with it."

I backed off a step and aimed the gun at him. "Off with your uniform."

"No, I won't."

Matteo's eyes widened as if questioning me. Oh, hell, not now. Matteo was losing his nerve. I must be the one to act.

I shook the gun, aiming it at his head. "Don't make me use this."

"You're crazy. Everyone will hear."

He was right—I couldn't fire on him—and he knew it. I shifted my grip to the gun's barrel, moved in, and swung it. Thud, it landed on the side of Nino's head, above his ear.

Nino crumpled to his knees. His eyes swam loosely in their sockets. This wasn't the plan, but Matteo had left me no choice.

I grabbed a tuft of Nino's hair and held on tightly, jerking his lolling head up. I slapped the gun on the desk and said to Matteo, "Take it, and give me the knife."

Matteo handed off the knife and grabbed the gun.

I held the knife against Nino's throat. "Now, take off your shirt and pants."

Slowly and clumsily, Nino unbuttoned his shirt.

Matteo set the gun aside, knelt beside Nino, and knocked his hands away. "I'll do it."

Thank God, I thought, *Matteo's found some backbone.*

A groggy Nino let Matteo yank off his shirt. Then Matteo removed Nino's belt and holster and undid and stripped off Nino's pants. Matteo tugged his flimsy pants off. He used one leg of his prisoner's pants to tie Nino's hands behind his back, the other to strap his legs together.

Matteo shucked off his shirt, ripped off the identification number, and outfitted himself in Nino's uniform. He gagged Nino with his prisoner's shirt.

I unloosed Nino's hair, hurried to the back room, and retrieved an empty mail sack. I wiggled it around Nino's feet, ordering him, "Get in."

Matteo pushed Nino low into the sack, knotted its top, and shoved the bundled Nino under his desk.

I gently brushed my hand over Nino's head. "Keep quiet and you'll be fine. If I hear a whimper out of you, I'll use the gun again. Remember, your mama is waiting for you to come home."

I shook a finger at the gun Matteo had slid into his holster, hoping he'd understand he must use it if necessary.

Matteo and I let ourselves into the back room. I wriggled into one of the mail bags, and Matteo tugged it closed. I tucked my knees up against my chest and concentrated on slowing my ragged breathing.

I heard Matteo walk out to the office and speak to Nino. "When you're found, you must say two men overpowered you. That they hid their numbers. It'll be better for you that way."

Finally, he'd remembered our plan. The escape was in his hands now. Damnation, I hated hitting Nino. I hadn't wanted to harm him, but Matteo's hesitation had forced my hand. With each slowly marching minute, I silently pled, *Matteo, please, just do as we planned.*

Finally, I heard the rumble of the lorry shifting gears and maneuvering into place, then the clunk of its engine halting. Matteo hurried into the sorting room and shut the door to the office. He opened the dock doors and whispered, "Get ready."

I gripped my arms tight around my legs and tucked my head to make myself compact. I heard the lorry gate drop and felt Matteo dragging me. He slid me onto the lorry bed. Thank God he had the strength to move me. Being on kitchen duty had helped him keep on most of his weight. And I'd lost weight; I was as skinny as I'd been as a youngster.

The lorry's cab door opened. A gruff, unfamiliar voice asked, "No Nino today?"

Matteo closed the dock door. "Everybody's getting shifted around. It's been a free-for-all. In fact, I'm to go with you today. To get a report filed."

"It'll be tight in the cab."

"Don't worry about me," Matteo said. "I'll travel in the back."

Matteo stepped onto the lorry bed. Up swung the tailgate. The cab door slammed shut. I felt Matteo's body against mine as he sat down. The lorry's tires bit the road, halted, and twisted as the lorry swerved away from the dock. Clang sounded the camp's gate. We'd made it out of the camp.

The lorry picked up speed on the straightaway as if freed of its ballast. I reveled in the dusty scent of the road, its dry earthiness, even the stink of exhaust.

We must have traveled eight to ten kilometers when Matteo loosened the cord of my sack. "We're coming up on a twist in the road, to the left. Roll into the ditch on the right."

I felt his hands pulling the bag down past my shoulders. I lifted my hands out of the sack and, laying down on my side, pulled it over my legs and feet. I dropped the knife into the sack. The lorry slowed as it bounced over a gully.

"Now," he said.

He rolled himself over the tailgate, keeping his profile low. I copied his movement. With a clunk, I hit the packed earth and rolled with the shock of it. On elbows and knees, I scrambled into the ditch several feet from Matteo. I heard the lorry slowing down. Had the driver noticed the lightening of the load?

I hunkered down in the culvert and whispered to Matteo. "Keep low."

I couldn't see from the ditch, but then the lorry's occupants couldn't see us either, unless they backed up.

Then I heard the truck trundle ahead.

I could hardly believe it: The plan was working. So far.

After a minute, all was quiet. I knelt and peeked up and down the road. No vehicles. "Let's go. Southwest, you say?"

"*Sì*," he pointed to the horizon. "To those mountains."

We hurried into the brushy countryside, baked powder-dry by late summer's heat. I checked the gloomy clouds ahead. Rain might obscure our movements, but the thought of a downpour chilled me. We steered clear of the occasional house or villa, sometimes slipping between rows of grapevines to make our way undetected. How would we ever explain ourselves—me in a prison uniform and Matteo in a guard's outfit? Then again, Italy was in chaos just now, with the Allies advancing from the south and Mussolini ousted.

Once we'd walked a few kilometers, I stopped and slumped over. "I can't keep up this pace."

"But they could start looking for us any time."

"We'll go steady, but you must let me set the pace."

Matteo nodded and hung his head. "I almost ruined our plan back there, with Nino."

"But it worked." I straightened up and peered into his eyes. I needed him to be strong. "You have more endurance than I do. You must keep playing the good comrade."

"*Sì*," he nodded.

I stared into the brushy stretch of land between us and the mountains. I stepped forward, picking my way around the low-lying bushes. Matteo strode along beside me. I was grateful for his silence. I didn't wish to speak to him just now.

We walked on, shoulder to shoulder, the only sound the crackling brush under our feet. At the far-off roar of a vehicle, we hunkered down into a dry creek bed. I reached into the bag and grabbed the knife.

Tugging the corner of my number patch loose, I slit its threads and stripped it off. I shoved it in the sack.

I dropped the knife back in the sack and looked to Matteo. "You should turn that shirt inside out. It's giving me the heebie-jeebies."

He raised his head. "All clear."

We stood and brushed ourselves off. As we walked on, he stripped off the shirt, turned it inside out, and put it back on, leaving it unbuttoned. He looked all disarranged, his shirt showing its seams, a gun and holster on his hip, military pants a few inches too short, and beat-up shoes.

"Back there," he asked, "were you afraid you might have hurt Nino?"

"I never intended to kill Nino. But I've been taught how to strike to kill."

"Have you ever . . . ?"

I knew what he was asking, even if he couldn't get the word out. "No, I've never killed a man. God help me if I ever have to."

"I don't know if I could have done what you did," he said.

"I've been trained—to act, not think if my life depends on it. My problem is I sometimes can't stop thinking."

Matteo slipped his hands into his pockets. "What did you do to get arrested in the first place?"

"Honestly," I said, "they never found out what I did. The Fascists wanted to turn me. And you?"

"I hid resisters in the church. And got messages back and forth."

We trudged on through the countryside, avoiding roads and houses. My heart thumped with exhilaration. But my mouth was dry as sand, and my head throbbed—from hunger, thirst, and the jar and strain of slogging over the rough ground. When the rain started, I licked the rivulets off my arms to refresh myself. We rested frequently, but I couldn't decide which was worse—trudging along in wet clothes or pausing and catching a chill. At dusk, just as the rain let up, we came upon a farmer's property with a stone well.

"Let's stop here," I pleaded. "I can't go another step."

We gorged ourselves on well water, but that didn't satisfy my gnawing hunger. From a hedge beside the farmhouse, we kept watch on the goings-on. When lamps lit up inside the house and darkness obscured our movements, we crept up to the side of the house for a better view.

Matteo whispered, "It looks like just one woman."

I, too, had seen only a stocky older woman. She walked with a lilting gait, as if landing on wide-splayed feet, busying herself at chopping something on a countertop and throwing it into a skillet. "We'll frighten the wits out of her if we approach now. And maybe there's someone else inside. In another room."

"*Sì*," Matteo said. "We'd better wait until morning."

We picked a spot under the house eaves, in case the rain started again, spread out the sack, and bedded down on it. It was a lumpy bed, our clothes were damp, and the night was cold, but I snuggled against Matteo's back, and exhaustion overtook me. In the depths of darkness, I woke out of a twilight sleep, gasping, startled by a vision of the Nazis pummeling Marianna.

Matteo twisted around and looked at me, startle-eyed.

"Sorry," I whispered. "I was dreaming about Marianna."

"I was afraid you'd heard something."

"I can't stop thinking about all the others still in that place."

He shifted onto his back and pulled me into his arms. "*Sì*, I'm not surprised. You are full of compassion. Try to forget now. Don't torture yourself."

I let my head rest on his chest. Forget the others? No, it was easy to say but hard to do. And I suspected he knew it as well. "You're right. We do what we must."

Come morning, at the first signs of stirring within the house, I knocked on the door and stepped back. The woman cracked it open. At the sight of me, she asked, "Who are you?"

"*Signora*, I am newly released from the Detention Camp." I flashed the crumpled patch with my number on it, showing only a zero. "Can you spare some food for my companion and me?"

"What companion?"

"Him," I motioned to the corner of the house. "He didn't want to alarm you. He's a priest, a gentle priest."

Matteo stepped into view. He'd stashed the gun and holster in the mail sack and draped the sack over his shoulder to hide his shirt uniform. But his pants were obviously military issue. I hoped my gray prison garb would convince the woman we were in earnest.

The woman eyed Matteo, then turned back to me. She spoke without emotion. "If you'll help with chores, I'll give you some food. But you can't stay long. I don't want any trouble."

"*Grazie*," I said, "that will be fine."

Matteo did most of the helping. He cleaned up two rows of her garden, cultivated them, and planted garlic bulbs. Then he fixed a misaligned door frame and patched its gap, even humming while he worked. Such surprises, I thought. He'd always struck me as staid and pious, but circumstances sometimes brought out another side of people. Heaven knows the camp had put a damper on my usual joviality.

I had no strength for heavy work and asked if I might do some housekeeping. I swept the floors and washed windows while the *signora* prepared a late breakfast for us—eggs cooked with peppers, a half loaf of bread, even some ersatz coffee, probably of roasted acorn. It all tasted wonderful. After breakfast, Father Matteo said he'd like to bless some holy water for her. That inspired her to offer us some clothes—"things from my husband that I don't need anymore." Matteo buried his uniform and my prison clothes in a deep hole in the garden.

Then, provisioned with two bottles of water, a hunk of bread, four carrots, and two kohlrabis, we renewed our trek toward the mountains of Monti Martani. We planned to track down fellow partisans—before the encroaching Wehrmacht or Italian Carabinieri discovered us.

THE MONTI MARTANI MOUNTAINS

SEPTEMBER 1943

Matteo and I followed the winding route of the Tiber River south and west. At nightfall, we reached the outskirts of the village Corbara and bedded down on the grassy grounds of an olive grove. After a breakfast of water and bread, we started our trek from the river's plateau up the rocky ravine.

I struggled over the uneven terrain, cramming my worn leather shoes into footholds and grasping outcroppings with trembling hands. When I paused to mark my progress and look down the craggy slope, I imagined myself toppling down, and my stomach flipped. Turning to face the cliff, I scrambled on hands and knees up a rocky stretch until I reached a fern-laden patch of ground. I plopped down and called out, "I need to rest."

Matteo backtracked and eased down beside me. "Hard going?"

Nodding, I looped my arms around my knees and collapsed over them.

He undid our sack. "Food and water will revive you."

Huffing to catch my breath, I said, "I can hardly keep up with you."

"I managed extra helpings at the canteen. But you, you're skinny as a rail."

"You can't go barging ahead without me. I'm too weak."

"Fine. Now eat." He handed me a carrot.

I chewed slowly, but the bits landed like gravel on my belly. What was wrong with me? Perhaps my stomach needed time to appreciate raw food again.

Finally, after trudging through low brush and veering around dense thickets of oaks and beeches, we reached the mountain crest and a meandering trail.

I straightened up, tightened the rope holding up my loose trousers, and rubbed my palm over the small of my back. "That was exhausting."

"It'll be easier from here, and I doubt we'll meet any military," said Matteo. "You can lead. Go as slow as you want."

We plodded along the ridge, taking in the plunging ravines, forested slopes, and valleys below, here and there sidestepping rock lumps or striated cliffs. I hardly had the energy to hold up my head.

At the top of a rise, the vista opened to a bouldered meadow, and Matteo grabbed my arm from behind. "Stop."

I looked up. Eighty feet ahead stood two men, partly sheltered by a rock cluster, their rifles pointed at us. One of them hollered, "What are you doing here?"

In a flash, I knew: They were partisans. Reaching my arms high, I stepped forward. "Looking for you, comrades."

Faintness overtook me; pinpricks of light pierced my field of vision. I slumped to my knees. Everything went blank.

———

I woke, fuzzy-headed, lying on my back under a blanket. My stomach felt hollowed out, my body woozy. Voices drifted into focus like bubbles rising from deep waters.

I heard an unfamiliar voice, hurried and high-pitched. "If I could've gotten close enough to shoot, by God, I would've."

"Did you have a plan?" That was Matteo.

"I didn't need a plan, just a gun. But the men around me kept saying, it's not possible, he's in hiding, don't be stupid. They're the stupid ones—not listening to me. Ought to be ashamed of themselves. Where's their courage?"

"Maybe they wanted to have a sure plan."

"Damn cowards. The government had him, and they let him get away."

"He got away?"

"Hell, yes. Hitler's aces swooped in and saved him."

Mussolini, I thought. They're talking about Il Duce.

"They should've strung him up when they had the chance," the man continued. "What in Christ's name were they waiting for?"

"Where is he now?" asked Matteo.

"In Salò, on Lake Garda. With Hitler pulling his strings."

I blinked my eyes open. I was in the middle of a meadow. Scores of men milled around the grassy swath, some carting wood, others bending over a

makeshift table, and several sitting on the ground in circles smoking and jaw-
ing. Three barrels with metal skirts, probably for collecting water, stood near the
table. A few patches of canvas set up on posts formed canopied shelters. Up the
slope from the meadow, two large canvas tents occupied a level plateau. The sun
was low in the sky, and chill air whooshed down the nearby hillside.

The man Matteo was speaking with asked him, "Did you hear about the
German general who wanted a pig?" After a pause, he said, "He demanded an
Aryan pig, and the farmer asked what that was. He said, 'It must have bristles
like Hitler, a snout like Goebbels, and a belly like Göring.'"

That sent the man into thigh-slapping laughter. He composed himself and
asked, "How do you test a bridge in Italy?"

"Tell me, my friend," said Matteo.

"Watch a truckload of Germans drive over it. If it collapses, it's a good
bridge."

The man laughed so hard I wondered if he'd fall over, drunk on his own
words. It seemed I'd landed in the middle of a Gilbert and Sullivan act. I rolled
onto my side so I could see Matteo.

"Ah, you're awake," he said. "Feeling better?"

"Yes, but weak."

Matteo said to his companion, "Tell The Raven to come over here."

"Greetings, *signorina*," said the roly-poly man, rising and bowing deeply.

The jokester marched off, and Matteo turned to me, nudging his chin
toward the encampment. "How do you like this place? Peasants and soldiers, all
of them partisans."

I smiled at him. "It's like heaven."

"Hah," Matteo said. "After that camp, a jail would feel like heaven."

I spotted a man trotting toward me. *Santo Cielo*, it was Luca Rospigliosi. I
could hardly believe my eyes. I threw off my blanket and clambered to my feet.
"Luca, my friend."

He scooped me into his arms, lifted me off the ground, and twirled me
around. Plunking me down, he kissed my cheeks. "Finally, you managed to
escape. I thought you only got others out!"

I couldn't help myself. I'd worried about him since the day of his escape.
Tears welled in my eyes. "It's you. It's really you."

"We can take up where we left off, Toto."

Tears streamed down my cheeks—tears of joy and relief. I was free. And so
was Luca. I grasped his hands. "My dear Luca."

"Only you mustn't call me Luca. Here, I am The Raven."

The Raven, I thought, brushing at my wet cheeks. The name suited him, with his shiny black hair, sharp nose, and lean features.

"I'm so pleased to see you—free and healthy." I couldn't stop crying—after months in that terrible camp, I was finally free.

———

After a community dinner of watery polenta and bread hunks, Luca spread a blanket on the ground next to the tin field kitchen, and the two of us settled beside its smoking stack, soaking up its warmth. We talked from sunset until deep into star rise. Such things I learned from him that evening. The very day that Badoglio had signed an Armistice with the Allies, Hitler was ready, as if he'd expected Italy to switch sides. The Wehrmacht stormed Rome, forcing Badoglio and the royal family to flee. And Germany had also marched on northwest Italy, intent on protecting its homeland and the oil fields in Romania. An Italian division had turned against the German army, trying to halt their southward march, but the Germans captured and disarmed them. The lot of them, minus a few who escaped, were shipped to forced labor camps in France.

I did not find the news particularly assuring. "And Mussolini got away?"

"*Si,* SS commandos rescued him. Now, Hitler is forcing any Italian man with a leg to stand on to build military defenses or work in German factories."

"It sounds like mayhem." In the dark, I could only make out the depth of Luca's eye sockets beneath his brow.

"*Si,* everyone is on the run. The Italian army, Italian Jews, even Badoglio."

"What positions do the Allies hold?"

"They've taken Sicily. They're bombing Rome." Luca flapped a hand in the air. "But the Wehrmacht are everywhere. Hitler grows soldiers like farmers raise wheat. Fields and fields of them."

"And the Italian army, what's happening to them?"

"Many are hiding out. Some have found their way up here."

"This camp," I asked, "what operations does it engage in?"

"Mostly sabotage. The men, they're all devoted, but the resources are limited. Not enough ammunition, not enough explosives."

"Do they have communications with the Allies?"

"Yes. And we help downed flyers get out of the country. We don't see many shot down in this area, but we're moving them through here. I interpret for them. Sometimes I travel with them. But it's dangerous for me."

"Are you being hunted?"

"Yes, I have a bounty on my head. Mussolini couldn't keep me, thanks to you, but now the Nazis are after me."

"If British and American flyers are getting out, why can't you?"

"I'm too valuable here. I help with communications."

"But there's so much more you could do. You know all the resistance groups, all their leaders."

"*Sì*, the Allies are probably working with Badoglio, but he's not the only one they should make contact with."

"You mean the Communist and Socialist Parties?"

"And the Christian Democratic, Liberal, and Action parties. They all oppose Badoglio's government and Mussolini's Republic of Salò. Some of them are trying to band together, but they all want something different for Italy. The Allies need to understand how complicated it is."

"You should get out. The British government needs to know all this. And I have information about Badoglio, too."

"What do you know?"

"Father Matteo found out his confessor is Monsignor Nunzio Falco. The Monsignor is a sympathizer. He probably wouldn't break the secrecy of the confessional, but he'll do what he can to help the partisans. Galeazzo Ciano told me a great deal about Badoglio, not recently, but I still think it's relevant. I'd like to get this information to the British government—I have contacts I can put you in touch with."

"God willing, this war will end soon. The Allies have been pounding away, but the Wehrmacht is like an octopus that keeps growing tentacles."

I nodded gravely, looking around the camp. "I just hope the Allies soon cut those tentacles. And save everybody here and in the camps."

—◦—

The next morning Matteo and I were summoned, separately, to the leader's tent on the rise above the encampment. My turn to meet the leader, known as Giant Gianni, came first.

A bearded man, short and burly, rose from behind a table to greet me. His name was obviously ironic, at least with respect to his stature.

"*Signorina*, I have heard about you. Come, sit." When he spoke, his scruffy mustache flicked like the tail of a wary dog.

A tattered gold-brown rug in the middle of the tent formed a sitting area. We sat across from each other on stools of hewn branches.

"Tell me about Massa Martana camp. I've heard only second-hand reports."

I recounted the conditions, approximate numbers of prisoners, and the events of my last week there.

"The Raven tells me you know many languages," he said. "We always need those who speak English and German, even French."

"I am happy to interpret."

"So, you got The Raven out of Camp Bolsena." Pulling his head back, he squinted at me. "Why?"

I might have been offended at the question, but to a partisan, everyone was suspect. And heaven knows I couldn't blame him. "I feared for his life. His torturers were brutal."

"And how did you do it?"

I explained the plan to him, except for its aftermath—how my hands were tied afterward.

"But that is not how you got out?"

"No, Father Matteo and I escaped on a mail truck. The plan for The Raven could only work once. I couldn't ask the women in my barrack to take another chance."

He nodded thoughtfully, with lips clamped, as if debating whether to believe me.

That, I decided, he'd have to come to on his own. Why should I waste breath proving my loyalty? I braced a hand on my knee and gave him a hard look. "Is there anything that can be done for those still in Massa Martana? Before the Germans reach the camp?"

"It's too dangerous to liberate it. The guards can easily shelter in the buildings and fire on us. The best we can do is disrupt the Wehrmacht's advance."

"Do you have enough ammunition and material for explosives?"

"No. They're hard to come by. But we get some drops from the British."

"What about other supplies? Food and petrol?"

"It's all rationed. And expensive. We work with shops in the villages. The Blackshirts threaten people who work with us. Sometimes we have to scare them into supplying us."

"I can contribute money," I said. "Do you have a bank or bureau I could get money wired to?"

"Yes, there's a village not far from here, Colonnetta di Prodo. It's isolated. The army mostly leaves it alone."

"And can you help me get messages out? So I can make a connection with the British government?"

"*Sì*, we have a wireless operator. But we move him around to keep safe, especially now that the Germans have brought in radio-detection units. It'll take a day or two to get your messages to our radioman."

"I'd like to get The Raven out. He can help more on the outside. And it's dangerous for him because the Nazis want him."

Gianni gave his head a decisive swing. "No, he's needed here."

"Why?" I asked, though I knew the answer.

"To speak to the British and American airmen who are shot down. To explain to them the safe houses and escape route. Sometimes he travels with them."

"I could do that now."

"You don't know the area well enough. And you're weak. Look at you—a rack of bones."

Now he'd thrown down the gauntlet. "Why don't you try me? You know as well as I that women can move more freely than men."

"True, but the Germans are on the watch. Our women have already done much, and they are suspect now, too."

So, I would need to work around Gianni. "Then let's start with money. I can help with that. Do you have a person I can have money sent to?"

"Yes, Renata Ferrari."

I composed a telegram on the spot to my bank manager in London, one of only a few people who knew my code name: "Wire to Renata Ferrari, Banca Colonnetta di Prodo, monthly check amount in lire. Cher Fox."

Then I ascertained what supplies Gianni and his fighters needed.

My next telegram was to Randolph Churchill, under his code name, Overdog. I told him I was safe with partisan fighters, sent coordinates of their drop location, and requested plastic explosives, detonators, fuses, Hawkins grenades, and Sten guns.

That night, I selected a spot on the ground at some distance from the men. I wanted quiet and privacy.

"Mother," I said. "Finally, I'm safe and free. And ready to fight on."

My mind buzzed with memories of Java and my mother; I recalled the day we hiked to Borobudur Temple. We wended our way along a trail through the forest of umbrella-topped trees. Wind rippled the leafy branches, and sun rays glanced through the patterned treetops.

We'd stopped to rest under a big tree that overreached all those surrounding it. "Look up," Mother said. "See how the branches spread out, see how they arrange themselves to share the sky?"

From my perch beneath the tree, I studied the splayed branches, the shooting rays of their arteries, logical as geometry, so neatly apportioned they might have discussed how to cooperate in soaking up the sun's splendor.

"Be as wise as the trees, my dear. They are older than all the peoples of the earth. Your pride and true purpose will find its way. You need only trust your intention."

"Yes, Mother, I have found my purpose and courage again. Next, I will find a design to use them."

THE ENCAMPMENT AND COLONNETTA DI PRODO

OCTOBER–NOVEMBER 1943

I spent the next several days learning about the partisan group's work: taking out stretches of rail tracks with either explosives or brute force; ambushing small units of the German army; helping Allied flyers get back to the fight; and acquiring, by various means, food, petrol, and ammunition. In the evenings, the camp's over two hundred men and I, the lone woman, dined on scrounged supplies, like roasted chestnuts, boiled carrots or potatoes, bowls of rice or polenta, an occasional helping of meat, and sometimes even local wine. Although it was a pleasant relief to have decent food set before me and to break bread with comrades, my stomach refused anything but small portions, and my weakness persisted.

After a few weeks in the camp, Giant Gianni arranged for me to go to Renata Ferrari's house in the village. "There," he said, "you can get strong again." I agreed, with the understanding that I would maintain communications with the camp via a messenger and continue to contribute. So, I bid goodbye to Father Matteo.

"I must thank you," Matteo said. "For getting me out of Massa Martana. It still bothers me that I almost ruined the plan."

"But you got us here, to this camp. Together we managed."

"I'm learning to use a rifle," Matteo said. "And I will fire it if I must."

"Will Jesus understand?"

"I believe so. The Germans will kill us if we don't kill them. And this is our country."

Luca, however, I didn't want to leave behind. "I will get you out of Italy," I told him. "You're needed in London."

"But I'm helping here. Translating and working with the aviators."

"It's too dangerous for you to stay. Don't you understand this?"

"*Sì*, only I hate to leave my countrymen."

"You must consider yourself and the contribution you can make." I'd need to think of a way to get him out, despite his reluctance.

After making final arrangements for communications with the encampment, Giant Gianni summoned a young man. "Hey, Good-as-Dead, come here."

A scrawny youngster threw a pack on his back and tipped his hat to the men standing around the fire pit.

I hadn't noticed this youth before. He was much younger than the other partisans.

The gangly youngster loped toward us and held his head hunched forward as if he were unsure of himself. Shyly, he greeted me. "*Buongiorno, signorina.*"

"Take the *signorina* to Renata Ferrari," Gianni said. "She's expecting her."

"But that is near my father's house."

Gianni slapped him on the back. "You're good as dead to him, so what does it matter?"

The youngster pointed to the meadow's edge. "We will take that path, *signorina*."

We struck out, walking side by side. I asked, "They call you Good-as-Dead because of your father?"

"*Sì*, he doesn't like me working with the partisans. But I wish they'd use my name." He shuffled along, his hands plunged into his pockets.

"What's your name?"

"Sandro."

"Where do you live? I've not seen you up here before."

"With my uncle, outside Colonnetta di Prodo. But I work for Giant Gianni. I bring them meat from the butcher when they can afford it. And I take messages up and down the mountain."

"You're a brave one." The path narrowed as we came to the edge of the meadow. I motioned him forward. "Lead on, Sandro."

———

Renata Ferrari took one look at me—at my filthy, matted hair and haggard clothes—and marched me to the rectory at Chiesa di San Giovenale for a bath.

It was heavenly, a private room with a deep metal tub filled with water so hot I had to stir it to suitable warmth. I sudsed my tangled mop of hair twice and held my head underwater as long as I could. But afterward, Renata still combed my hair with olive oil to get rid of the lice. She gave me fresh clothes, undergarments and a thick cotton dress that smelled like crisp fall air and soap—real soap made from lard, olive oil, and thyme. How wonderfully comforting it was, having a woman tend to me and being clean and warm, to say nothing of having my freedom back and contributing in some small way to the resistance.

Renata lived on a winding street on the edge of Colonnetta di Prodo, in a stone house with windows too high on the walls to see out from. The next morning, while slanting rays slowly warmed the kitchen's thick stone walls, she bustled about, boiling water on a one-burner stove for a coffee-like brew, slicing bread, and retrieving a jar of jam. She commanded me to sit for breakfast and told me she'd be out all day.

"Just rest," she said. "And stay indoors."

"What if someone knocks?" I asked.

"Keep quiet and don't answer the door." She swept her hand toward a pile of newspapers stacked in the corner. "Catch up on the news."

Gianni had told me Renata was like an older version of myself, but I didn't see it. Yes, she was thin and quick of movement, with an oval face and dark hair. But there was a buzzing energy about her and a reluctance to settle into anything but sharp, quick exchanges. Perhaps hiding me at her home made her edgy, although Gianni had explained that her home was a good safe house. And I imagined that Renata's position as housekeeper for the parish priest guaranteed respect in the village and allowed her freedom of movement.

Over the next few weeks, I read many newspapers. Although the reports were dated, the news was detailed—and encouraging. Renata also had a radio; in the evenings, we took it out and listened to Radio London to learn of the war's progress. Technically, the channel was forbidden, but neither Germans nor the Fascist Army had visited the village in months. A few other villagers sometimes dropped by to listen with us. I greatly enjoyed interpreting Churchill's speeches and commiserating with comrades about the Allies' advances.

After a month of Renata's cooking and forced rest, I regained my energy, some semblance of healthy weight, and my impatience—especially after Renata supplied me with fake papers. Together we concocted a new life story for me: I was a war widow from a Sicilian village. I'd fled the Allied advance and adopted the village as my new home. Renata gave me the name Julietta, with a southern surname, Cicirello.

———

One evening in November, Renata informed me, "The Raven is passing through tomorrow."

Luca had two downed flyers to escort to the next safe house. They arrived late the next day, Luca limping in alongside two young men in peasant clothes.

Renata asked Luca, "What happened to you?"

"Just a little ankle problem. I'll be fine."

Renata insisted on bandaging his ankle. "It's badly swollen. You shouldn't walk on it. A day of rest will be good for you."

Both the aviators were RAF men, one a pilot and the other a bomb-aimer. It was wonderful speaking English again and hearing them talk about their homes in England, in Chester and Swindon. They seemed quite young, with their light-whiskered, gleaming faces.

"How old are you?" I asked.

The round-faced pilot, Ralph, said, "I'm nineteen. I have a brother in the infantry. I can hardly wait for us to be home."

Luca laughed. "First things first, young man. With any luck, we'll get you back to your unit."

"Ralph's as impatient as a child," said the other man, Scott. He brushed a hand through his sandy-colored hair. "First, we have to beat Jerry."

I asked Ralph, "How much training did you have before duty?"

"I was a pilot before I went active," said Ralph.

"Not enough training," said Scott, "seeing as we got shot down."

"I can't wait to see London again," I said. "Sounds like it'll need some rebuilding."

"Bloody Germans are bombing the hell out of it," said Scott. "But we've got them on the run now."

Ralph asked, "Can you get any books in English for me? The only ones I've been able to find are from American soldiers."

I'd not seen any on Renata's shelves, but I asked her, "Are there any books in English in the village?"

"Maybe the school teacher has some. I can check."

I told Ralph Renata would check for her.

"That's swell," he said. "I have this to trade." He reached into his pack, pulled out a slim red-covered book, and handed it to me.

It was *They Burned the Books* by Stephen Vincent Benét. "I've heard about this, this indictment of how the Nazis burned books," I said. "Can I keep it?"

"Yes, I've read it so many times I know some parts by heart."

I asked, "What is your favorite part?"

Ralph pitched his head back and thought a moment. Folding his hands, he recited, "Books are not men, and yet they are alive. They are man's memory and his aspiration, the link between his present and his past, the tools he builds with, all the hoarded thoughts, winnowed and sifted from a million minds, living and dead, to guide him on his way."

I smoothed my hand over the volume. "I think I will translate this into Italian. For the partisans and people in the villages."

— — —

The next day, Renata prepared a mid-day feast for us—pasta with squash and sweet onions and fresh-baked chestnut bread.

After the meal, Renata brought out a map of the local area. Luca, who'd traveled the route before, traced it for his fellow travelers. "We'll follow the shadow of this road, passing behind the village of Orvieto, and at night we'll stay at a farmhouse two kilometers beyond the village." He planted his finger on the map. "I'll leave you there for the next courier."

Late that evening, I insisted on some private time with Luca. We sat on the back step of Renata's home, in the alley. "You must leave Italy. This is your chance to get to London. I'll radio ahead. We can get you out on a Lysander."

Luca inhaled his Gold Flake cigarette, taking obvious pleasure in it. "But I'm still useful here."

"I will take your place interpreting and getting the flyers out."

"Are you strong enough? Do you know the countryside yet?"

"I'll go with you on this trip and learn it. I can do this."

"No, you're not ready, Toto. Get stronger and take the time to learn the route well."

"Such a stubborn man you are," I said. "And you mustn't call me Toto. I am Julietta now."

We all settled in for the night, me in my narrow bed in the central room, and Luca and the two Brits bedded down there on the floor. In the early morning, before sun-up, three short raps, followed by a clunk, sounded at the door. I knew it was the safe signal, but not wanting to take chances, I motioned for the men to head for the back room.

Renata, candle in hand, cracked the door and peeked out. She ushered Sandro in.

Huffing and puffing, he asked, "Signora Ferrari, The Raven and the airmen, are they still here?"

"*Si*, what is it?" She plopped the candle down on the side table.

Sandro said, "There's a contingent of Germans heading for the village. Maybe they know about The Raven. He must leave now, him and the pilots."

Renata turned to me. "Tell the men to get ready—and not to leave any trace behind. I want them out in ten minutes."

I went to the back room and told the men to prepare to leave. Then I returned to Renata, who was gathering bread and bottles of water for them. I told her, "This is the chance to get The Raven out. With the aviators."

Renata and I had talked about my plan, and she agreed with me.

She scratched her brow. "He'll slow the others down with that ankle. We'll drive him to the farmhouse."

"Drive in what?" I asked.

"The priest's truck. He lets the partisans use it for errands." Renata turned to Sandro. "Do you know the Pelagrilli farmhouse outside Orvieto?"

Sandro nodded. "*Si*."

Luca joined us around the kitchen table. "I can still take them there."

Renata snorted. "Don't be ridiculous. You'd slow them down. I'm in charge here. We'll drive you to Orvieto. And then you'll leave with the aviators. I'm not bringing you back here."

I retreated to Renata's bedroom. I didn't bother to remove my sleeping gown. I pulled my thick cotton dress over my head and put on my shoes.

Renata joined me there. "There's bread and water on the table. Pack it for the men while I get dressed."

Within minutes, Renata had organized the lot of us. She sent Sandro and the two flyers on their way, out the back door and down the alley.

Luca, Renata, and I left by the front door. Mere glimmers of dawn appeared beneath breaks in the cloud cover, and the morning air was cold. I buttoned my sweater to ward off the chill. We spoke not at all as we traveled the quiet streets. I spied just a few windows with lights on. Even the dogs still slept. It was slow going with Luca, who limped along, but it took only ten minutes to wend our way down the dark narrow streets to a shack on the village's outskirts.

Renata opened the double doors of the shed. Inside was a dull-black lorry. Its elaborate chrome grill looked out of place on the truck's beat-up body. Renata grabbed a crowbar hanging on the wall, opened the driver's door, and motioned to Luca and me. "Let me show you how to lift the seat."

She tucked the crowbar under the lip of the bench and sprung it loose. "See this little notch here? That's where the crowbar fits. Otherwise, if someone's inside, he can pop it open by pushing with his feet, right in the middle."

Luca asked, "Has the lorry ever been searched?"

"*Sì*, but just the bed."

I asked, "What if Germans are on the road?"

"We'll stop at a farm along the way and load up some food for the market," Renata said. "We have plenty of time. It'll take Sandro and the others four hours to get to the other side of Orvieto." Renata motioned to Luca. "Hop in."

Luca lay down on his back in the compartment, with his knees bent, and Renata popped the seat back into place. We drove west out of Colonnetta di Prodo, along winding switchbacks, down the hilly countryside.

"This route is easy to learn," Renata said. "You can only go north or west on the main road through Colonnetta. Sandro and the others are on a trail just north of the road."

"I can't believe Luca wanted to walk this," I said. "The terrain is rough."

Renata spoke loudly, no doubt so Luca could hear. "The Raven thinks he's some kind of superman."

I felt a thud from beneath the seat; Luca had banged on the top of his hiding place. He said, "The Raven has many lives."

After a few twisting kilometers, we pulled onto a long dirt drive and followed it to a farmhouse nestled in a valley fold. The sun, only now rising over the hills behind us, glowed like a ripe peach.

"Remember this place," Renata told me. "There are some thick trees up the hill to hide in. The people here don't like me to give their names. Just know this makes a good stopping place. I will show you a few other houses between here and Orvieto. You must memorize the stops, not keep any notes."

Renata and an old man and woman loaded burlap bags onto the back of the truck. All Renata said as we loaded up was, "Julietta may come by herself next time. She can be trusted."

Then we were off again. The truck trundled down the winding road and reached a straight flat section as we approached Orvieto. There were a few vehicles on the road ahead of us, and they slowed and stopped.

"Damn," Renata said. "Germans. Have your papers ready. Good thing we've got a load of potatoes."

My gut tightened. The only Nazi I'd ever encountered was Lieutenant Wolff, who swore I'd never go free. I forced myself to breathe slowly and stay calm.

Our vehicle inched forward until the raised hand of a German soldier halted us. He came around to Renata's side of the lorry. "*Documenti*," he said.

Renata handed him her papers, and I held mine out as well, keeping my head bowed to signal a subservience I was far from feeling.

He asked, in German, "Where are you going?" Perhaps he only knew one word of Italian.

Renata looked at him questioningly. I wasn't about to erupt into German and draw attention to myself, so I spoke to Renata in Italian. "Maybe he wants to know where we're headed."

Renata turned to the man. "*Mercato*, Orvieto."

He walked around to the rear of the truck and hopped onto the bed. He thudded around on it, probably checking the load, then hopped off again.

I stared at the hilly countryside dotted with borders of low-lying trees, stone houses, and bare vines. Renata drummed her fingers on the steering wheel.

He handed our papers back to us and signaled us ahead.

When we'd put some distance between the Germans and us, I spoke loudly, for Luca's benefit, "The Raven does indeed have many lives."

COLONNETTA DI PRODO

DECEMBER 1943–MAY 1944

I t took me three weeks to translate *They Burned the Books* into Italian.

"I want to get this printed properly," I told Renata. "Is there any place in the village with a printing press?"

"No, for that, you need to go to Orvieto. But I do not know if it is safe to ask at the newspaper there."

"Tell me what you know about the people at the newspaper."

Renata explained that a family ran the newspaper in Orvieto, and they only printed local news and stories from the government. "They play it safe."

"Do you know if they have ever informed on anybody?"

Renata gathered our breakfast plates and rose from the table. "That I do not know, but Orvieto does not have many Blackshirts. It is too small, with no manufacturing, for the government to care about."

"Then I will take a chance on it. Can I use the truck?"

I set out that cold December day for Orvieto and found my way to its newspaper office on Corso Cavour. I asked to speak with the editor, Tomaso Gobbini, and was directed to his office.

"Signor Gobbini," I said, offering my hand, "I am Julietta Cicirello."

Gobbini was an older man, perhaps fifty, with piercing blue eyes and thinning hair brushed back from his high forehead. He invited me to sit. "How can I help you?"

"Do you ever print circulars or accept orders for private printing jobs?"

"That would be unusual, *signorina*. We are busy with the regular news and printing."

I carried the translated papers in my satchel and only intended to show them if he expressed a willingness to print them. "Is there another printing press in Orvieto that might accept such jobs?"

"No, I'm afraid not. You would have to go to Perugia for that."

"I would prefer not to travel that far." The fact is, the more miles I traveled, the greater the risk of being stopped and searched. That I dared not risk. "Would you consider a small printing job? I would pay for it."

"What is the nature of this job?"

Already the glum-faced man was pressing the issue with me. "It is merely a transcription of an essay about books."

"And yet, I sense it is more than a mere essay." He plopped his forearms on his desk and leaned over them. "Is it a political treatise?"

"The Nazis would undoubtedly label it political, but I believe most Italians would consider it a celebration of books and knowledge."

"There is no need to be so coy, *signorina*. Why don't you just show me this treatise so I can judge for myself?"

"Can I count on your discretion in this matter, *signor*? If you are at all inclined to disclose the nature of this material, I would prefer to leave your office now."

"If it cannot be disclosed, why should it be printed?"

"So I can distribute it to those who value the ideals it espouses."

Gobbini rearranged himself in his chair and brushed a hand over his brow. "Is this some kind of trap? Are you testing my political leanings?"

"I can assure you I am not in the least interested in your political leanings. I am only asking you to run a printing of this essay for me to take away with me. I would keep the matter completely private, as I would ask you to do."

"I am not in the business of taking private jobs. Nor do I wish to court the kind of danger inherent in printing political materials."

He was forcing my hand. I would have preferred not to use the information Renata had shared with me about his son's partisan activities, but I was determined to have this material printed. "Signor, I'm afraid none of us can afford to adopt neutrality these days. That includes you. And your son."

The color rose in his cheeks. He glared at me. "Why do you bring my son into this?"

"We are all citizens, not just of Italy, but of the world, Signor Gobbini. Your son is a brave man, and I believe you know his actions have saved the lives of many."

He flared his nostrils. "I do not like being threatened."

"And I abhor standing by in the face of ignorance and injustice. I am asking you to run a hundred copies of this essay, turn them over to me, and never say another word about this."

He moistened his lips and sighed. "Very well. But you must give me a week to do this."

I returned a week later to pick up the printed circulars. The lorry had a good hiding place—under the seat—so I did not fear being apprehended at any checkpoints. The printed copy looked good. It fit on a single two-sided sheet of newspaper, with the columns nicely laid out.

"This is nice work, Signor Gobbini."

"It is a good essay. I have kept a copy for myself."

"*Mille grazie* for your work. May you and your family keep safe during these difficult times."

Now I would have to distribute the circulars around Colonnetta di Prodo and the outlying farmhouses. Renata helped me make a list of people to get it to—school teachers and some sympathetic officials—who would appreciate it and pass the ideas on to others. Handing it out in the village would be easy; no Blackshirts patrolled Colonnetta di Prodo. I just carried it around to the addresses Renata shared with me and knocked on doors. I stumbled the first time I called.

A school teacher asked me, "Why are you giving me this?"

"It is a gift, something you can keep for yourself. And maybe teach about if you wish."

"Who knows you are passing this out?"

"Only me and one other person, and we will both keep your identity secret."

After that, I made up a little speech to allay peoples' anxieties, handed them the circular without giving my name, and quickly departed. This approach worked well, and the first day I handed out a dozen circulars.

But getting it distributed outside the village presented more obstacles.

"Orvieto would be a good place," I told Renata, "but I might encounter police or even Blackshirts there."

"*Si*," Renata agreed. "Maybe it is best to just hand it out through our safe houses in the area. Those people will know which locals to get it to."

——

In the months that followed, I took up Luca's job ferrying Allied flyers to safe houses around Orvieto, driving if there was only one or, if more than one, walking with them or giving them a map to find their way. Renata drew the maps on cloth, which I sewed into the sleeves of their jackets. This was a trick I'd learned from Stewart Menzies—fabric didn't make noise like paper, and sleeves were seldom checked. Along the way, I distributed circulars to the safe houses. It was making its way nicely around Umbria and maybe even beyond.

The business-like Renata and I made a good team, but she told me I would have to move on sooner or later. It was too dangerous for a stranger to stay in the small village indefinitely. But the decision was made for me one day in May when a man approached me outside the bank in Colonnetta di Prodo. He was a blond, blue-eyed man, probably around forty, dressed in a clean tan shirt and black pants.

He walked right up to me, blocking my path. "You, I have to talk to you about some important business."

There was something louche about him. I hesitated, asking, "Who are you?"

He switched to English. "I am with you; I'm British. Come, let's talk."

He sounded and looked like he could be British. But I'd received no communication about any British agent making contact, so I was suspicious. This was probably an ambush. A villager who'd discovered I spoke English must have betrayed me to the Blackshirts or Germans. Maybe they paid him. Nobody could be trusted these days—not with food and petrol rationed and everybody scrounging to fill their belly. I must warn Renata there was a traitor in the village.

It seemed the man was alone. At least I didn't see anyone watching us. I looked around furtively. "I must run an important errand first. I'm sure you understand. Can I meet you in an hour?"

"Yes, meet me at the café then."

Once out of sight, I ran for Renata's house and let myself in the back alley, checking, as usual, to be sure no one saw me enter.

"Renata," I called. "It's time for me to leave."

I couldn't risk another day in the village—not as an escapee, partisan, and Allied spy. My sunny days in Colonnetta di Prodo had run out.

VENICE

MAY–JUNE 1944

enata drove me to the train station in Perugia, and I boarded a train for Venice. Finally, I was making my first visit to the city of canals. So far, no bombs had touched Venice, and it had fallen to Germany without bloodshed. Even though Nazis had overrun northern Italy, including Venice, I reasoned the city was large enough to make for good hiding. And I had an old friend there, Contessa Natalia Zamboni, whose home I visited upon arriving. She was not expecting me.

A maid ushered me into the entryway. I seated myself at the base of a winding staircase, admiring its graceful curves and the etchings of canal scenes on the walls.

"Toto," Natalia said, her heels clicking down the stairs. "Whatever brings you here?"

We exchanged kisses on the cheeks. I asked, "Can we speak privately?"

She escorted me to the room off the entryway, a parlor that looked out on the Grand Canal. She offered me a seat with a view of the rippling water. I could hardly believe I was in Venice, a city I'd longed to see for so many years. If only the circumstances were not so dire.

I sat down and faced her, weaving my fingers together on my lap. "I must tell you I'm on the run. I escaped from Massa Martana Camp last fall. I'm hiding from the Fascists. And the Nazis."

Natalia's hand flew to her chest. "You can't stay here. I'm billeting a German officer and his aide. They could return any time."

"I'm sorry if I have put you in danger. Do you know a place I can stay?"

She stood and paced. She paused at a side table and rapped her fingers on it. "Perhaps Hotel Danieli. I know the manager there."

I could not have asked for a lovelier hideout than Hotel Danieli—with its gold-tinged lobby, marble columns, and wide, beautifully decorated halls. The manager gave me a private room on the top floor, a cozy one with plush red drapes and serviceable furnishings—a soft bed, a comfortable chair, and a small desk. It did not look out on the canal, rather on the hotel's back side, onto the narrow street below. But I thought it was just as well that I couldn't sit at the window and show my face for hours on end.

Once alone in my room, I stretched out on the bed. I had to think: How long had it been since I'd known such luxury? The last time I'd stayed at a hotel was in Florence, in January of 1941. My God, it'd been over three years. Nearly three and a half years I'd been imprisoned or on the run. Would this awful war never end?

I wanted to see Venice, to get out and wander its piazzas, bridges, and canals, but I knew I must be careful. The next day, Natalia brought me some dresses; she said my peasant clothing would draw attention. Then, I took a few days to get oriented, established contact with my bank, and shopped for a nice pair of shoes and a few more items of clothing.

One day at dusk, I risked some sightseeing. I wandered to the Piazza San Marco and settled at an outdoor café. It was springtime in Italy. Unfortunately, it was also a time of occupation, and Venetians didn't linger long around the square, perhaps finding the presence of strutting Nazis distasteful. The Germans had requisitioned a nearby hotel, the Palazzetto Pisani, as their headquarters, so the square was lively with Nazis marching to and fro.

I stayed in the piazza only long enough to savor a half bottle of Champagne before returning to my hotel. It was the first Champagne I'd had in years; it brought back memories of my London times, particularly when Lord Beaverbrook and I shared a bottle of 1914 Dom Perignon. And it made me woozy. Carefully, I walked back to my hotel, unsteady on my feet and wary of being scrutinized by Nazis frequenting the square.

After a week of respite, I was ready to get back to work. On the drive to the train station, Renata had promised to make arrangements for me to rendezvous with a Venetian partisan, a man named Mario. We were to meet at his parish church, the Chiesa di San Geremia, a church on the Grand Canal in the northern part of Venice. I made my way there by vaporetto on the designated evening and found Mario, as arranged, in the fourth to the last pew.

I slid into the pew and sidled up to him. "Have you come to pray for the peasants of Veneto?"

"*Si*," he said, "and also for their comrades in Monti Martani."

"Mario," I said. "It's a pleasure to meet you."

"Come, Julietta. We can talk in the sacristy."

I followed the elderly, hunch-backed Mario up the side aisle. I loved the hushed reverence of the church's airy arches and white stone columns. Although I knew little about the Catholic faith, I greatly admired the beautiful architecture, paintings, and statues of its churches. We walked up the altar steps, through a door off its side, and settled in chairs in the vestibule.

"So," he said, studying me with penetrating brown eyes beneath white eyebrows, "I have to tell you we are being very careful these days. Venice is crawling with Nazis. They feel safe here because everybody has agreed not to bomb Venice."

"I understand they're imperious wherever they're found. They must be insufferable here."

"*Si*, we mostly coordinate with our field fighters, diverting supplies for them."

"If you need a translator, I speak English, German, and French."

"That is good to know. I will tell the others about you."

"What about the Jews here?" I asked. "Isn't the Jewish Ghetto nearby?"

"It's practically in the church's backyard. The Nazis have been rounding up Jews who live outside the Ghetto. Next, they'll probably empty the Ghetto."

"Are there any operations to get them out?"

"A few have escaped to Switzerland or the south. Church families are hiding some others."

"I would like to help them. What can I do?"

I pushed and prodded, but Mario said the parish had already exhausted members willing to take in Jewish families. And the partisans were so busy sabotaging Nazi troop movements in Veneto that they couldn't spare any time to sneak Jews out. He thought the best way to help Italy's Jews was to undermine the Nazi war machine.

"Is there nothing I can do?" I asked.

"I will think on that and talk to the others," he said.

We arranged to meet again in two weeks. It sounded like the partisan network here was well organized and doing what it could to route the occupying Nazis. That meant I could turn my attention to Venice's Jews. I knew that Hitler and Himmler were obsessed with rounding up Europe's Jews and sending them to camps—whole families of them. I wanted to do something to keep them out of Nazi clutches.

The next day, I rose early, put on a simple blue dress, and took out my map of Venice. I traced the route I'd need to walk to get to the Jewish Ghetto. After a breakfast of ersatz coffee and pastry—how I enjoyed these simple pleasures—I set out for the Ghetto.

I found the dark alleyway entrance at Calle Ghetto Novissimo and wandered through it into the world of Venice's Jews. Quiet pervaded the stone-patchwork square. I could only stroll the streets, hoping to find someone to speak with. Then I came upon a woman dressed in black letting herself out of a narrow door.

"*Signora*," I called out, walking up to her. "May I have a word?"

She jerked around toward me, her eyes wide, perhaps startled at encountering an intruder in her neighborhood. "What do you want?"

"Only some information. I am a friend from Chiesa di San Geremia." Since the church had helped some families, I thought this introduction might assuage the woman's worry.

"What kind of information?"

"I want to help at the school. Can you tell me where it is?"

She hesitated, maybe suspicious of a strange woman asking about a school for Jewish children.

"*Signora*," I said, folding my hands and bowing slightly, "you can trust me. I know the Nazis are watching Venice's Jews. I only want to help. I am taking a chance, too. Tell me before someone sees us talking."

That seemed to allay her misgivings. "It's in the middle of that street there, Calle Ghetto Vecchio, behind green double doors."

I pushed open the doors to the school and found myself in a narrow hallway lined with glass-windowed doors. It was surprisingly quiet for a school. I could hear only murmuring conversation from behind the closed doors. As I walked down the hall, I glanced into the rooms and noticed children, very young ones seated in a circle with their teacher, older ones bent over desks, and teachers at blackboards or bulky desks. I was struck by the hushed intimacy among the children and teachers—how the children respectfully regarded their teachers, how the teachers bent their heads toward the pupils, how somber they all were, perhaps especially at this time. Would they be suspicious of me?

The hall turned to the right, onto a suite of offices. I knocked on the door marked "Head of School Rabbi Elijah Padova."

I heard a man's voice. "Yes, come in."

I opened the door to a narrow-faced man with close-set eyes. He was around forty years old, and his black suit draped loosely about his thin frame. Perhaps he'd recently lost weight, or maybe he was wearing hand-me-down clothing.

"*Buongiorno*, Rabbi, may I have a few minutes of your time?"

He motioned for me to sit in one of the chairs in front of his desk. "How can I help you?"

I'd given myself a new surname, one common in the Veneto. "I am Julietta Bonato, and I want to help some Jewish families and children hide from the Nazis."

He cocked his head and narrowed his eyes. "Who has sent you, *signorina*?"

"I come of my own accord, though under the auspices of Chiesa di San Geremia. And I work with Giustizia e Libertà."

"How do I know I can trust you?"

"I know what is at stake—I myself was imprisoned by the Fascists. The Nazis are already rounding up Jewish families. I have a plan to help."

Over the next two weeks I visited the school often, teaching the children a little German and explaining it would help them navigate Nazi rule. One of the first children I met was Galilea, a petite six-year-old with spindly limbs and hair almost as dark as mine. She was an only child, and I thought she and her family would be good to get out first, if her parents would agree. She was sweet, dutiful, and intelligent, the kind of child who would quickly endear herself to others.

One day as I left the Ghetto, a German soldier stationed at the entrance stopped me. "Are you a resident here?"

"No, I'm helping at the school." He'd spoken to me in German, and I responded in kind.

"I see you know German," he said, frowning at me. "Are you a Jew?"

"No, I am not Jewish. I have been hired to teach the children German."

"This is forbidden—working for Jews. You will not do this anymore."

"Yes, officer, I will let the school know this is not allowed. Thank you for informing me."

Now every time I went to the Ghetto, I needed to avoid any patrolling officers. They were tightening the noose around the Jewish Ghetto. In all likelihood, they'd soon begin emptying it. I must act quickly.

The next day I contacted Natalia and asked if she knew anyone who might be willing to hide some Jewish families. She arranged for me to meet with her daughter-in-law and a few of her friends, but she couldn't promise they'd cooperate.

Natalia's daughter-in-law, a beautiful young woman named Carlotta, welcomed me to her home off the Grand Canal.

"It's lovely of you to invite me, Carlotta," I said, offering her a bouquet of white lilies.

"I'm pleased to meet you, Julietta." She handed the flowers off to a maid. "Natalia said I must ask you about your favorite opera houses."

"There are so many. I'm looking forward to the next season so I can see Venice's house."

Carlotta walked me to a lovely parlor and introduced me to her friends—Isabella, Elena, and Sofia. She served us Cinzano and bruschetta, and I asked about where in Venice they lived and the history of their families in the city. Then I broached the topic I'd come to discuss.

"I want to talk to you about the state of the war and the Nazi occupation. I'm sure you know that the Allies are making inroads now. Soon they'll force out the Nazis." I paused to let them take that in.

Carlotta nodded. "They can't get here soon enough. The Nazis are diverting our food to their military, causing even more shortages."

"*Si*," I said. "And soon the Allies will retake France. Their offensive is going well in the north. The tide has turned. Germany will fall. It's only a matter of time."

I set my empty glass down and looked around at the women—all so nicely attired and well-mannered. These were modern young women from wealthy families who probably wanted to get back to normal living again. Now I must tell them I wanted their help.

"I'm sure you're aware of the Nazi's intent to round up Jewish families and send them to camps. I had hoped Italy's Jews would escape this fate, but no, they're being taken from their homes, just like the Jews in all the other countries under German control."

"Yes," Sofia said. "My sister knows a Jewish family that was taken away recently. They ran the bakery in her neighborhood."

"The Pope's encyclical condemns the Nazi's actions against Jews," I said. "He has put the weight of the Catholic Church behind his words. I'm looking for people who can take some Jewish families and keep them safe until after the war."

Carlotta leaned toward me, clasping her hands. "Natalia told me you might ask for some help with this. You must know this is a dangerous thing you're asking."

I took in and released a deep breath. "Yes, I know anyone who harbors Jews is at risk, but their lives are at stake. If they can be kept safe just a little longer, they can survive the Nazi campaign against them."

All four of the women fell silent. Isabella and Elena studied their feet.

Finally, Sofia spoke. "But why should we take a chance? And put ourselves and our families at risk?"

"You are respected citizens of Venice. If you say you have some family visiting, no one will question you. You could even say they lost their house in a bombing campaign. Everyone knows homes are being torn apart by this war."

Carlotta said, "But answering questions from our neighbors and friends might put us in danger."

"I understand this," I said. "But you would be honoring the Pope's encyclical, saving lives. Will you help?"

Sofia shook her head. "I would have to speak to my husband. I cannot make such a decision without his consent."

I sensed them slipping away from me, starting to think of excuses. I would have to ask for less than I had proposed, which I'd planned out beforehand. "I appeal to your sense of humanity and justice. Would you consider just taking one or two children—saving some young lives at least?"

Still, they sat quietly. I rushed in to fill the void. "I can provide some payment, enough to cover the cost of food for them. And if it doesn't work out, I will take the child and find another home. Please don't turn away little ones in need."

I looked at the women. I feared I was losing them. "Sophia, will you speak to your husband?"

"Yes," she nodded. "But I doubt he will agree to this."

"Isabella," I turned to her. "Will you consider helping?"

"I must think about this. Can I let you know later?"

"Yes, you can let me know through Carlotta." I looked to Elena, who'd not said a word the whole time. "Elena, are you willing to help?"

"No, I have my own children to think about. They are too young to keep secrets."

Carlotta spoke up. "I will help. But only with one child. I will tell my husband some story. It is best I am the only one to know."

"Thank you, Carlotta. This is a wonderful thing you're doing."

I hated leaving the evening on such a note—with three of the four refusing or hesitating. I needed to get them to consent in some small way to help with this effort. I shook my clasped hands and circled my eyes from each to the other. "Will you all agree to keep this meeting a secret among us? To tell no one else about it—except those whose help you may need if you hide a child?"

I studied each by turn. "Please, I need to hear from each of you about this."

One by one, they nodded their assent.

A few days later, as arranged, I telephoned Carlotta to ask if any of her friends were interested in me delivering flowers to them. This was our code for taking children. She told me no, none of the others wanted any flowers. I had only one home for one Jewish child. I'd obviously have to scramble to find more.

———

When I met Mario two weeks later, I asked, "Have you found any more families who can help Venice's Jews?"

"Father Volpato said he might be able to find a few more families to hide some individuals. But they don't have enough room for more than one person in their homes."

We were tucked away in the sacristy. The air still held the smell of incense from the day's Mass.

"That is something at least," I said. "I have found one family who can help, and I will keep trying to recruit more."

"But how will you get the children out? The Nazis are watching the Ghetto."

I knew he was right about this; I myself had been stopped and questioned. "I thought I could use a gondola and take them out at night. The small children will be easy to hide. Do you know a gondolier who might help?"

He stroked his brow as if contemplating some weighty matter. "Are you sure you want to do this?"

"Yes, I have to help. I've seen two Italian camps. I'm sure the Nazi camps are much worse."

"The gondoliers I know are concerned about the Nazis," he said. "They are being searched. You would probably have to pay them."

"I can do that." I could see much of my monthly allowance would go to this campaign.

Mario arranged for me to meet a gondolier with partisan sympathies. The gondolier said it was too dangerous to risk traveling the Grand Canal with forbidden cargo, that he would only transport children on the minor waterways. I had little choice but to agree to his terms.

VENICE

JULY–OCTOBER 1944

Galilea's parents agreed to have her hidden with a Catholic family. I couldn't tell them the name of the family that would take her in. Carlotta insisted she would only keep the child if no one else knew her identity. I told Galilea's parents that the family taking her would know their name and address; they would bring their daughter home as soon as it was safe to do so.

I decided to bring Galilea out on a Sunday night, when the city was at its quietest. I had to go to her family's home before the evening curfew and wait until after dark. The family served me a nice dinner, and we talked with Galilea about what to expect.

"I'm going to start calling you by your new name," her mother told her, "so you can get used to it."

Her father cupped a hand over her head. "What do you think about that, little Julietta?"

Galilea smiled and looked at me. "If I am little Julietta, you are tall Julietta."

We all chuckled at that. We passed a quiet evening, visiting, and then the parents said their goodbyes to Galilea.

"Be a good girl," her mother said, hugging her. "We'll see you very soon again."

Her father stroked her cheek. "You're going to visit some nice people for a little while. It will be a pleasant visit for you."

They looked at me with pleading eyes as they handed Galilea off. I could see they were both trying not to cry—for their daughter's sake.

The gondolier agreed to meet me at the Ponte de Gheto Novo at ten. We nestled a sleepy Galilea into the gondola's bow. I covered her and her little bag of clothes and personal items with a blanket.

"Ready?" the gondolier asked.

"Yes, please go quickly." I tucked the blanket snugly around Galilea.

I dreaded the possibility of a Nazi accosting us as we left the Ghetto. I'd seen them patrolling periodically, and I could only hope we'd chosen a safe time.

The gondola glided along the still waters, rocking gently with the motion of the gondolier's oar strokes. I trained my eyes on the sides of the waterway. The gondola cut ahead and turned right onto rio della Misericordia. Now we were passing out of the Jewish quarter and had only to make our way to rio di Noale. I thought if we could make it there, we would be safe. I uncovered Galilea.

"We are on the way now, Julietta," I said. "If anyone speaks to us, you let me do the talking, *si?*"

In the darkness, the water looked inky and foreboding. I could hear it lapping against the embankment. *If stopped,* I thought, *we'll pretend to be a mother and daughter returning home from a visit.*

The gondolier let us off at Calle Stua Cannaregio, a short distance from the Grand Canal. From here, we would meander our way to Carlotta's home.

"Come, Julietta," I said as we disembarked, "take my hand." Her little hand fit neatly in my palm. She trusted me, and she was being so brave—she hadn't cried at all when she said goodbye to her parents. Perhaps the poor dear didn't fully understand she'd not see her parents for at least several months. She was so sweet and innocent; I almost wished I could take her to my hotel room and keep her myself.

"Do you know where we are?" I asked her. "Is this place familiar to you?"

"No. Momma always leads the way."

"That's fine. I know where we're going." But I'd walked this area only once before. Although I'd memorized the route from here to Carlotta's, it was dark now. I cursed the way Venice's streets and canals bent around; it was hard to keep my bearings. But I strode on, making my steps sure, but not so hurried as to tax Galilea.

And then, finally, we were there—at Carlotta's doorstep. "We're here, little Julietta, at your new home."

———

Over the next several months, I managed, though with difficulty, to recruit four more families, each of whom agreed to take one child. The easiest part was making contact with Jewish parents; they knew it was only a matter of time before they'd be removed from their homes. By August, I had gotten five children safely out and settled with Catholic families around the city.

Everything was going well, though I knew I must be careful and space out my clandestine activities. Then one morning in September, the hotel desk telephoned, saying they had a message for me.

"I'll come down and retrieve it," I said. I trotted down the stairs, wondering who could be contacting me. No one except Natalia knew where I was staying.

The desk clerk handed me an envelope. I settled in a chair in the lobby to read it.

Dear Julietta,

I overheard the colonel billeting here. The Nazis are planning to search your hotel tonight. They may be listening on the telephones and watching the hotel. Stay in your room for now. I will think of a plan and send another message later.

Natalia

I tucked the message back in the envelope and walked briskly across the lobby to the stairs.

I felt frightened and powerless. If I could be assured they weren't watching the hotel, I'd have gone to Chiesa di San Geremia to hide. But Natalia said they might already have the hotel under surveillance. I couldn't risk leaving. I'd have to wait to hear from her. I hated nothing more than inaction. I felt jumpy. I wanted to bolt out of the hotel and lose myself in the streets of Venice.

I let myself into my room. I tore the message into tiny pieces and flushed it down the toilet. I looked around the room. It'd be impossible to hide here. Might there be some place in the hotel I could escape notice if it were searched? I only hoped Natalia would come up with a good plan. Or that she knew the manager well enough to solicit his help hiding me.

I checked the street below. I saw no Nazis there, but I could see only a portion of the street. It was possible soldiers were already guarding the hotel exits. I paced my room, waiting to hear back from Natalia. A half-hour passed, then an hour. Surely she hadn't abandoned me. Finally, I heard a knock on my door.

"Who is it?" I asked.

"Bellhop, with a message."

I opened the door and took the message, giving the young man a tip.

I tore the envelope open.

Contessa Natalia Zamboni requests the presence of Contessa Julietta Bonato at a dinner to honor the district leader and five other dignitaries.

Dinner is at eight in the hotel dining room. I have made all necessary arrangements with hotel management. Check out of your room before coming to dinner. The desk will hold your suitcase.

I could only try to stay calm through the afternoon and early evening hours. I took a long bath and dressed for dinner. Then I packed my clothes and personal effects and rang for the bellhop.

When he arrived, I instructed him to take my suitcase to the front desk for storage.

Dressed in my best evening gown, I strode into the dining room at 8:10. There, in a private room off the main dining area, I saw six Nazis in tan uniforms. And there was Natalia—in the middle of the gathering, charming the lot of them. She spotted me and waved me in.

"Ah, Contessa," she said. "We've been waiting for you."

Now I had a title to go with my new name.

"Lovely to see you, Natalia," I said, taking her hand and exchanging kisses on the cheeks.

"Let me introduce you to our esteemed guests." Natalia knew these men by name. They formed a circle around us, and I shook hands with each of them.

When we sat down to dinner, Natalia motioned for me to take the seat beside the district manager, Gauleiter Paul Giesler. His Italian was impeccable, which was perhaps the reason he'd been given a post in Italy.

"How are you finding Venice?" I asked him.

"It's a charming city. And you, are you from Venice?"

I had taken time to think through my cover story, knowing I must speak without hesitation. "No, I visit often, but my villa is in Treviso."

"And your husband—the Count—is he at the villa?"

I cast my eyes down. "I'm a widow. But let's not dwell on sad topics. Tell me about your hometown."

That sent him off on a description of Munich, which I encouraged. Next, I asked where he'd learned his excellent Italian. As a schoolboy, he said, at his mother's insistence. And, I asked, do you enjoy Italian opera? Or do you prefer Wagner?

"I love Wagner. He is my favorite composer."

"And which of his operas do you love best?"

"I vacillate between *Tristan und Isolde* and *Der Fliegende Holländer*."

"That is a dilemma," I said. "In my opinion, the lyrics of *Tristan und Isolde* are labored, often repetitive, though the music is more transcendent."

"I am inclined to agree with you. And what is your favorite Wagner?"

"*Tannhäuser*," I said without hesitation. "It marries the music and themes beautifully. And I love the female characters. They are both strong and true to their natures."

"You are a connoisseur of opera, I see."

The evening went off without a hitch. The whole dinner was a convivial affair, with the German officers well turned out in their tan uniforms. Gauleiter Giesler, in his burgundy piping and red sleeve insignia, looked every bit the man of the hour. Absorbed as I was in dinner, I saw no sign of the hotel search. But I imagine the searchers had not dared to interfere with a party for the district leader. Natalia's plan to hide me in plain sight had worked. After the dinner party, which went on until nearly midnight, I went to retrieve my suitcase.

The young man behind the desk shuffled the key to my room over the counter. "The manager says it is fine for you to return to your room now, *Signorina*."

I slept well that night.

———

Over the next several weeks, I managed to place two more Jewish children. Soon I would run out of families willing to take them. The Nazis had begun to empty the Ghetto, so I needed to act quickly. One afternoon, I decided to visit Father Volpato at the Chiesa di San Geremia to see if he could find more families.

The minute I stepped out of Hotel Danieli, two Nazis approached. One of them said, "Signorina Koopman?"

"No, I am Julietta Bonato," I said.

"We know who you are. We have orders to bring you to headquarters."

VENICE AND RAVENSBRÜCK

OCTOBER 1944

The Nazis had caught up with me. How I did not know. Perhaps they had a photo of me and someone had recognized me on the street or in the hotel. I dreaded dealing with them—I feared they'd be crueler than my Italian captors had been. The two Nazi escorts brought me to their headquarters at Palazzetto Pisani, where my interrogator stared me down across a carved-wood table.

The bull-necked Lieutenant Becker sliced the air with his hand. "We know you're spying for the British. What have you told them?"

"I know only as much as the ordinary citizens of Italy, Lieutenant. I'm sorry, I cannot help you."

He stood and braced his hands on the tabletop, looming over me. "Your life depends on your being honest with me."

But I knew that revealing any spying or partisan activity would doom me. I had to maintain my innocence. I choked down my fear. "I don't know what you mean. I can only say I am no spy."

"Then what have you been doing since you escaped from Massa Martana?"

"Trying to remain free," I said. "You have no right to detain me. I have done nothing."

"Where have you been hiding?"

"At Hotel Danieli."

"All this time?"

"I only came to Venice last May."

"And where were you before then?"

"In a little village. Since you think I am a spy, I won't say where. I refuse to endanger innocent Italians."

He harangued and slapped me, told me I'd regret not cooperating, and insisted I'd feel Himmler's wrath if I didn't reveal my spying activities. But he clearly had no evidence to set before me. The Abwehr was operating only on a hunch—or their knowledge of my previous relationship with Lord Beaverbrook. They apparently knew nothing of my activity hiding Jewish children, or they would have brought it up.

After two days of interrogation, I was loaded onto a train, a boxcar occupied by Jewish families from Venice. "Where are we going?" we asked each other. But none of us knew. We sat on straw and shared a bucket of water, which we drank up in two days. Some passengers had brought food, but they didn't share it outside of their families. I was so hungry I started thinking about food all the time and dreaming about it when I slept. My lips cracked and bled from not having any water. Dribbles of my own blood were my sole sustenance.

Along the way, more prisoners were loaded and Nazi documents shuffled. Soon the car was so crowded it was impossible to lie down. Now we mostly sat or crouched in our little spots, trying to always use the same corner of the car to urinate or defecate. The car smelled awful—like shit and piss and the stench of fear—and we took on this smell, too. Each time we stopped, the doors swung open. I crowded the door, straining to spot landmarks: snow-laden mountains in Innsbruck, the aging train station of Augsburg, the forests surrounding Aalen. We'd traveled through German-occupied Austria and into the heart of Germany. After several days of taking on more prisoners, the train began to make stops where some prisoners were ordered off. But not me.

— —

After eight days of transport, on October 11, 1944, two weeks before my thirty-sixth birthday, the train stopped in the cold, forested north of Germany. Two women guards in grey dress uniforms and caps ordered the women in my and the other cars out, including a mother and her infant. It was late in the day, and a few inches of fresh snow blew about.

We all shuffled down from the train car. I was so weak from hunger and thirst that my legs buckled and I struggled to stand. Six more guards, four men and two women, converged on us. They stomped their thick leather boots and yelled, "Line up. In rows of five."

Chill wind whistled through thick pine woods lining one side of the train tracks. An immense brick wall loomed on the other side. We milled about, wide-eyed and cold. I scooped up a mouthful of snow, as did many others, even though guards were prodding us to line up. There must have been four hundred of us.

Then I saw the sign on a tall metal gate—RAVENSBRÜCK. I hadn't heard of the place, but now we whispered the name to each other in urgent voices. Dear God, it was a camp, a concentration camp.

Three of the guards carried whips; they brandished and cracked them like lion tamers. We jostled against each other as we tried to fall into rows. Two big German shepherds growled and snapped the air as their handlers clenched their leashes.

Once we assembled into rows of five, the guards marched us through the towering iron-barred gates and swung them shut behind us. We found ourselves inside a compound surrounded by the brick perimeter wall, a thick wall about fifteen feet high. A wire fence lined the wall; it bore high-voltage signs and black placards showing a yellow skull and crossbones.

In the slanted, late-day light, I could make out a massive camp. The guards marched us across an open, packed-dirt area about three hundred feet square. Beyond it stretched rows and columns of grey wood barracks, enough barracks to hold thousands of prisoners. I saw no signs of vegetation on the grounds, not even trees.

The camp was eerily quiet, with only a few dozen women in wide-striped blue and dull-white gowns crossing the open square. They shuffled along, regarding us with blank stares, as if they had little energy to spare. They were all skinny, some near-bald and others with hair sticking out in stiff patches or heads covered with cloth.

The guards herded us into a long building and ordered us to take off our clothes. I was cold, and I didn't want to. I, along with the others, hesitated. But the guards with the whips cracked them and barked at us in German, "Take off your clothes, shoes, jewelry, everything."

I knew not all the women on my transport spoke German, so I told those around me, in Italian and French, "We must remove our clothes and jewelry."

A nearby guard let her dog lunge toward us. It barked and strained at its leash. We all looked around with big eyes, staying close, packing ourselves tight together.

I took off my coat, my dress, and my undergarments, like all the others. We stood in the middle of the building, naked and cold, our clothes in heaps beside us, guards all around. Some of the women had brought bundles or suitcases and set those down, too.

The woman with the baby grasped her infant to her, and the baby started crying. A guard stepped forward and grabbed the swaddled infant. The mother tried to hold onto her baby, but another guard stepped forward and shoved her away.

The mother ran toward the guard holding her infant, but the guard pushed her back and said, "We have a place for babies, we will take care of it."

The mother crumpled to the ground, crying. *My God,* I thought, *what kind of Nazi hell is this?*

The guards prodded us into the next room and lined us up in rows in front of tables with more guards, some males and some females. As we stepped forward, these guards gripped electric shears with thick black cords. I stood there, humiliated and spread out, letting a man shave the hair off my head and pubic area. He scowled as he gripped my thigh and ran his shears over me. I felt like a dog cowering before a cruel master.

Behind the shaving stations was a table with blue and white striped gowns. A guard handed me one. The next table contained an array of colored patches. The guards here had papers, and when we stepped up, they asked our names. I gave my name, and a guard gave me a needle and thread, a patch with a number, and a felt badge with a red triangle and the letter N.

"Sew it on your sleeve," the guard ordered.

I stood naked, stitching the badge and number to my rough cotton robe. I put the gown on. At the next station, a guard handed me a striped jacket, white headscarf, and shoes, clunky and ill-fitting wooden shoes.

My life as prisoner number 77370 of Ravensbrück Concentration Camp had begun.

My name and past life no longer mattered. I was a mere number, one among thousands.

RAVENSBRÜCK
OCTOBER-DECEMBER 1944

My home was Block 27, one of the blocks for Dutch women. The head of our barrack assigned me to share the bunk of a woman named Jean Bommezijn. Jean had brown hair streaked with gray and the sunken cheeks of someone who'd been starved month after month. There was no doubt in my mind that many in the camp were succumbing to prolonged starvation.

"How are our numbers assigned?" I asked her.

"By when we arrive. Mine is lower because I arrived here last year."

"And what does my red badge stand for?"

"Red badges identify political prisoners, like partisans and communists, and the N tells you are from the Netherlands."

Jean said there were thousands and thousands of women imprisoned here, probably over thirty thousand, with more coming and going all the time. Other blocks held Polish, French, German, Russian, Greek, Slovenian, Italian, and even some British women. Also in the camp were many Jewish women, Jehovah's Witnesses, and Gypsies.

"There are so many languages here," Jean said, "that many prisoners don't understand the guards. They get treated the worst."

About one-hundred-sixty women crammed into my block. Three-tiered bunk areas lined the side walls, with wooden planks about thirty inches wide that two or three of us slept on. Each bed had a mattress of wood shavings, but many of these mattresses were filthy from prolonged use. In the middle of the block were twelve washing basins and twelve latrines, not nearly enough for the rush of women who needed to eliminate and clean in the morning. The toilets' stench permeated the block, and I was nauseous until I grew accustomed to the smell.

On my third day, I started getting up in the middle of the night to wash. I felt it was important to keep clean to preserve my health and dignity. I decided that only by steeling myself could I survive this place. If I didn't, I would go crazy. I remembered the story from my childhood of the turtle who charmed and escaped its captors. I would be like that turtle now. I would harden myself against the guards, keep my eyes open, and learn how to avoid notice.

The daily routine was punishing and unerring. Every day but Sunday, we rose around four, and a siren called us for *appell* at five sharp. We mustered into rows of five outside our blocks, always rows of five, and stood until the guards were satisfied with the roll call.

Sometimes, if guards had to root prisoners out of the block, *appell* took up to an hour. While the guards searched the block, we stood there freezing, trying not to slump or fall down. When the guards found women hiding, they shoved them outside, beating them as they joined our ranks. But the numbers in the blocks kept shifting, so sometimes women who hid were overlooked and able to avoid work for a day.

On Sunday, only the Jewish women had to report for work. The rest of us were free until the mid-day *appell*. Afterward, we took forced recreation along the Lagerstrasse, with German music piped throughout the camp.

We were allowed to write one letter a month, and the first letter I wrote was to Randolph Churchill. I hoped the authorities would see I knew someone in the British government and treat me as a special prisoner. I asked Randolph to send garlic and onions because I needed extra food and because they had medicinal qualities. I shared my shipments, which arrived almost weekly, with Jean and a few others. We ate the onions and garlic when they came because there was no place to hide food; it would be found and eaten if we left it in the block—either by other prisoners or by the rats. Still, I began to lose weight because our food rations were pitiful—two hundred grams of bread and some awful soup each day. I hated the gnawing feeling in my stomach. It made me feel desperate and afraid—afraid I would not survive this place.

I worked on the excavation crew. It was exhausting, back-breaking work. We had to shovel frozen, sandy earth onto the back of trucks to be hauled away, only to shovel it back off again. It was busywork with no real purpose, except maybe to work us to death. Sometimes my crew worked on road maintenance. If we didn't smooth out the road as we dug, the whip came down on us. After we repaired the road, we pulled a big metal roller to tamp it down.

Several guards, always two with dogs, watched over us to be sure we didn't sneak into the woods. We could tell by how the dogs yanked at their leashes that they were trained to attack on command. No one wanted to take a chance on being mauled. I never doubted that the guards would send their dogs after us.

As I worked, I looked around. The forest was thick here. But if I tried to run and hide, the dogs would surely attack. And even if I managed to escape by straggling behind as we returned from work duty, where could I possibly hide—with my striped prisoner gown in the heart of Germany? The camp's interior was even more forbidding, with its electric fence and high brick wall. Jean said the voltage was strong enough to kill anybody trying to climb over it.

One day a woman on our work crew collapsed. Those around her urged her to get up, but she was too weak.

The guard kicked her, yelling, "Get back to work." She lolled on the ground, like putty beneath the guard's boots. He took out his gun and shot her.

I sunk my shovel into the frozen earth. Just work, I said, just keep shoveling. Pace yourself to keep going.

In the distance, over the treetops, the tall smokestack of the crematorium belched gray smoke—always working, always burning the dead. Were the distant gunshots I'd heard some evenings firing squads? Or was the rumor about a gas chamber outside the camp true? Amid all this random cruelty, I knew I must keep my strength up, my head down, and my fellow prisoners close.

———

One day in early December, a guard pulled me from the excavation crew and marched me to the *Revier*. All the sick were kept here, on narrow cots, and I saw both prisoners and guards tending them. The *Revier* smelled cleaner than my block; the latrines and wash area were in separate rooms. I glanced at the prisoners in beds and noticed the bandages were relatively clean. It was hard to believe after all I'd seen in my block—the filthy mattresses, rats, dysentery, and prisoners' dirty clothes—that there was one place in the camp that was actually somewhat clean.

I didn't know why the guard had brought me here, but I didn't like being singled out. I could only hope that being brought to the *Revier* was better than being put on a lorry and driven away.

The guard directed me to an office in the rear; he told me to sit and wait at the desk. Metal file cabinets packed the wall behind the desk. While sitting alone there, I considered opening a drawer and seeing what kind of records the Nazis kept. But with all the sounds of activity outside the door, I dared not risk it. Still, I knew Germany was in retreat and that this information might prove valuable after the war. If I had a chance to see the documents, I would. Otherwise, I'd observe as much as possible to tell afterward. I surprised myself—thinking about spying in the camp when all that really mattered was staying alive. Maybe I still had a little courage.

A man with a white gown entered the office, marched around the desk, and plopped down.

"I am Dr. Clauberg." He pitched forward over his elbows and eyed me. His face was pockmarked; he was ugly as a warthog. "I understand you are Dutch."

I spoke my finest German. "Yes, Herr Doctor, my nationality is Dutch."

"Your German is excellent, I see."

"I am fluent in German, Dutch, French, and Italian. I am also a nurse." In the few minutes I had been in the *Revier*, I'd decided it would be a desirable place to work. And I knew the chances of the Nazis checking on the credentials of prisoner 77370 were nonexistent.

He leaned back in his chair, jutting out his chin. "Where did you take your nurse's training?"

"At St. Mary's Hospital in London. I would like to use my training for the camp."

"That is something we can discuss later. First, I want to know about your nationality. You are perhaps not all Dutch. Your skin is not the color of the Dutch people."

"My father was Dutch. I even have Dutch royalty in my blood."

"And your mother? What race was she?"

I feared revealing I was not pure Aryan, but I didn't know how to explain my dark skin. So I lied. "My mother was also part Dutch."

He cocked his head. "But, I assume, not one hundred percent."

"That is true."

"I am asking what race your mother was. You will answer me now."

I saw I could no longer deny what his eyes were telling him. "Part Indonesian."

"That is better." He stood. "It's as I thought. Come with me."

"May I ask where you're taking me?"

"To the surgery preparation. You can have a shower first."

"What kind of surgery?"

"Sterilization. It's a simple procedure."

"I'm past childbearing age. Surely this is unnecessary. I beg you."

"I have orders from Berlin. There is nothing to fear."

I could hardly believe my ears. Female sterilization was major surgery, requiring removal of the female organs. I remained seated. "May I ask the method?"

"I will dilate the cervix and inject a substance into the uterus, observing the effect via X-ray. It's a new procedure."

"By new, I assume you mean experimental. I have not heard of such a technique. Is it dangerous?"

"You may call it what you wish. Many have gone before you, and they are all fine."

I doubted he was being honest with me. "Are they here at the *Revier*?"

"Most have returned to their blocks. As I said, it's a simple procedure. Now, enough of your questions. I have work to do."

I could see there would be no convincing him to spare me. I rose. "Herr Doctor, can we speak of me serving in the *Revier* afterward?"

"I will refer the matter to the head of our nursing department. Now, follow me."

On wobbly legs, I made my way out of his office down a narrow hall. If only I could run away, but there was no place to hide. I felt as defeated and powerless as a leashed dog.

The doctor turned me over to a female guard who took me through surgical preparation. While I was showering, I washed my uniform with soap and warm water. Then the guard brought me to the operating room.

A nurse strapped me down on a metal table, securing my torso, arms, and legs. They gave me no anesthetic. The doctor inserted a cold speculum-like device into my vagina. Instinctively, I seized up. He'd opened my vagina so wide I felt stretched to tearing.

"It will be easier if you relax," he said.

I cringed from the pain shooting through me. I felt a piercing sensation and screamed.

"I said, relax. You're making it harder on yourself."

"What are you doing?"

"I'm opening the cervix."

Stabs of pain roiled my abdomen—as if I were being knifed from inside again and again.

"Please stop," I cried out. My insides screamed with pain. I tried to think of something, anything other than the pain. I let strains of *Tannhäuser* run through my mind, trying to concentrate on threads of the "Pilgrim's Chorus."

I heard the doctor's voice. "Just another minute."

The stabbing stopped, and the cramping started—wave upon wave of hard twisting sensations.

The doctor removed the speculum.

"Please, unstrap me. I'm cramping badly." I wanted to curl up and protect my belly.

The nurse undid the straps and helped me off the table. I buckled over and clutched my abdomen.

She took my arm. "Come with me."

She dragged me to another room and stood me up against a bulky machine—an X-ray machine.

"We need to keep you still for the X-rays." Again, she strapped me in place, all stretched out. I wanted to bend over my cramping abdomen, but the straps held me spread out. The doctor came in and operated the X-ray machine.

"Hold still," he ordered. "Or I will have to keep you strapped in longer."

Again, I tried to distract myself. I thought of the "Grand March" from *Tannhäuser*, which helped my mind soar above the pain. Yes, I thought, keep playing the music.

After this, clutching my still-damp uniform, I hobbled to a bed in the *Revier*. I lay on my side and curled into a ball, moaning from the severe abdominal cramping.

"It'll only last a few hours," a woman on a nearby cot said to me.

While I lay there, I saw a young girl, possibly ten or eleven, coming from the operating room. She was screaming and clutching her gown over her pubic area. Blood streamed down her legs. My God, were they sterilizing girls?

I asked the woman on the bed across from me. "That girl. Was she sterilized?"

"Yes, she's not the first."

"But why?"

The woman looked around, perhaps not wanting to be caught telling me. "Can't you see her badge? She's a Gypsy."

Dear God, it seemed that girls and women who did not meet the Nazi definition of pure Aryan were being sterilized.

The day after the procedure, the head of the nursing staff came to me. "You can go back to your barrack now. Tomorrow, you start a new work assignment as a nurse."

"I will report here?"

"No, not the *Revier*," she said, "Block 6."

I would not work in the relatively clean *Revier*, which was obviously kept sterile not for the prisoners' benefit but for the sake of experimentation. Block 6 was different—it housed the sickest of the sick.

RAVENSBRÜCK

DECEMBER 1944–APRIL 1945

Block 6 held about three hundred prisoners—all crammed together in filthy conditions, many sick with typhoid or dysentery, some wedged head-to-toe on narrow cots. It stunk of festering wounds, sour sweat, and diarrhea.

Six nurses with white armbands worked on this block, all of us prisoners. Scurry as we did, we couldn't possibly attend to all the moaning pleas—for water, for bread, for simple comfort—forcing us to choose which ones to assist. After nine at night, guards locked up the block and left the prisoners on their own.

Since I was the newest nurse, I took over the most gruesome job, removing gold teeth from the dead. Anytime someone died, we had to carry the body to the back room and prepare it for the crematorium. This meant removing the woman's clothes and checking her teeth. If we saw any gold teeth, I had to use pliers to pull them out. There was a locked wooden box with a hole on the top to put the teeth into. Each day a guard came and emptied the bin.

It was grisly work—clutching the dead woman's head like an inanimate object, finding a good angle to grip with the pliers, and yanking with all my strength. I hated the cracking sound of the tooth severing from the jawbone. I cringed with each tug; I couldn't help thinking this was a person—a murdered person. I kept telling myself this woman was no longer suffering. And that my job was better than dying a little each day from the grinding labor of shoveling sand.

The prisoners in Block 6 rarely saw a doctor. They were the castoffs, too weak to work, some hanging by the last thread of faith, others praying for release from their agony.

The head nurse, a French woman named Genevieve, told me a new Nazi doctor, Adolf Winkelmann, had recently arrived from another camp. He visited the block every day to collect a list of the twenty sickest prisoners.

I asked, "What does he do with this list?"

Genevieve had a long, sad face and deep-set eyes. "These prisoners are taken away to the Youth Camp. He claims this is for recuperation, but we all think it is for gassing."

"Is there no way to save some? Can we keep some from this?"

Genevieve and I decided to be more systematic in discharging our duties, and we enlisted all the other nurses to help. Some patients were too ill to eat their rations, and we gave their share to those we hoped could recover. We removed the dirty bandages of those with wounds and, since bandage supplies had run out, used paper, which was cleaner than used cloth. The paper didn't last long, but it was better than nothing.

One Monday, when we were making up the list, I suggested we add the numbers of prisoners who had already died. Winkelmann always wanted us to put twenty numbers on the list, so this way we could save a few of the sick. Genevieve and I recorded the numbers of the women who had died the previous day and were laid out in the back room, ready to be taken away.

When Winkelmann came, we gave him this list. He left with it, and then, later in the morning, the driver came and went around looking for those whose numbers were on the list.

I walked around with him and showed him where the women on the list were. He checked off their numbers. After he had taken away fourteen women, he asked, "Where are these other numbers?"

"They died after we made up the list," I said.

He eyed me suspiciously. "Show me."

I walked him to the back room and pointed out the dead women and the numbers on their gowns.

I was afraid he'd inspect the dead and notice they'd been dead longer than a few hours, but he didn't. We were lucky that time, and we started saving a few prisoners each day with this ploy. Sometimes we hid one or two prisoners in the lavatory when the transport came to take them away. We told the driver they'd gone back to their blocks and work assignments.

We were all taking risks with these ruses, but we hoped we could outmaneuver Winkelmann and the transport drivers by working together. The camp was large and growing bigger each week. The prisoner identification system became even more disorganized, and some of the newest arrivals weren't even assigned numbers. This helped us in our subterfuge.

One day I said to Genevieve, "Let's put on a fashion show—to entertain the block."

Genevieve chuckled. "I don't feel especially stylish in this sack."

"I can use gowns to design different looks. It'll be distracting, if nothing else."

I devised ways to alter waistlines and make sashes, stoles, even headwear. As the nurses paraded up and down the rows of cots, I narrated in French, German, and Italian, pretending we were at a real fashion show.

"Here we have the latest design by Toto Koopman," I said of my favorite creation—a gown with a diagonal sash and jaunty headpiece. "You're seeing it here for the first time. I predict it'll soon take Berlin by storm."

The sick women clapped and laughed. It was a happy day. We all tried to think of little things like this to keep up morale. We knew our survival depended on our solidarity.

———

There were so many stories in Block 6 and, for that matter, across the whole camp, thousands of stories: a French woman who watched her mother dragged away on a transport, never to be seen again; several Gypsy girls who died from the sterilization procedure; a Jewish woman who was mauled to death by a dog; a Russian woman who went crazy and threw herself on the electric fence; and a Czech woman who'd witnessed the execution of the men of her village—as retribution for the assassination of an SS officer. So many stories that will never be told, so much sadness the world will never learn about.

A Polish woman in Block 6, Krysia, offered to draw a portrait of me. She was weak from overwork and undernourishment, but her spirit was strong. She had a severe limp that caused her to walk with a lurching gait. While I sat on her bed and posed, I asked her about her time in the camp.

"Two years ago, the guards took me and several other Polish women to the *Revier*, about eighty of us. The three doctors wanted to see our legs. We didn't know why, but they were very cruel, laughing at us as they ordered us to lift our gowns.

"Several days later, they called us back for more inspections, and they selected ten of us. I was in that group, and we were all terrified, fearing we'd been selected for transport. But no, they took us to the showers in the *Revier*, and then they shaved our legs. Next, we got an injection. It was an anesthetic. Then they operated on us. We were guinea pigs for these three Nazi doctors, two men and one woman: Rosenthal, Schiedlausky, and Oberheuser.

"When I woke up, my leg was in plaster and '111 TK' written on it. The others had marks on their leg plasters, too. Then the pain started, terrible pain in our legs. Over the next few days, our legs swelled up, pushing against the plaster. Oberheuser, the woman doctor, visited regularly to inspect our legs and take blood from us. The swelling was so bad they had to take the plaster off. Then we saw what they'd done to us.

"Our legs had been cut open and infected. They put dirty objects in our wounds—nails, glass, and wood splinters. We took these things out when the plaster came off, but our legs were full of pus and terribly swollen and painful. We were all thirsty, but they didn't give us anything but the usual soup and bread. Our wounds were foul and stinking, and flies buzzed around them. I was in so much pain I kept passing out.

"Then they brought in more women to be operated on. Those of us who already had the surgery helped them as much as we could after the doctors left for the day, fetching water and bringing around bedpans."

Krysia was only twenty-three, a compact woman with strong bones. She had probably once looked sturdy. I wanted to give her hope. "You must live to tell your story."

"Yes, I hope it will be told, if not by me, by someone else." She sketched my portrait with charcoal on a piece of cardboard scrounged from the storage room. I'd propped her up with a blanket so she could draw.

I said, "Show me your leg, Krysia. I want to see."

She pulled up her gown, revealing a ragged scar that ran from above her knee all the way up her thigh. The scar tissue was white and lumpy.

She covered her leg up. "They scraped our wounds and tried different treatments to see if they could defeat the infection. I was fortunate. I got a treatment that worked. But several of the women died from their infections. Some got lockjaw and died a very painful death."

"How many died?"

"I can't know for sure because there are so many Polish women in the camp, more than from any other country, and they took us from several blocks. But in my block alone, six women died. We call ourselves the rabbits because they experimented on us and because we hopped on our good leg after the procedure."

By the time Krysia finished her story, my portrait was complete. Even though it was on rough cardboard, it was a lovely drawing. I kept it under my mattress for safekeeping.

———

In January, news circulated that the Red Army was marching across Poland and would soon reach Germany. Someone in a nearby block had managed to find a Nazi newspaper, *Völkischer Beobachter*, which told of battles the army was fighting nearby. We sometimes heard planes flying over on their way to or from air attacks.

At the end of January, some women prisoners arrived from another camp, Auschwitz. They said the Nazis were closing the camp since the Russians were getting close. Many had died during the march, before the rest boarded a train that brought them to Ravensbrück.

One day in early February, we heard explosions from bombardments and knew the end of the war was coming. Now we all just wanted to hold on. We thought it would be a terrible tragedy to die with liberation so near.

Everyone was agitated and jittery. The guards started to look nervous, maybe because they wanted to save themselves from becoming prisoners of war or being tried for war crimes. We knew what they were doing in the camp was criminal. A rumor went around that they wanted to kill all the rabbits so they couldn't reveal the experiments on their legs. But the rabbits just hid in other blocks, and the women in these blocks willingly took them in, so they escaped execution. All the prisoners started working together now, feeling we finally had some power and hoping that the guards wouldn't dare conduct mass executions so near the end.

As the bombardments came closer, the guards became more and more desperate. They spoke to each other excitedly, with heads bent, as they walked across the yard. Discipline began to break down since prisoners knew they could avoid orders by hiding.

Jean and I and others in our barrack talked over our meager rations each day, pooling what we'd learned from others.

Jean said, "I heard guards are siphoning off food meant for the prisoners' kitchen. Maybe the supplies from outside aren't reaching us anymore. Because the Allies are cutting off the routes."

"I'm glad they're not eating any better than us," I said. "They deserve to know hunger."

Our pitiful food supplies had dwindled to potatoes and some kind of poorly milled flour. We all feared starving to death before we could be rescued.

A woman sitting beside Jean said, "Some women who had marched from the Königsberg camp say the Nazis burned it behind them."

Jean said, "I pray they won't march us out of Ravensbrück. I heard they kill the ones who can't keep up."

"We just have to hold on," I said. "It can't be long before the Allies reach us. Even if we're marched out, we could meet them on the road."

Another woman said, "Someone in Block 27 told me a lorry was going around during the day grabbing women for transport. Just randomly selecting prisoners."

"The crematorium can only burn so many each day," Jean said. "We'd best keep our heads down and avoid the guards."

Then, at *appell* the next day, the guards started looking at women's legs, going down the rows and asking prisoners to lift their gowns.

"What are they doing?" I asked. I still felt new to the camp. Nearly all the Dutch women in my block had been brought here many months, sometimes years, before me.

Jean said, "They're probably checking for those who might not be able to march."

As if to confirm this, the guards singled out eight scrawny women and ordered them on a nearby lorry. They made the rest of us stand there, even though they had completed roll call. They did this sometimes, like they were subjecting us to a sort of endurance test. After an hour of standing like this, a few prisoners just gave up and lay down in their rows. Those around them tried to get them to stand, but they were so weak they no longer listened to our messages of hope. They, too, were taken away on the lorry.

Then, one night in March, guards ordered women in some of the blocks to help remove papers from the *Revier* and headquarter buildings. Guards started a bonfire in the Lagerstrasse, and the prisoners formed a chain, with documents sent down the line to the fire.

Along with many women from other blocks, I gathered to watch. A French woman standing near me said, "I heard the Red Army is stalled not far from our camp, but the Americans and British are squeezing Germany from other directions."

"Good," I said, "now the German army has to fight two fronts."

"Liberation must be near," she said, "if the Nazis are destroying documents that can be used against them."

I thought maybe this bonfire was my chance to steal some records. I found a spot in the line of women and started handing the papers along, watching the guards as I did so.

Prisoners across the camp soon joined the spectacle, many standing around the fire, talking and enjoying the blaze's heat. Some guards moved close to the fire, too, so fewer watched the chain of women passing documents to the bonfire.

Whenever papers or files came into my hands, I quickly scanned the German text to see what information the material revealed. Many of the titles were cryptic and administrative in nature—block numbers, census reports, and guard lists. Then I saw a file with Dr. Carl Clauberg's name and the words "Sterilization of Gypsies." I bent over, lifted my gown, and tucked the file into my undergarment, hoping none of the guards had seen me. After the papers quit coming down the line and the blaze died down, everybody disbursed. I walked back to my block, holding my arms over the file hidden under my gown.

Back in the block, I showed it to Jean. "Look, I stole this file."

"What is it?" she asked.

I hunched over and opened it. The light was dim, so I held the pages close to read them. There were eight sheets of paper listing prisoner numbers and ages. "It lists all the Gypsies Clauberg sterilized. There are hundreds here."

"You'd better hide it," Jean said. "Don't tell anyone you have it."

I slipped it under our cot, where it hid beneath the portrait Krysia had drawn of me.

———

By the end of March, food distribution started breaking down. Meals weren't at regular times, and food rations shrunk even more. Knowing the guards were stealing our food supplies made us feel even more desperate. We wanted so badly to hold on. We were all becoming fatalists—some sure we would be liberated and others too dispirited to entertain any hope of freedom.

The weather was warming, and it, too, brought small hope. One day my fellow nurses and I helped those suffering from tuberculosis out into the sunny yard. They sat and leaned against the building, soaking up the heat and smiling.

Then, on my way to Block 6, on the morning of April 5, I saw guards emptying the two blocks with French women and making them stand in the Lagerstrasse for *appell*. Along with some other prisoners, I stopped to watch.

The guards had set up a table in the Lagerstrasse and called out numbers, lining these women up in front of the gate. Then I saw why they called up the women: Outside the front gate stood a row of Red Cross buses. The guards ordered the prisoners to stand still until their number was called, but the women kept turning around and talking to each other and smiling at the ones who joined the line. They were all antsy and maybe worried about being excluded from the line to the buses.

The day before, guards had ordered us to clean up our blocks, and they locked the room holding the dead in Block 6. Now I knew why: The Nazis

wanted the camp to look clean and hospitable for the Red Cross. But the prisoners' conditions told the real story, and we hoped that somebody from the
outside world would now see what was happening here.

That day the Red Cross took away about four hundred French women.
After that, everyone only wanted to talk about the Red Cross and whether the
rest of us would be saved. A few days later, more Red Cross vehicles evacuated
the Swedes and Danes. Now we knew that some countries were negotiating
with Germany.

We hoped this was a sign that everyone in the camp would be released. We
prayed we wouldn't be marched out of camp or taken for execution before more
Red Cross buses or the Allies reached us. The time for sealing our fate—either
for the best or worst—was near. Anxiety bore down on us, and we regarded each
other with one ever-present question: Will you be among those who live or die?

RAVENSBRÜCK

APRIL 1945

On April 23, a rumor flew around camp that the Red Cross would arrive to evacuate Dutch women the next day. My friend Jean and I were too excited to sleep and stayed up all night. The guards no longer patrolled after our work hours, so prisoners had started roaming the camp and talking to each other in the evenings. It was a pleasant spring day, and Jean and I sat outside our stinking block and breathed the fresh air. Air that now smelled like freedom.

"When I get out, I'll go find my daughter in Amsterdam," Jean said. "She has a new baby girl."

I said, "I think I'll go to Switzerland, a nice safe country."

But deep down, I was afraid to believe we were really going to be released—afraid we'd be disappointed or that the Nazis would trick us into boarding vehicles that would take us to our death.

April 24 seemed to drag on endlessly, and I worried we'd been forsaken. Finally, late in the afternoon, six guards, two with dogs, came to our block and ordered us to form rows of five. I grabbed my portrait and the file I had stolen and hid them under my robe.

Guards marched us out of the gate, around the side of the camp, and along a road leading away from the camp. I'd never been in this area before and kept looking around, trying to figure out where we were going.

Ahead, beyond a line of pine trees, I spied a concrete building, a square, low-lying building with no windows.

A woman in front of me turned around and gasped. "I think that's the gas chamber."

The prisoners at the front of the rows must have thought this, too. They balked and stopped marching. We all jostled each other, afraid the guards were marching us to our deaths. The guards with the dogs yelled at us, "Marching formation. Everyone, back in formation."

We bumped up against each other, trying to retreat. Some of us hollered at the guards, "Where are we going? Where are you taking us?"

The head guard said, "To the Red Cross. Just line up. Order, order."

The guards with guns trained them on us and forced us back into rows of five. They marched us forward—past the concrete building. We continued until we reached a paved road in front of the SS living quarters. The guards stopped us there. I thought, *now is the time: Either this is the end of my life or a new beginning.*

Then we saw a white bus with red crosses on its door and bonnet round the bend in the road. We started cheering and jumping up and down. More buses followed this one. It was a caravan of the Red Cross. We broke from our ranks and waved as the buses pulled off the road and stopped near us.

The drivers got off the buses and stared at us. They wore the blue and yellow emblems of the Swedish flag. We waved to them, and they smiled and approached the guards. We were ecstatic and could hardly contain ourselves. We buzzed with excited talk.

"Order, order," the guards hollered. They lined us up again and called our numbers. When we stepped forward, a guard tore the colored badges and numbers off our sleeves. For the first time, we could reclaim our names and not just be known by numbers.

In our ragged robes, we boarded the buses. I stepped onto the third bus and took a window seat near the rear. Everyone was very civilized until the last bus filled up.

There weren't enough buses for everybody.

The waiting women broke from their rows, trying to board the already crowded buses. The drivers stepped up and helped the guards calm the women. The women looked at us and started crying. We waved at them. My heart was breaking for these poor women.

The drivers climbed on the buses, and our driver greeted us in Dutch. He looked clean and handsome to me, even though he was a short man with stocky legs. He had healthy, rose-colored cheeks, and he was speaking our language. He was our savior.

"Don't worry," he said. "More buses will come tomorrow and get the other Dutch women. No one will be left behind."

He walked down the row, calming us, and, as he passed, women grabbed his hand in thanks.

He returned to the front of the bus and faced us. "I must tell you we'll be traveling through a war zone. So please, everybody, follow my orders along the way."

Then he started the bus and turned it around. The bus headed back in the direction it had come from. Our little caravan was carrying us away from this place. The women on the other side of the bus crowded to my side. We all waved to our friends as we drove off. We looked at the Nazi guards and laughed and made faces. I felt light as a feather. We were free, finally free. I only hoped all the others would also be released. I had seen so much cruelty in the camp. I prayed the guards wouldn't kill more prisoners or burn the camp and force the last of the women on a death march.

The sun was setting, and the road turned darker and darker. The bus driver turned the headlights off, but there was a full moon, so the road was easy to see. For many hours we traveled like this.

Then we heard rumbling in the distance, and our caravan pulled off the road into a field. The driver told us to be quiet and stay in our seats. The roaring sound came closer, and then we saw British tanks, cannons, and trucks full of soldiers passing by on the road. It took almost a half-hour for all the vehicles to go by. We had noticed the field was sprouting with grass, and we begged our driver to let us off the bus.

"Very well, just for a few minutes. But stay close to the bus, don't let it out of sight."

We got off and started grabbing handfuls of the grass and eating it. It tasted so fresh and full of moisture, like a little feast. My stomach started churning, so I quit eating. I rolled around in the grass; it felt soft and clean, like springtime. Then, overhead, planes roared.

"Everybody," the bus drivers hollered, "take cover. Run for the trees."

The drivers raced for shelter, and we all dragged ourselves after them, but some women didn't have the energy to move fast and lagged. The planes roared down over us, and we heard whistling and the rat-a-tat of guns and saw dirt spitting up where bullets hit. The aircraft kept diving at us and shooting, swooping up and down, their engines thundering and echoing all around us. I could tell by the markings they were British planes. They must have thought we were Germans pretending to be Red Cross.

I saw some women flail like rag dolls and fall, shot by the planes' machine guns. As the aircraft moved on, the roaring trailed off. Then it was quiet, an eerie and hollow kind of quiet. No one moved. We were too afraid to come out. What if the planes circled back?

After a few minutes, the drivers ventured out and told us to get back on the buses. They tended to the injured women. They loaded all the dead and wounded on the buses, about fourteen women, and we started up again. I was safe; I only had to live through this war zone and I would be free.

When morning dawned, we reached a French POW camp and stopped to rest. American soldiers took the dead and wounded off the bus. The rest of us they directed into a slapdash building, and as we filed along, the soldiers stared at us and asked us where we were from. The American soldiers looked so fresh and vital, with ruddy cheeks and firm shoulders. Some had tears in their eyes, like they were overwhelmed by how we looked. They let us use the latrines and washbasins, and then they fed us porridge with warm milk. It was so sweet and creamy it made my mouth ache.

I was free, finally free.

GÖTEBORG AND ASCONA

APRIL 1945–APRIL 1946

From the French POW camp in Denmark, we were taken to Fraaburg port, and then we were loaded onto a big British ship, a recommissioned battle-ship bound for Göteborg, Sweden. I had a cot all to myself, which was a great luxury. Military doctors and Red Cross workers tended to us. I took a shower and afterward donned a clean hospital robe. Simply being clean and treated with kindness filled me with gratitude and happiness.

By the time we reached Göteborg, so many war refugees were flooding the city that the Red Cross had to improvise places to put us. I went to the Natural History Museum. I slept on a cot by the dinosaurs, and I loved looking at these creatures' gigantic bones. It was a wonderful diversion from the thoughts of everything I had lived through.

The Red Cross nurses were careful to feed us only small helpings of food. Our stomachs couldn't handle rich food or large servings. The nurses were lovely—kind and devoted to our care.

I was weak and racked with many emotions. Waves of fear over how close to death I'd come coursed through me, followed by relief over finally being safe and free. Sometimes I just lay on my cot and let the tears dribble down my cheeks. I was so overwhelmed—I had to let my feelings out somehow.

I got word to Randolph Churchill about where I was housed. A week into my stay, I woke to find him sitting beside my cot. He looked handsome in a navy suit and white shirt. I noticed he seemed older. Even though he was my age, his temples were flecked with gray hair. Still, he looked healthy—wholesome and robust.

"Good morning, sweetheart," he said. "I hope they're treating you well here."

"I couldn't ask for better care."

"Thank God you made it here."

I knew I looked a sight—emaciated, pale, and with hair as rough and dry as straw. I could tell he was trying not to stare, not to show how surprised he was by my altered appearance.

"I brought some presents for you." He reached into a cloth bag and pulled out an aqua blue dress with simple lines. "Pamela helped me pick it out for you."

"It's lovely." I reached out and touched the fabric—a soft and supple cotton. It was probably a bit too large, but I wasn't in any condition to gallivant anyway. "Once I put on a few pounds, it'll fit perfectly."

"And one more thing." He pulled a wig out of the bag—it was the shiny blue-black color of my hair when it was healthy.

I teared up. "Oh, Randolph, whatever made you think to bring this?"

"I, uh," he stuttered, "I saw pictures in the newspapers of camp liberations and noticed many of the prisoners were bald."

"Well, it's perfect."

"I've also brought some cash for you. And I'll help you with the paperwork when you're ready to join the living again."

I slumped down on my pillow. "I can't believe how tired I am. How much I'm sleeping."

He pulled his chair close to my cot. "I'm so sorry. So sorry for all you've endured."

"I can hardly believe I'm free."

"I never forgot you, Toto. I had an agent tracking your movements in Italy. He was code-named WD—for Watchdog."

"You had me watched?"

"Yes, I was worried. After you escaped the camp in Massa Martana, we lost track of you. But then you got Rospigliosi out, and he confirmed you were still hiding in Colonnetta di Prodo."

"So much happened after that."

"I hope you'll tell me sometime. When you're ready." Randolph leaned forward and gripped my hand. "I can't imagine what you've endured."

I remembered the file I had brought with me and reached under my bed. "Look, I managed to steal a file showing how many Gypsy girls and women they sterilized. They used an experimental technique—I know because they used it on me."

His eyes got big as he took the file and opened it. "It's evidence. Hard evidence. I'll be sure it gets to the tribunal."

I could speak of it now. I was safe. I no longer needed to be strong for my fellow prisoners. "In some men, there is no humanity."

"The horror stories coming out of the concentration camps are shocking the world."

"I'll never be the same. I'll always wonder if I made a difference."

"You did. Because of what you told us, we bombed factories making planes and tanks. You helped save the lives of many flyers trapped in enemy territory. And you freed Luca Rospigliosi; he helped us connect with Resistance leaders and push our way through Italy."

"In Venice, I saved some Jewish children. Hid them with Catholic families."

"You did make a difference. Never doubt it."

"But was it enough?"

———

What makes a soul, and how is it some lose theirs? Even now, a year after my liberation, the question confounds me. I see the parade of people I encountered during the war—souls both brave and depraved. I can only imagine those who committed atrocities had their mercy and humanity frightened out of them. At least I hope they hadn't freely surrendered these qualities.

As for me: I have to ask why I'd involved myself in the war effort and if, knowing what I'd experienced, I'd do it again. My reasons for choosing to work for the Italian Resistance and Allies were not reasoned out. Honestly, the decision came to me in a rush. The worsening conditions on the Continent occupied me like rising waters; once they spilled over, I felt I had to act. I only knew that if I simply stood by and watched, my life would have no meaning. And what good did it do to torment myself now with the question of whether I'd do it again? This long nightmare of war was finally over. I could live again.

Still, the terrible things I saw will haunt me forever. I can only pray to make my grief pure and untainted by hate. But I'll never forgive the perpetrators. I hope justice will be served and the worst of the worst punished. The world must see that people who commit such horrors will pay the price.

I only know now that I must surround myself with loving people, people with compassion. Otherwise, I'll never regain that most sacred of things—hope. That was what kept me alive, hope and faith in human goodness. For we are all singular beings—all of us connected to the great wash of humanity.

AUTHOR'S NOTE

TOTO KOOPMAN was deeply affected by her experiences during the war. After recuperating in Göteborg, Sweden, she retreated to the small Swiss village of Ascona on Lake Maggiore. There, in 1946, she met the woman she would spend the rest of her life with, Erica Brausen. Although German, Brausen had violently opposed the Nazi doctrine and lived out the war in London. Toto moved to London to live with Brausen in 1946. Together, they opened an art gallery and discovered the painter Francis Bacon.

During her time in London, Toto rekindled friendships with her old London crowd, including Randolph Churchill. She reconnected with Lord Beaverbrook's son, and they renewed their relationship. She also had an affair with the Italian journalist she had helped escape from Fascist clutches, William "Luca" Rospigliosi. Her relationship with Erica Brausen was an open one, with both of them taking other lovers. Toto also tracked down her fellow student acquaintance in Florence, Elisabeth, and they remained lifelong friends.

Fascinated by the dinosaur specimens she observed at the Natural History Museum in Göteborg, Toto enrolled at the Institute of Archaeology at the University of London. During the 1950s, she worked with two internationally known archeologists, often accompanying them on expeditions to the Middle East.

In 1959, Toto and Erica Brausen bought property on the small Italian island Panarea in the Tyrrhenian Sea. They built a villa there and, although both traveled extensively, it became a frequent refuge for them.

In May 1991, Toto broke her hip and was hospitalized in London. She never completely recovered and died at the Eaton Place home she shared with Erica Brausen on August 27, 1991, at the age of 82. Brausen died a year later. Both are buried in London's East Finchley Cemetery.

ACKNOWLEDGMENTS AND RESOURCES

The primary source for this novel was Jean-Noël Liaut's biography of Toto Koopman, *The Many Lives of Miss K.* Little is known about Toto's actual intelligence work during the war. Toto avoided discussing her war experiences afterward, and those who knew her during those years have all passed. Thus, much of this novel is pieced together from Liaut's work and ancillary sources—or imagined.

I'm grateful to Melissa Danaczko for introducing me to Toto and to Juliadi Two for sharing her knowledge of Indonesia. I wrote this novel over a five-year period, with numerous other writers providing helpful feedback and encouragement, including Kim Taylor Blakemore, Laurie Alberts, Vanitha Sankaran, Connie May Fowler, and the writers attending Fowler's 2016 Yucatan Writing Conference. I must also acknowledge the *Writing With Color* and *Writing the Other* websites (https://writingwithcolor.tumblr.com and https://writingtheother.com) for valuable guidance on writing respectfully about persons of color. I appreciate the steady hand of my gracious and competent editors at Sunbury, Chris Fenwick and Sarah Peachey. As always, I am grateful to my wife and editor, Deborah Zita, for her support and the many friends who are willing to pick up any book I write, regardless of the story, and support my writing career.

BIBLIOGRAPHY OF KEY RESOURCES

Arenson, Refael Paul. *Use and Evocation of Non-English Languages as Elements in English-Language Fiction.* Montpelier, VT: Master's Thesis, Vermont College of Fine Arts, 2014.

Ciano, Galeazzo. *The War Diaries of Count Galeazzo Ciano: 1939-1943.* London: Fonthill Media Limited, 2015.

Deighton, Len, & Hastings, Max. *Battle of Britain.* New York: Penguin, 1990.

Delzell, Charles F. *Mussolini's Enemies: The Italian Anti-Fascist Resistance.* Princeton, NJ: Princeton University Press, 1961.

Gallo, Max. *Mussolini's Italy: Twenty Years of the Fascist Era.* New York: Macmillan Publishing Co., 1973.

Gallo, Patrick. *For Love and Country: The Italian Resistance*. Lanham, MD: University Press of America, 2003.

Gobetti, Ada. *Partisan Diary: A Woman's Life in the Italian Resistance*. Translated from the Italian by Jomarie Alano. New York: Oxford University Press, 2014.

Hastings, Max. *Inferno: The World at War, 1939-1945*. New York: Alfred A. Knopf, 2011.

Helm, Sarah. *Ravensbrück: Life and Death in Hitler's Concentration Camp for Women*. New York: Nan A. Talese, 2014.

James, Jamie. *Rimbaud in Java: The Lost Voyage*. Singapore: Editions Didier Millet, 2012.

Knox, MacGregor. *Hitler's Italian Allies: Royal Armed Forces, Fascist Regime, and the War of 1940-1943*. Cambridge, UK: Cambridge University Press, 2000.

Knox, MacGregor. *Mussolini Unleashed: 1939-1941*. Cambridge, UK: Cambridge University Press, 1982.

Larson, Erik. *The Splendid and the Vile*. New York: Crown Publishing, 2020.

Liaut, Jean-Noël. *The Many Lives of Miss K*. Translated from the French by Denise Raab Jacobs. New York: Rizzoli International Publications, 2013.

Manning, Molly G. *When Books Went to War: The Stories That Helped Us Win World War II*. New York: Houghton Mifflin Harcourt, 2014.

Moorehead, Caroline. *A Bold and Dangerous Family: The Remarkable Story of an Italian Mother, Her Two Sons, and Their Fight Against Fascism*. New York: HarperCollins, 2017.

Origo, Iris. *A Chill in the Air: An Italian War Diary, 1939-1940*. New York: New York Review Books, 2017.

Pugliese, Stanislao G. *Fascism, Anti-Fascism, and the Resistance in Italy*. Lanham, MD: Rowman & Littlefield Publishers, 2004.

Wilhelm, Maria De Blasio. *The Other Italy: The Italian Resistance in World War II*. New York: W.W. Norton & Co., 1988.

Wolff, Isabel. *Shadows Over Paradise*. New York: Bantam Books, 2015.

ABOUT THE AUTHOR

MARYKA BIAGGIO, PHD, is a psychology professor turned novelist specializing in historical fiction based on real people. She enjoys the challenge of starting with actual historical figures and dramatizing their lives—discovering what motivated them to behave as they did, studying how the cultural and historical context may have influenced them, and recreating some sense of their emotional world through dialogue and action. Doubleday published her debut novel, *Parlor Games*, in 2013. *Eden Waits* and *The Point of Vanishing* were published by Milford House Press in 2019 and 2021. She lives in Portland, Oregon. You can visit her website at marykabiaggio.com.

Printed in Great Britain
by Amazon

35738323R00144